OZ

THE RAMA ROWDYS

BOOK 2

MICHAEL OSBORNE

Inquiries and Book Orders should be addressed to:

Great Writers Media
Email: info@greatwritersmedia.com
Phone: (302) 918-5570

ISBN: 978-1-957148-87-8 (sc)
ISBN: 978-1-957148-88-5 (ebk)

Rev 3/03/2022

ACKNOWLEDGMENTS

Special appreciations are to the many articles I read about the martial arts training as I completed my lifelong training in the arts. I owe the novel *The Classical Man* by Richard Kim, as well as his wonderful stories of the past masters in many kung fu magazines. Also special thanks to Master Alan Lee on his article "The Deadly Secrets of Kung Fu." All my readings were from articles printed in the 1970 *Kung Fu* magazine.

Some friends who are mentioned in this story are based on true accounts. Their names have been changed. I have contacted each of them, and they felt honored to be mentioned in my story. Some other characters are strictly fictious and not to be confused with persons with similar names. Most of the adventures are true and based on my life growing up in Georgia. The Atlanta gangs and bikers are purely fiction.

The Rama Theater once was a place I worked at. Most of the ushers and their involvement with the story is fiction. Operations of the theater are facts. Their duties are true, but the individuals are not. The stories and adventures with the ushers are fact. Those usher names are fiction, and their characterization is intended to represent real persons but just to portray a story line theme. Some of the persons working at the Rama may feel they were one of the characters mentioned in the story. I can positively assure my readers that they are fictional character names.

This is my second book I hope of many stories to come. The third book will pick up from the jewelry store and proceed to Atlanta. Mike will continue his training and meet two bikers that will add to his abilities in ways that seem almost impossible to believe. Mike will learn a truth that has only been hinted at about the bikers. This truth will change the life of Mike in the following books to myths level. A war is brewing. It will be epic.

INTRODUCTION

THIS IS THE CONTINUING STORY of Mike, a young boy who, in a year, traveled on foot from Virginia to Georgia. He braved many hardships and many injuries trying to get back to his family. Believing his mother was killed and not wanting to end up in a foster home, he decided to run away, leaving his sisters with neighbors. Discovering his mom was alive, he was astonished to find his mom sold the house to pay the debtors and move to Georgia.

After months of living from trash cans and learning backwoods skills of fishing and trapping from the many people who he befriended, Mike makes it home, home with his mom and two sisters, only to discover the man he saved from being robbed and possible killed by a vicious city gang chased after him out of revenge. They discovered where he lived from a magazine article describing some of his incredible adventures.

Returning home from school, he meets a biker gang he made friends with. They helped him stop a life-threatening attack on his family by the Atlanta gang. After that attack, the leader of the bikers had Cho, one of the most dangerous men alive, secretly train Mike in his martial arts. Mike was totally unaware of the purpose of Cho choosing him and another biker Stephen's training regime in survival skills over the coming months, which created a child with amazing skills of combat.

Mike continues his adventures with friends he made at school and later at the Rama Theater. Many hair-raising adventures led to the boys being given the name Rama Rowdies at their school.

Believing all the past problems were behind him, Mike soon discovers it has only been delayed. Before Mike's training is complete, the most dangerous adventure lay ahead. This time Mike was not alone. His friends, the Rama Rowdies, were to be drawn in this fight for their very lives.

FIRST DAY

"**G**OOD MORNING, GOOD MORNING." THIS was said to each student passing through the homeroom door by the teacher Mr. Adams. He would personally greet each one every day. Rarely did any student who preceded Mike offer him a reply.

"Good morning," he said to Mike with his friendly smile.

Mike immediately returned the greeting with one of his own. "Thank you, sir. How are you?"

"I'm doing just fine. A pleasure to have you in my class," came his reply.

"Thanks," Mike replied, making his way through the middle row, finding a desk near the front of the class. Most other seats in the rear of the class were already taken. *It seems no one wants to sit in the front*, Mike quietly thought.

Mike pulled a chair out and sat down. In front of his desk was a pretty girl with short brown hair. She just sat lifeless, as if no one was sitting behind her. On Mike's right was a chubby boy wearing a red flannel shirt. He had a haircut like Mike had before his mom let him have it cut his way. He grew his hair long enough to part on one side. With a crew cut, there weren't hair long enough to cover the scalp, just a tiny layer hovering above the scalp.

Mike stared at this boy on his right, and he looked back at Mike and smiled. He seemed friendly. Mike was glad to have someone who was friendly. It helped in making new friends.

To Mike's left was another boy slouching deep into his desk. He was taller and thinner than Mike. Mike thought himself a bit on the thin side until he sat down beside this taller slouching kid. His hair was longer and red as a cherry. Mike gave him a nod. He returned the nod, and both turned their attention to the front of the room.

The last student walked in about that time. He found a seat next to the wall on the other side of the chubby kid. He noticed Mike right off. Like thin boy, he gave a nod with Mike returning a nod back.

Mr. Adams walked to the center of the room. He was slightly taller than Mike with little hair upon his head. He wore glasses that gave him an even more academic look. He stood erect like an athlete, scanning the room. Watching him, one could see his eyes light on each student's face. He peered at each student with an intense look, then to the next until each student was catalogued in his mind. He made a subtle *hmm* sound, and only the closest sitting near the front of the class could hear. A long pause followed that sound.

The class was too busy scanning the room to see who was in their class with them from the following year. Soon, they were all talking to each other. Everyone was trying to talk to their friends and continued to talk as the teacher stood in the center of the front of class. Once he made the *hmm* sound, it was like someone turned off the light. All but one person went quiet.

Mike thought to himself, *I am glad of the silence.* It appeared to him that all the students were talking to friends from the prior year; they all seemed to orient their gaze toward Mike. It appeared they were talking about him.

"Mr. Abbot!" Mr. Adams called out with a high squeal in his voice. "When you are finished, please let me know so I may continue."

This was announced to all the class, but Mr. Abbot got the message. It was intended for him, the only one still talking. Mr. Abbot turned to see the teacher with the whole class staring at him. After viewing the entire class staring at him, he stopped his talking, but not entirely. It was when the person he was talking to put his finger to his lips, making the "shh" sound, did he completely stop. Abbot was the last to come in and take a seat.

"Good morning, class," Mr. Adams repeated a second time to the class as a whole.

The girl in front of Mike along with several others sitting in the front of the class responded with a good morning to Mr. Adams.

"Well, I see from your response, many of you have the respect to return my greeting. I hope as this year continues, you that did not respond with a greeting will learn the importance of good manners. It will serve you well to learn this if you continue to aspire to achieve your goals in life," commented Mr. Adams to the class.

Mr. Adams looked around with his hands on his hips to see if anyone had made an attempt to acknowledge his remark. Nothing, the same response after his first greeting to the class. No words, just a few nods.

After seeing the little response to his remarks from his students, he considered to attempt another approach to introductions. These students apparently were lacking the need to attend school. He wanted them to realize in his class, they will learn and be expected to participate in the learning process.

This time, Mr. Adams walked to the middle of the class and turned around in a circle, similar to a ballet dancer. With a quick and sudden stop, all eyes turned toward him. The student next to Mike spoke softly, but not low enough from preventing Mike from hearing his quip concerning the spin of Mr. Adams to another student.

"That is weird. He is odd. That's what they told me when I got stuck in his class," came a snarly remark from the tall thin slouching kid.

Mr. Adams spoke, "I usually like to start the class off with a get to know you, but today I think it would be a better idea to share a story with you. I will begin first with a quick introduction of who I am. I do this not to brag, but to allow you the understanding that you are capable of doing many things and acquiring any goal you want to achieve simply by not sitting on a fence."

Every face had a questioning expression, even Mike.

Mr. Adams paused just enough for that remark about sitting upon a fence to soak in. "Class, before I went to college to get a degree, I started working at a fast-food store to earn money to buy a ten-speed bike."

A short pause elapsed before he continued. As the story progressed, this became the norm, a statement followed by a pause.

"I stocked beer and cigarettes through the summer. That money I earned went to help my mom pay the bills. My father died when I was young. We had a rough time. My mother worked several jobs just to put food on the table. She never once asked me for any of the money I earned from stocking beer. I gave her the money freely. It was my family. I felt my duty to help out. Yes, I could go and spend it on whatever I needed or wanted. What I wanted was my family not to go hunger and my mom killing herself trying to get us all we needed. I want you all to know what you want and what you need are two very different things."

Mike perked up when he noticed the similarity of their lives.

Mr. Adams went on to say he lived in a duplex home—again like the house Mike was now living in. "We moved to a real home with a bedroom for each of us to have for our very own. I had my own bedroom," he told the class. "It was mine, no one to share with, just mine.

"Every day, I walked fifteen minutes from school. Whether it was cold, raining, hot as sin, we walked to school. We could not afford the bus or have our mom drive us to school. We just walked. Rarely did I have a coat that would keep the rain or cold out. When we got to school, we had to wait outside for another ten or maybe twenty minutes before they would open the doors to let the students in.

"Standing out in the freezing cold taught me my second lesson. Ignore the pain and focus on other things. Don't dwell on things you have no control over, only on the things you do have control to change. Anything else is just wasted effort," said Mr. Adams.

Mike began to like this teacher. He spoke of the same lessons he had learned on his trek home. Never once did Mike complain about his bad luck. It was what it was and a trial to fight through to reach his home. In many ways, a lesson was learned, with each lesson having provided skills for the next challenge to come.

"Every day I would walk past this kid's wooden post–fenced home across the street from our new home. Every day, even on the weekends, several of the neighborhood kids sat on that fence. They would sit on the fence for a while, returning from school with theirs books. Finally, one by one, they got off the fence, picking up their books, taking off to go home. About an hour later, they all would return and take up where they left off, sitting on the fence. Soon as time went by, I started to stop and talk to them. You know, getting to know others in my neighborhood.

"Not long after that, I too was taking up the post-sitting trend they sat. Everybody that lived on my street or the next street would gather at that fence to sit and talk. That's all we did every day of the week.

"Well, I got tired of just sitting doing nothing. I wanted to go somewhere and do something. Every day, I would ask them to go somewhere or do something. 'Hey, guys, how about we walk around the different streets?'

"'Nah, nothing to see,' was their typical response.

"'Okay, how about we play kickball or do some ball catching?'

"'Maybe tomorrow.'

"'Well, we can go to the school gym to play basketball,' I countered.

"'Not now, it's getting dark.'

"Anything I suggested, they had an excuse not to do it.

"This went on for the year through the winter and spring. By summer, I had enough. I applied to be a paperboy delivering newspapers. Every day, I came home from school to roll papers, got on my bike, and delivered newspapers. The first house I delivered was the house with the wooden fence. Man oh man, did they lay it on me.

"'A paperboy? I can't believe you want to deliver papers. That's so lame. There's got to be a better job than that. I wouldn't ever be a paperboy,' was their taunts to me every day.

"I kept that job until I got a job at a store for less than minimum wage. I was too young to get full pay. This job was given to me by a friend of my mom. Well, once the boys learned I was still getting less than normal pay, they taunted me even more.

"'Didn't you learn from your first job? You never will amount to much if you keep taking low-paying jobs,' came more taunts.

"Before my senior year in school, they were still sitting on the fence. Not one of them ever had a job. They all had big dreams they wanted to do in life."

Mr. Adams continued. "I got a job learning to repair appliances for less than minimum pay. I thought it was good experience, that this knowledge would one day pay off. With money I was earning, I saved a thousand dollars and put it in a savings account. I still helped my family out. I bought a used car. It wasn't much of an old car. Of course, they made fun of my car.

"What they didn't know was I established credit and was able to get a credit card. I was only seventeen now. Not many people my age had credit nor a credit card.

"Every day, I walked down to the store to get a Coke or candy bar. They always asked me to buy them one. Sometimes I did. After a while, I quit doing that. It was the same for my car.

"'Hey, where are you going? Can we go with you, or can you drop me off here or there?'

"Not one time did they offer to buy gas or even buy me a cola.

"'Hey, you got money, buy us a cola,' was the way they thought and told me.

"Reaching seventeen years of age, I took boxing lessons at the corner house in military housing. I competed and won several events. The military guy took me skydiving. When I graduated from high school, I had achieved a lot. A thousand dollars in my savings account, helping my family, learned several skilled jobs, learned to box and skydive. Finally, establishing credit. I went to college. I paid for college myself. After four years going mainly at night, I received my BA degree."

"What were these boys—I mean men doing?" Mr. Adams asked the class.

The whole class answered his question, shouting out in unison, "Sitting on the fence, Mr. Adams!"

Now the entire class was focused on Mr. Adams's story. He would walk from one side of the room to the other to keep each person's attention on him. Mike saw they were paying attention to what he was saying.

"That's right, sitting on the fence. One boy wanted to play in a band, do you think he ever did that, class?" Before they could answer, Mr. Adams began with what each person wanted in life who sat on the fence. "Another one had no idea what he wanted to do. Just get a job was his intent after graduating. A third boy wanted to be a sports star playing soccer. Not one ever achieved any of their goals. Does anyone in this class know why?"

Again, the whole class shouted out, "Sitting on the fence, Mr. Adams!"

"Years later, I returned to the area. One who wanted to play in a band was living at a church. He was homeless. The other guy wanting a job got his job. He put bottle caps on soda bottles at a bottling plant. The sports star dug ditches, working on a road crew in prison.

"So, remember this story when you decide an education isn't nothing or it's too much work. If you want something, you have a choice: either sit on a fence or get off that fence."

Silence followed his last words. Mr. Adams stood gazing at all of his students. In each and every one of them, he saw them pondering the lesson told to them. Mr. Adams could visualize what was passing through their minds. *That's not going to be me, no way, I want to do something with my life.* The key words that echoed back to him was what he believed each thought, something, nothing, but something.

Walking back to his desk, Mr. Adams picked up his roll book and began the call of each person by name. Each person responded with a *here* or *yes*. Once everyone was called up to Mike's name, all eyes turned toward him. He did not know anyone in the class. Apparently, they knew him.

Mr. Adams recognized Mike as a new student and made a welcome remark for him to the class. He asked the class to make Mike welcome to their school. "Everyone, say hello to our new student, Mike."

All eyes turned to face Mike. A short hello was echoed from the class.

"Next, each one will stand and introduce themselves. I want you to say your name, what you did for the summer, and one thing you like to do, and finally what your goal will be once you graduate from school," was Mr. Adams's final remarks.

Patricia was the first name called by Mr. Adams. She was the girl sitting in front of Mike. She stood; only then could Mike see her. She wore a pretty blue dress with a belt wrapped around her waist. Mike could see she had a good figure. Her hair was long, hanging down past her shoulders t. Her desk seat back made her hair seem shorter.

"Hello, my name is Patricia. My dad works a lot, and I had to stay home most of the time keeping up our house. My mom is divorced from my dad. I read a lot, and one day would like to be a teacher."

"Very good start for the class, Patricia. Nice to have you in my class," responded Mr. Adams.

Patricia sat down with a dainty movement.

Most of the girls liked to sew, dance, or desired to become an actress. The boys wanted to be a sport star. Basketballers or footballers seemed to be the most common choice. Some boys had no idea, or it seemed to Mike, listening to everyone who came before him make one up quickly.

A grand total of one doctor, five teachers, six nurses, two firemen, three policemen and the rest sport stars or "I don't know" made up all the options to become after graduating school.

Then came Mike's turn. He stood and looked about. He began with, "I traveled a lot most of the year. My dad was killed serving our country in the navy. I always wanted to become a geologist. That was it. Simple and to the point was his final remark.

The class acted as if Mike was going to tell them more than what he did tell them. Mike didn't want to get into the long journey he been on. He repeated that story so many times, and by now, he just couldn't bring himself to retell it one more time.

Next came Ron, the tall thin boy sitting across from Mike. He stood, speaking meekly. "I stayed around the house. My family and me went to the lake most of the summer. I like fishing and playing the guitar. Maybe one day I might join a band."

Jon stood next. He was on the other side sitting next to Mike. He was the heavy kid wearing a red checkered shirt. "I stayed around the house taking care of my two sisters. My mom works and expects me to tend to them. I just want to graduate so I can leave and do what I want to."

Through the morning hours, the class received books, writing their names in them. Next, each was assigned a locker to store the books and stuff in. Then they marched to the gym, art room, and music class. By lunch, the entire class was glad for some free time.

Mike didn't have a lunch or money to buy a meal. Neither did his sisters. So he sat at the tables with the boys he soon would call his friends, watching them eat.

"Hey, Mike, don't you have a meal? Aren't you hungry?" asked Jon.

Each person at the table apparently didn't hear the other ask Mike the same question. Mike soon felt embarrassed with each repeat of the question. Soon, everyone in the cafeteria was watching Mike and his sister sit at the table with empty places where trays would have been laid.

"No, I rarely eat lunch, and I'm really not hungry. I usually eat a large breakfast. Once in a while, when Mom hasn't time to prepare us a breakfast, she makes us a lunch." That was the usual comeback both him and his sister would tell each person.

Mike didn't have much food in their house and couldn't make lunches was the real reason. So Sharon and Mike decided to tell everyone this story to prevent any embarrassing questions.

After several weeks passed by, the teacher pulled Mike aside along with his sister. Mr. Adams told them they were allowed to walk home for lunch. "Your mom called the school to get permission." So every day thereafter at lunch, Mike and his sister would get together to walk home for lunch. When they got there, Mom wasn't home, and no lunch was made.

Boo could be heard halfway down the street in their neighborhood. He seemed to have sensed Mike was coming. First thing Mike did was to take Boo out and walk around the block. The second thing Mike did was sit with him, allowing Boo the freedom of the front yard. Being all cooped up every day gave him cabin fever. He went a bit wild when Mike took him out for his walk. Slowly, he began to accept Mike's family and usually was sitting with Mom when Mike came home after school.

Mom left them a note on that first day. "Make a sandwich." Of course, to make a sandwich, bread was a main ingredient. Sometimes there was bread, sometimes nothing. Crackers were used if they had them. Usually, a mayo sandwich or a glass of water was their lunch. Some lunches, Mike and his sister had peanut butter sprinkled with sugar as their sandwiches.

Mom started working at a dry cleaner and stayed on the job for a year. That was a good time. She stayed busy, and it seemed like a good life was ahead for the family. Her drinking was less and less.

Dodie was a year ahead of Mike and Sharon in school. She had to attend another school. She got off for lunch, and all met up at home sometimes. They would stay home for about twenty minutes and head back. That's when Boo would raise Cain. He would bark and keep it up until Mike was halfway back down the street.

On one day in class, just after lunch, Mr. Adams broke the news to everyone. "Class, I will be away for two weeks."

Every face looked puzzled.

"I'm getting married and will be on my honeymoon."

Hands shot up from the class immediately. "Mr. Adams, where to? Oh, we are so happy for you! Who is she? Will you bring her to class so we can meet her?" Those were most of the responses the class offered to him, Mike noted.

Mr. Adams didn't expect the avalanche of questions pouring on him. Stepping back as though a crowd was shoving at him, he held up his hands to quell the onslaught.

"Oh, hold on a second, one question at a time. First, we are going to a lonely island. I've known her for three years. She teaches at another school. Her name is Charlotte, and yes, when we get back, you all will be the first to meet her." With one quick reply, he answered all the questions posed to him.

One week went by, and the principal came to their class. "Class," he addressed them. He stood in the center of the floor with another teacher. Both of them had sad expressions on their faces.

"Class," the principal repeated, "I am here today to pass along some sad news. Mr. Adams was killed along with his wife in a terrible car accident last night. He was leaving the ocean liner he was on in a cab. A large semitruck overturned, smashing into his cab. Both were killed, quick. This is your new teacher. Please accept her into your arms as you did Mr. Adams."

That was it, quick and simple, to the point. The class sat there in their seats shocked. No one could say a word or think of questions to ask.

The new teacher was younger than Mr. Adams. She was tall and sporting short hair. She appeared to be a nice person on the outside. Some teachers in the school had a mad look on their faces, while for others, it was harder to read their faces. All the teachers had a report made on them by the students. Each received good or bad reviews. This teacher was new and yet to have a review done on her.

"Hello, class. I knew Mr. Adams and was very impressed with him. He was a kind and generous person. I will sadly miss him as you all will as well. My name is Mrs. Bently. I hope to live up to his high principles he set."

Not much was said for a few weeks in class.

At home, Mike started to experiment, making rockets using match heads stuffed inside a tape-wrapped cocoon as fuel. He would roll paper into a tube, tape on fins, then take it outside to test-fire. He had several successes, but not as well as he hoped for. Most of his rockets when ignited would fly off for several feet, but none would reach the height he dared dreamed. He drew many designs while in class. Mike had prided himself on his final and best design. It was a sled tethered to a balloon that would float up and launch his rocket into the stratosphere. He dreamed that NASA would one day call about his balloon rocket launcher to launch one of their rockets.

On this one day, Mike brought one of his rockets to school. Ron, the thin tall boy Mike first met, now sitting across from him in the class, became a new friend. Mrs. Bently rearranged the desks, splitting them with half on one side and the other on the other side, facing each other. Ron sat at an angle to Mike several seats down. Johnny, the chubby kid, lived near Mike. They lived in the same neighborhood. He sat beside Mike.

Ron, seeing the rocket, kept egging Mike all day to light it up. After lunch, he finally got his wish. Mrs. Bently left the room.

"Come on, Mike. You said you were. Do it!"

"Hold your horses, Ron. Johnny, keep an eye out for the teacher," Mike requested. "Ron, get over here by the window. Now hold on to the rocket while I get a match lit." Mike dug into his pocket, seeking a match.

"Wait a minute, it might blow up." Ron's attitude suddenly changed when he was told to participate in the launch.

"Oh, I light it and take all the risks so you can have some fun. No way, buddy. If you want to see this launch, you are going to help me," Mike quipped back to Ron.

Ron stood by the window. His hands started to shake. Mike could see in Ron's face he was running scared. "Okay, okay, hurry it up, Mike."

"What, you afraid, Ron?"

"No, just hurry, Mike."

Jon was by the door. Mike called out to him, "Jon, see anyone?"

"No, but you better get it done quick."

Mike had the match out and was waiting to strike it. After he heard Jon's response, he quickly lit the end of the rocket. This rocket was Mike's newest design. It had two boosters alongside of the main rocket. He had to light all three at the same time. If not done correctly, Mike expected the rocket to spin like a top into the air.

Ron held the rocket in place just long enough for Mike to strike the match.

"Let go, Ron! I have it!" Mike shouted.

The students surrounding the two of them quickly backed away.

Slowly Mike put the match to the rear of the rocket. He wasn't too sure what to expect. Couldn't anticipate the reaction of his rocket. Every test-firing resulted in a different response. This time was different. Mike almost dropped the match before lighting. Once lit, he stepped back from the reaction that came.

The rocket took the match quickly. He barely had time to move his hand from the burst of flame erupting from the tail.

"Yeow!" Mike screamed out as the fire burnt his fingers.

"Mike, watch out! The rocket ain't going out the window!" yelled Ron.

"What?" Looking down where all the smoke was coming up at him, Mike could see it on the floor. It started to swirl around, emitting so much smoke, all the girls began to scream.

Jon screamed, "She's coming. Run!"

Ron turned around, seeing Johnny running to his seat. "Mike, Mrs. Bently's coming back. We are in for it now!" Ron yelled.

Mike stomped down on the rocket. He bent down to pick it up and had barely enough time to reach his seat. He flopped down hard in his desk just as Mrs. Bently walked in. All went quiet.

Johnny was sitting in his chair with his face planted on the desk-top, pretending to have woken from sleeping as the teacher walked in. To all the students' dismay, she said nothing. Smoke and the odor from the sulfur lingered in the air. The class expected some kind of an outcry to the smoke and smell; instead, she walked over to her desk and picked up something lying on the top. Turning around to face the blackboard, she began to write down an assignment to complete before end of day. Placing the chalk back on the board, she turned toward the door. She left, closing the door behind her.

Mike suddenly felt the sharp prick of something stinging him on his left hand. *What could be causing that stinging pain?* Mike looked down at his hand. Sticking straight up was a small needle. The needle looked as if it had wings. He pulled it out and let out a cry. Laughter came roaring from the opposite end of the room. "What the, who the…" And before he could finish what he was trying to say, Ron called out, "Man, I'm sorry."

Looking about to spot where the call came from, Mike saw Ron raising his arms to get his attention. It was him.

"Mike, I didn't think it was going to stick you. I was afraid when I threw it, it was going to git you in the face. Sorry, really I am."

"Hey, Ron, that's cool. It was a darn good shot to git me in my hand. I'm okay. Do me a favor, don't do that again. It might have hit me in my eyes." Mike had responded to Ron's apology not exactly the way Ron had expected him to.

For the next couple of days, Ron just kept saying it was an accident and was sorry. It really made him feel really bad. Mike tried to assure him it was okay. That incident made both good friends.

THE WHITE STORM

MRS. BENTLY WAS ABSENT ON this day. The class had a substitute teacher. During lunch, Sharon and Mike walked out the rear door of the school. They would pass by the men's restroom window when leaving from school to go home to eat lunch. Ron called out to Mike as they were nearing the restroom window. They stopped to see what he wanted. He started to talk about Patricia, the pretty blond girl they would see at recess time. "Mike, what you think about Patricia?"

"Well, Ron, she's the prettiest girl in school," Mike remarked.

Ron responded, "Well, that's all you can think. She is going steady with Mark."

"Okay, Ron, so what?"

"Well, Mark told me you better not try to take his girl."

"No problem, Ron."

"Where you going, Mike?"

I told you, home to lunch, Ron."

With that reply, Ron spat at Mike.

"Why'd you do that, Ron?" cried Mike with a stunned look on his face.

"Just thought I'd try and give you a go-to lunch package."

Then Mike spat back at him. The spit wad went in the window and hit Mark on his face. The blood rose in Mark's face, and he yelled loud, so loud, it was apparent to Mike he missed Ron.

With a sudden rush to the screened window, Mark yelled down to Mike, "I am going to kick your ass!"

"Hey, Mark, I thought it was Ron I hit! It was an accident. I'm sorry, man."

"You ain't going to be half as sorry when you git back. I'm going to kick your butt," responded Mark a second time.

"Mike, what you going to do?" asked Sharon, his sister.

"Sharon, I can only hope he cools off. It was an accident."

"Are you going to tell the teacher what he plans on doing when we get back?"

"No, Sharon, hopefully he will calm down and nothing happens."

Returning from lunch, Mike took his seat in class. The substitute left the room. Before the door was even shut, Ron had in his hand a large wad of paper he chewed on. "Hey, Mike, look what I got here?"

"What's that, Ron?"

"It's the world's largest spitball."

"I hope you don't intend to throw that at me!" Mike shouted.

Everyone looked at Ron when Mike called out to him.

"Yep."

"Don't do it, Ron. I'm telling you, there'll be war. Don't do it."

Too late. To Mike's misfortune, that wad of spit paper was in the air. It came flying at Mike with hyper sonic speed. The wind created passing by his ears ruffled the hair on his neck. It hit one of the girls behind Mike on her dress.

Ron made the mistake of telling Mike he was making a spit wad on the way to lunch. When the class was in line to get lunch, Sharon and Mike would get together and leave to go home. Before walking out the school doors, Mike went in the cafeteria with the class line. While he was waiting in line, Mike secretly reached into the box of straws, grabbing several before he left.

When that wad hit the girl's dress, Mike revealed to Ron his straws. Ron had depleted his arsenal and, to his dismay, lacked the firepower, becoming weaponless. All his effort went to making that huge spitball.

The girl with the wad splattered on her dress screamed out across the desk. "You ass, Ron!"

Ron called to Mike, "Please, I surrender!" It was all he could say with a silly smirk across his face.

Johnny had a straw Mike gave him, also two other students. Between the four of them, they lay forth a wall of flying, high-speed spitballs. The white wad had one target and one target only—Ron.

The first salvo hit the mark. Within a minute or so, it was figured Ron had received direct hits with fifteen to twenty spitballs. He tried to get up and duck under anything he could hide from the missile attack. Bad mistake.

Everyone got out of their seats, leaving him exposed. Only then did he beg for them to stop. "Please stop."

"I told you, Ron, not to throw that. Didn't I tell you, you would regret it? I knew you were going to throw that at me or one of us. I decided to prepare for the battle before I went home to eat," Mike explained to Ron.

"Mike," Johnny called to him, "look. Look at all the spitballs all over the classroom. While we were engaged in a war with Ron, the others in the class jumped into the fray. Spitballs went flying all across the room."

Looking at his body, there were about six or seven stuck to Mike. In fact, everyone on his side had spitballs covering them. Everyone in class had spitballs somewhere on the bodies. No one escaped that fight.

The girls who had run to a corner to escape the white flurry had signs of spitballs landing on them. One girl had the biggest wad plastered on her dress. She stepped out of the corner, walking over to where Ron was cowering. "You clean this off my dress," she demanded.

There was no covering this up. Nor was there any pretending not to notice by the teacher. When the substitute teacher entered the room, she stood by the door. The horror of the event took a few minutes to sink in.

Softly she spoke, "Class, I am going to step out of this room for a total of three minutes, and when I return inside, there best not be one spitball in sight. I mean not even a stubble of a part of one visible. Now, class, is that clear to you?"

Quiet was heard. Only nods were seen by the teacher before shutting the door. When she stepped back in, not one spitball was evident. All clean.

Recess came thirty minutes later. The class thought for sure recess would be cancelled. To their relief, she had them stand to take them out to recess. Mike figured she had enough and wanted to allow them to vent all their pent-up energies.

On the way out, Mark's class met up with Mike's class. Side by side, they all marched to the rear door. Nothing was said between the two. Mark turned to Mike. Mike never met this Mark before, not until the incident in the bathroom window where he accidentally spit on him. A screen in the window prevented a good look at him. He stood evenly tall beside Mike and about the same build. Mark certainly had the look of someone you wouldn't want to mess with. He seemed to carry a mad-at-the-world look scarred to his face, Mike thought, looking at him with suspicion.

Mark spoke in a subtle whisper across the two lines of students heading outside for recess. "Remember what I told you, Mike."

Mike could see from Mark's eyes he was going to do just that.

"When we get outside, I'm going to kick your butt."

No sooner said when the door opened, they stepped outside, and Mark grabbed for Mike's shoulder.

Quicker than lightning, Mike threw his arm around Mark's neck and shot his hip under Mark's gut. With a quick twist, Mark flipped over Mike's hip hard on the ground. Mike had grabbed around Mark's neck to make his flip. He kept holding on when they landed on the ground. His arm was tight around Mark's neck, squeezing hard. Mark was caught good, and no amount of struggling was going to free him of Mike's solid grip. He squeezed hard. Mark's only recourse was to cry out to let him go as his face grew blue.

"Yeah, you really think so," Mike responded. "I'm going to jerk your head off if you don't surrender. Surrender, surrender!"

Ron walked about looking like he had a camera in his hand, pretending to take pictures of the two of them rolling on the ground.

Upon looking up, Mike saw Ron rotating his arm in a circle on his make-believe camera, and it kind of calmed him. Many of the class were gathering, watching the conflict unfold. Some laughed at Ron's moviemaking prank.

To Mike, it had a calming effect as he tried his best not to laugh. Mike was mad when Mark said he was going to kick his butt. Madder when Mark repeated his threat going outside. Then boiling mad when he grabbed Mike's arm. Thank the lord for the teacher. Mark surrendered just before the teacher tore them apart. Ron brought Mike back to a nicer person with that stunt of pretending to be filming with a camera before he hurt Mark real terribly.

Mark got up and brushed himself off. Mike followed his actions. The teacher told them to shake hands and apologize to each other. They did. Mark went his way, Mike went his. It wasn't over. Mark was the kind of kid who wouldn't let it drop, Mike suspected. Both went to opposite ends of the playground.

Jon and Mike walked home together just laughing at the spitball battle. Each argued about who hit Ron the most. Neither one of them ever decided who won. It was fun.

Before they crossed the street to get home, a loud roar of engines was heard coming up the street. It was a large number of motorcycle riders driving past. To Mike's amazement, he saw Chopper on the lead bike. Behind on the back of his bike was Bell. She held tight to him. Only after they were almost past him did Bell spot Mike standing on the corner.

"I never saw so many bikers riding bikes," Johnny quipped to Mike. Every bike had long-reaching forks on the front wheel. The bikers rode two by two, side by side. Some wore a helmet, many just a bandana around their foreheads. Over half had a woman on the back of their bike.

Jon made a comment about only seeing one woman riding alone on a bike. It stood out from the rest. It was the only pink bike on the street. Mike saw the lady on the lone bike all dressed in lace. Before half the bikers had passed by, a yell rang out on the lead bike.

Bell could be heard screaming, "Mike! There he is! Stop, Chopper!" With a quick jerk on Chopper's arm, she screamed out to him again to stop. "There's Mike. There he is. Stop, let's go back, babe."

With a sharp turn of his bike, Chopper steered into the incoming cars to turn his bike. One car swerved to one side of the road. The other cars managed to pass around the rest of the bikes without a single ding or dent made on either vehicles.

No less than twenty bikers turned facing the wrong direction in the road. It was a marching band of moving bikes exactly following each other. It was a beautiful sight to behold when they made a slow turn. Not one, no one in the group broke the rank in formation. Even when they stopped, it was a perfect stop followed with unison kickstand clinks. They stopped right there in the road where Mike and his friend Jon stood.

Razor was off his bike before Bell and Chopper had the kickstand down. He came up to Mike, grabbing him in his huge arms. Jon got scared watching a giant, burly, whiskered man take Mike in his arms.

"Boy, we've been looking all over for you. Chopper told us, he said he would check on you. He's a man of his word, kiddo."

Mike looked as if all the blood rushed out of his face from the hard squeeze Razor had him in.

Bell finally got over to Mike, and not a second too soon. "Damn, Razor, let go of him. He turning as pale as a sheet. You're squeezing the life out of him."

Razor dropped Mike like a hot potato, and before his feet could hit the ground, Bell had Mike in a hug.

Bell was a tall woman with a big bust. Mike never truly realized that until the hug she gave him. She buried his head between those large melons, as Chopper often referred to them. Mike had to pull away to get his breath. Between the slaps on his back and all the arm shaking from the men and all the women having the same way as Bell of showing Mike their happiness to see him, it left Mike weak upon his feet, mainly from the lack of air.

Jon, seeing these huge men in jackets and carrying some kind of a weapon under their jackets or belt, said, "See you later, Mike." Johnny was a timid sort, and these guns and knives he spotted the bikers carrying made him very nervous.

"Yeah, Jon, catch up with you later." Mike just had time to wave him bye before Jon scurried across the road. Not once did he look back.

On the other side of the road, Jon went from a fast walk to a near full-out run from sight.

"Bell, quit your hugging long enough for the rest of us to say hi, please," commented a large man stepping from behind Bell.

Chopper grabbed Mike's hand to shake it. Slowly behind Mike, without a sound, a huge powerful grip took hold of his shoulders.

Mike yelled out, "Bone Breaker! I never forget that grip. I'm still bruised from the gentle assisting you offered me in that bar."

"Yeah, I do leave that impression on people."

"Hahaha!" everyone laughed.

The street looked like a party was taking place with all the bikers milling around. Soon cars began honking their horns. Some nasty shouts were made from several motorists.

Turning around to face Bone Breaker, Mike was surprised by what he had growing on his face. The last time Mike remembered seeing him was at the bar. He had a shadow of facial hair. Now, before him, Bone Breaker had a full-grown beard. Lifting up his sunshades, one could see the happiness on his face looking down at Mike. Mike couldn't help himself, giving him a hug. Bone Breaker was just as pleased and returned the hug, just a little gentler than his comrades.

Before Bone Breaker walked up on Mike, Chopper and Bell also had a change in their appearances. Bell's hair was longer and blonder than red. She looked to have put on more weight around her tummy. Chopper was the only one unchanged of the group. What change Mike noticed was his weight gain. Razor was clean shaven and a bit thinner.

"Well, Mike, I told you I would check on you. Here I am." Chopper took Mike's hand, shaking it hard up and down, but not before he crushed what was left of it after the vise grip of Razor's. Mike nearly bent down to his knees from Chopper's power grip on his hand. Instead, he held tight and reasserted his grip. It was a futile effort. Mike's hand succumbed to the fatal cramp and gave in to it. For the most part, Chopper hadn't changed much. But remembering back, Mike only remembered him sitting down or him looking up at him from the floor. Standing near him only did Mike realize his true girth. He was a big man. Many of the bikers seemed larger than the mere normal man. Seeing them massed the way they were milling around was almost scary.

Soon, all three bikers at the bar and a few not there seemed to mill about Mike. It was like they heard some story that awed them and wanted to see who that person was. He felt a bit awed by their attentions.

Honking cars was the one thing that took their minds off Mike. Soon every biker was shooting a middle finger to all the cars along with some foul language. One man apparently seemed so upset, he opened his car door, only to meet with a sharp slamming shut by a biker standing near with his foot.

"Hey, you guys, get off the road!" one man yelled out from another truck. Another one said, "Move it, bub. Move it or lose it."

"I'm in a hurry. I ain't got no time for bozo family reunions!" came a shout from another car.

That was a wrong way to talk to Chopper's bikers. One thing Mike recalled in the bar talking to Chopper, he demanded respect. Bone Breaker was all too happy to teach Mike all about respect. So it was with that man who made the mistake of calling them bozos. Bone Breaker didn't need no invite from Chopper. Like a dutiful biker, he went to enforce respect.

The truck driver saw this huge mountain of a man with a smile of "you just screwed yourself" march toward him. He didn't seem smart, was Mike's first thought. He immediately rolled up his window and locked the door. After that, he did begin to show some smarts. The click of the lock was very audible from where Mike stood. Bone Breaker's grin turned into a sinister smile of joy upon hearing the lock click on the door.

Any car or truck driver or passengers or passersby along the street stopped and stared at the advance of this huge man-made mountain walking up to the door of the truck driver. Taking hold of the handle with one massive hand, Bone Breaker looked at the man through the window. It was almost as if Bone Breaker was waiting to see if the man would open his door.

I know what the driver is going to do. I wouldn't open my door, Mike thought, watching the scene.

After what happened next, Mike thought twice and reconsidered that he would have opened the door, but as quickly as that thought came, his prior thinking still prevailed to keep it shut. It didn't matter what your inclination was, whether to open or keep the door shut.

Either way, the decision was made to what Bone Breaker meant to do to that man making the unfortunate mistake of calling them bozos.

When the door was flung across the street, all eyes were watching Bone Breaker. It must be said, Mike would have bought a ticket to this show. Bone grabbed that man by his neck. Now, try to visualize a huge mountain grabbing a huge mountain of jelly, yanking that slushie mass of overweight truck driver into the air with one arm. That jelly bowl of a man was pulled out of his truck with little effort. Bone Breaker held him off the road with one hand. You could see the truck driver's face turning blue and both feet squirming.

Mike could sympathize with the lack of air the driver must be feeling after his reunion with the biker females.

Bone Breaker turned to Mike with a nod and a wink and swung that man in a half circle, throwing him over a car onto the other lane, going in the opposite direction of the traffic he was heading. That man rolled three times and stopped just as an oncoming car in the direction away from them slammed on his brakes. The car bunked the man, bouncing back from the impact. The man quickly got to his feet. Slowly, he turned toward Bone Breaker with a nasty look on his face. It looked like this guy was going to cross back over the street to give Bone Breaker a beating from that nasty look he launched at him.

Bone Breaker was about to take a step to meet up with him. That man became conscious enough to realize that was a bad idea and turned around. For a man his size, it surely was remarkable the way he could waddle away. Bone Breaker was going to give chase until Chopper signaled for him to come back to where they were. The honking car horns ceased honking.

A police cruiser pulled up to where the bikers were standing. Chopper saw him coming; apparently, this was the only reason he stopped Bone Breaker from chasing after the truck driver, Mike noted to himself.

A policeman opened his door and emerged from the front door of the cruiser. He stood by his car for a second without any thought of who he was dealing with and, by any other's reckoning, didn't care much. He walked through the bikers as if they were not there with a defiant stride, making it known he was the man. The bikers didn't make way for him either. Not on biker moved. He found he had to shove through toward the big man he perceived as their leader. He managed to work his way through the bikers up to Mike and Chopper.

Stopping in front of Chopper and Razor, he not once said, "Good day" or ask what the problem was. He just barked out an order to get those bikes off his road. Now!

Now, Bone Breaker, ever by the side of Chopper, showed up and stood beside the police officer. Slowly and much gentler, Bone Breaker placed his hand on the officer's shoulder. To the officer's merit, he looked at him and turned back to Chopper and repeated, "I mean now, mister," in a softer tone of voice!

The officer looked again at Bone Breaker after Bone's hand was felt crushing his shoulder. Mike never saw the other officer approach. The second officer left his car stopped on the other side of the street where roly-polies waddled away. He walked up to the back of Bone Breaker and gave him a tap on his head with a black baton.

The officer's baton was found on the ground near both officers' feet snapped in two. Bone, with an unbelievable speed, twisted then shot his second arm at the shoulder of the second officer. Both officers' shoulders were being held in a vise grip. Both faces were contorted from the subtle squeeze Bone was applying to each shoulder. The more they squirmed, the harder the grip got. Soon, they realized the futility of trying to resist.

"Bone Breaker, let those two officers go," commanded Chopper.

Neither officer could say anything for a few minutes. They kept busy rubbing their shoulders. Finally, the second officer spoke. Turning to face Bone Breaker and easing his right hand to his revolver, he unsnapped his holster. "Mister, you just made the worst mistake of your life. You just assaulted two law officers."

The first officer slid to one side, backing up the second office as he approached Bone Breaker. Both officers suddenly became aware of the mass of bikers circling them and crowding them.

Chopper, seeing what was about to transpire, quickly acted to defuse the situation. Raising both of his hands for the officers to plainly see he was unarmed, he softly spoke up. "Now, now, officers," Chopper said. "He was only trying to help me. Why don't you just let this be a warning?"

The first officer turned to Chopper. "Mister, no one but no one treats an officer of the law like he did and gets away with that."

"Hey you, big guy, put your hands out," commanded one of the officers. The second officer pulled his handcuffs out and slammed them against Bone Breaker's wrists. The cuffs could not snap close. Bone Breaker's wrists were no mere average-man size but twice as large as one man's wrist.

Seeing how hard the officer slammed those cuffs on Bone Breaker's wrist made Mike cringe in pain from the sight. Bone Breaker never once gave the impression it hurt, even after the third attempt to slap the cuffs on him. Finally, the officer just took hold of the cuffs and squeezed them over his wrists. Blood surrounded the wrists as they began to turn blue.

Chopper again tried to reason with the two officers. "Officers, let's be reasonable. You were very impolite talking to us in the first place. Second, you shoved my people around. You assaulted us first. Now, you nearly break my friend's wrist the way you put your cuffs on him. I got plenty of witnesses here to say this to our lawyers. We will press charges if you press charges against us."

Thinking about Chopper's words, both officers gave a nod of agreement. The second officer turned to Chopper. "Fine, just get your bikes out of the road, please."

"Whatever floats your boat, officer," Chopper answered with a slight disrespect in his tone. Chopper turned to Bone Breaker, and with a quick outward shrug of his shoulders, the cuffs snapped off his wrist, falling to the ground with a clink.

The first officer started to say, "You broke my cuffs. You going to pay." Before he could finish that remark, the second officer grabbed his partner's arm and gave him a look that said, "Don't say anything more, you fool. Didn't you just see what that guy did to them cuffs?"

The first officer was bright enough to get the meaning of his look and shut up.

Both officers walked back to their cars standing beside each driver's door. The first officer got out a light, then walked to the center of the road. He began to direct traffic around the bikes.

Chopper signaled his people to get on their bikes. He then turned toward Mike, saying to him, "Mike, you get on Bone Breaker's bike."

Suddenly, one officer watching Mike straddle Bone Breaker's bike called out, "Hold on, mister, where do you think you are taking that kid? Is he your son? If not, then he's not leaving with you. Unless you want a kidnapping charge." This was the same officer who first approached Chopper and had a smart mouth.

"Nothing of the sort, officer. We know each other, and this is the reason we are in this town of yours. We are old friends." Chopper turned to Mike and placed his hand on his shoulder, helping Mike remain on Bone Breaker's bike. Carefully, Chopper kept his eyes on the officers to maintain control. Both officers allowed Mike to remain on the bike.

With a quick foot stomp and throttle, Bone Breaker revved up the bike. All bikes started up, and not until Chopper got on his bike with Bell and start his bike did he signal for the bikers to pull out.

Both police officers stood out in the street to control the traffic. About twenty cars total had been stalled in the road for nearly twenty minutes.

Chopper took a slow U-turn, going back in the direction they first were heading until Bell spotted Mike. As he made his turn, he called to Bone Breaker to follow him, and to Razor, he told him take the bikes to a place they planned to hang out while in town.

"Where you live?" Chopper yelled out to Mike above the loud roaring engine noise.

"Well, Chopper, not far from here!" Mike shouted across the two bikes riding side by side. "In fact, turn right down this street." Mike swiftly jutted out his hand to signal a turn. Two bikes made the turn. Again, Mike called out to Chopper, "It's on your left at the corner, up ahead is my home."

Two bikes roared through an old, worn community of duplex homes. Many were unoccupied. Most needed repairs and a good coat of paint. Some children played near the street. Jon watched the two bikes pass his house. He saw Mike on the back of one bike, holding on to a giant.

Suddenly, Mike's heart almost stopped. He pulled hard on Bone Breaker's back to stop. He stopped just like that. Chopper and Bell pulled up next to them with a curious expression.

"Hey, Mike, is this your home?"

"Ain't much, Chopper," Bone Breaker said softly to him.

Bell put her finger to her lips to quiet his remarks about Mike's home.

"Just ahead is my home." Mike pointed. Mike heard the softly spoken remark about his home and ignored it. It was true, and somehow, this embarrassed him when Bone Breaker quipped it out.

Mike pointed to the three men walking sneakily up to the side of the house. All three wore a bandana and short-sleeve shirts. One had a gun in his hand, which was spotted by Chopper. He signaled to Bone Breaker, pointing at the man with the gun. A quick nod of acknowledgment came back from Bone. The gunman was made.

Before either biker had a chance to make sense of what was happening at Mike's home, Mike jumped off the bike. Quickly, Mike ran up to a tree ahead of the bikers. Looking back, he could barely see them sitting on their bikes in the road. The clump of bushes beside the tree Mike was standing behind hid him well from both the bikers and the three men advancing on his home.

The bikers sat there curiously watching what Mike was doing. From their viewpoint, they could see his house but probably not Mike.

The leader of the three bandana men got to a window and looked in. The other two separated. One went to the rear door of the duplex; the other gingerly made his way to the front door. The one at the window turned around to see if it was all clear.

Mike for the first time saw the face of the man at the window. That face was the same face he bear-clawed back in the city. Somehow, they found out where he lived. Why were they after him? Was it for revenge? Mike began to ponder all possibilities. Yeah, revenge, he finally acknowledged to himself.

They followed him through the city out of revenge. He thought for sure they learned their lesson. Mike recalled the incident in the park that night. He set traps for the gang members chasing him. He watched them from atop a hill overlooking the forest below. They crossed the stream, spotted his trail left for them, and followed it as he planned. Traps were laid along the path. Being city boys, they fell for each trap.

They were so intent on getting their hands on him, the briars, poison ivy, smoke, and howling only frightened them, not deterring their revenge. He launched one attack after another, inflicting many small wounds and leaving long-clawed bloody marks on each man. It ended when he hit the leader hard with his bear claw gloves, knocking him down the hill. His men ran screaming, thinking it was a bear attacking them. The police were waiting on the other side of the stream.

Guess they didn't learn their lessons, Mike thought. Mike still carried his knife under his shirt, even at school. Mike eased his hand up under his shirt, sliding his blade down and out. When that gang leader started to pry into the window, he knew it was time to act—and quickly. His family was home.

Mike broke from his cover, running at him. Mike shouted out to his family to call the police. "Someone is breaking in! Call the police!" he called again and again as he ran toward the leader.

Boo heard the sound before he heard Mike. He started to yip. When he heard Mike's voice screaming, he went wild.

Leader man at the window heard the yell. He couldn't turn fast enough to prevent Mike's leap onto his back. The knife dug into his arm still raised, lifting the window open. The blade was sharp as it was when first made. It slid through the shirt sleeve and easily into the entire thickness of leader man's arm. The tip of the knife's point poked through to the front of the shoulder with the tip sticking out, dripping blood.

"Ahh!" leader man screamed out. He swung about to throw Mike off.

Mike had remembered how the bear had thrown him off. That was when the bear could strike back at Mike. He was not expecting what the bear could do. Not this time. He held him tight. Both fell to the ground.

"Get off me, kid. Get off me! I'm gonna kill you. I'm gonna kill you and all your family. Nobody does what you do to me and gets away with it!" leader man yelled out to Mike.

He was mad, crazy mad. So mad to the point he just twisted every way he could without thought to the best way to shuck Mike off. He really meant what he said. He was trying his hardest to get Mike off.

Mike could feel the gun he had in his back pocket. Leader man's hand greedily became reaching for his gun once it became apparent he wasn't going to shake Mike off.

Mike held on tighter than he had ever done before. He knew this was life and death.

Leader man yelling at Mike caused both his partners to stop and turn back. The one in front met with Chopper. Chopper grabbed his wrist with the knife in it. Bell, not wanting to be left out, kicked the front of the man square between the legs. His face turned white. Both eyes opened wide from the pain. Soon, they closed tight when the left hand of God said good night. Teeth went flying out of his mouth after he hit the ground, and what was left in his mouth were soon kicked out by Bell's second kick.

The second gang member or backyard man was introduced to Bone Breaker. The awe he felt from viewing a mountain of the largest man he ever saw was truly inspiring. He might have wanted his autograph if given the opportunity. Mike only wish he could have seen his head crashing through the wall into their shed near the duplex. His feet stopped wagging shortly after a minute. Now both legs lay limp, drooping along with his shoulders not in the hole.

Chopper got to Mike first, but not quick enough, to his regret. Leader man had gotten hold of his gun concealed in his back pocket. "Hold on, Mike!" Chopper screamed, hurrying to get to him.

Mike lost his grip from the leader man twisting and shoving on him. He yelled toward Chopper. Chopper was in full gallop, speed racing around the corner of Mike's house. Compared to Mike, he could outrun Chopper's full speed backward. His age and riding on a bike most of the time didn't allow his legs to run as fast as he once could. Plus, maybe that belly fat flapping up and down with every step might have slowed him a tad.

"I can't, Chopper, he's got a gun!" Mike yelled as he lay on the ground, waiting for the gun's trigger. Leader man was to his feet, pointing the gun at Mike's head. Slowly, Mike could see leader man squeeze his gun's trigger back. It seemed a long time was passing as that trigger finally reach the rear of the trigger guard.

Chopper yelled, coming around the corner of the duplex, seeing a gun readying to shoot.

Bam!

The gun went off. The bullet flew into the ground by Mike's head. Mike was able to squirm as the trigger was released. It was enough. The gun sound stunned Mike's ear, causing him to ease up on his hold of leader man's ankles. It was just enough. Leader man swung Mike partly off him with a wild kick. He heard the yell from Chopper. Turning, leader man saw who was calling to Mike.

Chopper was just several feet away. Leader man raised his gun to fire at the two people racing toward him. His gun pointed not at Chopper, but at Bell, who quickly appeared beside Chopper. Bell caught up to him as he rounded the corner to where leader man was standing.

Bam!

Mike had fallen to the ground, still holding on to leader man's legs. He took his knife and attempted to stab at his foot. Mike saw the bullet hit the ground with dirt flying up, and he knew if he didn't do something quick, the next bullet would be fired, and the person running to his aid would also be down on the ground bleeding.

Still holding to the leader man's ankle, he raised his knife as he was twirling on the ground from leader man's kicking and spinning. He planted the knife as deep as he could into the foot. It stopped only when he ran out of blade in his foot. Blood leaked out like a faucet turned all the way on. Mike could feel leader man's pain all the way down to the ground.

The pain shooting up into leader man caused him to turn from the person still coming toward him. He was mad as heck and wanted Mike before the other person could stop him from doing just that. For the third time, Mike watched the trigger being pulled with the gun aimed at his face. The cylinder turned. A bullet rotated into the trigger's path. Leader man's finger slowly pulled back the trigger. Mike knew when the finger stopped moving, he would never hear the sound of the bullet fired. Hopefully, he would not feel the impact of the bullet entering into his face and the shockwave blow out the back of his head.

"If it's the last thing I do, I'm going to blow your head off, kid. Say goodbye," snarled leader man, looking down at Mike. The gun came down and touched Mike on his head. It would be Mike's last memory.

Mike heard what he said and looked back up to that growl on leader man's face. He felt a sense of satisfaction knowing when that gun was fired, he saved his friends and stopped those men from killing his family.

Within seconds before the third shot and between that space of time, Chopper had closed the gap. When the gun tapped Mike on his head was when Chopper's left hand shattered another jaw. This time Bell didn't need to follow up with a kick to remove the rest. His teeth all went flying in the air. Some stuck into the side of the wooden walls of the duplex. After several spinning laps on his feet created by the powerful punch Chopper landed, leader man dropped like a rock. He fell in a small condensed pile.

Reaching down, Chopper pulled the bandana off his head. Lifting the bandana, he flapped it open, then laid it across leader man's face. Mike squirmed from under the leader man's falling body.

"Oh." Somewhere came a soft moan, and again, another moan was heard. This time Mike heard the moan as Chopper turned to follow the sound back to its source. Over to one side of the duplex was where it was coming from. Softly the sound seemed to rise. Both Chopper and Mike turned to see where and what had caused that moan of pain.

Unbeknown to Chopper, when he ran to Mike's aid, he did not realize Bell had followed behind him. When leader man swung his gun to fire, he believed it missed him. He was still charging at the leader man when Bell caught the bullet.

Chopper raced over to his love. She was lying on her back with one hand across her shoulder. Blood oozed out between her fingers.

Bending down to cradle Bell's head in his arms, she moaned as her head was lifted onto Chopper's lap. Mike had gotten to his feet, walking over to where Bell lay. There he stood looking down, watching how gentle Chopper cradled her in his arms.

Bone Breaker appeared and stood beside him. Mike felt his strong grip watching Chopper and Bell, and it tightened with each moan from Bell.

"Shh, Bell, honey. It will be all right."

"He shot me, Chopper." Bell stared up at Chopper, and both their eyes met. Each had tears forming in them.

Chopper placed his hand on top of hers, pressing against the bullet hole. The blood eased up.

"Yeah, I can see that, honey. Now lie there and be calm while I check the hole." Slowly, he peeled back her black leather vest, seeing blood oozing out of her left shoulder. Chopper unbuttoned her shirt and pulled the shoulder sleeve down to expose the hole in her shoulder. He reached behind her back to feel for an exit hole. "You'll be fine, honey. The bullet went clean through. It didn't rattle around inside you." Turning to look at Bone Breaker and Mike, Chopper barked out two orders, one to Mike and one to Bone Breaker. "Mike, run to my bike and look in my saddlebags, git the box with the red cross on top. You can't miss it. Now, quick with you.

"Bone Breaker, go and put those three men somewhere safe. If the police show up, I don't want any explaining to do."

Bone Breaker looked about to locate a good hiding place for those limp gang members lying on the ground.

Before Mike left, he pointed to the home, a duplex. One was empty, having no residents. "In there, Bone Breaker! No one's living there!" Mike yelled to him.

Mike turned, running quickly to Chopper's bike. In the saddlebag Mike first looked in was the white box with a red cross sign. Grabbing it, he ran back to Chopper and Bell.

With one hand, Bone Breaker had two gang members' arms in one of his massive arms. The other hand held leader man by his leg. He dragged them to the rear door of the duplex next door. It had three steps up on a porch leading to the rear door. Each step formed a bump to leader man's head.

The other two gang members had an easier trip up the steps. Once at the top of the deck, the two gang members' gentle trip Bone Breaker gave them ended with the door being opened. It took two knocks at the door before it opened. Each knock at the door was from both gang members' head tapping at the door. On the third tap with both heads swinging like a whip snapping, the door flew open. It shut as Bone Breaker entered with all three bodies inside. He swiftly tied them with ropes before leaving.

Chopper had plugged the hole in Bell's shoulder. "Now, baby, this is gonna hurt a bit." He pulled out of the first aid box a roll of gauze. He placed it in her mouth. "Bite down hard while I pour this alcohol over your hole."

It hurt. Bell screamed, but not loud enough to make a scene. She was one tough woman, Mike thought, watching them.

"Mike, we need to get her inside before someone comes along."

Mike's house faced the road and at an intersection. If need be, Chopper could make a getaway quick enough. Mike looked at his house. No one had come out. *Maybe, just maybe, my family wasn't home*, Mike thought.

"Give me a second, Chopper." Mike ran to the rear porch steps of his home, opening the back door. Inside were his two sisters standing in the kitchen, looking out the window.

"Mike, what happened out there? Who are those two guys? Is that woman hurt?" Sharon asked.

Boo ran to jump on Mike. He had to make him stop until he was able to hold the door open. "Good boy, you did really good." Mike petted Boo, praising him. Boo wagged his tail to the fact Mike recognized his warning and alerted Mike's sisters. "Boo's yelping startled those guys long enough for me to strike at the leader man," Mike said excitedly to both sisters. "Listen, did you call the police?" Mike quickly inquired of his sisters.

"What? Why would we do that?" Dodie replied.

Mike heard this reply, stunned by them not hearing him cry out to call the police. "You mean, you didn't hear me yelling to call the police?"

"No. We were in the living room watching TV. Boo went crazy. We got up to see what he was barking at." Dodie was amazed and surprised hearing her brother was calling her to phone the police.

Mike quickly told both his sisters what they needed to do. "Dodie, whatever you do, pretend to know these people. You too, Sharon. Chopper is with his woman on the ground. Bell is her name. She's been shot by three men who were about to attack this home. They were after me, to kill me and my family."

"Who?" Dodie seemed to be full of questions. To many questions, Mike believed. He needed them to quit asking questions so he could get them ready for what may follow.

Mike quickly tried to explain to his befuddled sisters. "Remember me telling you what happened in the city? Those gang members chasing after me. I clawed them in their faces. I told you they had followed me across the city to a park. The police arrested all of them or tried to. I believe they got free escaping deep into the city back streets. Well, they followed me here.

"Chopper and Bell and the big guy were the biker gang that helped me out in the mountains. They are friends. Chopper is the leader and told me he was going to come by and check on me when I get home. He found me crossing the street from school."

"Big guy? What big guy?" Dodie turned around to look for anyone out the opened door. Sharon went to the window. Both of them said, "We don't see anyone outside."

Mike, standing by the back door, waved at the two people slowly walking toward their home.

"Hey, Mike, where can I lay Bell down?" asked Chopper, walking up the stairs carrying Bell, who was clinging to him with both her arms wrapped around his shoulders. Chopper was standing in the door, holding Bell in his arms.

Sharon and Dodie turned. They were shocked at what walked through the door.

"Oh my!" cried Dodie, seeing Bell in Chopper's arms with blood covering her arm and shirt. Dodie acted quickly. "Over here, lay her on the couch." Dodie picked up the two end pillows, laying them at one end for Bell's head to rest upon the couch. Chopper gently carried her to the couch, laying her down. Bell was awake and in pain.

"Is she going to be okay, sir? Can I do anything else to help her?" Dodie asked Chopper.

"No," replied Chopper as he put his hand on Bell's hands. Then looking back up to Dodie, he replied, "Yes, there is, can you get her a blanket?"

"Oh, yes, sure." Dodie was still trying to process the events that transpired but began to act. Sharon remained by the back door, holding it open. Mike moved to where Chopper and Bell were telling Sharon to keep the door open.

Boo jumped on the couch. Chopper was about to shoo him away until Bell raised her hand to stop him. "Let him be. He is trying to help. He's so cute. What's his name?" she asked to anyone nearby. Bell looked straight at Mike; tears were welling up in his eyes.

"It's Boo, Bell. I found him on the road, coming home. He was tied to a tree half starved. We been together ever since."

"He's a good dog. He warned your family." Bell smiled at Mike.

"Yes, he sure did try to warn them. He also helped me when I ran at the leader man. He distracted him long enough for me to jump on him."

Bell noticed the tears in both Chopper's and Mike's eyes before making a comment. "You two men are supposed to be big and strong. I'm the one hurt and should be crying from all this pain, instead you two are welling up full of tears. If you going to cry, do it outside. I got this warm blanket covering me and don't want it all wet from your bawling. I'm fine, don't worry."

Chopper had removed his jacket and laid it across Bell.

Dodie rushed to the bedroom nearest her, picking up one of the few blankets they had. Quickly returning, she handed the blanket to Chopper.

"Thank you, uh, Dodie. Is that correct?" Chopper asked.

"Oh yes, that is my name." Dodie was Mike's older sister. She did most of the chores around the house. Mike's mom stayed drunk when not working. Dodie had to learn how to write checks to pay the bills.

"Well, thank you. You have been a great help," Chopper said.

Mike looked at Chopper and was awestruck by his kindness expressed to his sister. He thought Chopper was one tough dude having little kindness left in him. A small smile crossed Mike's face listening to what he heard coming from Chopper.

Dodie, after receiving this small compliment, lowered her head as to cover the blush she was having from his remark.

Sharon, still standing near the back door, reached for the knob. She grabbed the door to shut it. Half closing the door, it stopped. Her eyes were still fixed on Chopper and Bell. Pulling the door back, she slammed it again to close it, but it still stopped. Turning, she saw the reason why the door would not shut.

A large foot was preventing the door from closing. Her eyes drifted vertically upward to the point the ceiling was just short of touching a huge man having a beard covering his face with two big angry eyes staring down at her. Sharon stepped back, then stepped back a second step.

Bone Breaker took up the whole visible area of her sight. Too much of him was still not visible until she took that second step back. Once back, she could see the entire person that he made up. It was almost too much of an effort to keep from letting out a scream of astonishment. Instead, she simply covered her mouth. Sharon's second step and with her hand against her mouth had her nearly tripping back on her feet, looking up at Bone Breaker. If not for the huge hand reaching out to stop her rearward tipping on the brink of falling, she would be looking up from the floor at him.

"Sorry about the foot, but I needed to get inside, little girl." A big grin beamed across his face.

Sharon at first thought he was going to eat her. Then she realized he was smiling.

Mike heard Bone Breaker enter the house and turned to see his sister nearly falling to the floor from seeing his appearance. He called out to him, "Bone Breaker, that is my twin sister, Sharon. The other one is my older sister, Dodie."

Dodie turned around to see who Mike was talking to. She too had a similar experience as Sharon with the sight of him. She stood silently and could only watch him enter through the back door into the house.

"Chopper, I got them three men in the other house. I tied them with a rope lying around. It should hold them until our gang gets here." Bone Breaker had a booming voice when he spoke, so there was no misunderstanding him. Even if you didn't get what he was saying, you didn't want to ask him to repeat the message.

"Right, now get on your bike and get some of our boys back here as fast as you can. Try not to draw the law back with you. Got it?" commanded Chopper to Bone Breaker.

Bone Breaker nodded, turning to leave out the rear door.

Before Bone Breaker got out the door, a police siren and lights were out in front of the duplex. Dodie walked to the front window, calling out, "It's the police. Why are they here? What are we going to do?" She was in a near panic.

Chopper walked over to her, putting his hand on her shoulder and telling her to be calm. "Everything will be okay. Mike!" Chopper called out.

"Yes, Chopper?"

"Go out and greet them. I will be with you soon as I get Bell up and looking fit."

"Sure." Opening the door, Mike walked out. It was the same two officers on the street. Same one as before, one walked up to Mike, and his hand was on his revolver, same as it was before. Before Mike could remark as to why the visit, the officer asked him a question.

"Hey, kid, aren't you the same kid at the road?"

"Yes, sir." Mike followed his reply with a nod.

Chopper exited the door at that time. The two officers seeing him realized the bikes parked near the road was theirs. "Oh, and what are you doing here?" asked the same officer who asked Mike his question. The second officer spotted Chopper and swiftly approached next to the first. Side by side, they stood looking at Chopper and Mike as if they committed a crime.

They are right, a crime was committed, but not by us, Chopper thought. "What's the visit for, officer?" he asked, not understanding why they came. Chopper was good at keeping what his thoughts and actions were from the law.

Mike looked at him in awe. He was good at not revealing anything to them.

"We got a call that shots were being fired. Some neighbors called, they heard gunshots."

"Oh, I see. Naturally, seeing me and my bikes here, you assumed someone had been shot by us."

The first officer led the questioning. "Yeah, you might think that way. Has there been any gunfire, Mr. Chopper?"

"You can see for yourself. Please inspect the area. Just wasting your time."

"Our time, sir."

"Hey, officers, do you want to come inside and inspect my home while you're at it?" called Mike to the officers, who were turning to inspect the yard.

When the officer got to the steps, he stopped long enough to eye Mike's appearance. "What happened to you, kid? By the looks of you, it seems to me you been in a fight or tussle."

Quickly, Mike responded, "No, sir, not a tussle. I get home, and my dog wants some quality time. I just got inside the house from playing with him on the ground."

"Thanks," the second officer responded for the invite as he finished with his first inquiry with Mike. He walked up the steps and passed Chopper and Mike as the two of them parted to allow him access through the door into Mike's home.

Chopper gave Mike a soft pat on his back, turning to follow the officer into the house. "Nice move, Mike," he whispered, passing along his side.

Mike nodded back, following him into the house.

Inside, Bell was sitting up, and Dodie sat near her, holding her hand. The officer nodded his head and asked Dodie where her mother or dad were. "Is your mother home, young lady?"

Dodie replied, "No, sir. She's at work and won't be home for another hour. Our dad was killed serving our country in the navy. My mom is a widower."

Bell spoke up. "Officer, we plan on staying here until she gets home."

"Did anyone hear a gunshot sound?"

Dodie shook her head. Sharon, standing next to Bone Breaker, also shook her head. Chopper spoke up. He stood half in and half out the door with his hands folded across his chest. "Officer, you said someone reported gunshots. Well, they weren't gunshots, maybe it was our bikes backfiring when we arrived here."

"Hmm." The officer turned around, eyeing the room he was standing in. "Well, there sure doesn't seem to be anything wrong going on in this home. While you are here, I hope we don't continue to make house calls on you while you remain in this town." After several seconds of staring at Chopper for any sign of suspicious activities he might be concealing, it gave way to nothing happening on the expression on his face. The officer was convinced nothing was nefariously going on, and he turned, walking out of the house.

Seeing his partner return from walking about the outside for any signs of suspicious events happening, he waved to him. They both stood talking for a minute.

Chopper and Mike stood on the porch watching.

"Well, you all have a good evening." Both got into their cars and drove off.

Returning inside, Chopper went and sat by Bell. He turned to her. "You did good, babe. Now you lie here and rest." Looking up at Bone Breaker, he asked him, "You still here?"

Bone Breaker got the message and left out through the rear door.

Chopper stood away from the couch where Bell lay, turning back for one more look at Bell. Mike could see the concern in his eyes for him and Bell. "I need to check on those men next door, Mike. Keep an eye on Bell."

"No need to leave her, Chopper," Mike returned. "I can go and check on them. Bone Breaker said he tied them up. They ain't going to give me any trouble. I stick my head in and make sure they are still there tied up. No need to worry. Be back in a second. Sharon, shut the door behind me. When I come back, let me in."

Sharon shut and locked the door as soon as Mike was outside.

Mike quickly went down the steps and ran next door with Boo on his heels. Opening the door, Mike saw two of the men still lying on the floor, out like a lamp. The leader man was sure one tough dude; he was standing up and nearly had his bonds off when he saw Mike. His jaw hung limply from the rest of his mouth, just dangling down. He tried to speak, but to no avail. His eyes turned a vicious red with hatred filling his expression, looking at Mike.

Like a mad dog frothing from his mouth, he stumbled toward Mike. The ropes slowed his advance. When he got within range of Mike, a memory of what Sensei taught Mike flashed through his mind: "To keep an opponent off-balance, blind his seeing you move. His focus changes from you to the obstruction of his sight. Strike quick and hard before he gets his sight back. Your movement will seem invisible to him. Your movement will be but a flash, and fear will fill his heart. The unknown of an attack makes one feel helpless, no matter how strong he may think he may be. Your hand in his eyes will hold him fast, his sight of you will be obstructed, and before he can remove the obstacle, it will be of little use."

Suddenly, Mike's next move came rushing into his mind. With an open hand, he flung it at leader man's face. Mike's hand grew in size as it neared leader man's eyes. Anything beyond Mike's hand was invisible to leader man. Without touching leader man, Mike made him helpless. That was when Boo reacted; he charged, biting the bad foot where Mike stabbed it. Two things were beyond leader man's sight; the other thing was sounds of a barking dog confusing him. Two threats needed to be dealt with. Between Mike blocking his sight and Boo's bite, he was at their mercy.

He raised his arms to move Mike's hand from his view. Before realizing his mistake he was led to make, Mike's other hand raced out to his throat. His waving arms prevented Mike from clearly seeing where his hand landed. He felt the soft skin of leader man's throat. His dangling chin was knocked to one side as Mike's cupped hand sank deep into that throat.

A sharp wheeze came immediately from leader man. Both his hands grasped at his throat. His eyes bulged from their sockets. For a second, Mike thought he might have maybe caused a severe hit bad enough to kill. Leader man started to suck in air while looking at Mike. The thought in Mike's mind that he might have killed him soon ran out.

Leader man attempted to lash out at Mike standing before him. He didn't get a second chance to grab Mike; he was struck again by Mike. A quick kick to his kneecap took him down.

Mike could see the pain in leader man's contorted face when his leg bent in the opposite direction the good Lord had not intended it to. He almost felt sorry for him before kicking him in his gut with a follow-up front snap kick. Everything leader man ate that day in his stomach came heaving out his mouth. The jaw dangling directed some of the puke back up into his face. He fell flat facedown in the puke that just came flying out of his mouth. Both the puke and a puddle of blood mingled, swirling in an eddy, in and out of his gaping mouth.

as he lay there squirming in pain, trying to cry out, Mike quickly grabbed both arms, holding them behind his back. Boo changed from biting his leg and tore into his hanging jaw. Once Mike retied both hands, he had to pry Boo off leader man's mouth. Not too soon, he almost pulled it completely off. It was bleeding bad, but still attached, just dislocated with a few teeth remaining.

Chopper came charging through the door. Looking down at Mike on top of leader man was all that needed to be said to him. He could see what Mike did. The only question he asked Mike was how he did it?

After a short explanation, Chopper reached to pick up some rope. "Here you go, Mike. You did this to him, you get to tie him up. This time, do us a favor and do a better job than Bone Breaker. Oh, by the way, you can rub it in when you see him," sniped Chopper to Mike.

"No way, Chopper. I will leave that up to you. My shoulder still is a bit sore from his welcome on the street today." Mike double-checked the other two still wrapped up and used the rope Chopper handed Mike to double up on their ties.

Turning to Chopper, Mike asked him a question. "Chopper, what are you going to do with these guys? When they get back to the city, they will be coming back for me and my family and maybe after you bikers. Why didn't you let the police take them?"

Turning to Mike, Chopper stared into his eyes. It was his eyes and what he was thinking made apparent on his face that said it all to Mike. It didn't need saying.

Mike wanted to know anyway; he had to know. "Chopper, tell me, please? It's my family," Mike begged.

"Okay, Mike. I plan on taking them on a bike ride. They won't be bothering you or your family again."

"But, Chopper, their gang members might know where they went and come looking for them."

"Mike, do you trust me?"

"Yes, I do, but—" replied Mike.

"No buts, Mike. I can assure you their members will know exactly where they are and won't come a-looking. Now take that worry out of your mind. Come now, let's get back inside with the ladies. We don't want them worrying what has become of us. It has been a busy day. You think?"

"Yeah, it has been a bit busy today, Chopper."

Together, they walked back to the house. After about thirty minutes, one could hear the sound of bikes approaching. The roar of the engines stopped when they got to the house.

Chopper walked over to the window, pulling the curtain back. "Hey, Mike, all your worries will soon be gone." Then he turned to look at Bell. She was still sitting up on the couch with Dodie. "Honey, Bell, you feeling a bit better?" he asked her.

"Sure, whatever was in that shot you gave me sure helps."

When they got back in the house, Chopper grabbed his bag. He was about to take out a vial to give to Bell when he suddenly felt the need to rush over and check on Mike at the other house where the three gang members were being held. He gave her a shot of painkillers, he called it, returning back to Mike's home. It worked just fine. Soon as he administered it to Bell, she went into dreamland, only to be woken by a familiar sound of bikes roaring to a stop.

Razor entered the room as Chopper opened the door. A sigh of relief whistled from his mouth. "The way Bone Breaker was telling what happened, we hurried here half expecting a bad scene." Looking at Bell and back at Chopper, he continued, "Well, looks like everything is fine. Guess we are too late. The danger is over."

"Talk for yourself," Bell quipped back. "You ain't carrying this hole in you, Razor."

Bone Breaker went to the other house. Looking at leader man, he quickly realized what happened before he left. Hurrying over to the house, he rushed in through the door. Everyone turned to see him enter. Through panting breaths, he asked if Chopper was all right.

Chopper, hearing this, replied, "Of course I am. Why the worry?"

"Well, I went to check on them fellows, and leader man got loose. I figured he may have caused some harm to someone, or I thought that before you retied him up. I guess I was wrong. Everyone looks fine. My bad."

"No, you were right. It wasn't me but Mike here. He went to check on them. Leader man got loose."

Bone Breaker turned his gaze to Mike. A curious look appeared on his face.

"Mike took him down?" Bone asked Chopper. "What? How? No way, the kid did that to him?" Looking back at Mike, he asked him, "Really, you did that?"

"Yes."

"How? Man, that guy is bigger than you."

"Tell him, Mike. If you don't tell him, he will plague me all the rest of the year. So do us a favor and tell him how you took him down," Chopper said.

"My sensei taught me how to fight. One of his many lessons was to disable your opponent by removing his sight. Fear will enter your heart to the unknown."

"Wait, you took out his eyes? I didn't see his eyes missing!" exclaimed Bone Breaker with wonder on his face.

"I didn't take his eyes out, just kept him from seeing me."

Puzzlement was expressed on Bone Breaker's face with each explanation Mike gave. Bone Breaker couldn't believe that a small person took down this tough punk.

"Do you want me to show you?" Mike asked Bone Breaker.

Bone Breaker stood there contemplating what he should respond with.

Chopper called out to him, "Go ahead, let him show you. You ain't afraid of a small kid, are you?"

Bone Breaker stiffened up and stood tall. "Go ahead, Mike, show me what you did."

Walking over to where Bone Breaker stood, Mike stopped short of an arm's length. "I am not going to hit you, so please don't kill me," Mike timidly said.

Bone Breaker nodded back not to worry.

Looking at this huge man still made Mike worry how he would react. Mike asked Bone Breaker in a low and polite manner, "Okay, you ready?"

Another nod.

Before he finished his nod, Mike shot out his open palm at Bone's eyes, quickly sidestepping to one side of Bone Breaker. When Bone reacted to remove Mike's hand from his sight, Mike was behind Bone Breaker, reaching up between his legs. Looking down to where Mike once stood, he felt and saw a hand. It was in the place that was most vulnerable to any man, even one as big as Bone Breaker.

Chopper called out, "Look between your legs."

Looking down, Bone Breaker saw Mike's tiny hand reaching up and stop. Quickly he closed his thighs, but not before Mike gave Bone a gentle tap where it counts, then removing his hand before Bone could snap his thighs on it.

Everyone let out a laugh.

Bone Breaker reached behind himself before Mike had a chance to get out of his range. With a firm but gentle tug, he pulled Mike around to face him. Then staring down with an expression of madness across his face, he bursts into laughter. Then he twirled Mike around and slapped him on his back, flinging him over to Chopper.

Chopper stopped Mike from crashing into him. "There now, Mike, that wasn't so bad. He took that quite well. Don't you think, heh, Mike?" quipped Chopper.

Bell started to laugh, then she cried from the pain it caused her arm. Still, she couldn't stop laughing just thinking how easily Mike slipped behind Bone Breaker and grabbed at him. Throughout the night, she would wake and begin to laugh again from that memory.

Everyone was still laughing at the demonstration when Mike's mom walked in. Seeing all the bikes in the front yard gave her some concern. Passing through several bikers standing outside on guard duty, she entered her home. Beside the bikers, Mom appeared to be a child. *Every biker stood a foot taller than Mom*, Mike noted to himself.

Chopper, seeing her for the first time, remarked to Mike, "Hey, kiddo, your mom's a looker." He turned back to Mom. "Now now, before you lose your cool, let me explain," Chopper quickly spoke at her.

Mom stood there near the front door dressed in a pantsuit with soft-soled shoes. Her hair was cut just short of her shoulders. Her black hair hung down with a wave and a curl at the end. She still kept her hair parted down the middle. Standing next to Razor, she seemed to be smaller compared to her standing next to her children.

After looking around and seemingly calm to all the strange men in the house, she staunchly placed her hands on her hips. "Well, somebody better talk, and do it quick."

"Yes, madam," Chopper replied with a new sense of respect for her. "See, it's this way. I made a promise to Mike I would check on him. After we gave him a ride home, Bell got shot, and Mike, he took down the leader man. All three of them are resting next door."

Mom's face seemed shocked. A million questions came flooding in upon hearing that jumbled mess of occurrences. *It's a wonder that I was able to understand her puzzlement and shocked look on her face*, Mike thought, watching her.

"What in the hell did you just tell me? Three men? Bell who? Shot? Why? And who in God's name are you?" All those questions in one breath were bellowed at Chopper.

Dodie, Sharon, and Mike stood back and found the table to sit around. They just watched, trying to avoid her wrath. They saw her get mad many times, and the symptoms were well known to them.

If Chopper didn't speak quickly enough, all hell was going to be let loose on them all.

Before another word was said between parties, a calmer, softer voice spoke up. "Mrs. O, your son, if I may explain, was befriended by us in the mountains. He was sick and hungry, we aided him, and in doing so, we all became his friends. We told him before he left us, we would come by his home to check on his well-being. You have a brave and strong boy. We are greatly pleased to call him a friend."

Mom turned to see a woman sitting on her couch. She had tattoos covering every exposed skin with pictures usually found on sailors. She noticed her arm was bandaged. Boo was lying in her lap. Other than the tattoos that decorated her body, Bell looked pretty. A bit on the rough side with what she was wearing, but pretty.

"I don't know the extent he had discussed with you his many adventures and if he had mentioned us. Hopefully, he has mentioned Chopper, who you are talking to. I'm Bell, and this man is Razor. Over there by the back door is Bone Breaker."

"Bone Breaker? What, who is a bone breaker?" Mom asked with curiosity.

Bell pointed to where he stood.

Mom turned to see him.

True to his name and the response he gets, Mom too was in awe. She stood there for a minute with her mouth open, just looking at him. Only when Bell began her explanation did Mom come back from her shock.

Turning, she saw Bell on the couch. This time, she took notice of the red spot on her shoulder. "What happened to you? Are you all right?" Looking back to Chopper, she said, "Shot, you said Bell was shot. Is that what you mean? A gunshot! Was anybody other than Bell shot?" Mom's questioning started becoming rapid. Mom turned to look at her three kids sitting at the table.

They all responded together. "Mom, we are all fine."

A slight relief went across her face. She turned back to Bell. "Did anyone call a doctor?"

Chopper interrupted Bell before she started to speak. "Mrs. O, that might not be the best idea."

"What?"

"Hold on a second. Bell, she is fine. We tended to her wound. It is not that bad. The bullet went straight through and out with little damage. We cleaned the wound and packed it. Bell was given an antibiotic and a sedative shot. She will need to stay here for a day or so." Chopper was barely able to complete the last sentence before Mom hit him with several more questions.

"What, stay here? Who is going to take care of her? I will be going to work. You can't leave her here unattended."

"I will be here as well," Chopper answered her.

"You are kidding. Look around, this is a small home with two bedrooms. We have little food, barely enough for my children. I can't afford to feed and take care of Bell." Mom looked at Bell with an "I'm sorry" look.

"No worries, Mrs. O, we will provide everything we need and help out with all the food," responded Chopper.

"But, but..." Mom tried to think of something to say.

"Mrs. O, we had the police here before you arrived home. If they saw the three gang members in the other building, there can be a lot of questions you don't want them to ask." Bell quickly responded to Mom's multiple questions fired at them.

"Really, like what can they ask?"

"We were attacked by three men bent on trying to kill your son."

"What three men? Where are they? Are they dead? Oh my god!" Bell's reply of three men suddenly made an impact in Mom's mind.

"Mrs. O, what Bell is trying to convey is those questions will come out in the news. The men have friends. They will most likely come and avenge them. You will never be safe. Mike will be taken into protected custody and possibly your whole family. This will only be until the trial is over."

"After the trial, what then?"

"Mrs. O, we want only to help you and Mike through all of this," said Chopper.

Mom stood there shaking her head back and forth.

Seeing her concerns and worry written on her actions, Chopper spoke up again. "Mrs. O, we can protect you and prevent any of this from ever being known."

Mom's face turned ashen at what she suddenly realized what Chopper was going to do with those three men. "You mean you are…"

Chopper quickly realized that she thought they were going to dispose of the men, kill them and hide the bodies. "No, Mrs. O, none of that." Chopper continued to explain. "You need to understand, those types of men are killers. They have killed, and they will kill again. This won't go away by calling the police. We live in this kind of environment. Believe me when I say to you, this is only the beginning. We need to end this before it gets started any further. We have ways of dealing with this. Trust us, when we leave, you will not need to worry—ever.

"Now to reassure you, we will continue to pass through this town and follow up with a check on your family. Mike is part of this family of mine, and we take care of our own."

Mom was standing next to Razor. He raised his arm and laid it across Mom's shoulder. For a moment, it gave her a sense of relief with Razor's arm holding her.

Dodie, standing up, spoke. "Mom, it will be okay, we can do this for them."

Then Sharon spoke up. "Mom, they helped us."

Mike stood and put his two cents in. "Mom, they saved our lives. Those men were about to break into the house and would have. You might have come home with all of us dead. If not for Chopper, Bone Breaker, and Bell, we just might have been." Mike walked over to Bone Breaker and put his arm around him. "These people are good people. If they leave, I am leaving with them," Mike stated.

"Now, none of that, Mike." Bell continued to speak, but with more difficulty. The drug seemed to be having some effect on her. "Mike, this is your home, and your family needs you."

"Bell," Chopper interrupted, "Mike may be right. If we leave and not take care of this business before we leave, well, it will be best if he does come with us. To protect him and to keep the others from coming here." His final remarks were said staring into Mike's mom's eyes. No words came, just a strong sense of assurance was given to her through their eyes meeting.

"Okay, okay, I will agree to your terms," Mom blurted out. "But—and I mean *but*—no harm comes to those men you have. I want your promise, and if you don't promise, I will take my chances with the police."

Razor turned to face Mike's mom. "Mrs. O, I will guarantee the three men we have will not be harmed any further once we leave here. We never break our promises." Razor had eyes that could melt ice when he looked at you.

Mom melted some when he looked at her.

"Mom, that's right, they never, ever break their promise." Mike gave her a smile, turned, and gave Chopper a nod. He already told Mike what he intended to do. Razor gave his word, not Chopper's word. Also, he said no further harm will come to them when they leave.

In truth, they won't feel a thing and will be at peace, was Razor's thoughts to Mike's remarks.

After all was said, Mom walked over to the table. She asked the three kids if they were hunger. Lifting her head, she turned to ask the others if they were hungry. "We have little to offer as a good meal to feed you. I will do my best to have enough for you and your men."

"No worries, Mrs. O, that is being taken care of as we speak." Bone Breaker had walked over to the kitchen refrigerator. Looking inside and at the empty shelves, he silently gave Chopper a signal as Mom was talking to him.

Turning to Razor, he whispered in his ear. Razor turned and opened the front door. Before he walked out, Mike told him he wanted to go with him. Mom put her hand on her son's shoulder to halt his walk toward Razor. He looked back at her and said, "It will be okay."

Chopper followed up with, "He will be just fine. Besides, after what he went through, it will probably do him some good. My experience after such things, alone time is the best cure to find your way back in coping with pain. Razor knows this as well. Mike can have another man to talk this incident out with."

Razor waited for Mike before they both walked out the door. Mike got on the bike with Razor. One other biker started up his bike to travel along. The other two men by the bikes went into the house with the three men as the sun began its slow descent.

Before the two riders got to town, it turned dark. Several bikers passed them by on the way to town. Mike tapped Razor on his back. Razor knew what was about to be asked by him. "Mike, they will help with those gang members. We need to get them as far away from this town before daylight. It could be hard to explain to any law dogs if they pass by them riding on the back of our bikes. Each one will be tied to a biker to keep them upright and to prevent them from getting any bright ideas about jumping off."

"Where and how—?" Mike started to ask.

Razor stopped him in midsentence. "Least you know, the better, kid. Know this, we tend to send a message back to the city. It will help to mislead them and keep them from following up any further." Razor slapped Mike's leg, then revved up the engine, giving Mike a jerk back on the bike.

He grabbed hold of Razor for dear life.

First place they stopped was the Big Apple store. They both walked to the store while their companion waved to Razor and drove off back to the house. Mike looked at Razor as to why the companion was leaving.

Razor again read Mike's mind. "Mike, Baby Face is going to get some hot food. I motioned back to him as we passed a fish house to drop by, get us all supper."

"You mean the Shrimp Boat on the left just up from my home?"

"Yeah, that's the place. Is the food good, kiddo?"

"Yeah, Mom gets us dinner once a week from there. They got the best hush puppies you ever ate." Mike smiled back at Razor to confirm his answer.

Thirty minutes later and after a filling up a cart full of food, they walked up to the register to pay.

"That is a lot of food to put on the bike," Mike said to Razor.

"No problem." Then to Mike's surprise as the total was rung up, Razor pulled out of his pocket the largest wad of rolled money Mike thought possible to come out of a pocket.

"My god, where, I mean why?" Then Mike realized that might not be the right question. "Do you carry that much money around?"

"We do a lot of moving around. Haven't got the time to stop at a bank to make deposits. Also we would need to do that in every town we go to. Most towns don't always carry the same banks. Also, might I add, they tend to ask questions with this amount of money. They want to know where all the money comes from. The government might wonder when they see a large amount enter in a bank. Just too many questions. Might need to get money quick anytime," Razor explained.

After paying for the food, both carried two bags of food to Razor's bike. Razor had two compartments on both sides of the rear of his bike. Looking at them as they neared his bike, Mike couldn't help to ask him a question. "Aren't those already filled with your stuff?"

Sure is, but there is always room for more." Opening the first compartment, it looked full. Not for long. Razor grabbed hold of his clothes and lay them across the rear seat. Then, like magic, he put his bags inside. Taking one of Mike's bags, he finished the packing. "Now, Mike, watch this." Stepping around to the other compartment, Razor shoved all the stuff to one side and put the last bag he held into the empty spot. Then the clothes on the seat were laid on top. With a bit of effort, the lid closed.

"See, easy as pie."

"Yeah, easy as pie," Mike returned the quip.

"Now, Mike, get on, and back home we go."

Hopping on back, Mike asked Razor to pull to the other side of the parking lot.

"What's up, kid?"

"I…I…"

"Let me guess, kid. You a bit upset with what just happened back there at your home."

"Not really, Razor. I been through a lot of stuff, and that fight did bother me much. I guess what really bothers me is they might come back here? I did not travel all this way home to lose my family for something I did on the road." Mike finished with what his concerns were that were building inside of him.

"Hey, kid, you helped save a man's life in an alley from them gang is what I been told. Ain't nothing wrong with that. In fact, that was a good thing. Not many people would have put their life on the line for a stranger. Heh, not even for their own family. Many would cower and beg for their life. Do you regret saving his life now?"

"No, no, I don't. I just was thinking if I hadn't, maybe—"

Razor interrupted Mike's sentence. "Quit that maybe. You can maybe on that all your life. What's important is you did right. Besides, how do you truly know if you didn't save his life, they would have chased after you? Remember, you were in that alley with them before that man you saved showed up. Instead of running away when they turned to face that guy, you remained. That took guts, kid. If I ever had a kid, I wish he would be half the kid you are."

Mike grabbed a hold of Razor, holding on to him tight. Tears began to form in the corner of Mike's eyes. "Thank you, thank you all. I'm proud to know people like you."

"Ahh, kid, cut that out. You going to make me regret everything I said about you." Razor tugged on Mike to sit up. Mike held on tighter. "Okay, you hug on me a little bit more. Just don't you go and tell them other biker rats I was all fatherly. You got that, kid?"

Mike gave a little nod.

They sat on the bike for several minutes.

Back home on the porch, the door was opened for them. Chopper was standing by the door holding it open. "About time you guys got back. Your supper's getting cold. For a minute, I was about to come looking for you. What happened, you get lost?"

Razor looked at him and quietly said, "We had a moment."

Chopper nodded back.

"How's Bell?" he asked.

"She ate some food. Then before she finished her whole meal, she went to sleep. Over on the table is what's left for you two. Bone Breaker takes three meals to fill him up. I had to stop him before all of it was gone. In fact, I was just getting Baby Face to leave to get a refill." Chopper looked at Baby Face getting on his bike.

Baby Face wore a vest and no shirt. He had a hairless chest and no facial hair.

Chopper told Mike he was twenty-nine years old and never had to shave, hence his name.

"Be back in a second!" Baby Face shouted to all. Turning his bike, he was off with his long hair streaming, flying in the wind behind his head.

Mike along with Razor and Chopper entered the house. Bell lay on the couch asleep like Chopper told them. Mom and Mike's sisters sat at the table. Bone Breaker was finishing off all the rest of the food.

"Are you filled?" Chopper called to him sarcastically.

"Well, maybe a bit more to top off. You know I get hungry when I have to do all that fighting."

"What fighting? All you did was slam that one guy's head through the shed's wall," responded Chopper.

"He was heavy and hard to lift, Chopper." Bone Breaker peeked over to Mike's way and winked. "Oh yeah, I had to carry them three guys to the other house. Besides, the one stuck in the hole in the shed, he was hard to get out. I had to hold him up just to pull his head out. It took me three good yanks before his head popped out of that hole."

"Yeah, well, you going to have to fix that hole before we leave. Don't worry, I told Baby Face to bring extra food for you."

"Sure, sure, Chopper. Whatever you want," said Bone while licking his fingers. "Thanks, I could use a little more for the long trip back to camp."

This time, Mom laughed at what Chopper said, along with the rest of them.

Mike walked over to Chopper and softly whispered in his ear. "Where are the other bikers?"

Chopper replied, "They are taking care of our problem." That was all he said about that for the whole time they remained with Mike's family.

Baby Face returned with more food. Chopper made Bone wait until the others had all they wanted to eat. After the meal was eaten, night came.

"All you kids get your baths and get ready for bed."

"Ah, Mom!" retorted all the kids.

"No ah moms, just do it," commanded Mom. "Mr. Chopper, you can stay in the house with Bell."

Razor spoke up. "Mrs. O, we intend to sleep over at the other house next door. We are used to sleeping out. Besides, we need to check on our group and will be off for a few hours. Before the night is over, we will be back. So see you all in the morning." Giving a handshake to Chopper, he walked over to Bell and patted her, saying good night, and turned, walking out the door followed by Baby Face and Bone Breaker, waving goodbye.

Everyone in the house all waved back, saying, "Good night."

Leaving the room, Mom walked over to Chopper. She took his hand in hers. "Thank you, thank you for saving my family." Now, tears filled her eyes.

"Know this, Mrs. O, your son did most of the saving this day. Weren't for what he did and when he did it, might have been too late before we were able to save your kids. We were still sitting on our butts astride our bikes, watching and wondering what he was up to. He ran at those men screaming out. We saw only him where he stood behind bushes and not what those men were up to. His quickness stopped them, allowing us time to get there to assist him. That is why we care so much about Mike. He has guts, and he is a good kid. No, a great kid. We will do anything for him. Believe me, when we leave, we won't forget him or this family."

"I know, Mr. Chopper I can tell from the way you talk to him and…and…"

"Yeah, you don't need to say it, Mrs. O." He looked at Bell. "She cares about him as well as the whole gang too. I believe she wished he was her son."

"Mr. Chopper, Mike lost his dad, and in many ways, you and your men seemed to have found a way into him as father figures. I hope you really feel that way."

After twenty minutes sitting with Bell and Chopper, a shout was heard.

"Mom!" Dodie called out to her.

"Yes?" responded Mom.

"We all have taken a bath. Can we come out and say good night?"

"Yes," Mom answered her back.

All three walked out wearing their sleeping clothes. Chopper quickly noted that none had pajamas or nightwear. He was glad Bell was sleeping. Her life was much the same in her home. All three kids came down the short hall back into the room where everyone was standing. Each of them said good night to Mom and Chopper. Mom told Chopper he could clean up next.

"Thanks, I'll use the backyard hose and a bar of soap."

"Are you sure?"

"Yes, it's how I wash almost daily. We often don't have a house or a place to stay most times. Oh, a towel if you could spare one, Mrs. O."

Chopper walked to the back door and down the steps, and soon he located the hose. Removing his shirt, he began his nightly ritual of cleaning.

Mom headed to the bathroom and began her shower. She and Chopper finished bathing at the same time. Both reentered the living room where Bell lay asleep. Once Bell was checked on and found to be okay, Mom said her good nights.

Chopper took the blanket Mom left and laid it at Bell's side on the floor.

Everyone woke early the next day. Even Bell was sitting up. When the kids entered the room where they were, Mom was serving them coffee. They had some toast with peanut butter and jelly. Saying goodbye, the kids left to go to school. Mike gave Bell a hug before leaving. Mom noted Mike hugging Bell and not her. So did Chopper and Bell.

Bell asked Mom, "Is that what they usually eat for breakfast?"

Mom, caught off guard by the question, was slightly embarrassed to answer back. "I'm afraid that is for the most part. Our money we get is used to pay rent and other bills. What I make working helps with the other necessities."

What Mom didn't tell them was that what was left of the money was spent on beer and cigarettes. Apparently, Chopper got up at night when Bell began to groan to find a glass for water. Looking in some of the shelves, he saw her two cartons of cigarettes and a six-pack of beer. He told Bell what he saw in the morning as they awoke an hour before the rest of the family.

"Babe, I'm afraid I know why they lost their home and had to come to Georgia."

"Yeah, I guess I know what you think," Bell replied back. "Babe, you know I left home because of my mom drinking all the time. We had nothing in the house except for all the yelling she gave us. Her booze and cigarettes meant more to her than my sister and I did. I couldn't stand it anymore. When you and the others came by, I got my chance and left with you. Chopper, I never looked back."

"Bell, I am only going to tell you this one time. Keep out of this. I know you feel their hurt, and I know full well you want to help them. But don't. No matter what you think you may be able to give them, it won't make them want to leave their mom. Kids have that bond with their parents. Now, you remember when you were young. I mean younger than when the time we showed up. Remember you telling me how you and your sister used to fight the teachers when they tried to help? Remember how you threw things and cursed at your neighbors when they tried to help? You two loved your mom.

"Never in a million years would you leave her or let someone take you away from her. She was Mom. Mike and his sisters feel the same way. You try to take them away, and they will hate you forever. Now remember this, we will stop by time and time again to check on them. If they need anything, we will be there for them. Right?"

"Right, babe," Bell agreed, but seeing this home and Mike's mother tore at her every day they remained.

"Mrs. O, if we can offer any help, you just let us know. Mike will know how to contact us. Please call for us anytime. We mean it," Chopper informed her before she left for work.

"Thank you, I will be going to work in a few minutes. Help yourself while you're here." Writing down a phone number, she handed it to Chopper. "This is my number at work. Mike and Sharon will be coming home for lunch. I should be home around five." Mom wore the same outfit from the other day. She went into the bathroom. Several minutes later, she emerged with her hair combed and face made up. Then she walked out the door and drove to work.

"Well, babe, here we are. You hungry?"

"Yeah, a bit," Bell replied.

"Want some eggs?"

"Sure, Chopper dear."

Chopper, now familiar with the layout of the kitchen, located the eggs and pan. After several minutes, he returned with six fried eggs and toast. He sat next to Bell. Both began eating.

"This is good, babe. I can get used to your cooking more often."

"Don't go getting any ideas, Bell. You still the cook. I ain't dying from my cooking."

Just then, Razor, Bone Breaker, and Baby Face walked in the front door.

"You eaten yet?" Chopper inquired.

Bone Breaker spoke first. "Sure, boss, we left early and went to this all-you-can-eat place."

"Yeah, they were damn glad we left after all the food he put away," replied Baby Face, taking a poke at Bone Breaker.

Razor spoke up. "We stopped by the gang's roosting place. After some questioning, we got what we needed to know."

Again, Baby Face spoke up. "Yeah, that leader man didn't want to talk much."

Bone Breaker butt in. "You think? With a broken jaw and no teeth, I guess it was hard to say anything."

"Well, Chopper, the other two did most of the talking. Leader man did a lot of nodding to agree with what they were telling us."

"Yeah, only after we gave him some incentives," spoke Baby Face.

"You going to tell this or am I, Baby Face." After a sharp retort and a nasty look from Razor, Baby Face stopped his butting in.

"It is as you guessed, they are from Atlanta. They have a gang of about twenty to thirty men. We know where their home place is and who controls what places around them. Apparently, this leader man gone a bit rogue coming here for revenge. No one came with him except those two stooges. They are at war with some other bigger gang and didn't see any reason to leave. They might not be able to go back to their turf."

"Where did you leave them? Are they alive, Razor?" Bell inquired.

"Yeah, Chopper told us not to kill them. He made a promise to Mike's mom."

"You mean they are alive? Won't they come back later?" Bell followed up with indignation learning those three men were still alive.

"Never. We weren't that dumb to think they would leave and not ever return. Leader man has a broken jaw, a hole in his arm, and another in his foot. After what Mike did to him in the other house, a broke knee or I think it is broken from the looks of it."

"Razor, don't forget, no teeth."

"Thanks, Baby Face. Some teeth missing, Bell."

"Anything else, Razor?" asked Bell.

He hesitated and started to fidget some on his feet.

"Go on, tell him, Razor."

"Baby Face, I told you to let me finish. Is this going to be a problem?"

"No, sir," quipped Baby Face.

"Well, we decided to help him not forget, and a few of the boys made sure he will not be having any wet dreams ever. Get my drift?"

Bell gasped and put her hand over her mouth, realizing what Razor said.

"That took care of leader man, but what about his two friends?" inquired Chopper.

"Chopper, the way I see it, they gonna have a hard time finding their way home carrying leader man and with one eye missing from each of them."

"Don't forget the missing ears. Each one has one less too, boss."

Razor looked at Baby Face, but not quick enough to keep him from reminding Chopper they also had no teeth. Razor just shook his head, saying, "He's hopeless. Yeah, Chopper, the guys and girls all thought they should have matching dental work. We left them about a thirty-minute walk from a small town."

"Well, maybe several hours the way they were walking," Baby Face piped up.

"Well, you done good, men. Pass that along to the guys for me. One other thing. Let me guess what if they or when they get back to the city, can we be sure they are done with this?"

"Yeah," Razor replied. "There is always a chance that leader man will try this again. He does seem to have a hard head. Got to give him that. Well, not to worry, Chopper. I sent a few of our men ahead to have a sit-down with the members of his gang. What they tell him and who else they may sit down with will depend on how they answer the questions. I think once they understand the situation and outcome of any further actions down here, they will know what needs to be done. Anyways, that leader man won't be their leader man anymore."

"Razor, you and the boys can go on to the hangout. Leave me Bone Breaker."

"Tell you what, Chopper, I do one better. I'll leave you Baby Face as well."

"Huh?" Baby Face quipped.

"That's for you interrupting me," Razor quipped back at Baby Face.

"Razor, come here." Bell beckoned to him.

"Yeah, Bell, what you need?"

Looking up to him, she reached out with both hands. "I want a hug before you go."

"Dang, Bell, this gunshot has made you a little bit of a sissy pants," quipped Chopper, watching Razor grudgingly walk over to Bell. Chopper wanted to take that remark back, but he was a bit too slow.

Old age, probably, but still too late. A sharp slug to his ribs from Bell changed Chopper's mind, shutting him up.

"Now off with you. See you in a day or so," Bell told both of them.

"We will be waiting for you. Say bye to the kid for us."

"Sure, Razor," Chopper replied.

Within seconds, the roar of the bikes could be heard and soon became a distant faint sound, then total silence was left behind.

Bell slept some while Chopper went walking around the yard. Coming to the shed, he noticed it still had a hole on one side. By the time Mike and Sharon came home for lunch, the hole was patched.

Mike along with his sister walked inside their home. Bell was sitting up playing solitaire. Mom often played it late into the night.

"Hey, you're home." Bell greeted them with a smile.

"Yeah, we come home for lunch every day," replied Sharon.

"Well, what do you want to eat?"

Sharon answered back, "We usually don't eat anything, maybe some water and buttered bread."

"That all?"

"Well, it's not much left to eat. Besides Dodie, she gets to eat at school. Mom makes her a lunch. The school will not allow her permission to walk home for lunch. Our school will."

"You mean she eats a lunch, and you two get nothing."

"No, we eat at home."

"But you just said to me, you usually don't have anything to eat here."

Again, Sharon responded, "We have water and bread."

"That's all." Bell was near fuming until she saw Chopper about to walk through the rear door. That took the fire off the kettle raging inside her.

Sharon continued her menu items they chose from. "Well, we put butter or mayo on bread. Peanut butter if we have any. Sometimes, there are leftovers from supper. We find something, usually."

This time Mike answered. "Besides, Bell, we are used to not eating a lot for lunch."

Chopper walked in, and the questions stopped.

Grabbing hold of the couch's arm, Bell stood up.

"What the heck you think you are doing, Bell?" Chopper barked out.

"I am getting these two something to eat. I'm fine. Shut up or help me," she commanded.

"Now that's my Bell."

Within minutes, both Mike and Sharon were seated at the table. Two sandwiches that could have fed four people were place in front of them.

"Eat, and I mean all of it."

"Yes, madam," responded the two.

Sharon dug into her sandwich without a second thought. Mike looked at Bell standing beside him.

"Eat." Bell gave him a direct order and a finger pointing at the sandwich.

He picked it up and ate it.

"While we are here, you are going to eat good. Got that?" Then she looked at Chopper and repeated her remark. "Got that?"

Chopper nodded back.

"Good."

Once both finished and began to leave home, Mike turned to Bell. "Thank you. Are you feeling better today?"

"Feeling much better," Bell replied, then smiled.

They walked out, but not before Mike gave Boo a hug. Every day after that, Mike and his sis came home to a cooked meal. Bell made every meal herself.

On the third day, both Bell and Chopper met them at the door as they were leaving to go to school. "You three kids are something else. We are going to miss all of you. Remember, we will be dropping by time and time again. We are not gone forever," Bell said with a slight sadness.

Tears filled all of the kids' eyes and Bell's. Mike and both of his sisters hugged her. Mike walked over to give Chopper a hug.

"Now, Mike, you are the man of this house. You proved that. No more of them hugs. Just shake my hand. That's what men do." Chopper made it a point to remind Mike of that responsibility as to imply a meaning. Mike would ponder about the meaning on the way back to school.

Mike let loose of Chopper's hand, turning to leave. Out the door was Bone Breaker.

"Well, you going now, Mike? Ain't I getting a goodbye?" Bone Breaker stood by his bike and offered to give both a ride back to school. Sharon didn't want any part of riding on a bike. So Mike had to refuse the offer. Then it occurred to him what Chopper implied. *My family needs are important, and that means walking with my sister back to school.*

Mike went over to the big lug and hugged him. It didn't matter if he was a man. This was goodbye, and Mike was still a kid for now.

Mike and his sisters left. They could feel the three bikers' eyes watching them walk down the street. Mom shook Chopper's hand and turned to give Bell a hug. Bell offered her hand instead. "Mrs. O, I hope you take good care of those sweet children you have."

Chopper gave Bell a sharp pat on her rear.

Bell got the message.

"I will, Bell." Walking them out the door, she stopped to thank Bone Breaker. Mom watched them get on their bikes with Bell grabbing hold of Chopper. With a loud roar from starting up, they gave one last wave goodbye.

"We will be seeing you again!" Bell shouted to her as they drove off.

CALM BEFORE THE STORM

SEVERAL DAYS HAD PASSED SINCE the bikers rode off. Mike and his sisters were getting back to the same old grind going to school. Every day they would wake up, get dressed, walk to school. Jon would walk with Mike and his sister when they passed by his home. Most times, he was waiting on the porch for them. Seeing the two approaching, Jon would walk down the steps to meet up. Sharon would walk on one side of her brother and Jon on the other.

Getting to school, Sharon went to her class and Mike to his. Mrs. Bently didn't meet him at the door daily as Mr. Adams had done. Ron would meet Mike at the door, and the two went to their assigned seats. After the bell rang, Mrs. Bently would enter the room. She tended to leave the room a lot. That was all well and fine by everyone. Everyone did their thing when she wasn't in class. Mike got to believe she left on purpose knowing full well hell was raised in class. It was believed by most of her students that she didn't know how to handle them. The class was wild.

After the rocket incident, spitball fights were common. It ended when she rearranged the room. Now Ron and Jon and Mike sat next to each other. Can't have a spitball battle sitting so close.

The students soon settled in on classwork. Someone must have given her advice when she moved everyone around. It stopped most hijinks. But not for long.

Ron was always daring Mike to do something. Jon would egg it on. Sometimes Mike took his dare, and other times Mike would challenge him. Most times Ron would back down. Mike most times took the dare on. One such dare started early and continued for two days. A constant barrage of "I dare you" all day came from Ron. Finally, to end his relentless daring, Mike had to take it on.

The dare was for Mike to jump out the window. When Mrs. Bently took one of her leaves from class after lunch, everyone met at the window. In fact, most of the class stood by the window watching Mike.

Outside the window, the ground was a bit lower than the class floor. In other words, it was farther down to the ground than Mike first thought. Mike suddenly wished he hadn't accepted Ron's dare.

"Well, Mike, when you going to jump?" Ron kept up his taunting.

Jon, needless to say, followed with the taunting, and soon the whole class was chanting. "Do it, do it!" They all joined in.

"Give me a second, Ron," Mike quipped back. "I want to figure out just how to jump out of this window." Mike stood there looking down the window and then back at all the kids watching him. Then Patricia walked up to him. The prettiest girl in class. The same girl who got him into a fight at the bathroom window a while back with Mark.

"Mike, you shouldn't jump. You might hurt yourself," she said while looking out the window to the ground.

Women are all the same. They let you know they care about you, and boom, you do something stupid. I guess they are born with that trait, Mike thought to himself as her tempting blue eyes portrayed a sincere caring for him.

Boom, he did something stupid and jumped out the window. He hit the ground hard. "I misjudged the distance!" Mike called up to the gawking faces poking out the window.

Everyone started poking their heads out the window when he disappeared below the window ledge.

"Sort of made me feel even dumber for doing that," Mike murmured quietly to himself.

Looking up from the ground was a funny sight. Every head was vying to squeeze out the few windows that were opened. It sort of looked like chickens at a carnival show along the boardwalk in Virginia at Ocean View Amusement Park. Barkers would call to the people passing by to throw a ball through a hole. If they could, they would take home a baby chicken. Kind of made Mike wish he had a ball.

Trying to get back in was more difficult than jumping out.

"Ron, Jon, I can't get back in. I need help!" Mike shouted to them. Mike stood near the window; it was well over his head. He could barely reach the window ledge with his fingertips. Mike leaped up and was able to grab hold of the ledge. His feet had few surfaces to get a foothold on.

Ron reached out the window and grabbed Mike's arm. When Mike jumped up, he pulled at the same time, and zip, Mike was almost all the way in. No problem, every kid near Mike offered a hand. With all that help, he got in, flying several feet across the room in the air.

"Whoa!" Ron cried out as he pulled hard on Mike's arm to keep him from hitting the floor with a bang. The force was too powerful for Ron to completely stop Mike from being swung to the other side of the class. Ron did prevent the flight from going the distance. Of course, Ron was thrown with the force as well.

Mike landed face up caused by the flip by Ron's jerk on his arm. Ron ended up on his feet where Mike landed. Only a few desks ended up being disarranged. They stopped Mike's flight.

"Hey, you okay, Mike?" Ron stood looking down at Mike. Jon was beside him, standing close by, giggling.

"Sure, Ron." Patricia was standing near where Mike landed. With some luck, the toss flung Mike near where Patricia stood. Those beautiful blue eyes, blonde hair, and her smile just melted his heart.

"You're not hurt, are you?"

Mike looked at her, speechless for a minute, listening to the melodious song of sweet-sounding words.

"No, no, I'm fine. Thanks for asking."

She smiled at him then turned to walk back to her seat. It made Mike blush some. Jon was quick to make that point to him. "Hey, Mike, you are blushing."

"Jon, why don't you tell the whole class. You could have said that a might quieter." Mike gave him a keep-quiet look.

Ron, not to be left out of the little teasing, called out, "Hey, Mike, you are blushing."

The whole class had no problem hearing what he announced.

"Ron, I'm next to you, and I will make you pay," Mike replied, lifting himself off the floor.

The whole class, hearing Ron, turned to look at Mike.

"Hey, look, Mike's blushing," someone said.

"Hey, Patricia, he likes you," said another.

"Yes, and Patricia likes Mike," piped a girl.

Then the dreaded song came. A chorus of the whole class began to sing. "Mike and Patricia sitting in a tree," and so on and so on it went. Then Mrs. Bently came in. The day couldn't end fast enough. Mike prayed for it to end.

On the way home, everyone met up. At the street corner, Ron went one way, and Sharon, Jon, and Mike the other. When Mike and Sharon got to Jon's home, he said goodbye. Mike and Sharon walked the next block to their home. A sudden thought crossed their minds as they neared home. Neither Chopper, Bell, nor Bone Breaker was going to greet them at the door. Opening the front door, they walked in. It was only Mom. She was sitting at the table with a bottle of booze by one hand and a cigarette in her mouth.

Seeing Dodie standing behind her in the kitchen, the two walked over to her. Mom didn't look up. Instead, she lifted the bottle and poured a glass half full and took a huge swallow.

"Mike, Sharon, she's drunk. Been this way since I got home," Dodie quickly said.

"She is drunk again?" Sharon inquired. "God, I hope not. I don't want this to begin all over again. Dodie, what set her off?"

"I think she got fired from her job, Sharon."

"Why?" Sharon asked.

"Well, from what I gathered from the person who brought her home, she has been drinking at work. They warned her several times," Dodie said.

"Dodie," Mike asked, "I thought she wasn't drinking anymore?" I never saw her with booze since I have been home."

"Mike, she gets this way sometimes, and usually it is beer. When she starts on booze, all hell will break loose. She can stay this way for weeks."

"What are we going to do, Dodie?"

"I don't know, Mike. By the time we go to bed, it will get worse."

"What you mean by that?" Mike asked her.

"Mike, maybe not. Let's hope she goes to bed and sleeps this off."

"Has she ever?"

"No, Mike," Sharon tells him. "Uh-oh, she's starting up."

Mom looked over at her three children in the kitchen. "What the hell are you doing? Get this house clean," Mom slurred out with a nasty tone.

"Well, I'm going out. You two want to come, or are you going to stay in the house?" Mike asked both his sisters.

Sharon spoke, "I don't know. We are thinking about going to the rec center. There is a dance."

"Sharon, where did you learn to dance?" Mike was quick to respond to her dancing.

"At the rec center."

"Dodie, can you dance too."

"Yes, Mike. Sharon and I go there a lot of times when we are out of school. Why don't you come with us?"

"Nah, I can't dance. I feel silly standing around. Besides, I have some other place to go." Mike turned, walking out the door.

As he was about to head out, Mike's mom started yelling. "Get me a cigarette! Get me a drink! Where is my liquor, damn you? You better not hide it from me!"

Usually, Mike would go to Jon's house and hang out, playing different games outside with the other kids in the area. When the day ended and night came, they went inside Jon's duplex house. His mom worked at night. Jon and Mike usually stayed inside watching TV shows until around 8:00 p.m. Mike would then leave and go home. This usually was the time Jon's mom came home, and they ate supper.

Getting home late most of the time, Mike's sisters would have already eaten, and if there was anything left, it was his to eat. Many times crackers or a peanut butter sandwich was his meal. For a period of time, Mom started buying frozen TV dinners. Mike loved the chicken meals.

When Mom was eating, it was always a good sign; it was a sign she stopped drinking. She had several ways of letting them know her drinking was beginning and several ways of signaling she was stopping. Eating was one, Mike was told by his sisters.

"Where is my drink? What did you do to it? What have you been up to? Where were you? Get up, clean the house. Did you hide my cigarettes again?"

"We haven't, Mom."

On and on, all night long it went. In the middle of the night, Mom would scream, "Wake up, damn lazy kids! I got more brains in my little finger than the whole lot of you put together. Get up! I never slept this late, get up!" All night and into the morning it continued. Day after day and night after night until the liquor was gone. Silence followed the last drop of liquor. Then sleep. She awoke often hungry. That was the end of that bout. It would last a few days or, if they were lucky, several weeks, keeping sober before it all began again.

DR. STRANGE AND
THE MISSING BOY

A TALL SLENDER MAN WEARING A thousand-dollar suit sat at a large solid mahogany desk. His suit spoke volumes. This was what he intended. Everything about him spoke of power. He was in his forties, possessing the knowledge and talents of most of his peers. A writing pad sat in the center of his huge desk. It was a relic remaining in the office before he was born. Many people sat behind that desk. The desk exuded power. Power was what one needed to sit behind its massive frame. It was a wild mustang needing taming before one could ride it.

This tall slender man never minced words. Each word had command. He said sit, you sat. No second thought, only to comply with his command.

Pressing a button to the right of his desk pad, he spoke. "Get me Dennis." The voice came out the other end to his receptionist as powerful and direct as he intended it to be. His receptionist was quick to comply. This man demanded the best and got the best. Only after ten to fifteen receptionists within a week did he decide on Doris.

Doris was a pretty blonde. No other hair color was allowed for his receptionists. Blondes were a distraction to any person who came to that desk. He wanted any person he dealt with to be focus on his task. No chitchat to distract them when they passed through his office door. That changed when he realized a distraction allowed him to catch them off balance and unprotected from his questioning. Doris bleached her hair blonde before interviewing for the job.

Passing through those two large doors made you feel small and willing to be subjugated. If the doors were not intimidating, the long walk to the thin man's desk did. This long walk allowed the thin man to evaluate his visitor. One chair was placed directly several feet away in front of his desk. The legs of the chair were specially designed to have his guests sit lower than the level of thin man's chair. This gave him the appearance of height.

On either side of the desk were large curtains that draped to the floor. Between the curtains was a larger-than-life portrait of the thin man staring down at the exact place the chair was positioned.

"Mr. Howell, Mr. Dennis has arrived," Doris spoke through her com with clear and concise of words.

"Send him in." *Click.*

Mr. Howell's silence was interrupted from this com message. His thoughts rearranged their focus on the matter Dennis was sent for to discuss.

Doris stood up from her desk and walked over to the massive doors. Pushing one door triggered the automatic door opener, and slowly the double doors parted the full distance. Knowing where to push the door was Doris's job. This prevented any unwanted person from pushing his way into the office uninvited.

The first thing that was visible to any person entering the room was the full-wall picture of Dante's *Inferno*. Entering into thin man's office wasn't a straight walk. Upon entering, one would walk through an aisle, and at the end was a picture of fire and brimstone. A precursor to what was to come, one might take as they turned to enter into the main office space. This too was to imply what to expect if the thin man was crossed.

Mr. Dennis had walked through these doors more times than he had wanted to. His last count was one hundred. After that, he quit counting. He was the best in his field and knew it. Thin man liked that from all the people he held in high regard.

Dennis had been around the studios longer than most men. He'd seen it all. Some of the greats preceded him. They taught him well.

Dennis was a quick learner, quickly working side by side with the best in the business. Dennis earned the reputation as a man to go to. No waiting and excuses. He got the job done and many times below budget.

Dennis was a tall and heavy-built man in his early fifties. He enjoyed eating and eating well. He developed a taste for the exotic foods from the many travels to various countries the job often required of him. Dennis was like three men working, and few men could outpace him when he was at work.

"Mr. Howell, I assumed you called me here to discuss the venture you talked to me yesterday to consider. I have, and it is possible. I began the layout theme and have talked to several designers for the house. My boys were told and eager for this new challenge. Costs are being discussed as well as a time period to begin at the site. We have a price offered us for the purchase, needing your say-so."

"Good. It seems you have taken the first steps. Have you begun to learn to read minds? I have just considered the thought of undergoing this venture," replied Mr. Howell.

"Yes, sir, knowing you, sir, I have learned when you discuss a venture, it usually means you have made the decision to go ahead. What money spent so far is the cost of labor obtaining information. I should have everything by tomorrow or the next day, tops. If not, then heads will roll."

"You are making me feel you are in charge. You are going to have to let me think I am still in charge, Dennis."

"Always, sir."

"Then when you leave, have Peabody drop by."

"He's outside waiting to come in, sir."

"Really? How did he know about this venture considering we just discussed this yesterday?"

"Right you are, sir. I realized when you showed me the magazine article about the house in the swamps you would want to gather intel."

"Send him in."

Dennis abruptly turned, walking out of the office. He waved to Peabody as he was leaving Mr. Howell's office. "Mr. Peabody, Mr. Howell will see you now."

"Thanks, Dennis."

He nodded back to Peabody.

Mr. Peabody dressed accordingly in a two-thousand-dollar suit. He was the type not to be outdone by anybody, even his boss, Mr. Howell. He knew this annoyed him, but Mr. Howell only cared to impress thoughts he needed to.

Walking with his cane tapping on the solid marble floor with every step, Peabody slowly walked forward. Peabody was the total opposite of Dennis. Dennis dressed more in a working man's attire. Peabody was a dandy. He prided himself on wearing the best and looking the best. Seeing Peabody, one would see wealth and power. He earned his respect through his mannerism and shortness of patience. Anyone working for him knew good and well his quickness to point out their lack of performance, and if not corrected soon, they would lose a job without pay. He was a cold man with little to no room for frivolous humanities.

"Good day, Mr. Howell. Congrats on your new venture," Peabody, with his high, shrill voice, said. His voice was not a naturally inherited shrill. It took months to develop his irritating tone. Anyone hearing his talking knew right off who it was.

"Well, it seems everyone is aware of this venture. I will assume you have come prepared since you are here before I sent for you, Mr. Peabody." Mr. Howell leaned forward, placing both elbows on the desktop. It was to rattle the cages of a person he was talking to.

Mr. Peabody wasn't rattled. "That is correct. I read the article in the magazine. A Dr. Strange and his team happened upon the house with a bit of luck. They encounter a young lad along the road. That lad was the person who helped them locate the house. They had been searching for this mysterious house for several days.

"Apparently, people in the swamps heard about the place but were uncertain of its whereabouts or refrained from telling Dr. Strange's team. They came across this lad walking on the road they had driven on several times. That lad spent the night in the house. He encountered the occurrences firsthand. What the magazine doesn't say is the lad was injured. Also, it was left out of the article the encounters the lad had prior to returning.

"Dr. Strange felt it would lead others to the house and cause harm to the structure. I talked to him over the phone. He was cautious telling me what he knew. I believe if we send a person there to his university, we may learn more details. This house is haunted. It has many unexplained happenings, Mr. Howell."

"Mr. Peabody, what about the boy? Any info on who or where we can find him?"

Peabody stood unflinching telling his story, remaining stoic to any questions Mr. Howell tossed at him. "All we know for sure is his first name. Strangely, there was another article appearing in the magazine along with Dr. Strange's haunted house story. It tells of a group of gator hunters killing the largest gator ever to be hunted. What was interesting was a young lad accompanied them on this hunt.

"The boy was found sitting on a bridge when Dr. Strange's convoy of one truck and car crossed over. The road they were on was the same road Dr. Strange met his young lad on. Get this, Mr. Howell, both of the lads' name was Mike."

"Really, hmm, that is interesting."

"In each article, it describes the young lad having the same height, hair color, clothing worn, and nearly the same age. The one thing that clinched it was the jacket he wore. His jacket described in both articles was made of an animal skin.

"I have my boys cross-checking for any young lad in papers and magazines that might by chance mention a lad of the same description. Hopefully, this lad has left us more bread crumbs. If he has, we will find out who he is."

"I hope this boy is not a spirit but a real living entity. Continue with your search. Keep me up-to-date. This venture may well depend upon finding this lad, Mike."

"You got it, boss."

"Hmm, if this is a real kid, I got me a hit." A smile slid across Mr. Howell's lips. He leaned back in his red leather chair, hands folded behind his head. His body was engulfed in the enormous gold gilded throne he had made in his studio.

"Doris, get in here."

"Yes, sir."

TOO MUCH RAIN
CAN GET YOU WET

MIKE STARTED ROAMING THE TOWN. He walked across town and explored anything that might interest him. After school, he met several new friends. Steve, who was in his class, tagged along with him during recess.

Mike began to play football where most of the students were found. After a while, he got tired of chasing the quarterback around. He got pretty good at tagging him. He wanted to try throwing the ball.

The quarterback was the same kid Mike kept tagging. He could throw the ball really good. Mike asked if he could try passing the football. The kid had no trouble letting him throw the ball. Mike soon discovered that throwing a football took skill and practice.

That was when Steve and Mike met and got to know each other playing football. Steve was like Mike, and soon both got tired of chasing the quarterback around the field. He had an older brother who started to hang with them after school. Thus began Mike's adventure period after school and weekend exploits with Steve and his big brother.

One such adventure involved a journey down an old dried-up riverbed. On a Saturday, they left early from Steve's home. Across the street was only woods. After about thirty minutes clawing through the thickets, Mike, Steve, and his big brother came to this dried-up riverbed. It was ten feet lower than where they stood. To get down to the riverbed, they would need to jump.

"Steve, let's go down this and follow it to see where it goes."

"Okay, sure, Mike."

Steve's brother had another idea. He was the cautious one and stood looking at the dried sandy ditch. From his perspective, the ditch was surrounded on both sides with high-growing thickets. Little room to climb out if something went wrong. "Hey, you two, we don't know where this may lead. We are away from home. What if something happens to one of us?"

"Hey, don't worry, brother, we won't run into anything. Quit being a scaredy-cat."

"Well, it might rain, Steve."

"So what if it does? You afraid of getting wet a little?"

One could see from the way each talked to the other who was the boss.

"Well, Steve, he may have a point. If it rains a lot, we are in a riverbed. It might fill up with water," Mike quickly pointed out to Steve.

"Hey, Mike, look at it. It's full of dry sand."

Mike was first to jump down onto the sandy riverbed. "This river will never hold any water. Even if it does, it won't be anything we can't handle." Mike reached down, grabbing hold of dried hot sand in his hand. Holding it up, he slowly allowed the sand to slide through his fingers. "See, it is just loose sand."

Steve and his big brother jumped down to the sandy ditch. Neither of their feet sank when they struck the sand. Mike made a comment to that. "See, it is safe."

Big Brother still had his doubts.

It was about midday with the sun bearing down upon them like a blowtorch.

"Hey, guys, I don't know about you, but to me, it is awful hot. I'm getting thirsty. Did any of you two explorers think about bringing water or something to drink?" shouted a loud, booming voice from the rear of the group. Big brother was hot and sweating more than Mike and Steve.

"No, I didn't think we would still be walking this long. I thought we would get to a town or a street with a bridge," Mike answered big brother's questions.

"Mike, my brother is right. It is hot, and I'm thirsty too," responded Steve.

Everyone was sweating. None had dry clothes from all their sweating.

"Let us walk a little farther, guys. I sure hate to stop since we came this far. Anyways, look up, clouds are forming in the sky, and it should cool off soon."

"Yeah, Mike, or it means it's going to rain," clamored Steve.

"Well, you might be right, Steve. Besides, it don't seem to want to rain yet."

Looking up at the sky, the clouds began to form into larger and darker masses. About thirty minutes down that dry riverbed, Mike turned to Steve and his brother with concern on his face. He had to grudgingly agree with big brother's assessment about it raining.

"I think we journeyed far enough down this dried riverbed. I think it might rain, and I'm not too sure where we are. I wouldn't mind continuing on, but your mom might get worried if it starts to rain, and you aren't home, Steve."

"You're right, Mike. Mom will get to worrying."

"About time you two decide to go back. I'm thirsty and hungry," big brother quipped.

"Me too. Mike, let's get going back."

"Right, Steve." But it was too late. Stopping, Mike put his hand out, palm up. Again, this time more than one drop was felt. "Did you feel that?" As he held his hand out, another drop of water splashed on his palm. Then another.

"See, I told you two we were going to get wet," big brother quickly reminded them of his concerns before they decided to jump into the sandy ditch.

Now three drops then a hundred drops followed. Within seconds, everyone was totally drenched from the rain coming down. Puddles were beginning to form almost at the start of the downpour. A stream formed, snaking through the center of the dried river. Within ten minutes, all were up to their shoe tops. They began running. Water went splashing with every stomp of their feet on the swiftly filling dried riverbed.

Steve's brother started screaming at the two of them. "I told you, I told you! We are caught in this river. We are going to drown if we don't get out."

Rain was coming down in buckets. With every word they tried to speak, a mouthful of water filled them. Coughing and trying to make their way down the swollen riverbed, each person's feet began sinking in the sand. It was getting impossible.

Every step was made more difficult with the river water rising. Looking at the sides of the river, the walls were nearly covered thickly with shrubs as far as Mike could view on both sides. He tried to climb up and soon discovered it was too slippery. Steve pushed on Mike's behind as he struggled to get up, but to no avail. Mike kept sliding down the side.

Steve's brother was nearly in a panic watching Mike's attempts to get out of the river. "We are going to drown!" he screamed out. Turning to Steve, he grabbed hold and repeated, "We are going to drown!"

Mike had to grab hold of big brother. He broke free and continued to yell at the two of them. "We can't get out of this river! We are going to be washed away. Maybe even drown. We got to get out of here!"

Turning to look at either of them for any answer, big brother's face suddenly expressed a scary feared look. He was going to do something stupid from fear.

Mike was thinking, *I have to act quickly before he has a chance to do anything that could hurt all three of us.* Mike reached over and took one of big brother's hands then grabbed hold of Steve's hand. Both Steve and Mike looked straight into his brother's eyes.

"Calm yourself," Mike told big brother.

Steve saw the fear rising in his brother's eyes as Mike had seen. "Quick, let's make a run for it!" Steve yelled in his brother's face, which was dripping with streams of water showering down.

The heat of the day was rapidly replaced with a colder feel in the air. The heat cooled quickly like a fire being splashed with a pail of water, extinguishing it. All were wearing T-shirts with a chill starting to take hold of them.

Steve's brother began to feel the difference in the air first. Both Mike and Steve could see him turning pale as rain poured down as the river continued to rise.

Before Mike finished telling them to run, Steve's brother was ahead of them, running back up the river, kicking up waves. Steve followed, and Mike took up the tail position. They struggled with every step. First Steve stumbled and fell into the water. Once they helped him up, next was Mike's turn. Then big brother and back to Steve.

All three got a hundred yards from where they first entered the riverbed. The river waters now reached hip level. Steve slipped and yelled out. His brother turned to see Steve being dragged down the flowing waters. Big brother had managed to find a path through the thicket at a low water level bend in the stream and successfully climbed out of the water. His worst visions now were coming true. His brother Steve was being swept away by a torrent of fast-moving waters.

Mike yelled to big brother, "I got him!"

Big brother wasn't going to jump in and swim to aid as Mike hoped for; instead, he just jumped up and down, waving his arms.

Mike reached out his hand to grab Steve as he neared him. Mike slipped before he was within grasp. Now the two of them were being swept down the river. Mike rolled over on one side to grab a branch passing close to him. He came to a quick stop even as the water was trying its best to dislodge him from the branches.

Steve was soon floating past Mike again, but this time he got hold of Mike's arm. Immediately he swung Steve behind with the force of the water carrying him. With a hold on the limb secured, he told Steve to climb up over him to high ground.

"Hurry, Steve, climb up on the bank!" Mike yelled. He could feel the branch loosening its hold on the riverbank. The ground was soaked, and the dirt had become loose. Roots of the branch had little to keep planted to.

Once on top of the riverbank and safe from the on-rushing currents, Steve turned back to Mike. "Here, Mike, take my hand." Steve extended his arm down to Mike, their hands nearly touching. Before Mike could grab hold of the extended hand, Steve slipped back into the water. Half of him was in the water.

Big brother worked his way over to where both Mike and Steve were struggling to get out of the rising river water. It was amazing how fast the water rose in that dried sandy riverbed, Mike recalled later.

By the time big brother reached them, Steve was nearly out of the water again. Mike was slowly drifting farther down the river with the flow. The branch he clung to was straightened out from the hold it had on the river's ledge with the fast-moving water's pull. Both Steve and his brother were at Mike's aid. Too late for any good.

The branch tore from the shore, giving way to the yearning flow of the water's force. Mike let go of it to swim with all his might. Both Steve and his brother were scurrying as fast as they could through the thick river growth. They realized if they could catch up to him, he would be way down the river. In this rain downpour, seeing began to look hazy to the point Mike almost thought he lost sight of them several times.

It was lucky the river had bends; it allowed Mike to be swept near the shore. It was shallow enough for him to get a footing. Slowly, Mike was able to stand. He stood, tired and fully soaked from head to toe. He dragged himself out of the water. Lying there in the pouring rain, Mike saw Steve and his brother approach on the opposite side of the river.

"Man, we thought you were a goner, Mike."

"Me too, Steve," Mike replied weakly.

"See, next time you two will listen to me," big brother said with a satisfaction he was right.

"Next time? You are not going to tell Mom, are you, brother."

"Heck no, I don't want to explain all this and die in one day. We just tell her we got caught in the rain in the woods. By the time we got out of them, we were fully wet."

"Hey, Mike, you going to try and get over here on our side?" Steve quipped out to Mike.

Mike looked back at him with a queer look. Steve smiled. Mike smiled back, answering, "Not unless you two can give me your hands to pull me over."

"No, you stay on your side. We will follow along on this side."

Fighting their way through the wet trees and bushes was misery. Once they got clear of the woods, the rain stopped.

"Wouldn't you know it, now it stops," Mike quipped to Steve.

Together, they walked to Steve's house. Once there, Mike said goodbye. They tried to get him to come in. Mike didn't want his mom to give him her look and demand, "Why'd you take my boys into the woods and get them soaking wet?"

Mike got about three houses down from their home when the rain began again. It stayed raining all through the day and into the night.

NOT MUCH FUN AT
THE REC CENTER

ND SO IT WAS FOR the whole of school that first year. Every day after school, Mike would sometimes go home or just drop off at a friend's home.

Walking with Jon after they left his home on a Saturday morning, they looked for soda bottles to cash in. Upon collecting generally eight or ten bottles, the two boys went directly to the Quickie Store to buy a bag of barbecue potato chips and a soda. Sharing the soda and chips took care of any hunger pangs Mike had, and off they went to the rec center.

One day after school before the weekend, Mike and his sister Sharon wandered over to the rec center. Mike's sisters told him it had all kinds of things to do there. When Mike went inside, Sharon walked him through the center. There was a basketball court, a sauna room, and game room. Outside was another basketball court and a tennis court. Across the street was a baseball field.

"Sharon, this place has everything," Mike remarked.

"One more place I want you to see, Mike." Sharon led Mike past the basketball court, and behind a short wall was a swing set, merry-go-round, and slides. They ran to the teeter-totters their eyes caught sight of. Up and down they went.

"Sharon," Mike asked, "do you remember the time at the drive-in, in Virginia?"

"Sure do. I remember the times we played on these in the day before the drive-in was opened. We would sneak in and play on these and that huge snake slide. That was fun, Mike. All three of us and some of our friends used to sneak in all the time."

"I remember the snake slide. All of us would pile up and go down it together. We laughed so hard. Everybody squeezing each other."

"And climbing over each other too, Mike."

"Yes, that too, Sharon. We had fun, didn't we? We sat there enjoying the remembering of past fun until we stopped." After sitting, just going up and down on the teeter-totter, staring at each other with glee, Mike looked up at her. "I guess it's time to get home, Sharon."

"Yeah, I guess it is."

They left.

So one Saturday, Mike talked Jon into going with him. Jon generally never left his yard or the neighborhood they lived in. This was a first, and later several other such ventures out of the neighborhood for him.

Getting to the center, they walked through the double doors. In front sat an elderly woman at the desk. Mike asked her if they could come inside.

"Yes, just sign the register, please." She handed Mike a pen.

He entered his name. Over to one side, both noticed a table with balls on it. Walking over to the table, Jon asked this one kid watching two other older boys playing a game on it. "What are they doing?" Jon asked him.

"That's a pool table, they are playing pool."

Having a queer look and not understanding what the kid meant, Mike turned to Jon. "You ever played pool."

"No."

Mike tapped the kid on his shoulder. "Can anyone play, or is this for the bigger boys?"

"Yes, anybody can play. You got to wait your turn," he replied to Mike.

"How do you play pool?" Mike inquired.

After several lessons from him teaching both Johnny and Mike, the two older boys quit and left. Turning to Mike, the kid asked if he would play a game with him. Turning to Jon, not wanting to make him feel left out, Mike asked him if he wanted to try first.

"Sure." Jon already had a cue stick in his hand, waiting at the table for a turn. After several games playing with this kid, the kid quit and went in the back room. That left Jon and Mike at the pool table alone.

"Okay, Jon, it's you and me."

"Mike, we hit the cue ball, and when it bounces off the farthest rail, the closest one to the rail near us will get to break," Jon explained to Mike.

"Wow, look at you, the expert already, aren't we," Mike remarked to Johnny.

"Well, I have been playing while you watched."

Mike lifted his cue, striking the white ball. It rolled to the other end, bounced off slightly, and stopped just an inch from where it bounced off the rail. Jon had hit the cue ball first and was several inches farther from the rail than Mike.

"Okay, expert, I got closest to the rail," Mike snickered to Jon.

"Okay, shoot."

With a huge draw of the cue stick, Mike pulled back and released a thunderous hit on the ball. The ball hit the rack of balls, flying up and over the rack and to the floor.

"I win, Mike!" Johnny was quick to claim.

"What?"

"My turn now. You scratched on the break. It's the rules, buddy." No sooner than Jon hit the rack of balls, three older boys walked in the rec center. Immediately they walked over to both Jon and Mike playing pool. One boy, much bigger than Jon, grabbed his cue stick. The biggest of the three, that is the taller and more rounder kid, reached for Mike's stick.

Needless to say, Mike held tight to his cue stick.

"Let go, kid. We got this table now," the more rounder kid holding on to Mike's stick demanded.

Looking at this huge kid several years older and more than two times Mike's size, he shot back, "You have to wait your turn, just like we had to wait."

"Is that so? Well, kid, this is our rec center. We make the rules."

Looking at the lady at the desk, Mike called to her. Only thing she had to offer him was, "You boys need to learn to work out your differences."

"You're not getting my cue stick," Mike venomously told the round taller kid.

"Well, kid, you need to step outside so we can work this out."

Jon looked at Mike with his "don't go" face. All three of the older, larger boys stood at the door entrance for the two of them to follow.

Big boy yelled back to Mike, "Are you coming?"

First Mike and reluctantly Jon walked to the double doors. Johnny came out last. Everyone walked around the corner of the building to the rear.

"Okay, kid, one last time, you going to give me the cue stick, or are you wanting to fight me?" Big boy stood across from Mike. He was nearly a foot taller and several times his size. They stood two feet apart. Big boy's friends faced Jon and Mike. Jon stood several feet behind Mike. Johnny seemed to inch his way closer to the corner as if to make a dash for it if things went bad for Mike.

"You ain't getting my stick, Mike replied."

Before he could react, the big boy punched Mike in his face. He fell to the ground. The three of them walked back in. Mike sat on the ground holding his nose. It was hurting, but not bleeding or broken.

Jon walked over to Mike, offering him his hand and a remark. "I told you not to."

"Yeah, you did. I'm going back in."

"Are you kidding? I hope you don't think you are going to get to play pool while they're still there."

"It is still our turn, Jon. Besides, that punch hurt, but not as much as my pride will if I don't try again."

"Your nose, Mike. That isn't all that will be hurting if you try and play again," replied Jon.

Once inside, Mike walked up to the big kid and grabbed his stick big boy had taken from him. Mike held the cue stick on the end as big boy was going to strike the cue ball.

"What the?" big boy said with surprise. Mike had grabbed hold of the end of his cue, preventing him from striking the cue ball. He turned and saw Mike. "Hey, kid, git your hands off that stick, unless you want to go back outside again."

"I want my stick back," demanded Mike.

"Okay, let's go outside, kid."

This time Mike led the way out. In the back where they were just minutes ago, Mike turned to face big boy. The others formed a circle around him, as they had done before.

"Well, kid," he said to Mike, "this time I hope you learn a lesson."

This time Mike punched at big boy first, and it grazed him on his chin. Not hard enough with his first punch. He was mighty big around the center, and it made hitting him harder to reach with a punch. Therefore, the hit had little effect against the massive jaw.

Big boy stood looking at Mike, then returned a smile. He was quick in his response. Big boy punched Mike in his chest. The blow knocked Mike into the arms of big boy's two friends. It hurt, and Mike bent over, trying to catch his breath.

"You had enough now, kid?"

Mike took another swing at him. He was still hurting from the chest punch, and it slowed him considerable. He managed to punch big boy's round belly. That was when Mike realized that belly was jelly, and his fist only bounced off from the punch. Again, big boy stood there smiling from the punch he received.

"You ain't got what it takes to barely make my belly bounce, kid."

He was right, that belly never made much of a dent when Mike hit it. He was right for the second time; Mike didn't have the stuff to make it count. He did have brains and used them, and Mike thought quick. Then he spoke out.

"Never, I will never quit. You may beat me now and later when we come back out again. Each time I will learn and get better. Even if I can't beat you, I will wait for you when you leave. I will come up behind you with a stick and knock the hell out of you. You're never going to see it coming."

"You do that, kid, and I will beat you good."

"That may be, big boy, but that won't keep me from coming at you again and again. I'll throw rocks at you. I know I can outrun you. If you don't believe me, just go back in and take my cue stick. We'll be back out here again. After that, I will be waiting for you to leave." Mike stared into big boy's eyes with one intention, and that was to make sure he believes he meant every word of what he told him. Mike knew this would cause him to think about maybe this kid is just that crazy to do that.

He looked hard at Mike, then turned and walked over to his friends. While he was talking, Mike went back inside. Jon followed him. Inside, Mike picked up his cue stick. Johnny racked the balls. Three big kids walked back in. Big boy walked past Mike from his rear. Suddenly, Mike felt a slap on his back. Big boy walked past and sat down. His two friends stood by the table and watched Jon and Mike play.

After one game, Johnny quit. So with no one else to play with, Mike put the stick back on the wall rack.

Jon and Mike walked about the center, poking their heads in different areas. They soon came to the spa room.

"Hey, Mike, let's try them out."

"You mean get inside of it, Jon?"

"Sure, why not, Mike?"

"Okay, Jon."

Opening the door, both sat on a stool, closing the door to each of their saunas. To the right was a knob for time and another for temperature. Both of them turned them all the way up, the highest temperature to set. Within moments, both were scurrying for the doorknobs to get out. The air outside of the saunas was suddenly cold. Mike's and Jon's shirts and pants felt damp.

"Hey, Jon, any other bright ideas you got?"

"Nah, not right now, Mike. Besides, look who has bright ideas. That wasn't such a good idea going outside to fight that big kid."

"We got to play pool, didn't we, Jon?"

Both chuckled.

Leaving the sauna room, both went back to the pool room. All three of the big boys were not there. The two of them played some pool. After five or six games, it was getting late. Mike and Jon decided it was time to go home. They left before five.

This was for some time a place both usually went off to when they got home from school. Later, during summer breaks, it became one of their favorites.

TWO EARS AND TWO EYES

S EVERAL WEEKS CAME AND WENT. One day after school, Mike decided to visit his aunt. Walking down the road in the opposite direction from home, he turned to follow the road down another hill. At the bottom, he turned and walked up the next hill.

On one side of the road, Mike remembered there was a place he lay waiting for his aunt to come home. Memories began to flood in from his first meeting them. Uncle Dat met him at the front door, only to catch him falling into their home. He was injured running into the road to save his beloved dog, Boo. A car hit him and Boo. Mike wanted to rush to get Boo, but many people were gathering. He had no choice but to run into the swamp.

Mike recalled the pain; his ribs were cracked, and one leg was cut and bleeding. After spending the night in the swamp, freezing and being bitten by mosquitoes, he made it back to the road. Slowly, he hobbled away from Macon. He found a drive-in movie theater.

For many days and nights, he hid under the screen in a shortage area. Late at night, he emerged, checking the trash cans. Often hot dog buns and, with luck, the dogs were dumped in a can. A large bag of popcorn was always there.

Finally feeling well enough to continue his trek home, he managed to locate Uncle Dat and Aunt Gladys's home. Mike ended his long journey on that night. His walk from Virginia to Georgia was an incredible one fraught with dangers.

That last memory came rushing back to Mike as if it was yesterday. He soon drifted from walking down the hill to Aunt Gladys's house and focused on that last memory he had with his uncle.

Mom had called Uncle Dat to come by after work. That late afternoon, he came to the house. Uncle Dat was always smiling and cracking jokes. He brought some joy wherever or whoever he was with.

Mom greeted him at the door after Mike just got home from his long walk. "Dat," she said, "can you do us a favor? I know you and Gladys have been very helpful, and I hate to impose again."

"No such imposing on us, Evelyn. We are family. You can call on either of us anytime. What can I do for you?"

"Well, I was told we need to keep the grass cut, and we have no mower. Is there a way to get a mower where you work? Maybe allow me to make payments?"

"Now that will not be necessary. I think my boss will allow your son to work off the cost of a mower."

"You think?"

"Sure, I'll get back with you tomorrow."

The next day, Uncle Dat called Mom, having arranged for Mike to work off the cost of a mower. That Saturday, Uncle Dat dropped by and picked Mike up to meet his boss. He was working at a furniture store down the road from where Mike lived.

Uncle Dat was a tall lean man about fifty years old. He wore a waxed black handlebar mustache matching his salt-and-pepper hair. He was of Italian descent. He was always laughing when Mike was with him.

In the house, Uncle Dat asked Mike to step out on the front porch to have a talk. "Mike," he told him, "I want you to make a good impression on my employer. I am going to tell you a story that will be of great value for you the rest of your life. This will give you a perspective most people never acquire."

"Yes, sir, Uncle Dat."

"Hmm, now how should I begin? Ah yes, let me start at the beginning, hahaha, good place to begin, heh?"

"Sounds good to me, Uncle Dat." Mike sat by Uncle Dat's side on the edge of the porch. Both their legs hung over the ledge. The day was early, and plenty of shade offered a cool reprieve from the scorching heat.

"Well now, I used to do service work on office machines. I was sent to a hospital to work on one. Entering the office, a tall pretty woman sat behind a desk. She stood up and met me with a handshake. I introduced myself and why I was there.

"To my surprise, the machine needing attention was hers. From the way she looked, I thought she was a manager, not a secretary. She wore an expensive red dress with a bead of pearls around her neck. Nice shoes to match. She looked more like a model than a secretary. She explained the nature of the problem on her machine.

"I got to work quick. Pulling up to her desk, I ran a function test on the machine. She started to strike up a conversation with me. First thing she mentioned was the carnival that came to town. She told me it always amazed her how this man could look at you, guess your age, height, and weight. She would always look for the carnie man at every show and compare one man to the other man she saw last time. Sometimes she would dress differently to make him mess up, but to no avail, she cited to me. He knew every time her correct age, weight, and height.

"She asked me what I thought about that. I told her anyone can do that if they have two ears and two eyes to see with."

""Really, Uncle Dat?" Mike interrupted him.

"Now, Mike, if you are to learn anything from my story, first you need to let me finish it, okay?"

Mike nodded back. "Okay."

"Apparently, she wanted to test me, Mike. I told her I had to work and could get into trouble with her boss. 'Besides, if I say something that you don't care for, you may be offended and call my boss.' Let this be a lesson to you, Mike, be darn careful not to evaluate a person then tell them," Uncle Dat said.

"What you mean, Uncle Dat?"

"Never mind that right now, that is another story for later. Hmm, where was I? Oh yeah, she just kept on me until I decided to demonstrate to her. I began with telling her a few rules she had to agree to before I began. One rule was to tell me the truth if I asked her was I right or wrong about my guesses. Second, I said 'If I am within a year, inch, or a pound, you will consider me right.'

"Knowing she would accept my requests because one thing I learned, Mike, is a woman loves to be told things about themselves. Just curious creatures they all are." Uncle Dat put his arm around Mike and chuckled.

"I began with the basics, Mike. I told her age was twenty-four, and she silently nodded to me correct. Then her weight being 126 pounds, another nod yes. Her height was five feet six inches. Another nod. I stopped to ask her if she wanted me to continue.

"'By all means. How much can you tell me?' she asked.

"'Quite a bit, depends on how much you want me to tell you.' Now, Mike, she was really peaked to know how much I could tell her. She eagerly wanted more of my evaluation of her.

"So I began. This is some of the things I told her. First, she was married for six years and had one child, then I changed it to two children. One was a girl, one year older than the boy. The girl was six and the boy five. 'You were married at a young age. You have a small home. The yard is not kept cut. You own one car, new, four doors, and black.' She stood there quietly. Her expression on her face spoke volumes to me. So I asked her if I was correct. She nodded, then followed it up with a question. 'How do you know this?' I told her I will explain everything after I completed my assessment. She looked a bit peeved with my answer, Mike, hahaha.

"'Your home is messy inside. Dishes usually left unwashed. The house is untidy. You tend to throw your clothes on a chair or other places when you go home. Rarely hanging them up. Your husband tends to most of the housekeeping. You do the cooking, but you are not too good of a cook.' Again I looked at her, asking if I was too personal with my assessment.

"'No, no, continue,' she replied. She tried to ask a question again. Before she could, I put my fingers to my lips to signal her not yet. I could see what I was telling her was a bit disturbing. I continued with my evaluation. By this time, I found myself enjoying my success, and I wanted to find out how far I could perceive knowing things about her.

"'You have everyone dressed up to a tee when the family goes out to a movie, dinner, or church. People's impressions about you are important. You have a strong desire to achieve your goal of being successful. This makes you a bossy and demanding person at home.

"'You completed high school and went to college for maybe one or two quarters. Maybe even some technical school. You have ambitions. You are not a nurturing person, but a person who values herself and her needs over others. I am not trying to be disrespectful to you when I tell you this,' I told her. 'It is an admiral quality for a person trying to succeed.

"'You may view your family as an asset to aid you in achieving goals you set for life. The need for recognition in your job drives you. I am going to assume that your boss has made comments on your untidiness, and this digs at you. You come on strong with meeting people, trying to make an impression on them.'

"I went on with a few other things I will leave out due to your young age, Mike."

"Well, what did she think of your assess…assessment? Were you correct? The biggest thing I really want to know is how did you know all that stuff about her?"

"Okay, I am going to tell you this. Remember why I started this story, Mike?"

"Yes, sir, you said it was to teach me about hearing and seeing."

"Right you are. When I finished, she was dumbfounded from what I was able to tell her about herself. I explained to her that the first thing I noticed when we met was her posture."

Mike had a queer look on his face when he said that.

Uncle Dat pointed that out to him. "That look on your face was about the same on her face, Mike. I went on to explain the posture of a person sets a tone about that person on a first encounter. Watch me and tell me what you notice."

Uncle Dat stood up, yanked his shirt from his pants out, messed his hair up some, loosened his pants belt, and allowed his pants to hang low. Then he stood with a stoop and looked about. "Okay, Mike, looking at me, what does it tell you?"

"You look lazy standing like that, you must have just gotten out of bed. Your hair is not combed, and your pants need to be pulled back up. It makes me think you don't care what people think about you."

"See, you use your eyes, you see things. Now listen to me and what I tell you carefully." Uncle Dat spoke with broken sentences and ran them together without a break. Never once did he look at Mike while talking, usually looking somewhere off to a distant place. "Okay, now what did you hear, Mike?"

"Uncle Dat, you talked like you had little education. Mispronounced many words, constantly repeated many words, *the*. You seemed not interested in me, the way you kept looking everywhere and not at me."

"Now you understand when I say to use your ears to hear and your eyes to see? Most people never do this and miss out on much in life. How can you ask a person to listen to you when you come across not interested in them? People want to feel they are important, and what they know and say is too. Her posture was straight, she kept in shape and looked good. I took notice. She didn't overdress and displayed too many assets."

"What assets, Uncle Dat?"

"Female assets, Mike. She wore expensive style of clothes and shoes. Her makeup was perfect, along with professionally styled hair. She even had her nails painted with a design. On her married hand was a small wedding ring. The ring looked a tad bit out of place compared to the expensive clothes she wore.

"Next, I looked at her desk and the machine she complained not working properly. Asking some questions concerning her machine, she really seemed to have little interest or knowledge about it. Most people working with their hands know their equipment and want it in perfect running order. Having little interest in her equipment told me she didn't like her position. Her desk was the same. Messy, unorganized.

"The one thing that stood out to me was her wedding ring and no pictures of her husband or children on her desk. I did notice them on a shelf behind her desk. Now, Mike, what can you deduce from this information so far?"

"Well, a small wedding ring might mean she got married young, and they had little money."

"True. Go on, Mike."

"An unorganized desk and not knowing anything about her machine implied she didn't care. She'd rather be doing something else, I guess. Her interest was in her ambitions. Unorganized at work followed the path at home."

"Good. Now I will take over. A small ring put with the fact she wears nice clothes, has her hair and nails done, can be defined as taking care of her needs. The small ring is probably due to her spouse not wanting to upgrade it. Probably due to their income. Marrying young, why? Pregnant with most likely a girl child. Hence, I deduced a need to have a second child. Most husbands want a boy. This was a guess on my part. Her figure kept this fact from me.

"When you give it a second thought, she cared more about herself, leaving the husband feeling left out. She was bossy because of her ambitions. This also caused problems with her husband. He did most of the domesticate chores and worried about expenses. They kept growing to meet her needs. She wanted people to notice her, another worry for her husband. This is the reason for putting her private life hidden from view on a shelf.

"She had a strong drive, but not the same drive when it came to performance at work. Her charms and looks are what she held as her assets. Being unorganized can lead to a lack of planning and doing her assigned tasks getting done efficiently. She mostly likely depended on her associates to aid her. Taking credit from others to offset her lack of skill sets. Anyone remarking about her work she viewed as jealousy and not to her performance inaptitude.

"People who have strong nurturing aptitudes tend to care more about their family than anything else. They dress with less flare. More conservative. Have strong work ethics and are readily willing to aid others. Tend to be a self-sacrificing sort.

"Now to the education part. When she spoke, her language gave slight hints. The nomenclature she used was minimum. She spoke in general terms with little understanding about her job. Run-on sentences and verb disagreements. She had a strong regional drawl. Most people going to college tend to adapt to language of their professions. Usually acquire a speech similar to those they attend school with. I deduced she remained in school a short time. Little influence was imparted by her classmates in such a short time span.

"That is the lesson I want you to learn. When you meet my boss, what kind of impression will you set? Do you want a mower? You must make him think you will work hard for it. You go in to meet him dressed and acting like you care less, do you think he will allow you to work for him? Do you want someone to do a sorry job and pay him to do that? People who work for a living and want to be successful, getting raises, and promotion will work hard doing their best they are capable of doing.

"How would you like it if someone was lying around, doing little, taking a lot of breaks, not doing the extra time, or not taking courses at a school to improve themselves get the raise or promotion you earned? Kind of takes the fire out of you. It will make you want to stop trying or quit your job, right?

"The lesson is to hear with your ears and see with your eyes. People are always watching you. You might not think they are, but they are. When you go to a restaurant with your family, people see and hear you with your family. How you behave, your children behave. You make an ugly scene, and someone will see it and report it. Always there are eyes and ears turned to you.

"You look like a tramp, you are a tramp, you act like an ass, you are an ass. You are a fool once, the rest of the time you are proving it. Many people see what's on the surface, few bother to look any further. Successful people do. When you see my boss, your actions will reflect on me, Mike."

The next day early in the morning, around 7:00 a.m., Uncle Dat drove to Mike's home. Together, they went to his job site. Entering the front door of an old building, both walked into a huge warehouse of furniture. Together, they walked down a long aisle with furniture packed like sardines on either side. Arriving at a wall with a square porthole, a woman stood to greet them. Looking at Mike, she asked Uncle Dat, "This is your nephew? He is a handsome young man."

"Thank you, miss. You are a pretty woman," Mike said in response.

"Hmm, you are very sweet to say that to me."

Uncle Dat placed his hand on Mike's shoulder, saying, "His name is Mike, Nancy."

Mike extended his hand to greet her. They shook. Her hands were soft. She looked to be forty years old. She had short curly hair with more gray than brown.

While she and Uncle Dat discussed the morning trade, a short nearly bald man about fifty or so waddled up to the desk. He never took his eyes off Mike. How curious it was, Mike thought.

When he came to a stop, Mike automatically extended his hand with an offer to greet him. He took Mike's hand in his. He was small, about the same height as Nancy, and his grip was strong. Mike, not wanting to show weakness, doubled his effort with a stronger grasp. Mike was able to hold him to a draw when they broke off the handshake.

"Good morning, sir. My name is Mike." Mike turned to look at Uncle Dat. Mike said with a friendly smile, "This is my uncle Dat."

"Good morning to you, Mike, I am Mr. Burl. I know your uncle well."

Uncle Dat turned and offered his hand. Both greeted each other.

"I assume this is the young man who would like to work and earn a new mower, Dat?"

Uncle Dat placed his hand on Mike's shoulder and replied, "Yes, sir. He is a good boy and a hard worker. He will do a fine job for you."

"Well, Dat, if he doesn't, it will come out of your pay."

Both of them laughed.

Turning to Mike, Mr. Burl remarked, "Mike, I am impressed with you right off. You will work for me for two days. You will be with those two men leaning against the double doors over there."

Mike turned and saw two big men wearing overalls with a sign printed across the shirt pocket. It read Burl's Furniture, and under the logo was each man's name. That he couldn't read where he was standing.

"Yes, sir, I will work hard for both of them, Mr. Burl." Mike attempted to walk over to the two tall burly men, but halted, realizing Mr. Burl was still making his briefing. Mr. Burl wasn't finished, and Mike didn't want him to think he wasn't interested in what he had to say to him.

"At the end of the weekend, they will report to me. If they give me a good report about your work, you got a mower, Mike."

"Thank you, sir, you won't regret this. I will do an excellent job for you, Mr. Burl."

"Good. Now off with you." Turning to Uncle Dat, Mike heard Mr. Burl say, "He seems like a good kid. I think he will work just fine."

Reaching the double doors, Mike stopped and extended his hand to the one man who had the appearance of being in charge. He was.

"Good morning, sir, my name is Mike. Mr. Burl told me to work with you. When do I begin?"

"Hey, Jim, we have a real eager beaver here," said the fellow alongside of him.

Jim extended his hand. Mike shook hands, then offered his hand to the other fellow alongside Jim.

"Good to have someone who will help in the work." Jim gave a wink back to Bob.

"Mike."

Turning to the mention of his name, Mike said, "Sir?"

"Sir, Mike, let's get started on the right foot. Around us, there be no sirs, got that?" replied Jim.

"Yes, sir. Yes, I mean Jim." Mike quickly corrected his reply.

"Now you got it right. We start you off on some of the lighter stuff. Check you out. Gots to be a bit careful loading this furniture. Customers buy this and don't cares much about gitting it with all kinds of nicks on it."

"Yes, sir, got it, Mr. Jim," Mike sharply replied.

"Just Jim, Mike. Just Jim will be fine. You go with Bob to the truck. Me, I'm going to get the manifest of deliveries. See you two in the back."

"Come on, Mike, you'll be riding with me." Bob slapped Mike on his back and motioned him toward the direction to the truck. The two of them got in the large van. Driving to the back double doors, the truck backed up. Both opened their doors and stepped out of the truck. Mike closed his, and Bob left his door opened.

"Mike, come over here," Bob called out. "See all these smalls? We calls them that. You be responsible to git that into the truck. So git all this stuff up by the doors. Jim and me will be loading the big stuff."

Quickly Mike finished carrying all the smalls to the rear doors. "Hey, Bob!" Mike shouted. "You guys need any help with the furniture?"

"You finished already?" came an astonished reply. Mike nodded back. Jim nodded to Mike to help. "Sure, come in and help Bob and me move this stuff around to make room for all the stuff needing moved."

Within half the time usually spent loading, the men were ready to leave. Soon they were at the first site. Mike constantly got his job completed early and was always on the spot to offer assistance to Bob and Jim. They were ready to accept his offer and just as ready to remind him to be careful unloading furniture. No scratches and dings were always mentioned to Mike with every new assignment he asked for.

At lunch, the three drove and stopped back at the store. They walked over to their table after lugging their lunchboxes from the shelf along the wall. On the shelf was laid all kinds of tools and knickknacks. Mike went and sat by the doors.

After around an hour, they approached him. "You already ate, Mike?"

"Yes," he answered with a nod of the head. In truth, he didn't have a lunch.

On the movers' last stop, Bob and Mike started to unload the big couch to a new home. Jim went ahead to inquire from the owners where to take it. Bob and Mike were waiting by the truck. Bob was inside, and Mike stood on the down lift by the tailgate. Jim and Bob had moved the couch onto the platform with half of the couch hanging off the tailgate. Bob accidentally leaned against his end of the couch, causing it to slide back toward Mike, unbalancing it. Suddenly, it started to take a header straight to the ground. Bob reached for it without much success. Mike reacted by squatting under the leading edge in time to grab hold, preventing it from hitting the ground.

Mike screamed out from the sudden strain it put on him. Mike's knee buckled, but he held it.

Bob called out, "Are you all right, Mike?"

"Yes, but hurry, I don't know how long I can hold this couch up."

"Thank the Lord!" Jim cried out, hearing Mike's cries. He came out spotting Mike nearly being crushed by the large sofa. He was by Mike's side, lifting the weight for Mike to regain his stance. Together, Jim and Mike lowered the couch to the ground safely.

"You sit for a while, Mike. Bob and I will finish." Jim motioned for him to sit. Coming back out after placing the couch in the house, everybody went back to work.

"Mike, it is knock-off time, and you did good. We will see you tomorrow."

"Yes, sir, 8:00 a.m., Jim."

"That's right, Mike."

Next day, Mike arrived early. He walked to the store. It was the same loading and unloading of the van. There weren't many deliveries on that day. So Jim had Mike do some cleaning of the truck and after that the warehouse. Lunch was the same. Then several more deliveries, and the day came to an end.

Before Mike left to walk home, Uncle Dat stopped by. After talking with Mr. Burl, he walked over to Mike. "Mike, the boss has a full two days of work and needs extra help. He asked me if you would be willing to do some extra work?"

"Sure, be glad to, Uncle Dat."

"Okay, then you need to go and discuss it with him."

Walking up to Mr. Burl, Mike asked him about the work. "Uncle Dat said you needed extra men to work for you. I will be glad to if you would accept me, sir."

"Well, young man, I would appreciate that. My two men informed me of your good work and how dependable you were. Now, I know this was not part of our bargain, and I am willing to pay you by the hour for your time. Is it a deal?"

"Yes, sir, and, Mr. Burl," Mike said, "I don't want the pay."

Mr. Burl gave Mike a quick stare. Before he had a chance to ask him why, Mike told him it will be for paying the debt he owed him for allowing a kid the opportunity to work for a mower, Mike explained.

"Well, I'll be a turd on a fence post. Mike, I pay for work, and I am going to pay you."

"No, sir, I won't work then." Mike held tight to his demand to not get paid.

"Are you sure, Mike? I have no problem with paying you. It would make me happy if you would accept my pay." Mr. Burl caught sight of Dat at the counter, watching the two of them discuss work. "You stay here, Mike." Mr. Burl walked toward Uncle Dat. "Dat, I want to have a little chat with you."

"Yes, sir, boss."

"Dat." Mr. Burl was looking toward Mike as he spoke to what they were discussing. "He won't take any pay. Said he felt he owed me a debt. That boy has a lot of pride in him, Dat."

"Yes, he does, sir."

"I feel for him. His family could use the money, and it bends me the wrong way not paying him, knowing they may need the money. My two loaders mentioned to me he never ate lunch. Do you know something about why he doesn't eat lunch?"

"Well, the family has fallen on bad times, his mom being out of work. They lost their home due to hospital bills. They moved here, and Gladys and I help out as much as we can. They rarely ask for anything. I been to their home. Not much of anything in it. When they were in another room, I peeked into their cabinets and refrigerator. Not much there either."

"Sounds to me too much pride."

"Yes, sir, some of that."

"Hmmm. Is that it?"

"It's not my place to mention anything else. Family business, boss."

"I see."

Both of them walked back to Mike. Mr. Burl asked Mike if he would take pay for a second time.

"Thanks, sir, but I will not take any money." Mike left, and after Uncle Dat had words with the boss, he took Mike home.

So it was. Mike worked the two extra days. On the third day or first day of extra work time, Jim came up to him and handed Mike a sandwich. "Here, you need to eat something. Don't you turn it down. We know you hadn't eaten the whole time you been working here."

For those next few days, it was hard work, and Jim or Bob would bring Mike a sandwich and insist he sat with them at the table. The last day was long, mainly loading and unloading the whole day. They had a short lunch. Getting back about five thirty, well past working hours, Mr. Burl was at the back door waiting for them.

Mike shook hands and said goodbye to Bob and Jim. Mr. Burl waved to them as they walked to their cars. Once they left, Mr. Burl approached Mike. "Mike, take this." He handed him an envelope.

Mike took it. "What is it, sir?"

"I will not take a no. You will take this from me, Mike. It is pay for your work."

"But—"

"No buts, Mike, take it. I want you to take it. It will please me. You don't want to get me mad, do you?"

"No, sir." Mike didn't open it, just held it in his hand. Mike shook his hand and thanked him, turned, and walked home.

That was several months ago, and now Mike was coming to the bottom of the hill and turned to Aunt Gladys's house. He stood facing the home; he stood looking at it for a long time. It seemed not too far back ago, thinking back to the day he first came to the house, where he stood there on the same spot. A small house covered in ivy vines. White and plain as most houses along this street was. Her house had a bigger yard than most. Mike soon was to find out why.

Approaching the front door from the long path that led to it, Mike stopped short. He remembered Aunt Gladys telling him to go to the rear door if he comes to visit. Turning to one side, he walked on the barely covered dirt with little or no grass, trying to survive under all the trees surrounding the front yard.

Around the side and into the backyard, the ground changed to a green, grassy, evenly cut lawn. Onto the driveway, Mike walked to the screen porch. The door to the kitchen was opened. He knocked on the door, but no one answered. He called out, "Aunt Gladys, are you home?" Suddenly startled, he heard her voice coming from behind him.

Turning around, near the corner of her yard, bordering on the empty lot, was a small glass-covered house. Aunt Gladys stood in the doorway wearing an apron and gloves. One hand had some kind of scissors in a gloved hand.

"Hi." Mike beckoned to her, nearing the glass building.

Waving back to him, she replied, "Well I'll be. What do I owe the pleasure of this visit?" Aunt Gladys often spoke with a soft kindness in her words. Mike took this as being a gentle soul, but soon was to realize under that soft-spoken demeanor was one tough lady.

Looking away, not wanting her to see his face, Mike answered her inquiry. "Well, it has been a while since I visited you and thought I better get on over here."

"I sure am glad for the company. How is your mom and sisters?"

"My sisters are doing fine. In fact, Dodie has a boyfriend. Sharon, she's in love with some guy we haven't met yet. Mom, well, she's back to her old ways. We have good days with her and bad days."

"I understand, Mike. Is there something else?" Looking at Mike, seeing he couldn't stop fidgeting made it obvious to Aunt Gladys he had something else on his mind.

Mike realized she caught the undertone of his reluctant manner. "Well, I would have come long ago, but I kept putting it off. The longer I did, the harder it was to come by. I'm really sorry, Aunt Gladys," Mike said.

"Before we talk, Mike, let's go inside for some tea. Let me put these things away." Placing the scissors on a shelf, she removed her gloves.

"Aunt Gladys, what were you doing, and what kind of a building is this?" Mike looked up, down, and around, examining the place. "It's made out of glass. I never saw a glass house before."

"You never saw a greenhouse, Mike?"

Mike shook his head no.

"This building is made from glass to allow the sunlight and heat to enter and stay inside. It will stay warm all year round. These plants growing in here will die during the winter cold. Look around, most of the plant I grow need a warm, moist climate to live in."

"Why?"

"These are tropical plants, mainly from Mexico and Central America. Some like these are from Florida. This flower I was working on is the bird-of-paradise. Look, the flower has a shape of a bird, Mike."

"It does, I see that. Wow!"

"Hey, I kind of wondered why there ain't a house on this yard next to yours."

"Mike, have not I told you about that empty lot?"

"No."

"Well, that yard was once our home. Your uncle Bill was staying with us while investigating the air force base. One night, the house caught fire. He nearly was killed. All his papers were destroyed. He told us later that someone hit him on his head. That is why he has all those burn scars on his upper half of his body."

"I remember Mom telling us about that incident years ago. I never knew it happened in your home, Aunt Gladys. Did anyone else get hurt?" Mike inquired.

"No, Mike. We bought the home next door and never had the heart to sell the lot. Come now, I could use a glass of tea. I can see you need a glass too."

Both walked back to the porch. Along the walk to her porch, Mike glanced over to the firepit Uncle Dat, him, and his sisters sat, watching him burn all the yard clippings. *That was the first time we ever toasted marshmallows on a stick*, Mike recalled.

Walking past the firepit to the carport, Mike met his mom and sisters, who were coming back to Uncle Dat and Gladys's home from the hospital under the back porch. Memories began to flood his mind. Good memories, but still they made him sad. *Funny the way that is*, Mike thought to himself, entering in the house.

Aunt Gladys pulled a chair out and told Mike to sit while she started to brew some tea in the kitchen.

Sitting at the table, Mike noticed paper clippings scattered around. To one end of the table was a scrapbook. It looked like she was cutting and pasting the clippings inside. One clipping was near Mike's hand. He couldn't help but to reach and pull it over to read.

Looking back toward the kitchen to make sure Gladys was staying in there, he could hear her whistle as she was putting a pot on the oven. So it seemed safe to read the clipping.

At the top of the clipping in large print, it read, "One of Our Town's Most Beloved Citizens was Killed Last Night." It quickly got Mike's interest. He started reading it.

> On the night of June 14, a cloudless sky with a full bright moon, a dimness settled over this town. No matter how bright the moon and stars had shined, it could not compete with the darkness that had visited it. On the front yard lay a fallen beloved citizen. A man shot down while walking to the street to get his evening paper. This reporter knelt by his side slowly watching

the life ebb out of his body. My heart sank seeing a friend die lying on the cold damp ground.

This man was well known to many. Any and all who had the privilege to meet him instantly liked him. He was friendly to every person he met. A friend truly to all. All but one. The one person who took his life. I watched my friend's eyes dilate, heard his last gasp of breath he will ever take again leave out of him.

His wife crying, she was aided by one of the officers standing nearby. Within moments of the shots, the police were called. Only one call was made. It was by his wife. Not one of his neighbors called. They heard the shot and was apparent by their massing around the yard. Every person standing around was staring at this man dying. They stood there, and not one went to his aid. By the time the police arrived, they still were standing around. The man had died.

This reporter happened to be living across the street in the residence near his home and heard the shot. I was getting into my car. Once I realized the shot was nearby, I drove down his street first. Immediately, I saw the body lying on the ground. A man was darting away. Quickly, I jumped from my car and ran to the man's aid. He said one word. *Gladys*. I looked up and saw the front door opening.

I went to the door of his home as fast as my feet could carry me. He wanted Gladys. I was going to bring her to him. Only to arrive just as Gladys was coming to her door. She saw her husband fall after the fatal shot. Running to the phone, she called for help. I held her as we approached Dat.

I felt the tremble in her body. I heard her prayers. I felt the tears fall on my hands. I supported her when we reached Dat.

I couldn't do the one thing I wished I had done. I wished I had the strength to prevent her seeing him dying in her arms. She gently lifted his head, cradling it to her bosom until the police arrived. By the time they arrived, the yard was filling with many more spectators. I would have loved to say friends.

Friends, what does that mean? Look it up in the dictionary. What I witness this night didn't define friend as that. No one made an effort to aid her. No one, from what the police repeatedly said to me, had called for assistance.

This I will tell my readers. As one officer walked by me, I heard him say, "I heard the shot. I didn't want to get involved." Everyone he questioned had the same response. They didn't want to get involved. He was talking to another officer.

What have we come to? A nation of fear. Courage took a back door. Commitment to our neighbors and the area we live in went to the side. When did a fence replace trust? No more sitting on the porches or visiting neighbors. Now, many people remain inside watching TV.

Within minutes, the young man was caught. Apparently, another call went into the police station. It was a call telling the police where to find this killer.

A police cruiser with sirens and flashing lights came to a stop in front of the yard where the body of Dat Sebtin lay. The officer opened the back door, pulling out a young man about sixteen years of age.

Walking over to where the body lay, they stopped. I look at this killer, so young, but not as innocent as one might think. Wearing a T-shirt, his arms bare except for rolls of ink work dotting up and down both arms. I saw many arms similar to this young man. Tattoos with gang art and symbols decorated them.

I looked hard at those eyes. Those uncaring eyes. Eyes that appeared to be full of pride. Then a slight smile crept across his lips. Soon after that snarly smile, he spoke. "So, this is the man I shot. Hey, look there."

His eyes pointed the way to the single bullet hole. "How about that, right dead in the heart. One shot, one kill. So cool, man."

The officer almost took a slug at this uncaring, joking young man for the death he just took, but held back the impulse. Some woman standing in the crowd yelled out, "Stop, you are hurting him!" Another screamed, "He has rights!" Then one added, "Police brutality!" All were Dat's neighbors standing in the crowd, screaming to not hurt the kid. The killer.

Gladys, his wife, now his widow, looked at her husband. Suddenly, a horrific look appeared over her face. "I know you. You...you are Kevin. You were in my third grade class. Don't you remember me?"

"Sure, I does. That why I shoots him. I had to proves I could kill someone I knows."

Shock, then hate, followed by pity, then remorse reentered her. Gladys stood, looked up, rotated her head, then looked everyone in their eyes as she panned her yard of onlookers she once called friends and neighbors. Then she turned toward her home to begin the long walk to a now-empty home. I stood and walked along with her.

I ask the readers of this paper, if this happened in your neighborhood, would you be one of those bystanders watching, hearing the shot, do nothing, say nothing? Would you expect and want your neighbors to ignore your pleas for help?

Wow. Mike quietly thought, *I didn't know this. I was told he was dead, but not this way. Not him being shot down. No one, but no one there to help. Help him, the killer, but not the one shot down.* Mike felt the hate well up inside for the people who called Uncle Dat a friend and stood, stood by doing nothing but defending the rights of a killer. A heartless killer. A kid who took pride in killing and would again. *What kind of people have been born into this world we live in now?* Mike asked himself.

Aunt Gladys saw Mike reading the clip and just watched him, saying nothing until he finished. Then she came over and put her hands on Mike's shoulders.

Mike held his head low. Tears were filling both eyes. He began to realize even more so that he should have come sooner. She had no one to see her. Mom, she never went over. Mike heard his mom talking on the phone. Mom told all of them of Uncle Dat's death shortly after the phone call.

"We went to the funeral. Mom had us seated in the back row. I thought we were family and was to sit up front. I felt left out, even shunned. I don't know why I felt this way I did. I guess this is the reason I didn't come over sooner, Aunt Gladys," Mike said in a shaky voice. Mike looked up, turning his head toward his aunt.

She saw the tears flow down Mike's face. She just hugged him. She cried. They both cried.

SINKING SAND AND
FAILING FRIENDS

FOR THE WHOLE SUMMER OUT of school, once or twice a week, Mike went around taking on grass-cutting jobs. The money he made went into the jar. Where the money went, he thought for food or expenses, or he hoped it did. He kept some to buy gas and a snack. Sometimes, when Christmas neared, he put some money away for gifts.

Summer wasn't all work. This was to be an epic time of adventure for Mike. Once in your blood, it was hard to not want to roam about. Mike went fishing with little success and set snares out with just as little success. He caught a rabbit and took it home. Both his sisters screamed watching him gut and skin it. After all that work, neither one of them would eat a bite. Mom was drinking and seldom ate. It was good rabbit. That experience took the drive out of Mike to trap or fish. That ended going fishing for a long time.

Some time had passed when Mike decided to go fishing along a creek once again. He asked his friend to go fishing with him. Jon rarely went anywhere, but since the creek was nearby, he decided to go with Mike to end his constant prodding.

Along the way to the stream, Mike came upon some bamboo. Neither Jon nor Mike had a pole. Mike brought fishing line and hooks. Usually when he fished, Mike just threw a line into the water attached to a piece of wood as a float. Since this was Jon's first fish outing, he decided Jon would like to use a pole. Walking down the road, Mike pulled his knife out and began cleaning all the branches from each bamboo pole. After completing each pole, Mike handed one to Jon along with fishing line.

"Here, Jon, take the line. Tie it at one end of your pole like I do."

Shortly, after finishing attaching their lines to their poles, they reached the edge of the stream. Mike had scouted this place weeks ago on one of his many excursions. Having to walk down this long downhill road before they were close to the stream made Jon gripe. Going between two houses, they followed the stream along the ridge running parallel to the stream. They were nearly out of sight of the houses on the ridge, and following the meandering stream made for more griping by Jon. Finding a promising place to enter the stream to pole-fish, they walk down to the water's edge.

"Jon," Mike said to him, "now would be a good time to attach your hook. First, we will tie a piece of wood to the end of our lines, about ten inches from the end, then the hook at the very end."

Mike demonstrated to Jon what to do. Jon made a feeble attempt to tie the hook. Mike ended up completing the knot to stop his griping.

"Now we need bait, Jon."

"Where you going to get that?" asked Johnny with a sour look written across his unhappy face.

Mike was beginning to regret making him accept his demands to go fishing. "Follow me," Mike replied. "Bait is all around us. You just got to know where to find it, Jon." Walking over to a fallen tree Mike spotted, he called to Jon to help. "Okay, we are going to turn this tree over, Jon. Many times, insects live under the dead wood. They make good fish bait."

With little effort, they rolled the tree over to look. Jon griped about having to push the rotten log over. "That is nasty, the log is wet and mushy."

Mike replied, wishing now he never brought Jon fishing, "Look, we just need to move it a little. Quit your griping. Come on, give me a hand."

Sure enough, there was a nest of white grub lying near the surface. Mike grabbed several and told Jon to do the same.

"No way am I grabbing hold of them slimy, wormy bugs, Mike." Jon turned and backed away from the overturned rotted log.

Mike laughed at Jon being afraid of grub. "Heck, Jon, them grubs are more afraid of you than you should be of them."

"Why, Mike?" Jon was still keeping his distance.

"You can eat them, and they don't want to be eaten, Jon."

"You are kidding, aren't you, Mike? Whoever would eat them ugly disgusting bugs?"

Mike reached down, picked up one, and quickly placed it in his mouth, then began chewing.

Jon almost threw up at the sight of him eating bugs. "You're sick, Mike." Jon's face looked a slight green when he said that.

"No, Johnny, I had to live off stuff like this when I was walking home. It was way better than having an aching belly and headaches all the time. They are full of good nutrients for your body. If you don't want to pick up grubs, come over here."

Mike was standing near a soggy area. He took his knife out and started to dig a hole. "Over here, Jon, look at this." In the hole was a large worm. Mike dug more, and the more he dug, more worms appeared. Reaching into the hole, Mike pulled a worm out. It stretched for an inch before it popped loose. Holding it up for Jon to see, Mike said, "Now you grab one for your line, Jon."

Johnny did so reluctantly. Holding the worm an arm's length away, he asked Mike, "Is this good to eat too?" He was half-heartedly joking, expecting Mike to tell him they weren't.

"Yes, but they have dirt on them and can be a bit crunchy if you don't clean them."

"No way, man," Johnny replied.

Again, Mike took his worm and slid it in his mouth. With a single bite on the worm, he swallowed it whole. Mike then told Jon, "I don't much like the taste of them. It is better to just swallow them whole."

This time Jon hurled.

With their bait in hand, both Johnny and Mike walked to a cleared area to attach their bait to each line. Mike demonstrated his way of wrapping the worm to the hook for Jon to try. Again, as expected, Mike had to do the hooking for both of them. Mike used his grubs to have a different bait to try for a fish. Mike tossed his line in the water, and Jon followed with his.

After thirty minutes went by and no nibble on either line, Mike suddenly told Jon he was going in the water to try noodling for a fish. He asked Jon if he wanted to accompany him. The offer was moot; he knew Jon wasn't going anywhere near the water.

"Mike, what are you doing? I thought we were going fishing. What is noodling?"

"We are fishing. This is another way to catch fish. You walk near the banks searching for any holes with your feet or hands. When you find a hole with your foot, you drop down under water to put your arm down the hole. If you feel a fish, grab hold."

"What are you going to grab it with?"

"You put your hand inside the fish's mouth, take hold when the fish chomps down on your hand. Next, just pull with all your might. Many times, them fishes don't want to come out too easy."

"If you let go, won't the fish come out on its own?"

"No way, first, the fish ain't going to let your hand go. Got to pull hard, or you might drown."

Jon looked aghast listening to getting drowned. Jon thought about leaving.

Mike removed his boots and socks, then slipped slowly into the moving shallow water. Looking back up at Jon, he motioned for him to enter with him. Jon still refused the offer. Looking up to Jon, Mike said, "Okay, then you keep an eye on both of our lines."

"Hey, Mike, I thought you meant we were fishing using poles. I didn't count on getting into the water."

"We were, but we haven't caught anything, so I decided to try this, Jon."

"I ain't gitting in that water. There might be snakes in there, Mike. I think you better not git in the water."

"Okay by me, Jon. I thought maybe you might want to try noodling. But go ahead, use your pole." Mike called out to Jon, "Follow me downstream a bit, I'll show you where I caught some fish last time I came here."

Mike was wading along the edge of the creek, trying out his noodling skill. Jon followed Mike for a short distance. When he came to an area of thick brush, Jon opted to wait there instead of working through the briars. "It might have snakes in these bushes, Mike. I'll try fishing here." Jon made up his mind. Once Mike was out of sight, he would leave.

"Okay, you wait there." Mike went several hundred yards down the stream. Jon was out of sight. Bad thing for Mike, it turned out. The water began running deeper nearly to Mike's belly button. The bushes were not as thick by the edge of the shore, and the sand had a looseness or softness with each step.

Then without a hint, Mike stepped into some quicksand and immediately began to sink. Quickly, Mike reached for a hold of a low-hanging branch. It held him. Water was up to Mike's chest and moving fast. Mike screamed, "Jon, come quick!"

All he heard was, "I can't! The bushes are too thick!"

He yelled again to Jon, "I'm sinking and can't get out! I need your help. Go around the bushes. Hurry, Jon, this branch might not hold me long! Help, Jon!"

"Wait, wait there! I am going for help, Mike." Jon dropped his pole quickly, scooting away from the stream. Never once did he glance back.

Jon's voice was loud and seemed close by. Mike continued to yell for his help. Nothing came yelling back. Mike kept quiet, hoping to hear or see Jon making his way to get to him. Many minutes passed.

Mike yell back to him. Too late. Many thoughts ran through his mind. Mike guessed he took off and couldn't hear him.

Mike stood in that spot for nearly an hour. Soon, it was evident Jon wasn't coming back. "Probably got lost," Mike thought out loud. Hearing his own voice helped quell his fears. *I'll drown this day. Not really, just kidding*, Mike told himself. *Maybe I shouldn't kid like that, dummy, it might just happen. So, keep them thoughts out of your mind, kiddo.*

Not long, the water brought with it some floating branches. Mike had to let go of one branch to keep branches from running into him with the other free hand. One large branch slammed into his face. A small cut opened above his right eye. The blood oozed down into the eye. It burned; Mike had to continuously wipe at the blood. It finally stopped bleeding. Still, it didn't keep him from thinking of alligators might be in the water attracted to the smell of his blood. *Remember your training.* Mike had always fell back on them when things seemed most dire.

Mike was amazed with all of the stuff floating past him in the water. Suddenly, a snake appeared in the water. The one fear he had was swimming straight at him. Mike looked all around for anything to use to keep it away. He suddenly remembered his karate lesson to contain the fear. *When that snake nears, fear will well up inside. Don't allow the fear to take hold and control your action.*

Panic almost got hold when that snake floated toward him. Mike froze, just staring at that squirmy creature. It twisted around his body like it would a stump in the water. For a moment, he was sure it was going to climb up him and bite. Staying calm and motionless made the snake think he was a stump and did not need to defend itself. That didn't stop the snake from slithering up around his shoulders.

Mike was drawn back on the trail home from Virginia and his first snakebite. The trail was bad enough, but he wasn't alone to doctor the bite. He had found Mary. This time, he was stuck, and no one around. The snake was wrapping itself around his neck. Slowly Mike sank his shoulders into the water, twisting ever so slowly. The snake uncoiled and floated off his neck. Quickly, the fast-moving waters carried it far from him, to Mike's relief.

Mike struggled to free one foot from the soft sandy bottom but tended to sink from his efforts. With each attempt to push one leg down to lift the other, it only made the sand less hard. After several attempts at trying this technique, Mike realized the sand was softening, and if he could pull while stepping down, he might be able to pull free from the soft sand. The trick was to pull up before the sand pulled him down. Luckily, he got hold of another branch, and only after a strain taking most of his strength and will power, his foot was coming free of the quagmire.

He was tired and getting cold. Mike remembered what Bo told him about hypo, hyperhiberate, or something like that. Bo said, "Getting cold can kill you if you are wet and don't get warmed up."

"*Hypothermia!*" shouted Mike. The word finally came to him. It was his first win and made him feel great. "Now to beat this quicksand I'm stuck in!" he shouted.

With all Mike had left, he pulled and pulled with one giant effort. He began to feel his feet move up through that goo. "If the branch can hold me, I will be free." Mike kept telling himself this as the sand slowly let go of its grip. Night was coming fast. *I sure don't want to be in this creek at night*, he thought.

Finally, after what seemed a very long time pulling and tugging, he was able to drag himself out of the goo. Mike lay in the water, allowing it to drag his body along with the flow while clinging to his branch. It felt good allowing the soothing waters to caress his tired body.

The sun was near the ground, and being in this creek at night wasn't what he had intended to be doing. Dragging himself onto the dry land, he lay down for a time, warming off the setting sun. Mike made his way up the banks to the nearest home after gathering his belongings that were left where Jon was fishing. Upon reaching the house, he followed the fence until he found an opening to walk through. Mike swiftly was on the road to home.

The walk was longer than he thought. He was tired, hungry, and mad. He went by Jon's home; he was outside playing with his neighbors, to Mike's surprise and disgust.

Walking over to where Jon and the two next-door kids were playing, Mike was still wet from head to toe. He stopped. Neither of them noticed Mike standing on the curve in front of Jon's duplex. All three were having a grand time wrestling on the grass. Only when the dad of the two younger boys walked onto the porch with deer burgers had they stopped wrestling. The father quickly saw Mike standing wet at the road.

The father knew Mike because Jon and Mike often played with his two boys. He called to Mike, "Hey, Mike, what happened to you? Did you fall in a creek or something?"

"Yes, sir, I did. I almost drowned. Jon was to go and get help because I was stuck in quicksand."

Jon turned to see Mike standing as the father called out to Mike.

Seeing Jon turn to look at him, Mike yelled out, "What the heck, Jon! I nearly drowned, and you were supposed to get help for me!"

Jon stood there with a bit of "what the hell are you talking about?" on his face. "I did go back with help. You were gone when we arrived. I thought you freed yourself and went on downstream fishing."

"Well, for your information, I just freed myself only a few minutes ago with no help. I stayed in the water for almost two hours waiting. I didn't hear anyone yelling to find me."

"I did, you never answered me back!" Jon quickly answered back.

"Yeah, Jon, did you spot my boots and socks where I left them? Who went with you, is what I would like to know? Tell me who they were? I would like to hear what they got to say."

Jon stood there not saying a word. He lied and was caught in that lie.

The father spoke up as Jon remained silent. Jon turned to him and listened to the father of the two boys ask, "You been playing with Davy and James for more than a few hours. Why didn't you tell me this?"

Jon just stood there quietly.

"Yeah, Jon, did you bother to stop by my house to see if I got home, Jon?" Did you at least do that for me? Please say you did."

Nothing, nothing, and nothing was said by Jon.

Mike looked at him, and for the first time, he really saw Jon for what he was. A liar and a coward. *I guess it was my own fault. I made him a friend and should have expected no less or no more from him. Still, he left me alone and possibly in a life-and-death way. He gave up quickly on that search for aid. That is, if he even attempted looking*, Mike thought.

Jon stood alone in the yard. Both Davy and James were told to get in the house. The father said a few words to Jon before shutting the door. "Jon, I want you to not play with my sons again."

It was the last time Mike had anything much to do with Jon. He would pass by his home going to the store or if he was wandering off on an adventure. Jon, if he saw Mike, avoided his eyes and looked away. Some friends aren't worth having, and Mike was lucky to learn that before it was too late. Mike thought about that every time he went by his home.

WATERMELON MAN

PRIOR TO THE END OF his first summer, Mike gathered his troops. He left early on a Saturday morning to wander over to Steve and his brother's home. Greeting Steve at the front door after they had breakfast, he discussed with him another adventure.

"Steve, you up for a walk today?" Mike inquired. "I went down this back road and came across this large field of watermelons the day before. I was going to drop by Ron's to see if he wanted to go. I figured you might just want to collect some melons for home. So how's about it? You in?"

"You bet I am," Steve readily answered.

Steve's brother was sneaking a hearing to their conversation and blurted out to them, "I want to come too."

Steve looked at Mike. "Well?"

"Sure, the more the merrier, Steve," Mike answered.

"Yippy!" big brother replied. He turned and ran back in to tell his mom.

She came to the door. "Hi, Mike, so you three are off on a little trip? Remember the last time. These two came home soaking wet. Just try and keep dry on this trip. Mike, I am depending on you to be safe and get these two home before supper."

"Yes, madam," replied Mike. Mike remembered how he felt getting them nearly drowned and hadn't the heart to face their mom a second time if things went wrong.

Before the three set out to Ron's home, their mom called them back. She handed the brothers some money.

"What was all that about?" Mike asked Steve when they walked back.

"Oh, Mom wants us to have some money to call home if we need to. Also, for us to get a snack if we stay out too long."

They crossed the street over to Ron's home, which just happened to be almost on the other side of the street from Steve's home. Ron was outside sitting on his porch. He was like Jon, having to keep an eye on his younger brother. Mike rarely took Ron on any of his adventures because he only found out where he lived recently. After school, Ron went in another direction from Mike to go home. One day he went to locate Ron's home from his directions. He found it quickly. Ron was inside a fence playing with his brother. Mike continued to drop in more often after that. One day his family was going to the lake, and Ron asked him if he wanted to go.

"Mike, Dad is taking the family to the lake. Come and go with us," Ron pleaded.

"Sure, but I need to check in at home, Ron." Mike quickly ran home, and his mom told him it was okay.

The family left early as soon as Mike returned. On the highway, the sky turned black from the growing number of rainclouds overhead. They watched the rain pour from the sky off to one side of the highway.

"Mike, look at it, it's like a wall of rain."

"It fell from the sky like someone poured a bucket of water on the ground," cited Mike to Ron. It reminded him of the storm he experienced leaving Susie's town, recalled Mike.

They rode in the car for about an hour. The car turned off the road and onto a dirt road to a fence with a gate. Stopping at the gate, Ron's dad paid to enter into the lake. He drove by the large pond or lake. In the water were slides, swings, and rope ladders. When the door opened, everyone was off. They stayed in the water until Ron's mom called them to come and eat.

"Hey, Ron, I hadn't figured on eating. I ate a sandwich at my house, buddy. Not too hungry." Only after Ron increasingly pressuring Mike and then his mom calling to him did Mike reluctantly drag himself out of the water.

"Aren't you hungry, Mike?" Ron's mom asked, holding a sandwich in her outstretched hand.

"Not really, madam. I usually don't eat lunch."

"Well, you can at least have a sandwich."

"Yes, madam," Mike answered.

She handed him a pineapple sandwich with mayo.

Mike looked at the pineapple sandwich. He wasn't sure he wanted to eat it. He was hungry, but a pineapple sandwich? *Never heard of it*, he thought to himself. "I don't know. I never much liked pineapple," Mike said softly, lifting the sandwich from the tray it sat on.

Ron's mom must have caught his hesitation eating it. "Mike, you don't like pineapple sandwiches? You know it is not necessary to eat it if you'd rather not."

"Thank you, madam, it is fine." Mike ate it. Wasn't that bad, it turned out. One was enough.

Mike, Ron, and his kid brother stayed for two more hours playing in the pond. Suddenly, everyone was called to get out of the large swimming pond. Apparently, a child got bit by a water moccasin snake, they learned in the car while driving home.

They left the lake. Later in the car driving home, Mike was told that they shocked the pond with electricity to remove the snakes. The child lived.

Arriving at Ron's house, Ron hesitated when Mike asked him to go with the three of them. Mike could see the wanting in Ron's eyes. With a little pushing, Ron agreed to ask his mom.

After getting Ron's mom to approve, they were soon on the road. A new adventure, one last for the end of summer. One to talk about at school. Also, one that put them all in danger again.

Everyone followed Mike back to his neighborhood. From there, all left down the same road he and Jon traveled to go fishing.

They walked down a road with a steep hill. At the bottom was a creek. The same creek Mike got stuck in quicksand. That was when Steve's brother began his warning cries. *I told Ron and Steve about Jon and my fishing disaster at school—a big mistake*, Mike thought.

"I don't think we should go down that creek. It has a nasty look. See, look at the water along the banks." Big brother pointed at some yellow stagnant water in a shallow branch leading into the stream. "I hope you aren't planning for us to walk in that?"

Turning to look at big brother, Mike replied, "No, we can walk on the ledge of this bank up to the next road, then we will cross over."

"Where is that, Mike?" Ron asked.

"Just up ahead, guys. I told you this is a journey. We will be going through the woods," Mike reminded them.

Not long walking along the creek, they came to the bridge.

"Let's stop and take a rest here, Mike," Steve's brother quipped. Steve and Ron agreed.

"Okay, a short rest, and off we be."

The small stream was becoming a nice-size stream, several feet deep. "Farther down the stream was where I got stuck," Mike told the guys.

Ron mentioned the episode of Mike's fish noodling with Jon again to the group.

"We are not going over there," Mike made sure to tell big brother before he went crazy with fear.

Mike pointed up ahead to an opening path leading up out of this low level to higher ground. Steve's brother slipped down the path two, make that, three times. This was becoming a pattern with big brother. He would hurry ahead of the group and, like usual, end up fouling up. He was a bit awkward, Mike noted to Steve on several occasions. After assisting big brother up the hill, all finally got to the road to cross.

On the other side was the path Mike said he went down earlier. "Guys, we are nearly here. Look, the dirt road I told you about, Steve." Mike signaled.

Across the street was a dirt road barely visible. It was almost hidden, covered with a thick growth of bushes. You couldn't make out the entrance until you were several feet near it. It was nearly invisible from passersby who walked along the road. It was as if someone intentionally meant it to be hard to find. Mike told the group he only spotted the entrance to the dirt road when he saw a rabbit hop out and back, seeing him approaching.

"About time. I'm getting thirsty, Mike."

"So am I," Ron quipped, agreeing with Steve and big brother. Sweat was pouring out the two brothers more so than Mike and Ron.

"Just down this path, there is a well and a field full of melons," Mike told his pals.

"I sure hope this won't be like that other river trail we followed." Turning to look at the others, Steve jokingly told Ron about the heat and then the rain again.

"Dang, Mike, when did that happen?" inquired Ron.

Steve's brother spoke up. "Several weeks ago. I'm surprise he didn't tell you, Ron."

"I mentioned it," Mike shot back with a snarl on his face.

"Yeah, I bet you left a few details out," Steve's brother quipped back. Everyone laughed a bit.

"Yeah, I might have skipped some things." Mike was looking at Ron, and Ron was laughing. Both looked at Steve's brother. Big brother realized they were laughing at him and not the seriousness of what he said.

Walking was made harder once they left the hard dirt road for a sandy road. The heat rose up a notch, and so did the griping by big brother.

We're all getting thirsty, Mike realized.

Steve's brother started to get skittish coming to a part of the path covered by thick shrubs. "I don't think we need to go through all them bushes. There might be snakes, spiders, and maybe bears," big brother spoke with trepidation in his words.

"Bears?" Ron said in a shocked tone.

"I heard tell there are bears in the woods," replied big brother.

"Man, you got to quit thinking of things like that. I've been through all the woods around here and never once saw any bears," Mike pointed out to his team. Mike reached up under his shirt, taking hold of his knife. Holding it in front of all three boys, their mouths dropped open. Mike held the knife still sheathed. The beautiful sheath caught their eyes. It shimmered in the sunlight from the gold braided line that stitched along the edge. On the out-facing side was an embroidered face of a wolf.

"Wow, where did you get a knife like that, Mike?" Steve asked.

"Well, I helped make the blade, and the father of a friend while I was on the road crafted the handle. He was a metalsmith. That man could make all kinds of things. Mainly, he liked knives. When I stayed with them, he and his son taught me how to forge metal."

Mike held the knife up for them to see. Then he unsheathed the blade. Along the length of the blade was a wavy pattern.

"Why does your knife have wavy lines on it? All the knives I ever saw was shiny, Mike. Can I hold it, Mike?" pleaded Ron.

"Sure you can, Ron, just be careful, it is mighty sharp."

Ron took the blade from Mike's hands, holding it up high, admiring the craftsmanship.

"Those waves you see on the blade, Ron, are caused by the folding of the metal bar. The more you fold the metal, the stronger the blade becomes. After folding the blade, I twisted the red-hot iron like screw threads. It is a Damascus method of making steel stronger and creating the wavy pattern on the blade."

"Me too, me too," Steve's brother begged. Big brother grabbed for the blade like a small child seeing something pretty.

Ron twisted, pulling the knife away from big brother's grasping hands. Ron handed the blade back to Mike.

Mike started to give the knife to big brother but stopped. "Hey, you need to be careful with this. If I let you hold this, don't go swinging it around. It's not a toy," Mike reminded big brother.

Big brother grabbed the blade from Mike's hand just as he finished reminding him of the dangers of his knife. Steve asked his brother to hold it carefully. His brother's eyes grew in size holding the knife. He was awed by how easy it felt in his hand, almost like a glove. Steve's brother started swinging it around like a sword. After just missing slicing Mike, he had to take the knife away from big brother.

"Hey, hand it over, it's not a toy. This knife saved my life," Mike said to big brother.

"What you mean?" Steve's brother asked Mike.

"Both Steve and Ron saw my scars when we were swimming at the end-of-the-year school pool party. I told them about the encounter with a bear."

Steve snapped back before Mike could explain, "He killed a bear with it."

"Wow," big brother said.

"Show him your scars, Mike," Steve urged.

"Go on," said Ron. "Show him."

"I told you guys, I don't like to talk about that too much. I was told it disrespected the animal I killed. I didn't kill that bear for glory." Mike tried to explain, but to no avail. Mike could see he had to take his shirt off and show big brother. Mike handed his blade to Steve to hold while he removed his shirt.

"I will this time," Mike reluctantly agreed. He lifted his shirt, revealing the claw marks on his chest.

"Oh my, you mean you killed a bear? How big was it? Why did you have to kill it? It, it attacked you?" Just as Mike knew it, big Brother had a million questions he wanted answered.

"Hold on a second, I can only answer one question at a time." Mike retold the story just to shut big brother up.

"See, brother of mine, if we run into any bear, Mike's got that knife and knows how to fight a bear." Steve held the knife as if he was stabbing a bear, then handed it back to Mike. "Thanks, Mike."

Mike didn't say a word. He felt it might help big brother deal with his own fear. Truth be told, he would run as fast as any of them if they came upon a bear. *Once was enough*, Mike thought quietly.

Once they fought through all the limbs with no encounters with bears, spiders, or snakes, the group continued their hot walk up the path. Soon, Mike found himself returning to his old habit of daydreaming while walking.

Mike's mind started to drift back to arriving at Mom and his sisters' new duplex home. It wasn't much. Little to no furniture, two bedrooms, a table, four chairs, and a used TV. He remembered the days just being in the house. Days later, he cleaned out his pack and came across the letters put in his bag by the friends he made. It reminded Mike of the promise to them when he finally made it back home.

He couldn't write to Sam; he had no address to send a letter. All he could do is think about him, hoping and somehow feeling his thoughts. The letter Mike wrote that was the hardest was to Mary and Bo's Ellie and John. Ms. Ellie thoughts brought tears to Mike's eyes as he wrote it. He had stopped thinking about those letters written until those memories were brought back on this trail they were walking.

Around the next bend on the sandy road, an old house loomed ahead. From where they were walking, the house looked old but in one piece. The closer they got, the older it got and less livable.

Stopping at a well pump near the only door, Mike entered the old house. It looked even more of an eyesore.

"Mike, I thought you said it was a deserted house? Heck, this place been deserted forever." Big brother was quick to let his opinion be known.

"Yeah, I agree with my brother. This place looks broken down." Steve walked over to a side of the house and pulled on a loose board. It fell with little effort off the side.

"Mike."

Turning toward Ron's call, Mike answered him, "Yeah?"

"I'm thirsty, where is the water?" yelled Ron.

"Right here, Ron. What else you need?" Mike pointed to the well pump. Poking out of the ground was a handle with a spigot attached to a pipe extending down in the earth.

"Heck, that thing is all rusty," big brother quipped. "Ain't going to work, and even if it does, the water might be bad."

Mike replied to big brother, "The water is good. How is it going to get bad way down into that deep hole?"

Steve gave Mike a "don't know" nod concerning what his brother said.

Big brother just turned around and quipped out to Mike, "See, you got us in another mess, Mike."

Mike walked over to the well pump, taking hold of the handle. With several up and down strokes, nothing came out.

"See, I told you this would happen!" big brother shouted to all. Both of his hands were waving around to display his disappointment.

"Wait a second. It needs to be primed with water!" cried Mike.

Steve was now siding with big brother. "Sure, water. What water, Mike?"

"Look, give me some time, I will get it working." Mike grasped the well pump handle, twisting while lifting to pull the pump's rod out. The seal was about shot.

"What is wrong with it?" Ron asked after Mike quipped, "Dang it!"

"The leather seal that allows the pump to suck the water up is bad, Steve."

"Now what are you going to do, Mike?"

"Look, big brother—" Mike halted what he wanted to say, realizing he was wasting his breath. He turned to Steve, giving him a hard stare. "Will you take your brother for a walk so I can get this working? He is beginning to annoy me."

Walking over to his brother, Steve took hold of his arm. "Come on, big brother, give Mike a rest."

"Okay, but I'm thirsty and mad."

"Well, you didn't have to come with us on this trip."

So it went that way with them until they walked up the road away.

Mike and Ron went looking for any leather or rag to make a seal. Mike found a suitable cloth by the front door. It was an old shirt left by someone recently. Tearing a strip, Mike fashioned a round seal.

"Hey, Mike, what you going to do with that round cloth?" Ron inquired.

"Watch, Ron. I am going to slide it down over the old seal. Then I will place the washer back down on top of the rag. It looks good," Mike said to Ron. "Let's hope it will work."

"Mike, how did you learn how to do that?"

"Well, Ron, I stayed with a woman after I got a snakebite in the backwoods. All she had for water was this type of pump, one in the kitchen and another one in her bathroom. Every once in a while, the seal would go bad, and water wouldn't come out. She showed me how to fix it. Once I got the plunger out of the well, Ron, I saw right off the seal was torn. It only made sense to replace it."

Mike located some water in a broken bowl on the side of the house looking for a seal and told Ron to fetch it. "I saw it when I discovered the shirt," he told Ron. As soon as Ron brought the water to Mike, he poured it down the well head then pumped the handle hard. After about ten pumps, water came spurting out of the neck of the well. It was clear and sparkling.

"See, Ron, all it needed was some good ole know-how." Mike beamed with a big smile after telling Ron.

Ron let out a whoopy yell, then called to Steve and his big brother. "We got water! Hurry, come get some!"

Mike was about to take the first drink when Steve and big brother showed up. The water had a rusty, almost like blood appearance. When they came over to Mike, he was drinking the rusty water. It was iron giving the water the bloody taste. Mike knew it was safe. When Ron, Steve, and big brother drank, they complained it was bad after spitting it on the ground.

Mike said before big brother was about to make another nasty remark to him, "I knew you would complain about the taste. Don't worry, I can fix that too."

"How, Mike?" big brother said with a smirk.

"I'll show you a trick I learned on the road. You can boil water to make it safe is one way. It kills the bad thing living in the water. Another way and just as safe is to filter the water. Now, big brother, watch and learn something," Mike commanded.

Mike took the remaining piece of shirt and laid it across a chair without a bottom to sit on. Looking around, he gathered some burnt firewood near an old campfire. Mike instructed Ron to collect some dry grass growing near the sandy road and Steve to scrape up some clean white sand. "Now, it must be sand, not soil," Mike reminded him.

Big brother stood there watching Mike build his filter.

Having all the parts assembled, Mike explained to the three how to construct a filter. "First, you need to mount your cloth onto a place that will hold it off the ground. Second, you place this crushed burnt wood or charcoal at the bottom. The trick is to make layers for the bad water to pass through. Then a layer of sand, and the final layer will be the dried grass. The grass removes the big stuff in the water, sticks, bugs, things like that. Then the sand continues with separating the smaller stuff. Finally, the charcoal will purify the water, removing the harmful microscopic stuff. You can do this to most of the foul water you run into, making it safe," Mike explained.

Reaching into his pocket, Mike removes a small vial of Clorox bleach. Steve greedily wanted to drink the water after Mike poured the first amount of water from the well through the filter.

Mike stopped him. "The first couple of times," Mike explained, "I usually pour water through to allow the filter to get started. This first water coming out is safe, but wait a bit longer, the water will be even better."

Big brother looked at the first water dripping from the filter. "It looks dirty to me. That don't look that clean."

"It is. The filter will work better the more water we allow to pass through it, big brother. Watch and see, the water will get clearer and clearer with every bucket of water running through it."

Ron was the first to notice the little vial of bleach. "What is that, Mike?"

"Oh, this? It is bleach, Ron."

"What's it for?"

"Well, I usually bring this with me. It is a quicker way to kill bacteria in the water. Another thing that kills bacteria in water is sunlight. I was sure you three didn't want to wait that long for water," Mike replied.

After the third pass of well water through the filter, it appeared clear from all dirt. Steve was first to take the glass to drink. He slugged it down without a hint of trying to taste it first for safety reasons. Mike put several drops in the next container of water. The others slowly sipped at first, then they drank their fill. Finally, Mike got a drink of the pure cold water after it had been filtered.

Ron kept asking Mike how he learned all those things. He was amazed at Mike's knowledge. Mike guessed Ron thought he was some kind of a genius.

"Okay, Mike, where are those melons you said you found?"

Turning to big brother, Mike replied to his snarly request, "It's up that road you two walked while Ron and I were fixing the well. I guess you didn't go far enough." Mike pointed up the road.

Everyone stood up from sitting on the ground. Walking together, they went up the road. Sure enough, as Mike had told them, there was the prettiest fields of melons as far as the eye could see.

Not grabbing the first melons they came to, everybody, including Mike, ran into the open field after seeing hundreds lying on the ground to choose from. Mike was enjoying seeing all the melons. The others went wild running from one melon to another, not sure which one to cut from the vine. Soon, each of them had their perfect melon. It didn't take long for them to realize the heavier the melon, the harder to carry.

Everybody finally got back to the house carrying the largest melon they could. Everyone laid their prizes on the ground around the well. Each wanted to take their melon home. No one wanted to slice into their melons.

So Mike removed his knife, slicing his own melon open. Everybody reached for the first slice of melon.

Sitting on the ground chomping down their first slice, Ron quickly noticed another smaller knife in Mike's boot. "What you got in your boot?" he asked.

"It's my small hideaway knife. I put it on my stick I carry along," Mike told Ron.

"I always wondered why every time you come over, you carried that stick, Mike."

"Ron, this stick was a gift for me. It was made to mount this small boot knife."

"Let me see!" each cried out to Mike.

Soon all three wanted to hold the boot knife. This time big brother didn't get to handle it. Mike demonstrated how it fitted into the walking stick.

"Hey, it's a spear to throw!" Steve yelled out. "You ever kill anything with this spear?"

"No, I hadn't the opportunity to do that, Steve."

Inside that melon of Mike's was the reddish core of juicy sweet-tasting fruit. Mmm, it tasted good. The team went through that first melon in no time. Soon, they started on Ron's melon. By the third melon, there was little room to finish it off in their stuffed bellies.

Ron and Mike went back to the field. They fetched the first melon they came upon. Their bellies were too full to pick another huge melon to tote home, both agreed. After cutting the melon from its vine, neither Mike nor Ron saw the lone man by a truck.

"Stop!" came a yell.

Both Mike and Ron looked around. Both took a step backward, not spotting where the voice originated from.

"Stop or I'll shoot."

Mike looked at Ron, and Ron looked back toward Mike, "I don't know" expressions written on both faces. Ron wanted to take flight after the second shout to stop was given.

"Stop!" the voice called again. *Bang!* came a loud sound.

The melons both of them were holding up fell like rain to the ground to their feet. They turned to where the yell was coming from. A man by an old pickup truck had his shotgun pointed at them. He was wearing blue overalls and sported a long gray beard below his neck. He cracked open the double-barreled gun to reload. Before the first shell filled the chamber, Mike and Ron turned back in the direction they came, then lit off like two rockets at launch. It wasn't no slow burn and gentle liftoff. They were like missiles—*bang*, gone.

"Did you see that man, Mike?" Ron said in midstride of his run.

"Yeah, Ron," Mike gasped back, keeping up next to him. "Yep, did you see what he looked like, Ron?"

"Sure did, Mike. That beard was down to his belly."

"Got that right, Ron. That, my friend, is what I was told is a redneck."

"Well, Mike, I ain't staying to introduce myself to him."

"Me neither, Ron."

Around the bend they saw both big brother and Steve standing, watching them run toward them full bore. "What was that sound?" big brother yapped out.

"Ain't you ever heard a gunshot sound?" Mike yelped back to him as he and Ron sped past.

"No," both responded back.

Mike looked back, and the two of them were still standing where he and Ron passed them. "Hey, you two, if you want to meet the man who shot at us, you keep standing there!" Mike yelled, not stopping to see if they followed.

They all got a short way down the sandy road where they came upon going to the watermelon field when big brother stopped. "Wait, I hear something up ahead!" cried big brother.

"Maybe it's that redneck following us, Mike," Ron said softly.

Both Mike and Ron halted, looking back to where big brother had stopped and called out to them.

"No, no, it is coming from this direction." Big brother leaned down and pointed his finger toward the bushes near the woods where both Ron and Mike had come to a halt. "Hey, guys, I'm not kidding. There's something in the woods coming toward us."

Steve looked hard in the bushes to spot what his brother said he heard coming near.

"Not again," Mike retorted back to him.

Ron felt the same. "Hey, big brother, I'm tired and want to get home."

Steve followed with the same sentiments, then started to run up to Mike and Ron ahead on the road, waiting for him. Together they began a slow and steady trek a bit farther.

Again, big brother yelled up to the three ahead. "I hear something in the brush, Mike!"

"Okay, okay, everybody get quiet," Mike commanded. They listened for several seconds. Nothing.

Ron spoke up, "I want to get going."

Turning, Mike called back to big brother, "If it was something, it might have run off from all the noise we are making. You hear anything?"

Suddenly, a loud snort was heard a few feet from the three.

Steve took off after the second sound came, following his big brother. Mike and Ron were still standing, looking into the brush. A low snort was heard close to where they stood. Both brothers ran ahead several yards before stopping.

"I heard sounds like those before," Mike told Ron after another snort was heard nearing closer to where they stood. It was an animal approaching, Mike was sure. Then several sounds followed. Mike yelled to the three, "Find a tree! Hurry, get up a tree!"

Steve and big brother had stopped running long enough to listen to what Mike was telling them. Ron turned and looked at Mike with that queer "what the heck are you talking about?" look.

"Get in a tree! Quick!" Then Mike saw what made the noise. He yelled again to them, "Get in a tree, quick!" Ron, standing next to Mike, got a shove from him. "Go, Ron!" Mike yelled.

Still, they didn't move. They stood there watching Mike. Mike reached down to pull his boot knife out, attaching it to his walking stick. Not too soon enough.

First to appear was a small pig. It wandered up to Mike. He stood still. Mike knew from experience not to move or strike out at that baby pig. If it felt scared, got hurt, or panicked, the first thing that pig would do was to call for its mommy. Mommy—Mike didn't want to meet her.

Then—Mike would have made a bet on it—big brother yelled out, "Look at the baby pig!"

Mike silently thought, *I'd have won that bet.*

"Look over there, it's another baby pig. Then two more oinking piglets appeared!" shouted big brother.

Thank the Lord they're not squealing. Mike was relieved.

Unfortunately, big brother kicked at one when it got too close to him and his brother Steve. Then all hell broke out. Mike continued to scream at them to get in a tree. Big brother took his advice. Steve and Ron stood watching the pigs. Big brother kept up his screaming, "It is going to kill us!"

Ron yelled back, "We can't! There's the biggest pig you ever saw coming at us, Mike!"

"Run, guys, quick, get behind anything."

Big brother yelled to Steve, and at that moment, the mommy pig charged at Steve. Big brother was in a tree faster than any of them. Both he and Steve happened to be near a tree easy to climb up. He screamed the whole time as he climbed. "It's going to kill us!"

Steve was still by the tree when the first charge of that momma pig came. She was a big one, Mike thought as she emerged from the shrubs. He could see those tusks protruding from her mouth. What bushes that Steve was able to get behind was only turned into trash by those tusks. She mowed through them like Mike's power mower did cutting grass.

Steve screamed, "Shit, shit, shit!" As quick as a wink, he jumped behind the tree big brother had climbed up. Big brother was slow to shimmy up that tree. Steve kept yelling, "Get up the damn tree! This pig's trying to tear me up."

Mike could see the pig running over to where Steve was scurrying; momma pig was surely going to get him. Suddenly, a hand reached down and took hold of Steve. Big brother had lifted Steve up into the tree. The mommy pig ripped at his shoe and pants leg. It tore his pants but not his leg.

Mike could hear Steve ask big brother, "What took you so long?" Mike could barely make out exactly what was said after those words from all the oinking and screaming from everyone.

Momma pig, seeing one of the boys got away, turned to where Ron was hiding. He threw a stick to help Steve right at the time Steve got hoisted into the tree. Bad timing was all it was. That pig stood sizing up how to best get at Ron. The stick made the choice easy. It hit the momma pig hard. She lashed out to the closest person. It was Ron.

Ron ran to another tree. Momma was on him too fast for him to shimmy up it. He ran around the tree with the pig just inches from him.

Mike was in a full run to get to Ron. Ron was running around the tree. The mommy pig nearly got him twice. He had a stick, giving mommy pig two big whacks on her snout. Didn't do much good other than making her madder.

The piglets were following Mike down the road to be with the others. Mike wished they weren't oinking so loud. Mommy pig heard them. He wasn't ready for her to turn and charge at him.

She turned away from Ron, staring right at Mike. Mike saw nowhere to climb. Ron picked up a bigger stick. He was about halfway in his climb to safety when he spotted Mike, and the mommy pig was going straight at him.

Ron saw Mike lunge with his spear, only to miss. Mommy pig hit him with a glancing blow to Mike's boot. It tore open, and Mike felt some pain tumbling head over head to the ground. Ron, seeing the pig hit Mike from the tree he was safely up on, slid to the ground. He struck momma pig on her head with his stick. It happened quickly before she could turn and take another swipe at him.

Mike rolled to his feet from his tumble to face mommy pig with his spear.

Steve, in the tree safe, started ripping any limb he could get hold of. Soon, all three of them were attacking momma pig with anything they could hurl at her.

Lucky for Mike, the momma pig and Ron were all together near the tree big brother and Steve were up in. Mommy pig turned, and Ron ran. Momma hesitated running at him. She was getting confused with all three of them taking turns hitting her with whatever was in their hands.

It gave Mike the time he needed to ready his spear again.

Whap!

"What the heck?" cried Mike. A tree branch smacked him in his chest.

"I'm sorry, I'm sorry, I was trying to hit, to hit the momma!" Steve called down to Mike.

Mike yelled back to Steve, "Hey, I'm not momma pig!"

Ron ran to big brother's tree. Steve was still throwing anything he could tear from the tree at the pig. Two of his throws missed the pig and nearly hit Ron.

"Watch it, this pig's trying to kill me. She doesn't need none of your help!" cried Ron after getting swiped with a branch.

"Sorry, sorry!" Steve yelled down at Ron. "It's hard to hit the pig under the tree with you so near, sorry."

"Well, I ain't running out from here!" Ron shouted up to Steve.

Steve threw another stick down at momma pig. She stopped after the stick smacked her on the snout.

Mike ran with a slight limp toward her. Momma pig turned, staring at him coming at her. It looked like she was still confused from the whack on the snout. She stood there until Ron reached down to pick up the first stick thrown at the pig. When he did, momma pig turned to take after Ron. Just three steps Mike was able to make. She heard him. Again, she turned back to Mike. He saw her eyes stare with a burning hate. She was hell-bent on tearing one of them apart. Big brother kicked her child. She wanted revenge. Ron and Mike were on the ground. Decisions, decisions—she would need to make a choice. Mike or Ron. Looking at Mike, the choice was made. Mike was closest. Also, she smelled blood. Blood was oozing from his foot.

Thinking how stupid big brother had been causing all this while waiting for mommy pig to make her move made Mike mad. *I told him along the trail when he was afraid to enter through the brush to continue on the trail. Snake, there might be snakes in there. Maybe a bear or spiders.*

Having dealt with a bear, Mike told him, "If you saw one, whatever you do, stand still. Don't move, and he might pass you by. If he doesn't, then yell and wave your arms as much as possible to scare it. Most times, wild animals would rather run away than attack you. In any event, just stay calm and never touch them. They're not pets to pat."

Now, we all might get out of this hopefully without a scratch, Mike was praying. Both Ron and the brothers were safe. Mike was left in the open with this big mad-as-hell pig. She was tired but just as determined to get some satisfaction. She stood there still after that whack on her snout from Steve's limb he threw from his tree.

Ron yelled, throwing another stick at her. She was about to make her charge at Mike when he did that. She stopped and turned back to Ron. Too late for her to change her mind again. Mike let loose his spear. He thrust it with all his might. He could feel the depth of the spear pushing through her body. No bone he could feel; it went in almost like slicing through butter.

The thrust didn't knock her down. Mike guessed because it went in so easily. Not enough force to topple her over. Mommy pig didn't die quick. She pulled at the stick. Finally, the spear made its way through her body and out at the belly, then into the ground. It was as if he had driven a stake through her. She couldn't pull loose nor run.

Ron was quick to run to Mike's aid. They both held that spear. At one point, the spear felt like it was at its breaking point. When momma pig was twisting, Mike reached under his shirt, pulling the knife from its sheath.

"Ron, hold her, I'm going to end this."

"What?"

"Just hold her," Mike repeated.

"What you mean hold her?"

"Ron, grab her rear legs. Make sure you get both of them, Ron."

"No way, Mike."

"You got to, Ron. This spear isn't going to last long. Do it, do it, now, Ron!"

Ron let go of the spear and backed away from Mike and the thrashing mommy pig on the ground. He stood there staring at the sight of Mike holding on to the spear and momma twisting. It was the first time he saw the scene unfold before his eyes. Then and only then did it strike him of the danger they all were facing.

Mike yelled to Ron again, "Quick, she's going to get loose! Quick, Ron, grab those legs."

It was what Ron needed to hear that broke the spell cast over him. Fear caused him to freeze. But Ron didn't run like Jon.

Mike remembered the first time Sensei told him to not allow fear to take hold. "It is the mind killer. It will freeze your actions. Doubt will enter your mind. Time passes, giving your opponent control over you. Never allow this to happen. That is why practice and preparation during practice is necessary to prepare one's mind for combat." Memories rushed through Mike's mind of that lesson.

Ron bent down to grab the two legs. His first try was almost successful. He got one leg and almost the second. The sow kicked out; his weak effort made it easy for her to free one leg from Ron's grip.

"Ron!" Mike shouted at him. "Do it, don't think, just do it."

Hearing this, Ron grabbed hold of both legs. He pulled tight on them. In fact, so tight, it caused Mike to slip and land on his butt. The strain it caused against the spear thrust took the fight out of her, and she lay there in the sand bleeding out and panting. Mike knew he had to finish her off. He didn't want her to suffer. Removing his knife, he placed it under her chin then made the cut.

Her piglets ran off when big brother climbed down the tree and chased after them. Both Ron and Mike sat on the ground beside momma pig. Soon, the oinking from the piglets stopped.

Steve called over to Ron, "Quick, Mike is bleeding."

Ron looked at him. Both were staring at the dead mommy pig at their feet.

"Ron, you did good. Thanks, Ron," Mike said.

"Mike, your leg is bleeding," Ron said.

Mike watched Ron stand and Steve come at him. Ron was fine, not a scratch; only Steve was cut and bleeding. One arm had a long bloody scratch running the length from elbow to wrist.

"Steve, you are bleeding," Mike retorted.

Looking at his blood, Steve realized it was a cut from the tree. He tore off so many limbs, he cut himself several times in the process. "Ah, it's nothing. I got more cuts from that tree I was in than from that pig." Steve made a jest. Reaching down to his pants, he flapped it back and forth. "See, she got hold of my pants, but not a cut on me."

"Steve, thanks for the help. If not for you throwing those limbs at the momma pig, she was so confused, it kept her from getting either of us," Ron told Steve.

"Yeah, Steve, I appreciate the help," added Mike.

"Me too, Steve, even for the whop in my chest," Ron quipped.

"Thanks, you guys," Steve replied back to Ron and Mike.

"Yeah, those branches, man, you gots to work on your aim," Ron quipped back at him.

Mike sat up and untied his boot. Ron assisted with getting it off. Mike's sock was soaked with blood.

"Steve, bring me the water bottle," Ron requested.

Steve walked to where he dropped all of the stuff he was toting before climbing up the tree. He poured water onto Mike's foot, holding himself back from throwing up. All the blood from a huge rip opened on Mike's foot was making him sick.

"It hurts," was the only words Mike said with a grimace across his face. Mike never yelled out.

While Ron was washing Mike's wound, Mike removed the bleach from his pocket and handed it to Ron. "Pour that on my cut," Mike instructed.

"Hey, are you sure? This is bleach, Mike."

Sitting and holding on to his ankle above the cut, Mike explained to Ron why. "I learned one thing in the woods, if you get cut or bit by an animal, you need to clean it quick. Most animals have nasty things in their mouths. A bite not treated can be serious. So, Ron, pour it on, it will kill any germs from that pig's bite."

"Mike, it's going to hurt."

"Yeah, I know," Mike replied with a grimace.

It did. Mike held back from yelling for a few seconds. Then he let out a tiny yip. Ron kept pouring. Steve tore off some of his pants leg that was ripped by the momma pig. He wrapped Mike's foot. Both of them helped him get his boot back on.

Once Mike's leg was bandaged, big brother returned from chasing the piglets off. "What's up, guys?" he called out, nearing where Mike was sitting. Looking down at the blood around Mike's leg, he just said, "Oh."

Steve stood, pushing past his brother, and walked up to the dead pig. Steve pulled the spear from the momma pig, and big brother squealed at the sight of him pulling it out of the dead pig. It made a sucking sound as it was being pulled out. The entire boot knife was bloodred from its tip of the blade to the hilt. Steve poured the remaining bottle of water over it, washing off the blood.

"Thanks, Steve," Mike said, watching him clean his knife.

He handed it back to Mike. Mike removed the knife from the spear, placing it in his other boot. He used his stick as a cane on the way back home.

"What you think we might do with this pig?" big brother questioned.

Everyone remained quiet.

Mike spoke up. "Well, if I was on the road, I would gut and skin it. Then cut it into small strips to dry and smoke."

"You mean you would eat this pig, Mike?"

"Sure, big brother," Mike replied, giving a "what's wrong with that?" look to him.

"It could have all kinds of stuff wrong with it to eat."

"That's why I would dry out or smoke it. Smoking is best. It increases the drying and keeps the flies from laying their larva in the meat. Meat dried and smoked prevents it from rotting. It can last for a long time. Besides, big brother, it is always better than starving."

"Mike?" big brother asked.

"Yeah," Mike returned.

"Why did you keep calling this dead pig momma?"

"What do you think? She came a-running when you kicked at her babies."

"True, but she ain't no she."

"Huh? What?" Mike asked.

"Well, Mike, if she has a penis, then I guess you can't call her a she. Me, I thought only guys had a penis," replied big brother to everyone's amazement.

Ron turned to look at Steve and his big brother. Everyone walked over to where big brother stood looking at the pig. All stood there looking at the he pig.

"What does it mean?" Ron asked all fuzzily.

"I'm not sure," Mike said.

Then they all heard those sounds again. *Oink, oink, oink.* It was getting closer and closer. Mike turned sharply back at big brother. They all did. "Why did you have to chase them piglets?" he called out to big brother.

He threw up his hands and said to all of them, "I thought she—he was dead. So that was okay to chase after them piglets because we just killed their mommy, daddy pig," big brother remarked. "Well?"

"Well? Is that all you got to say?" Steve asked his big brother.

"Hey guys, we got to get out of here. Them oinking sounds are getting close," Ron butted in.

They started to run down the sandy road a second time. Steve led the way with the rest following in the rear. Mike's leg hurt, but not so much that he couldn't keep up. They got almost out of sight where they left the dead daddy pig. Turning back, they all stopped and looked. Barely out of sight from the slain daddy pig, a big pig broke through the brush. She started to sniff around the body.

Everybody turned and walked real fast, keeping close to the side of the path less visible for that big pig to spot them. Around the first bend, they were out of sight of her.

It was a long walk home. Most of the conversation was about Mike's wound and about the pig attack. Everybody laughed every time Steve brought up the stick that whopped the momma pig on its nose. One of the two, Ron or Mike, reminded Steve he had whopped not only the pig, but them too.

Once everyone got back to the road they previously crossed, Steve and big brother mention the melons. "Hey, we forgot our melons."

Everyone just laughed.

The first home they came to was Ron's home. Ron ran up to the house, calling out to his mom. "Quick!" he yelled. "Mike got bit by a hog. He's bleeding bad!"

Mike hobbled to the front porch step and sat down. Steve and big brother left for their home. Big brother wanted to leave and insisted. Steve wanted to stay but went. Waving goodbye, they walked across the street to their house.

Ron's mom called her husband to aid in removing Mike's bloody boot. She was a nurse. Upon examining his wound, she said, "Mike, this will need stitches."

"My mom's not working. I don't think we can afford to go to a doctor. If you got a bandage to put on it, I will wrap it when I get home," Mike said.

"Well, Mike, I can sew it up. I don't have anything for the pain. This wound will need more than a bandage, I'm afraid."

"If you can stitch it, I can deal with the pain. I been cut worse than this," Mike said.

"You ever had stitches?" Ron's mom was looking at Mike's leg, realizing how much pain stitching was going to cause him.

"Yes, madam," Mike responded back to her. A flashback to Sam's wife Leela sewing up the bear claw cuts entered Mike's thoughts.

"Okay." She went back into the house and came out with a box. "Mike, I am going to clean the wound before I begin the stitching. This will hurt."

Mike nodded back.

Ron stood next to his mom while she began washing Mike's leg. It burned, and the blood ran out of the wound. He gritted his teeth and barely made a sound.

"Okay, it is all clean." She motioned to her husband, and he sat next to Mike. "Honey, you need to help keep the wound closed while I begin sewing." She looked up, telling Mike, "It will take maybe ten stitches to close this cut."

He nodded back to begin. She took the curved needle and ran a string through the eye. Ron's dad held the wound on the skin closed, and she began with the first puncture of the needle.

Mike felt a small prick. "Wasn't so bad," he told her.

"I'm afraid it will get worse as I continue." She looked Mike in his eyes one last time. He never saw her eyes again until the last stitch. It seemed with every stitch, it had the same effect on her as with him. She knew it hurt and surely seemed to feel Mike's pain with each poke of the needle. Mike remained quiet and still. After doctoring his foot, they had Mike stay for about an hour.

"Madam," Mike told her, "I don't feel much of going right now." He was exhausted and glad they insisted he remain at their house for the time being.

She nodded back to Mike. "I don't expect you not to be tired. Most people who get stitches want painkillers and make all kinds of whining sounds. I am shocked by the way you handled the pain, Mike. My husband told me he could never have been as strong as you are."

Before Mike was ready to go, Ron's mom asked him to come inside and have a sandwich before leaving. Mike ate the sandwich. Not a pineapple one this time. It was peanut butter and banana. "Tasted pretty good," Mike said as he thanked her.

Ron walked with Mike to his home. He left him at the front door. He wanted to stay and explain what happened to Mike's mom. Mike wasn't sure if his mom was sober and really didn't want him to meet her if she wasn't. Ron left when Mike insisted it wasn't necessary to tell her what transpired.

Ron left as Mike walked in his home. Mom was sitting on the couch, smoking a cigarette and having a beer at the table. It looked to be the fourth beer from the count of empties.

Mike said, "Hello, how are you doing? Can I get you anything, Mom?"

Dodie came into the room hearing her brother enter. He walked to the kitchen. She saw his leg. He signaled for her to be quiet. "I'll explain later," Mike told her.

It got dark outside pretty quick.

Dodie walked back in from the kitchen carrying a hamburger they had for supper to her brother. It was cold. Didn't matter; he was hungry. It tasted good. He stood up and walked to his room. Blood was dripping from his boot. Ron's dad had stitched the boot from the rip it received from the daddy pig's tusk. It had little damage compared to all the ripping to his foot from the tusks.

ATLANTA WAREHOUSE

WHEN THE SUMMER ENDED, MIKE was entering a new school and a new change in his life. Neither Sharon nor he shared a room. Dodie was in another school across the street. Mike was a year older than anybody in his class. Some of the students from his other school was at this new school also.

Atlanta, Georgia

On the top floor was an office. Three men sat alone inside the office of an old warehouse with several members of their gang scattered around in a huge mainly empty space. Two skinny gang members were sitting alongside two women. One woman was sitting on a man's lap, kissing him. The other sat waiting for the smooching to end so they could continue a card game they were playing.

In another corner of the warehouse, smoke rose from pipes and hand-wrapped cigarettes. Some men were lying on the ground, a few sitting Indian style, puffing on weed. Everywhere one looked, gang members were seen doing one thing or another to pass the day.

Two men passed through a door and up the stairs to the office. They knocked on the door and waited until they were told to enter. Not a long wait before someone told them to enter. Opening the door, smoke poured out like a pitcher of water into a glass. They walked over to the three men wearing T-shirts and with tattoos running up and down their arms. One man had his jaw wired and lay sprawled across two chairs. A cane was leaning next to his chair. The other two were bandaged, and each had a set of crutches. All of the three men had most of their teeth missing.

Turning to see who was coming toward him, the wired-jaw man sat up. He was the only one of the three missing an eye. Murmuring through his closed mouth were barely understandable words. After repeating the words, the two men leaned forward to hear what the other words were that followed.

"Toll mee dis, you fiene thas kit."

"What you say?" one fellow asked.

One of the other men sitting next to wire jaw spoke. "He said did you find the kid?"

"Sure did. Found his aunt and uncle. It took a while, we had asked about town. Finally, this couple knew about this boy walking from some other state all the way to this man and lady's home. We was told they were his aunt and uncle. They knew them people and gave us directions to their house. We found the place and kept it looked upon until we gots the words from you, boss."

"Okey, dis you gek the jub up to git tho kis?"

"What you say?" the first man to talk to the wire-jawed man asked again.

Again, the man next to him repeated what was said. "He said did you set the job up? Also, did it go down as we told you to get done?"

"Sure. We have it all planned. We got a newbie to do the job. He'll do it. He wants to prove he's bad enough to join our gang."

"Wail he kept his mooth shoot?"

"What?"

"He said, will he keep his mouth shut? We don't want it to get back to us." Repeat man spoke, not waiting for the man to ask boss what again. It was apparent he had trouble understanding wire-jawed man talking. He also realized wire-jawed man had a short temper and would pretty quickly shoot that man if he asked him to repeat what he said one more time.

"Sure, but didn't you want a message sent to that kid? You know, so you ain't forgetting what you told him you was going to do to him? He's a dead man. How's he going to knows it was you who sent a hit on his family if we don't lets him know?" asked the first man, finishing his report.

"Thas kid smrt, he fig it aut."

"What?"

Again, repeater man relayed the message. "The kid, he's smart, give him time, he'll figure it out. Besides, if he don't, you got your men keeping tabs on him. We send him another message if that didn't git through."

Wire jaws turned and looked at his two members, remembering those bikers' lessons. He lifted his cane and threw it across the warehouse. "Sht, sht, them beeker go tu git it to," he murmured through his wired jaw. Thoughts of being thrown off the back of their bikes miles from any city ate at him. Anger welled up inside. His mind filled with foul words and thoughts he couldn't say.

If it weren't for some local yokel, they would probably have been dead. It took a week to get back to the warehouse. All that pain and most of his teeth missing gnawed at him. "That kad is goin' to pay."

The man repeating wire-jaw man's words quickly told them to make sure they knew that kid's every move. "Don't do a thing until we gets back to you. Just watch him."

They turned to walk out of the warehouse. Before they got a few feet, the repeater man yelled to them, "One thing more! We better get it quick. If any of them bikers shows, we better hear it quick. Not a day later or an hour later. Got what I said, quick?"

"Sure, we got it, quick. Anything happens, git it back here fast."

Turning, repeater man called some of his members over to him. Three gang members stood walking to his side, sitting by wire-jawed man.

Looking down at the three crippled leaders, one of the three asked, "What you need?"

Slowly raising his head, he pointed to the repeater, then snapped his fingers. Repeater man pulled a paper with a picture of some bikers passing through a town across the state, raising hell with some local cops. "Find them, follow them. Find out as much as you can. How many and mainly where they hang out. Get back to us quick like. Send as many guys you need. Git it done."

A LETTER COMES LATE

SMOKE FROM THE BARN FILLED the kitchen. Ms. Ellie laid a letter down on the table, then walked to the back door. She often had to call out loud to get John's attention, who was working at the forge. "Honey, come in the house!"

John heard her shout after the second calling came. Putting the hammer down then cooling the coals, he left the barn forge.

Ms. Ellie held out the letter she retrieved from the table. She was intending to walk out to the forge after her second call to him. Seeing him coming, she went back to the table and sat.

John entered the kitchen. He was still wearing his apron and began to remove it to hang it on one of the outside hooks. It was not permitted to be worn in the house. He obeyed that rule and others when it came to the inside of the home.

"What's up, honey? You know I don't like to be disturbed when I am making a blade. Unless maybe it's an emergency. It's not an emergency, is it?"

"We got a letter from Mike. I haven't opened it. I thought we should read it together."

"Great, thanks, babe." He reached for the letter, only to be denied. She held it and wanted to open it. He got the message and sat down.

Tearing open the envelope carefully so as not to tear the address, she pulled the two pages from its opening. Ellie held the sheets like one of her valuables. She unfolded the two letters carefully. Taking a breath, she began reading out loud.

> Dear John and Ms. Ellie,
>
> I am sorry to be writing this letter so long from my time with you. Many things happened to me on my journey home. I met a colored man. He and I had a run-in with a bear. I killed the bear with John's knife. That knife saved my life and Sam's. Sam and his wife Leela were really nice to me. In fact, the whole town they lived in, the people treated me great. The bear got a good swipe at me and left a reminder for me to carry. Sam and his wife nursed me back to health. I got a scar running down the side of my chest. It appears I will carry it as a reminder not to do something stupid like that again.

Ellie paused as she read that Mike was hurt.

> I was bitten by a snake and found another nice person to tend to my wound. I stayed and helped her around the farm for several months. Later, I walked into a swamp, and swampers had me assist them in catching the largest gator ever been killed in the swamp. You might have read about it in a magazine article. Also, in that same mag, they have a story of a haunted house. They mentioned some young kid. That was me. You can see I have had an adventure.

She continued to read the exploits Mike had mentioned in the letter to John. John sat there not saying a word.

> Tell Bo his teaching me how to noodle came in handy many a times. Rarely did I go hungry.
>
> I met these bikers in a bar. We got into a fight with another biker gang. I got knocked out. Next day, they gave me a lift to Georgia. Hey, I been ginseng

hunting. Jacob taught me all about ginseng. I made some money.

Looking up from the letter, Ms. Ellie asked John, "What is ginseng?"

"I think it's a root. It might be used in beers or added to food. You know that stuff you have in your seasoning cabinet, your spice rack. Is that all that's in the letter, babe?"

"No, there's some more. He says he rode on a train and went to Atlanta. Had some gang men chase after him after he helped save a man from being robbed."

"Dang that boy, he sure got into a ton of mischief."

"Quiet, honey. He tells about an older lady he stayed with and a dog he found. The older lady was dying. He remained with her to the day she died. He left her home in tears with Boo. Boo is the dog's name."

We crossed a street, and Boo got hit by a car. I thought Boo was killed. Another car slammed into me. I walked away with a broken rib. People were gathering. I ran into the swamp. The next day I found an outdoor movie drive-in where I remained for days under the screen in a shed. I ate good.

Every night I would wander out of the shed and look in the trash bins. I found popcorn in large plastic bags. Also, hot dog and burger buns. Sometimes I got lucky and ate hot dogs or burgers tossed out.

When I made it home, they were waiting, surprised. I arrived at my aunt and uncle's home. Both my mom and two sisters were there. We had a long crying time.

Oh, Boo was alive. A reporter was at my aunt's home holding him. He found my dog. I was told the man I saved in the alley was the editor of a paper. He sent this reporter to locate me. He spotted me and Boo at the corner of the street we crossed. He took Boo to a vet.

"John, Mike says he will write us again, and tell Bo to keep up his practicings."

"Well, I'll be. He made it, babe."

"I never once thought he wasn't."

"Oh, come now, babe. All you done for all this time is wonder when he would write us. You were so worried he wouldn't. What now, you going to write back?"

"No, not right now. I want to find that magazine he mentioned of the gator and haunted house."

John pulled his chair from the table and walked over to his wife. "Babe, you feel fine now?" Bending down, he gave her a kiss. "We will talk later when Bo gets home. I'll be in the forge."

"Supper will be in an hour, honey." Ellie stood and walked into the living room to the magazine rack. She took all the mags back to the kitchen table. For a long time, she kept scouring through the articles. Next to the last mag, she found the two articles.

NEW SCHOOL AT THE END OF SUMMER

FIRST DAY AT A NEW school. Everybody was required to wait outside until the correct time. Only if it rained would the school allow the students to come inside. All headed to the cafeteria. Once the bell rang, they hurried to each homeroom.

Mike's teacher was an old woman who chewed snuff. Her hair was as black as coal and looked uncombed. She wore only a black dress. The word was she was a newly widowed woman.

The first time Mike remembered approaching her desk for help answering a math problem was nearly his last time he would go to her desk. He put his paper in front of her, then explained to her what the problem was. She turned her head, opening her mouth to speak. Mike thought she deliberately put her mouth in his face as close as she could without touching him. Speaking, she spit out some of the tobacco she was chewing on. That breath could knock you back a few feet. The snuff spit on his shirt kept the smell lingering for most of the day.

"Excuse me, young man. Here is a tissue."

Mike took the tissue handed to him, wiping off the little bits of tobacco smeared across his face and shirt. She began to explain how to solve his math problem.

Mike turned to look for a trash can to spit out what landed in his mouth. The class was watching and giggled, seeing what transpired. With the tissue, he cleaned the rest off. After that first encounter, he made it a point to keep his distance. She was a good math teacher, and Mike excelled under her teaching.

After class, Mike would meet with Ron and walk home. Within weeks, Sharon and another girl were fighting in the hall outside of his room before class began. He didn't know it was his sister until squeezing through the crowd that gathered. Seeing her on top of the other girl, he grabbed her to pull them apart. Sharon had the best of her. The other girl looked more like a boy the way she dressed and acted. Once off the floor, the she boy cursed at Sharon. Mike held his sister back. That girl then punched Mike in his kidney. The pain was bad. Turning to her, Mike asked, Why you hit me?"

"You're her brother. My dad taught me how to fight. Just wanted you to know."

Mike hurt from that punch and was fuming mad. He told her, "If you want to act like a boy and look like one, I will treat you like one. Next time you take a punch at me, I will make that already ugly face even uglier. Got that?" That was a lesson Mike wasn't going to forget. Never, but never step between two people fighting.

This was the beginning of one of the most troubled school years he ever had. Mike believed he spent more time in the principal's office than he did in the classrooms. Mike's butt got, from what was heard around school, the most paddling than any other student ever received. Mike guessed he had the new record. His butt felt like it did, at least.

That all changed with one visit from Mom to school. The principal was going to expel Mike. Mom showed up drunker than a skunk. After that, Mike never went back to the office.

In the gym, Mike sat next to a new friend. They started talking about some movies each saw. "My mom watched movies all the time," Mike conveyed to his new friend.

The new friend told Mike he knew a kid who worked at the local theater. "They always need workers," he told him.

Mike's friend introduced him to Melvin. After meeting Melvin, he told Mike to show up at the Rama Theater after school. "Be sure to wear a white shirt and tie," Melvin told him. "You show up looking ready to work, Tad will hire you."

Mike did, and he got hired. He was never asked about his age. That was good. He wanted the job.

Mike remembered the first time he walked into the theater. This tall slightly plump man looking about in his early twenties met him, and they shook hands. He had a friendly face and carried a smile on it. Mike liked him right off. He seemed to be young for an assistant manager's job. Mike often thought of that first interview.

Tad was the assistant manager's name. He walked around showing Mike the candy counter and the girls who worked behind it.

"While you work here, Mike, you buy the first Coke and popcorn. Save your cup and box. You can eat all the popcorn and drink all the Coke you want after that. Also, you can attend any theater owned by this company, free."

"Wow, that's sounds great. I don't know if you can cook that much popcorn. I might have to put me on a limit," Mike answered.

Tad turned to look at Mike. "You eat all you want, but after you get enough, you will probably not want any popcorn, is my experience."

"I don't know about that. I surely love popcorn, Tad, sir."

"Your job will be to obey the doorman's orders and keep the area clean. Also, help assist moviegoers with their drink and popcorn. When we begin to get the people coming in, stand near the doors to the inside. Keep an eye on anyone at the concession stand for help with their drinks and food. Help them carry it to their seats, Mike."

"Yes, sir."

Walking over to a closet, Tad opened it. Inside, he pointed to the cleaning bucket and mop. "Between every movie, we sweep the lobby and sometimes the aisles between the seats. On the shelves we keep some restroom supplies. Toilet paper for you to replace. So check the restroom often. Keep them clean.

"This is where you can keep your cup and box for drinks and corn, Mike. Every day when you show up, you log your time in on this sheet. I prepare the schedule for all the ushers. Now, I will enter your name near the bottom. Can you work today, or would you wait another day to start?"

"No, I came to go to work today, if that is okay, Mr. Tad."

"Good, we need someone for this afternoon shift. I think you will work out fine. Now follow me to the storeroom." Tad waved toward the direction they were to go. Mike followed like a puppy dog. Together they walked around the concession stand.

The two girls watched them passing by through the window surrounding the concession area. The boys' restroom was across from the second entrance doors to the movie. The storeroom was next to the entrance. Tad opened the storeroom door, and both walked in. Against the walls were stacked boxes of popcorn, candy, and cleaning supplies.

"Mike"—Tad pointed at the boxes—"if you need resupplies, come in here and collect them. This is where we hang our red blazers." Lifting one off the hook beside several jackets, Tad handed it to Mike. "Here, try this on for size."

Taking the jacket, Mike tried it on. "It's a bit small," he said to Tad.

"Here, take this one."

Mike tried it on. It fit.

"Now, Mike, that jacket has no name label attached to it. We will give you a label to put on your jacket. That will be yours to wear while you work here. We wear these every day." Walking over to a shelf, Tad removed a flashlight. "Here, this is yours to use. You will need it when you aid people to their seats. We are one of the few theaters that escort our moviegoers to their seats. Always be polite." Tad patted Mike on his back.

Looking over at a box, Tad grabbed it and opened it up. "Mike, these are flyers we offer people to see what next attractions are coming. These bulletins and posters we put up along with marquee letters are also kept back here. Either the doorman or I will teach you how to lay these out. Now follow me." Tad led Mike back out the storeroom and turned to enter the movie seating area.

"We expect you to walk up and down these aisles several times during the show. Mainly to check to see if someone needs assistance or is causing trouble. If you see someone with their feet on the top of seats, ask them politely to take them down. If someone gets too noisy, politely request they lower their voices. If anyone causes you a problem, see the doorman or me. Got that?"

"Yes, sir."

"Now, I am going to take you upstage and behind the screen." Walking down and up on the stage, the screen was huge. Tad pointed to the projector room on the balcony. Walking to one side of the screen, he pulled back a curtain. "This is the rear exit. No one can come or leave this way. If a fire occurs, then you will go here and open the door for them to exit."

Tad led them down the stairs and back up the aisle to the lobby. Along the way, Tad explained when the balcony is used. "When the lower seating section is full, we open the balcony. One of the ushers will remain up there to assist people going up and down the stairs. Over here by the closet next to a door leading upstairs to the balcony is a button, Mike. The button is to signal the projectionist to begin the movie or to delay the movie. This is the door to the balcony. Outside on the other side of the ticket booth is another set of stairs leading to the balcony. We never use them. That leads to the main office. The doorman's job is to escort the ticket girl up to the office to count the tickets and money every night. Whenever you hear a buzzing sound, the projectionist wants you. Two buzzes mean quick. Come on, let's get up the stairs. At one time, Mike, this was the colored section. Only colored people could sit up here." Tad mentioned this casually.

"Really, Tad?"

"We still allow them to sit up here when they come to see a movie. It is not required now, but if they want to sit up here, it is permitted. You need to check on them just like you do with the patrons below."

At the top of the stairs was another set of stairs leading to the top row of the seats. Mike couldn't help to view over the railing; it was high.

"Mike," Tad said, "no one is allowed to stand by the rail or lean over them."

"Yes, sir."

They walked to the top row of seats. There was a door to the projection room. "Mike, before you enter, always knock twice. We try to keep people out." Tad knocked twice on the door.

A tall thin white-haired man opened the door. "Howdy."

"Hello, Mr. Deeks, I thought I would bring up the new usher to introduce him to you," Tad told him.

Mr. Deeks took Mike's hand readily and shook it vigorously. Smiling, he said, "Welcome, welcome, nice to meet you, young man."

"Me too, Mr. Deeks," Mike replied.

Tad showed the projection room to Mike. "Over here, this is where Mr. Deeks checks in new movies. He unwinds them and rewinds them. He checks for breaks in the film. He also attaches ads and trailers for coming shows." Turning to Mr. Deeks, he allowed Mr. Deeks to show Mike the two projectors.

"This, young man, are the projectors. Each will run a twenty-minute reel. When the bell rings, I have about two minutes to start the other projector. I look through these port windows. When I see my cue marks, I start the projector. When I see my second cue marks, I open the shutter to this projector. And it continues where the other reel left off."

Walking over to the side of the projector, Mr. Deeks lifted the side door. "This is where the light is created that shines the picture on the screen." He pointed to two pencil-size rods, one held on a moveable carriage that makes contact with the nonmoving rod that sparks both rods to light up. "These are carbon rods. When electricity is turned on, the light is so bright, to look at it directly could cause you to get a flash burn or lose your eyesight. If ever you open that door when I light these projectors up or the doors are left opened, don't look. These doors should always be close. I need to change the rods often. They are copper coated for the electricity to ignite them. Behind the rods is this convex mirror used to reflect the light through the film and down on the screen." Mr. Deeks continued talking, never stopping even to take a breath of air.

"Mike, we can always use someone to take his place when he has a day off or might be sick. We pay extra when you work the projectors. Think about that, you might want that job," Tad said to Mike.

"Okay, I guess that about wraps up everything I need to tell you about the projection room, Mike." Tad walked over to the same door they entered and stopped for Mike to walk over.

Mike turned to Mr. Deeks. "Thanks, Mr. Deeks." Then he extended his hand before leaving. Again, Mr. Deeks shook it vigorously.

Downstairs, Tad and Mike walked around the outside. Tad showed him the two marquees with the attraction and coming attraction spelled out. Then back to the front, he pointed out the different posters displayed. "This is a one-sheet, and on these larger boards, we place the number 3 sheet posters displayed in front under the awning." Turning back to Mike, he asked, "Mike, any questions?"

"No, sir, not at this time."

"Fine. You got on your jacket, and I will buy you your first drink and box of popcorn."

"Thank you, sir."

"Call me Tad."

"Okay, sir, I mean Tad."

With a drink in one hand and a box of fresh-cooked popcorn in the other, Mike entered the movie auditorium, taking a corner seat near the door. It was empty with no one watching the first movie running. Before long, one or two people entered. By 6:00 p.m., the movie ended. Mike made two rounds as instructed and entered the lobby once before the final show ended. When the last patron left, he began sweeping the carpet before Tad told him.

Tad watched him. "You are working out really good, Mike. Would you like to work the evening shift?"

"Yes, sir," Mike replied with a thrill.

THE RAMA THEATER

EVERY DAY AFTER GETTING HOME, Mike would immediately change clothes then walk back outside to his bike. It took ten minutes to ride to the Rama. The first paycheck was nearly twenty-two dollars. This money Mike put in a box to save. Mom was getting his government check. He still gave her some of his earnings if needed.

Dodie, Mike's sister, was dating this guy for nearly a year. Their first Christmas before Mike got the job at the Rama was bleak. Only presents was what Mike gave his two sisters. He handed them three dollars each to go to the store and buy something. Mike saved pennies from collecting soda bottles and kept a few dollars from his mowing jobs. Mom drank every Christmas before they came to Georgia and continued to keep her traditions of drinking during the holidays.

Mike always hated to go back to school. All the kids would talk about how many presents they got. Of course, they asked him what he got. It was the same answer he'd been telling them since they moved here: clothes.

This Christmas was coming quick. Mike had been at the Rama for several months. He was doing a great job. Tad had him tend the door.

"Mike, if you continue working hard, I am going to make you the official doorman. You'll be in charge of the ushers. I see you been doing the marquee most of the time," Tad said.

"Yes, sir, I like doing it."

"Well, take care. I saw you hanging from that ten-foot ladder reaching out to hang letters without anyone holding the ladder steady."

"I got pretty good at balancing on the ladder, Tad."

"That's beside the point. Try to have someone there when you put the letters up. I will feel better knowing there is someone there for safety purposes, Mike."

Mike nodded.

"Now, Mike, I need to teach you when and how to place the posters out front. That is the job that goes with this job of doorman."

After completing installing several new posters for the up-and-coming new flicks, Mike returned to the doorman's chair, looking out the front for any patrons. Usually, the afternoon show had few patrons. About halfway through the first showing of the movie, a young black man and his girlfriend arrived. After purchasing a ticket, they entered the side door outside the ticket booth and walked the steps up to the balcony.

Nothing much happened until Mike received a buzz from the projectionist. Mike quickly told one of the concession girls to keep an eye on the door while he went to see what the projectionist wanted. Going up the inside stairs to the balcony, he knocked on the door. The projectionist opened the door. It was Melvin. This was the first time he had been up to the booth and Mr. Deeks wasn't there.

"Hey, Melvin, I didn't know you ran the projectors too." Mike looked astonished seeing him up in the booth.

"Yeah, I'm the backup when I am not at the door, Mike." Melvin was also the doorman. He and Mike shared the job when Tad wasn't there. Tad was the assistant manager and would stand by the door to assist during heavy traffic.

Once inside, Melvin began to tell Mike the reason he wanted to see him. "Mike, I opened the door to get some fresh air and saw this man and girl in the corner."

"Yeah, they just got tickets, Melvin."

"Figured that out, Mike. But they are not watching the movie. Instead, they are having sex."

"What? You kidding me, Melvin?"

"No. What do you want to do, Mike? Mr. Cox is not here, and neither is Tad."

"Well, I guess it is up to me. Tell you what, Melvin. Give me three minutes to get downstairs. I need to get my flashlight. Now, you gradually start to raise the lights up." Mike explained to him his plan.

"But all the people—"

"Not to worry, Melvin. They are the only people in the movie."

"Mike, he might get violent if you interrupt them."

"That's why I want to get my flashlight. Besides, after three minutes and when you hear my voice, you come out of the projection room in case I need some help," Mike quickly explained. "Okay, now, Melvin, you start raising the lights. I'm heading downstairs."

Mike left quietly through the door he came in. Before he got to the stairs, the lights were getting brighter. He thought to himself, *Good, Melvin.*

At the bottom, he hurried over to get the flashlight left on his seat and to tell the ticket girl, Lindsey, where he was going and why.

"Wait, I want to go," Lindsey demanded.

"Who is going to stay down here in charge?" Mike asked. "This might go bad, Lindsey."

I don't care, I'll get the candy bar girl Debbie to watch the front. I'm going, Mike," she demanded.

"Okay, okay, follow me, and be really quiet. When we get to the top of the stairs, we need to crawl up the final steps on our hands and knees. I want to get right up on them," Mike explained.

Lindsey came out of the booth.

"Here, you take this flashlight." Mike handed it to her. "Wait till we get to the top, and when I stand, you stand and flash your light at them. Together we will flash them."

"Oh, this is going to be so cool."

Just before they entered the stairs outside, Rusty showed up early for his shift. Quickly Mike explained to him what was happening, and he ran and got his light. The three of them silently walked up the steps to the balcony. Slowly, Mike, on his knees at the top of the stairs, stealthily peeked around the corner to spot where the couple were sitting. He motioned to Lindsey and Rusty that the couple were at the top corner.

They all slowly began a silent crawl around the stairwell and to the steps leading to the top of the balcony. The lights were nearly all the way on.

All three approached the last step and began the slow turn into the aisle just below the top aisle the couple was in. Moans and a subtle squeal came from the couple. Once all three reached the last row of seats, Mike gave the signal, and they all stood together with their lights shining down upon the couple.

Mike yelled out, "Surprise!" That yell of Mike's could have woken the dead, and surprisingly enough, no one died from fright when he yelled.

Melvin, true to what was asked of him, opened his door, popping out of the projection room. Everyone had their flashlights on the couple.

Lindsey blushed; the boy stood trying to pull his pants up. The girlfriend screamed, yanking at her skirt. After the boyfriend pulled his pants up, he turned to face Mike. All the flashlight beams were shining in his face. He thought Mike was alone. Thinking it was one person flashing his flashlight at them, the young man said with an angry tone, "I'm gonna beat the hell out of you."

Mike lifted his light. "That would be a pretty stupid thing to do. I have a pretty big flashlight."

In fact, Mike bought his own weeks ago. He found a three-battery model. It was about twice the length of the first handed to him. It was nearly a club or bat in size and weight. It came with a belt attachment. Most times the flashlight provided by the theater was carried inside the rear pocket or side pocket. Sitting down proved a hazard to the light. Often it would either fall out of the pocket or get snagged and pulled out while getting out of the auditorium seat. Either way, when the light hit the floor, it was necessary to replace the bulb.

Mike went on to explain to the young man, "You might want to notice, I'm not alone. Look over at the projection room and beside me."

Knowing Rusty, Mike couldn't figure on him as much of a backup. The same could be said about Melvin. One thing was Melvin was a doorman, and if he had to, he would. Lindsey would; she had a mean streak in her and also a tomboy attitude. Neither of the three were the young black man's size, but they had the numbers, Mike knew.

"I want my money back," the boy demanded from Mike. His girl stood up next to him. Her dress was pulled down, and she had finished straightening herself, grabbing hold of her boyfriend's arm.

"Well, if you came to the watch the movie, I might allow you to have your money returned, but since you obviously didn't come to see the movie, there will be no refund," Mike responded to the angry patron.

"I still want my money," the man demanded.

Well, if you are so insistent, wait till I get downstairs and call the police. When they arrive, I will refund your money, and I will provide the theater's complaint we have with you two, sir. If you have a complaint, then you will be able to make one." Mike turned to Lindsey to go downstairs.

"Wait, wait, I changed my mind. Keep the money, we are leaving."

"Okay, but when I get down the stairs, I am still going to call the police. All I need is your name so I can give them your complaint."

"We are leaving, no complaints."

Before the couple reached the bottom and out the door of the Rama, all three stood holding back their laughing.

Melvin walked over to where they stood. "Were they doing what I thought I saw them doing, Mike?"

Lindsey was quick to answer. "They sure were. He was pulling up his pants so fast, I thought he was going to fall over on us."

Mike never knew if the story of this had been told to either Tad or Mr. Cox, but everyone on the floor knew it before the weekend. After that incident, all the ushers went and bought their own three-battery flashlight.

Soon, it became all the rage to see who could twirl the large flashlight the most times around in their palms without dropping it. Mike held the record for a long time. Still, it never ceased for someone to challenge his record.

One day outside, Mike was installing the up-and-coming posters. Ric dropped by to begin his shift. He was wild and was always playing pranks. He was several years older than Mike but acted more childish. Most of the girls liked him. He was definitely a lady's man, Mike thought.

Mike was working on the last poster when Ric snuck up from behind. "Yeow!" Mike yelled out. A sharp pain bit him in his butt. Mike thought it might have been a bee. No, it was Ric having fun with him. In Ric's hand was the second staple gun. He shot Mike in the butt.

Turning, Mike could see Ric laughing while holding the stapler. "Hey, man, that hurt!" Mike squealed.

"I didn't mean to pop you in your butt. I was trying to get you in your wallet. Hehehe, I missed. Hehehe," Ric explained.

"I won't miss either, Ric." With a sudden charge, Mike went at him. Both of them began a staple shooting battle with staples flying. Ric was the first to run. Mike chased and caught up with him before he got to the men's room. Mike got revenge, but not before Ric popped another into him. They decided to call it a tie.

As usual, they stopped by the concession and asked for their cups to be filled. Mike had the customary mixed drink and Ric an orange soda. Then came the telling of the jokes. Always the afternoon shows were slow with little patrons arriving. Many a times the ushers and candy bar girls would mill around the counter, sharing jokes or stories to pass the time. Mike got to learn a lot of jokes.

With Ric, one never knew what to expect. On this day, he was feeling his oats. Suddenly reaching over the counter, he grabbed hold of Kay's wrist. Then with a jerk, he pulled her to the countertop. "Mike, give me a hand!" he yelled out.

"What are you trying to do to Kay?"

"We are going to drag her across the counter, Mike."

Kay responded, "No way! Let go, you jerk!" She was screaming at Ric.

"Come on, Mike, we need to indoctrinate her. She is new. Come on. Hurry."

Mike reached and grabbed one of her wrists. Between the two of them, she came across easily.

Turning to face Ric, Kay remarked with a sour face, "That wasn't fun. I will get even with you two."

"Oh, come now, it was your first week. We do this with all the new girls," Ric quipped back to her.

"Well, not to me. We will see who will get the last laugh. I will get even with you two," Kay replied.

Mike stood there with nothing to say. He realized that particular prank was going to have some payback handed out. With candy bar girls, it wasn't always the best thing to do. If mad, they can get even in ways far worse than what the ushers could do to them.

When she got back inside the concession room, Kay talked to the other girl. Ann was one of the old girls. She had been at the Rama less than Lindsey. Lindsey had been at the Rama several years. Probably the oldest working person there besides Melvin and Tad.

Two days passed by. One day Mike went up to get his usual drink while putting on his red jacket. Without a thought, he took the drink handed back to him by Kay. He took a deep swallow. He nearly spit it out across the counter. Instead, Mike ran outside and spit it out in the road. Coming back inside, the girls were laughing. He knew he was had.

"Mike, payback. We got our tricks too," Kay said with a snicker and smiled.

Mike just smiled and said, "Even, I hope."

After that, Mike always sipped his drink before drinking anything.

One day Tad told Mike he needed another backup projectionist. Mike replied he would love to learn.

"It pays a dollar an hour," replied Tad.

"Heck yes," Mike replied.

Mike started going to karate classes between working and school just weeks before Tad offered him the projectionist job. He'd been learning a new style from that of his first sensei's style. He quickly learned and achieved several ranks quickly.

Melvin became Mike's instructor in learning to run the projectors. First thing was to learn to check in new film. Melvin put a reel on the winder and turned the crank. "Mike, I hold my fingers across the film to check for any cracks or splits. When I find one, I'll show you how to cut and glue the film. It's called splicing," Melvin told him. "Then once the film is checked and repaired, we can load each projector with a reel, Mike. Each reel runs for about twenty minutes." Melvin made a set of circular scratch marks near the end of the reel he was checking. Placing cue marks near the end of the reel would allow you to see when to start the second projector, and the second cue mark was for the final switch.

"Once the other projector takes over, we take off the finished reel and replace it with the next in sequence, Mike."

Melvin walked over to the wall by the door of the projectionist room was the light controller and the record player. Melvin called Mike over. "Every show, when the patrons begin arriving, we start the music, and before the flick starts, we slowly lower the lights. Dimming them allows the patrons' eyes to adjust to the dark. Mike, slowly turn this light knob once every minute or so. Once the auditorium gets dark, then it's showtime."

Mike ran the backup for the first show twice a week. Between the nights he wasn't running the projectors or working downstairs as the doorman, Mike was at the dojo practicing his martial arts. It became a religion the way he worked out. Not at the dojo or work, he was home in the backyard practicing kata or a weapon drill. One of Mike's favorite weapons was the staff and knife.

Every day and after work, Mike would be in his backyard practice-throwing his knife. He would set a goal of ten direct hits and no misses before he went on to the next sequence. Each sequence was stepping back two feet and throwing his knife ten times at the new distance. After achieving remarkable adeptness, he began to vary his distances and changing his knife. Soon he was able to throw any sharp object with control with fairly good accurate aim. With the staff, Mike could twirl it as good as any majorette at school.

One day Mike arrived at the Rama. To his surprise, outside the ticket booth was a young man dressed similar to the ones who came by his house to break in. Thanks to Chopper's aid, they stopped them. When Mike walked to the double doors leading into the Rama, the man turned and left. Mike walked over to Lindsey and asked what the man wanted.

"Nothing, Mike. He wanted to know when the next show started, was all."

"Lindsey, has he been around here before?" Mike pressed.

"Yes, I seen him several times. Oh. Why the questioning, Mike?"

"Just curious, just curious. I think he is someone I might know, Lindsey."

Saturday, Mike went to the Rama to see if they needed an extra person to work. It was his day off. Nothing to do at home and no karate class.

Ric came by. "Hey, Mike, just the guy I was looking for. You working today?"

"Nah, off."

"Good, Mike."

"Why, Ric?"

"Well, I am going to Alabama to see my aunt and to get some firecrackers. Could use the company. Want to come?"

"Sure, when?"

"Now! Hop in, Mike."

Down the road going past the speed limit, Ric cruised with his tape player playing loud "California Dreamin'." After the third rewind of the song, Mike lay back with his feet hanging out of his window. He started to sing the song with Ric following. Both of them went down the roads singing that song over and over. Soon, they were in Alabama, and the first store coming to, they stopped. Inside, both looked around.

"I never saw so many firecrackers in my entire life," Mike said to Ric.

"Come over here, Mike." Ric was still marveling at all the aisles in the store filled with fireworks. The cash counter was in the rear of the store. Ric walked through the aisles toward the front. "Here's what you would come to expect a store to have stocked on the shelves and made the long drive to buy," quipped Ric to Mike.

"What have you got, Ric?" Mike turned around to where Ric was plowing through a box of red tubular short sticks having a fuse in the middle.

"These are M-80, one-fourth of a stick of TNT."

"Wow," Mike replied.

"Here, grab a handful, Mike."

"I thought we came here for firecrackers. What are you going to do with these, Ric?"

"You'll see."

At the counter, Ric had twenty M-80s and two packs of black cat firecrackers and several dozen bottle rockets.

"Hey, Ric, I'm only going to buy two dozen bottle rockets and six M-80s. I don't think I could ever use this many, but you got nearly three times as many. Ric, what the heck you going to do with all them fireworks?"

No answer came to his question except for a grin on Ric's face.

Walking out the store, Mike turned to Ric. "Hey, you think we got enough to start World War III?"

"Not really, wish I had more money," replied Ric.

Walking out the store and to the car, Mike repeated, "What are we going to do with all of these fireworks, Ric?"

Once in the car, Ric finally explained to Mike what he intended to do. "These M-80s will wake the dead going off. We are going to set these out all over town. I got some plans when we get back, Mike."

After Ric's visit and lunch, the two of them drove back to Georgia. They came back to the Rama around five thirty that evening.

Ric parked the car in front. The show just let out. Every kid in town was sent to the Rama for the whole day on Saturday by their parents. In one way, the ushers were their babysitters. Mike usually worked on Saturday and enjoyed all the kids. He knew several of them by their names.

There was this special man around forty-five who would be dropped off at the door. Every usher was introduced to meet him on the first Saturday working at the Rama. He would come up to Tad, and the both of them walked over to the candy bar concession booth. Later, it was Mike's turn to introduce the ushers to this special man when Tad was off.

"Get me a popcorn and a large drink for Dicky, please," Tad would say. Then Tad would make sure he got a seat near the side door in the movie. Turning to Mike, he said, "Mike, whenever Dicky comes to the Rama, he gets in free. Have the girls give him a free popcorn and large drink. If he comes out and wants a refill, always give it to him. He is one of our special friends."

And so it was, on every Saturday, Dicky would be there when the front doors opened for the first show. He would stay until the last matinee played before the evening show would begin. On the last show ending, he would simply get out of his seat and say goodbye to Mike or

Tad at the door and stand by the curve. A car would drive up, and he would enter and leave, until the next Saturday matinee.

Once the theater was emptied and Dicky left, it was the hour prior to the night show cleaning. During that time, everybody had a broom in their hand and begun the march from the top aisle to the bottom aisle, sweeping between the seats. After the sweeping began the mopping. The girls were busy restocking and washing the popcorn kettle. There was plenty of help. Both shifts were either coming on or getting off. Neither left until the place was cleaned and prepared for the evening show.

That is when Ric and Mike showed up. Ric walked in and placed his bag down on the candy countertop. Then he pulled out his bounty. Everyone gathered around for the show. All mouths were agape.

"Where'd you get all the fireworks?" one usher asked him.

"Mike and me just got back from Alabama. I went down there to visit my aunt. Mike went with me. We stopped on the way there as soon as we crossed the state line."

Mike walked in with his smaller bag and laid it next to Ric's. "Wow, when are we going to light them up?" asked Mike.

Rusty walked over and began to finger through the booty that lay across the counter. "We want to see them too."

Ric blurted out, "I want to go and roll the vice principal's home tonight."

"Are you kidding?" Rusty remarked, looking at Ric and Mike in astonishment.

"No, we are going to do it after the first showing. Who's with us?" Mike declared.

Melvin walked in and sidled up to Ric. "When we leaving?" Melvin asked Ric.

"Well, Mike, he got a great idea for the rolling of the vice principal's house. Tell them, Mike."

"Well, instead of getting out of the car and throwing these toilet rolls around everything, if we take three of these M-80s and stuff them into one of these toilet rolls, it should do the job on the house better than we could by tossing them and taking the risk of getting caught," Mike explained.

Melvin spoke up. "I hate to ruin the party, Ric, but those M-80s have a short five-second fuse. How're you going to light all three at the same time and throw them out the car window before they blow? Remember the last time we tried that?"

"I do, Melvin, I was with you there." Ric wanted to show Mike how powerful these things were. Ric had one left before they went to Alabama. He decided to take Mike out and show him what it can do.

"What are you guys talking about? I didn't hear of anything like that," Rusty replied.

"Oh, it was the other night before we left to go to Alabama. Ric saved his last M-80. We got in Melvin's car and drove over to my sister's boyfriend's house. Ric sat in the middle and me near the window. When we got to my sister's friend's house, who by the way I don't like much, Ric took the cigarette lighter and touched it to the fuse. Well, it didn't light. That's what we thought until I saw the sparks from the fuse. 'Quick, Ric!' I yelled. 'Hand it to me.' No sooner than he did, I tossed it out through the open window. Thank the lord I had opened the window prior to him lighting that thing. It must have just left my hand when it blew, Rusty. Melvin hit the gas, and we came running back here."

"Yeah, that was close," quipped Melvin.

"Got that right, Melvin," Mike said. "That's why I came up with this idea. I don't want one of those going off in my lap."

"Me neither," Melvin answered back.

"Well, Melvin, I used to play around with firecrackers when I first came to town. A friend got some, and being the creative type, I came up with this idea from some cigarette bombs I had ordered from the mail. You take this small sliver and push it up the end of a cigarette. When a person lights the cigarette, he can take several puffs, and maybe a minute later, when that flame gets to that load, *kapow!* The whole cigarette blows apart," Mike explained.

Mike continued his story. "I timed it one time, and almost five minutes went by before it blew. Using a cigarette would be perfect. On other attempts, I used to take those wind-up rubber band planes and stick a firecracker between the rubber band and the fuselage. Then I threw it as high as I could. When the propeller unwound, the band got slack, and the firecracker would fall out. Only problem was, it might blow while still under the rubber band or fall when the plane makes a loop. I had a firecracker fall near me too many times instead of where I wanted it to. Still, it was pretty cool watching the kids run all around from where the plane flew. They had a lot of fun dodging the plane. That was my first inspiration to use a rubber band balsa wood plane. They were a tiny bit unreliable and could even return back to us, *kapow*. No thanks."

"Well, if I should peel back the plastic that is wrapped around the fuse and put a hole in the cigarette, of course we should light the cigarette first. It should work."

"We tested one before we came inside to show you all our fireworks. Ric, tell everybody."

"Where, Ric?" Lindsey asked.

"Oh, it should be going off soon." Mike turned back to Ric and answered Lindsey's question.

"You mean you put one out here?" Lindsey gasped with a hush and a hand over her mouth.

Within a short time, a loud boom was heard outside behind the brick wall separating the shopping center from the Rama and the parking lot.

"Oh my god," Anne quipped out. "Gee" soon followed, and a "holy cow!" was the final remark before everyone ran outside to see where the explosion occurred. Smoke was still rising when everyone made their way around the brick wall opening to get a peek at the carnage.

Back inside, Mike continued explaining the details to his toilet roll bomb. "When we get to his house, all we need doing is push the three fuses through the hole and toss it out the window. That is, of course, we light the cigarette first before we put the fuses through the hole."

"You guess, Mike?" Ric answered back.

"I guess," Mike replied.

Both were being a tad sarcastic to the other.

"Sounds like it might work. Can I go on this next trip?" Rusty asked.

Melvin spoke up. "Keep me out of this one. That was too close a call that last time. My heart might not take the strain a second time."

"Okay, Mike, I will drive. Mike, you will light the sucker. Rusty, you just sit in the back and keep an eye peeled for anybody," commanded Ric.

Mike spoke up and began giving directions. "Rusty, go get me a roll of paper. Lindsey, can I borrow a cigarette from you?"

She was the only person who smoked working at the Rama. Tad used to get on her when he caught her selling tickets. "Never smoke while serving the public," he often reminded her.

"Sure, I want to see how you will do this, Mike."

Mike reached down and pulled a small boot knife out from his boot and twisted it in the cigarette until it reached the other side. He took each M-80's fuse, slowly peeling away some of the outer coating. Once all three fuses were stripped, Mike twisted them together and pushed them through the small hole in the cigarette. Debbie, one of the candy bar girls, handed Mike some tape. Secretly Mike thought she was the prettiest girl there and had a crush on her. Mike attached the fuses to the cigarette.

"Why'd you do that for, Mike?"

"Rusty, I sure don't want this to come off, and these three M-80s fall in my lap or yours."

"Hey, you guys, after work, we are off."

"Where to, Ric?" Mike asked him.

"Where you think, Mike?"

"Ric, you sure you want to do this?"

"Yes, Mike, I do," Ric returned with a definite response.

"Okay, just checking is all."

"Come on, Mike, help us clean the aisle while you are here. Besides, you start to work soon," Rusty said to Mike.

At ten o'clock, nearly halfway through the last showing, Ric got antsy. Lindsey stayed late after she finished the count upstairs. Usually, about ten, she finished and left. Not this time. Standing around, she asked Ric if she could go with them.

Ric walked away from her, telling her two times, "No, you cannot go." But eventually, he finally agreed to let her go. Mike came to the lobby, and Ric told him Lindsey will ride with them.

"I will be back soon. I need to make a round before we leave, Ric," Mike replied with a snip. This was Ric's job, but Mike often found he was doing Ric's work and his most of the time Ric and Mike had been paired to a shift. Ric started before him at the Rama but never got the doorman's job.

Once the movie was over, it was Mike's job to close up. After turning off the lights and checking the door, he went upstairs to check on the projectionist. Melvin had the job this night.

"Melvin, Ric's in a hurry to drop this off. You mind if I leave? I will be back in about ten minutes. I would appreciate it if you would tend to the theater until we get back."

"Sure, I'll wait until you return. I want to know how it goes, Mike."

"Thanks, Melvin, be back in ten."

All four of them loaded into Ric's car. Ric and Mike were in the front seats, and Rusty was with Lindsey in the back seats.

"Be careful with that, Mike," Lindsey reminded the two in front. "There is a woman in the back."

"I am," quipped Mike.

"Whatever you do, don't toss that in the back with us, Mike. My girl will miss me, and besides, Lindsey will scream, and my ears couldn't stand her bellowing."

With that remark, Lindsey quickly punched Rusty in his shoulder.

"Yeow!" Rusty yelled out. "Dang, Lindsey, it was a joke."

"Next time, Rusty, keep your jokes to yourself."

"If anything goes wrong, Rusty, you sure in heck ain't getting in the front seat with us," Mike teasingly said.

Ric crossed Main Street and headed down two blocks. Turning right, Mike saw Steve's home. His dad got transferred about six weeks ago. Three houses down across from Steve's home was the target. Ric drove past the intended house. At the intersection, he turned around. Everyone remained quiet.

"Mike, you ready?" Ric pointed to the house on Mike's right. "There, right there is his home. Get ready. I will slow down for you to throw it out the window."

"Give me a second to get this lit, Ric." Mike held up the cigarette to his mouth and drew the lighter heat to the tobacco. After several strong draws, the cigarette stayed lit. Everybody was anxious about the M-80 lighting safely, and Mike plum forgot to wind the window down.

"Shucks!" he yipped out.

"What, what?" came yelling from the back seats.

"I forgot to roll the window down," Mike explained, then chuckled.

"Dang, roll it down fast! Roll it down!" Rusty yelled back.

"Hurry, hurry, it might go off!" yelled Lindsey.

Mike got anxious and became a bit clumsy. His hand was having trouble unwinding the window. The harder he attempted to unwind it, the harder it was to turn the handle.

Ric yelled to Mike, "I forgot to tell you the window is broken!"

Lindsey yelled, "What?! You idiot Ric! Throw it, Mike!"

All in one voice, even Mike, they yelled out, "Open the door!"

Before the last uttered syllable was heard from all, Mike opened the door. This time it was the window not working instead of a match. The M-80 was out of the car. If not for the slow burn of the cigarette, it was nearly burnt to the fuses when the door finally was opened. Mike tossed it out. Half in the flight to the intended landing zone, the M-80 went off. Ric floored the gas pedal, and off the car flew away.

The car with the four still partially stunned adventurers returned to the Rama. Everyone was a bit shaken up. Melvin was waiting at the door.

"That idiot nearly got us all killed!" Lindsey screamed at Melvin.

"Yeah, we nearly got blown to smithereens," followed Rusty's carp.

Mike was stepping out of the car and walking around to the other side.

"You ought to have seen us, Melvin!" Ric exclaimed.

"Well, how did it go, Ric?"

"We didn't stay to see what happened, Melvin."

"Why not, Ric?" asked Melvin.

Mike spoke up, "The window wouldn't open to toss the M-80 out."

"So that window never worked. I guess you didn't light it then," Melvin said in an unexcited tone of voice.

"No, no, he threw the dang thing!" Lindsey yelled back to Melvin as she began her walk to her car.

Ric yelled back to her., "Aren't you going back with us to see what happened?"

Lindsey just tossed up a finger sign back to Ric. "That idiot Ric didn't tell us the window didn't work. Mike had to open the door to toss it out. It nearly went off in the car." Those were her final words as she entered her car.

Ric turned to Rusty and Mike. "Aren't we going back to see what happened?"

"After I close up, Ric." Mike turned to Rusty. "You going with us?"

"Sure, why not. It didn't kill me, Mike."

Turning to Melvin, they all stood waiting to see if he was going along. He nodded yes.

Fifteen minutes later, the Rama was closed for the night, and they all packed into Ric's car. Crossing back over the street, they went past one street, then turned on the first left.

"The vice principal's home is on the right, Melvin," Mike explained.

"Guys, this route back to the house will be safer. If anyone saw us, they might expect us to return the same way. Driving this direction, we can check the house out from the other side. If there is a police car, we can spot it and keep on driving past. We're doing this just in case we were seen to leave the area. We are farther from the scene where the explosion took place and won't see the extent of what happened," explained Ric.

After circling the block in Ric's car, the scene was clear. No police and no one came outside to check out the big bang sound they should have heard. When they arrived at the house, paper was still falling from the sky. Every tree was covered with pieces of white toilet paper strips. It appeared to have been snowing. The whole front yard was covered with bits of toilet paper.

Getting to the end of the street, Mike told Ric to turn around; he wanted to see the yard again. Passing it the second time still put everyone in awe.

"My god, Ric, Mike's bomb, it worked really good," Melvin remarked.

"Oh my, I can't believe that one M-80 did all of that," answered Rusty.

"Me too, Rusty, but that was three M-80s inside the roll of toilet paper," Mike replied. "Look at the ground, you can't even see the grass! It is as if snow had fallen on the ground all night."

"Dang, Mike, that was the best roll job I ever did."

"Yeah, Ric, that was the first time I ever did this myself," remarked Mike.

Rusty remained stunned, and Melvin never looked away. "Wish I went now," he softly murmured.

Back at the Rama, everybody got in their cars and drove home.

The next day, Ric was working with Mike in the evening. Mike was by himself until then. At six, Rusty and Ron came to work. Coming through the door, Mike was at the candy bar talking to Debbie. He turned hearing Rusty come in. "Hey, Rusty, you're not working until tomorrow. You forget to check the time list?"

"No, Tad called me in to work. Ric had to stay late at school."

"Oh, why?" Mike had a sinking feeling hearing Ric was detained at school. Wasn't a good thing to hear.

"I don't know. When he comes in, Tad wants to talk to him."

"How do you know that?" quickly asked Mike.

"He told me to tell him when he came to work."

"Tad's not here, Rusty."

"Yeah, he said when he does come, he told me to tell you so you can make sure he sees him."

Turning to Debbie, Mike asked, "I wonder why?"

Lindsey, with the ticket booth door opened, asked, "What's going on?"

"We don't know," Rusty said.

Lindsey and Mike stared at each other. All three got together by her booth door and began to discuss what happened last night.

"Did you guys go back and see what happened at the house?"

"Yeah, Lindsey, we did." Rusty continued, "We did, and when we got there, Lindsey, you would not believe the way the house looked."

"What does Rusty mean by that, Mike?"

"When that M-80 went off, paper was still coming down from the sky fifteen minutes later, Lindsey."

"It sure was. It covered the tree in tiny white paper, and the ground was all covered with white toilet paper. Mike, tell her about the ground," urged Rusty.

"Okay, Rusty is correct, the ground was pure white. We left watching paper still falling, A snowstorm hit the yard, Lindsey."

"Oh my, just thinking about how close we came to that thing going off in the car. After what you two are telling me, it just gives me the shivers all over."

"Yeah, Lindsey, I feel the same way just thinking how close it was to doing that in the car. If Mike hadn't been able to get that out of the car in time, brrr." Rusty shudders.

After an hour passed, Ric walked in the front door from the parking lot.

Mike walked over to greet him before he went inside. "Hey, Tad wants to talk to you. What did you do, Ric?"

"Well, I had to go over to the vice principal's home and clean all the paper up. He had me leave school early. Either I clean it up or get expelled for a week."

"First thing is how did he know you did the rolling of his house, Ric?"

"I kind of went bragging around school what we did, Mike."

"What? Are you just plain stupid, Ric? I mean, I may not be the smartest cookie in the bowl, but at least I got enough sense not to do that. Well, I guess I will be seeing him in the morning when I get to school, Ric."

"Why, Mike? He doesn't know anything about who helped me. I didn't tell him anything."

"I wouldn't have been upset if you did, Ric. We all were part of it. The only thing is if you kept your mouth shut, you wouldn't be in trouble," Mike repeated.

"Yeah, I know. I had to tell someone, Mike."

"Why? If you got to tell someone, why not just the Rama guys? We could have patted you on your back if glory is what you are seeking. Did you get it all cleaned up?"

"Yep, I did, Mike. It took nearly all day raking the yard. It was harder to clean up after the dew this morning melted the paper to the grass and leaves."

"Ric, out of curiosity, how did you get the paper out of the tree?"

"Well, Mike, I had some trouble trying to knock the paper out of the tree with the rake and even tried to climb up the tree with the rake to get at the higher stuff. After nearly falling several times, I had a great idea to use the garden hose. With the hose, it took only minutes to get the paper out of the trees. Raking wet toilet paper was a bit more difficult to do."

"Well, I would have helped in the cleanup, Ric. Hey, I got a peachy idea, Ric."

Ric turned back from walking past Mike with a curious look. "What?"

"Let's do his house again tonight, Ric."

"What? I just spent the whole day cleaning it up."

"Yeah, I know, who would ever guess we would repeat the crime?"

A short pause and a glint of maybe could be seen wandering about Ric's mind with the idea Mike presented to him. "Not me. Besides, you said Tad wanted to talk to me, Mike. I guess the vice principal called him."

Ric was laid off work for a week. During that week, Mike only worked several nights. He had practice. He met this kung fu master at the dojo of his instructor. He took a shine to Mike. He wanted to practice with him solely. He seemed to think Mike had some good abilities. After practice time, Mike stayed for several hours. Sensei allowed the dojo to remain open for them to stay. He gave the keys to his kung fu student to lock up after practice. This went on for two months.

One day Mike came to work. Both hands were bruised and had many cuts.

"Mike, what in the world happened? Did someone beat you up?" Tad inquired.

"No, Tad, these bruises come from my kung fu instructions. We would practice fighting sets," Mike confided to Tad. "My sifu had me repeat each set a million times. Once he was content with one set, he would begin another set. Some sets we did kicking drills, other sets mainly fighting with me blocking. Then the rest of the final hour, Sifu would have me practice punching a roped board no farther than six inches. I punch then block or block then punch at the two boards. My arms and fist were bruised or bloody when I finished, Tad."

"Repetition will make muscle memory, Sifu would constantly remind me, Tad. Six-inch punches will develop power with little movement. Combinations of blocks and punches will prepare you for multiple attackers. That's all he would explain to me. When I wasn't punching at the board, Sifu would often spar with me. Over and over, we sparred. Often the training was so brutal, I got exhausted and lay on the floor. Didn't matter how exhausted I was, Sifu would drag me up off the floor and scream, 'Fight!'"

The first week, Mike almost decided not to go back. He made up his mind not to continue with his training and decided to tell Tad to get extra work. Sifu decided otherwise; he showed up at the Rama after the last show. He met Mike outside walking to his bike.

"We fight."

"What?"

"We fight."

"Now?"

They fought for thirty minutes. When the fight ended, Sifu said to Mike, "We fight here or at the dojo. Don't miss class."

"Yes, sir. I won't," replied Mike, still stunned from Sifu arriving at the Rama's parking lot to fight him. He didn't miss one class after that night. Sifu still showed up at the Rama Theater several times after closing its doors.

On one night, Tad saw a strange man near Mike's bike and decided to stay near the front observing Mike walking to his bike. He had a funny feeling, and he later told Mike about that first observing him fighting. When he saw that strange man waiting for him, Tad said he almost called the police.

Master Cho had walked behind the Rama and handed Mike a T-shirt to change into. After donning the T-shirt, both would bow and begin fighting. Tad stopped one fight night as they were about to begin. Tad walked around the corner of the building in time to see the two of them square off to fight.

"What's going on here?" Tad asked.

Mike quickly explained to Tad, "This is my master, Mr. Cho. He wants me to be prepared for combat."

"Here behind the theater?" Tad said in a stunned tone as Mike introduced his sifu to him.

"Mr. Cho shook Tad's hand and quickly explained to Tad, "This is part of Mike's training. Please allow this. This will be done in quiet and secretly without others viewing."

Tad wasn't sure what to say. "Well, you make sure no one sees you two practicing here," replied Tad reluctantly. "They might call the police, Mr. Cho."

"Yes, sir." Mr. Cho bowed to Tad. Mr. Cho and Mike began fighting. Tad stayed and watched after first asking Master Cho's permission. "Would you mind, Mr. Cho, if I remain to watch? It is for my feelings for Mike to make sure it will be safe and no harm will occur to my doorman, Mr. Cho."

Tad watched as two people went through a strange fight scene. Each person was trying to kick, punch, trip, or throw the other. It was fast. Tad had on several times never saw the times Mike was thrown to the ground or knocked off his feet by Sifu. Mike on his part moved just as quick and often attempted to throw or trip Sifu. Sifu was much too quick and avoided each attack.

After the fight, Sifu told Mike while Tad stood near him to run home and to work, not to ride his bike. "Mike, leave your bike and never use it for the time being. Bring a change of clothes when you arrive at work. We do not want Mr. Tad to complain to me of a foul odor reeking from you."

Tad nodded. "Thank you, Mr. Cho. That would be most appreciated by me and his coworkers."

Mike left on his bike while Tad and Mr. Cho remained to have a talk. This would be one of many talks they had. Someday, Tad would share with Mike of their conversations.

Between karate, kung fu, and working the projectors and working the floor, Mike had little time in the day to rest. Ric started back two weeks after the toilet roll incident.

Every night Mike had off, he spent at the dojo. Master Cho and Mike usually practiced to one side of the room. For several days each week, they were alone. Master Cho had permission to practice when the school wasn't opened. Why sensei allowed him to teach Mike during the days there was no classes, Mike was not privy too. Generally, sensei had class three days a week.

Mike felt honored to be chosen by Cho as his student. One night after the Rama closed, he went to the school to practice with Master Cho. The door was left unlocked on those nights they practiced. Mike had given Master Cho his work hours at the Rama, so he knew his schedule and would be waiting for him to arrive.

This night was different from the other night practices. Mike walked in the dojo, and there was no Master Cho sitting on the mats. Looking about the room, it suddenly dawned on Mike the lights were not fully on. One light in the middle portion of the dojo was the only light. Mike noticed a small box lying on the spot Master Cho would normally be seated.

Walking over to the box cautiously, he stopped and stood still. Something wasn't quite right. He sensed something lurking but unseen. Remembering his training to breathe and relax, Mike cautiously perused the area. He allowed his chi to extend out and tried to feel every wall and corner for any unusually out-of-place item.

Quickly, Mike sensed something in three areas of the dojo. Focusing his gaze toward the first and strongest area, nothing was seen. He remembered what his first sensei taught him: "See with your eyes alone, and you will see little. See with all your senses, and you will see all there is to be revealed. Not everything is visible to our eyes. Learn to see with your ears, your smell, your touch, and your taste. Each has something to reveal to you the others cannot. Once you master the sense of self, then you will learn to sense with your spirit. The inner eyes see things all five senses cannot."

Mike's old sensei was right. At a spot he first perused, Mike could feel a presence, and soon the other areas revealed a presence. There was definitely three persons other than himself in this room.

"Once one learns to see with his spirit, not only will it help you become aware of unseen people, but their spirits. With practice, those spirits will reveal their true intentions," Sensei had taught him.

Each of the three unseen persons in the room with Mike, he had sensed, also had a strong intent to harm him within their spirits. He could feel their chi wash over him. The force of their chi suddenly came rushing toward Mike. Each of the three persons now reacted and charged forward with a blinding speed. Their intent was pure. It was to harm him.

Mike had little time to prepare his reaction against the three oncoming persons attacking. He had to solely rely on his training. The first person's presence Mike became aware of was springing from where he now held his gaze. He was quick. He was dressed in black, mimicking the darkness. Only the pressure of his chi and the subtle air movement gave his attack substance for Mike to latch on to.

The black-clothed attacker leaped into the air. His attack was a flying sidekick. Mike allowed his legs to give way and quickly dropped below the incoming flying kick. He felt him soar above. No sooner than he was past, the second assailant sprung. This time, he charged in with a skipping side thrust kick. Mike simply lay back in his prone position on the ground. The second man, with his leading leg extended out fully at the empty air above Mike's prone body, sailed into a snap kick of Mike's. The kick hit the second man as he was directly over him, propelling the second man up over Mike and into the first assailant.

The force of the skipping sidekick coming at Mike exerted from the second assailant followed by Mike's upward snap kick to his groin caused Mike to roll. Mike allowed the roll to continue followed with a snap, a twist of both legs, spinning up on his feet. Mike's groin kick to the second man propelled his assailant faster toward the first man. The first assailant landed just in time to meet with his friend swiftly slamming into him. It was just in time for the third man to get within range to throw a strike at Mike's head. Quickly, Mike turned to block the punch with a powerful inside block, only to block another and another strike that followed in rapid succession.

Whoever the third man was, his timing was perfect. The first two attackers got Mike off center but not unprepared. Mike was forced to retreat, back stepping from each strike of the third assailant. By the fourth strike, Mike sensed he was going to kick.

True enough, and thanks to Sifu and all the practicing they had been doing, Mike pivoted off the fourth strike. His assailant's kick missed, and Mike rotated with a reverse spinning wheel kick to his third dark assailant's head. He attempted to block the kick. The kick was powerful. So powerful, the jolt from the impact threw the third man flying against the opposite wall.

The first assailant, now recovered quickly, charged and tackled Mike in a rear hold. The second man was readying to strike at Mike from the front. Both of Mike's arms were held tight from behind. Thinking of his training, Mike simply relaxed and became like a wet noodle. With a quick side twist of his hip, he slipped behind the opponent's rear. Mike brought up his arm under the chin of the first man. With his arm neatly placed below the chin, this allowed Mike to stand erect and apply an upward force. The first man's head gave easily to Mike's rearward movement. The second man struck at the same time Mike pulled the first man's head up to bring the assailant down to the ground. The knees would buckle from the rearward force pulling down. The kick made a direct contact with the first assailant's nose. The first man went down faster, slamming hard on the mat. He wasn't getting up to soon.

The second man received a front kick to his midsection followed with an upper-cut punch to his downward lunging jaw. Down he went with little assistance needed. The third man came rushing from the wall he was previously flung to by the reverse spinning wheel kick Mike presented to him. Suddenly, the lights came on. The third man stopped.

Appearing from the only corner of the room Mike felt was empty of a spirit was Master Cho. "Well done, Mike. You did well."

Standing with a puzzled looked, it suddenly dawned on Mike that Sifu was testing him. "Sifu, thank you for your wonderful training. I could have hurt these men seriously or they me."

"I know, and they were willing to be part of this test. You must always be prepared for combat. Each day this may happen. Never be so content that everything is safe. Danger is a part of life. In life, one must prepare to fight for survival, if one chooses to survive. This is the way of warriors. Be at peace. Peace gives you the presence to detect anger. So enjoy your peace before the anger comes. Then fight for life and live in peace later. Now go home and sleep in peace, Mike. Good night Mike," Sifu said.

All parties stood and slowly bowed to each other.

Every day for the next two weeks, this continued. On several nights after the final show at the Rama Theater, this occurred. Three men from a hidden spot waited for Mike. A sudden attack, then a fading away. Attack then fade away. The fight would end just as quickly as it had begun, and the attackers left. Only one time did one of the three hidden unseen men was able to land a single blow. It occurred when the second man who followed the failed attempt of the first man's attack rushed Mike, like he was going to tackle him. He did, and it drove Mike into a car. The third man was there and threw a roundhouse kick toward Mike's head. Mike swerved and deflected the kick. The second man threw a punch into the midsection as he broke free from his tackle on Mike.

Mike knew the punch was coming and flexed his stomach to take the brute force of the blow. Mike kicked out at him, knocking him away while simultaneously spinning around with a hook kick to the third man. His kick hit arm bone, and it sounded and felt like he may have broken the third man's arm. Not one sound came from the third man. He backed away quick. Soon all were gone, and only Sifu walking forward was visible.

"Hmm, you got hit."

"Yes, Sifu."

"Bad, Mike."

"I flexed to take the blow. It didn't harm me, Sifu." Mike hoped him explaining he sensed the hit coming and prepared for the impact would merit some praise. He was wrong.

"Hmm, Mike, it is not simply whether the blow harmed you, it is that you got struck. Each strike takes away your strength. If the fight had lasted longer, the more strikes you receive adds up to break down your strength. It matters not whether it is one or ten hits you endure. Time to recover, to heal, to continue is eroded."

"I think I understand your meaning, Sifu."

"Here, let me phrase it another way, Mike. Take a tree, tall and strong. Do you believe if you hack it one time with an axe, you could fell it?"

"Of course not, Sifu."

"This is true when you are hit, Mike. After many hacks from an axe, the tree will begin to fall. When the final chop is made, the tree will fall. How many chops from an axe will depend upon the height, width, and hardness of the wood the tree is made of.

"Mike, when you practice, you grow strong. Practice hardens your body and mind. Every blow you receive prepares your mind to deal with pain. You become mentally strong and prepared for combat.

"The same is true with your body. Practice builds muscle, memory, speed, and power. It also provides endurance to continue when you are nearly spent.

"So you see, every hit is that axe hacking at your body and mind. Every movement you make along with any strikes from your opponents weaken you. So the more you practice, the stronger you become. You change from a soft pine tree wood to a mighty tough oak tree wood.

"Every opponent you fight adds to the chops you receive. One man will be as two when they attack. He strikes at you, and you respond to him. That makes two. If two men attack, then the effort will increase to four times the energy needed to fend off their attack. Every minute that passes adds to the erosion of your abilities.

"That is why you must keep a fight short. End it quick. Don't concern yourself with their welfare. They are not with yours. They tend to want to harm you. Nothing more or nothing less. In a fight, you always consider winning. Losers won't have a second chance.

"Take the fight to them. Even when you defend, try to turn it back on them. They will expend more energy when they defend. You will cut their power in half. Do not ever allow an opponent to control you.

"To remain in control of yourself is to maintain your energy levels. Make them deplete their energy. Control them, and they will do what you command of them. Every movement must be with the intent to control the fight." After a short pause, Sifu turned and walked away.

Tad was standing by the double doors and waited until Sifu was out of sight. He walked over to where Mike stood.

Mike had noticed him coming without lifting his head to see his approach.

"Mike, I know you are taking lessons, but are these the normal things that happen in a karate class? I assumed this would be done in class, not in the street late at night. I have talked to Mr. Cho about these training times at the Rama. I wasn't prepared for what I just saw tonight."

"You are right about that. My master wants to make sure I am capable of receiving his training," Mike answered.

"Well, I must say, I am impressed with your skills. I still have my worries for you."

"Tad, I would appreciate it if you keep this training private. Between us. Please."

"Well, Mike, I guess I can do that, but you will need to let me know later why the secrecy?"

"I promise I will, Mike. But for now, it is very important you talk to no one or even mention anything you see. Please never mention this training you see, Tad."

NO BLIP ON THE RADAR

LATELY, MIKE HAD BEEN UPSTAIRS playing the movie. Everything was going pretty good. No major malfunctions. In other words, a film breaks during the show or a short carbon rod left in going out before the reel ended. Sometimes you might think a rod will last longer than expected, and it burns out while the film is showing. The movie keeps playing, but no picture is seen. Quickly you pull the rods apart to remove the arc burn, then raise the shield. Unscrew the short rod and close the shield. All that is left is to touch the rods to light them up.

The first sign a rod burns out is when you sit looking out the small port to watch the movie and no picture. Everything turns dark. You hear the sound but see no picture.

This was what happened on this afternoon shift.

Quickly, the movie went dark. Mike rushed to the rods and pulled them back. Raising the shield, the rods appeared to be the proper length. *What happened?* Mike questioned himself. Quickly he relit the rods then went back to the port. Still no picture. This time Mike did the worst thing one could do and was told to never do, which he just did. He lifted the shield. The flash of light was intense.

The light nearly blinded Mike as he let out a yelp, falling back against the second projector. Blindly, he reached out, grabbing the shield door. When his finger felt the warm panel door, he quickly brought it down.

Mike stood by the second projector holding his hands up to his eyes. He could hear the door open to the projector room. Someone entered and was laughing.

"Hey, Mike, what happened to the picture?"

Unlocking his hands from his eyes, he barely made out the figure passing through the door. A second person followed and stood beside the first person to enter near the door. Mike couldn't see the two figures who entered but instantly recognized that voice who asked the question.

"What, what you mean, Ric?"

"The picture went dark. We thought you were in some kind of trouble."

"Thanks, but I got it corrected, guys."

"I don't think so," Melvin rebutted.

Melvin, standing next to Ric, looked out the port window of the second projector.

"What do you mean, Melvin?" Mike could hear the reel running, and the bell hadn't sounded yet to switch over the number 2 projector.

Mike turned to walk over to the first port window; it was dark. No picture. He looked back at the first projector's shield and could see the light shining through the sides.

"What's wrong with this movie projector?" Mike quipped out to both Melvin and Ric. Seeing a smile on both of their faces, Mike took a second look through the port window. They both laughed.

"Okay, what's going on? What did you two do?" Mike stood facing his two friends and realized they were playing a prank on him. *How?* he wondered.

Ric spoke up. "I'll let Melvin show you. It was his idea."

Mike turned to Melvin, who walked over to the projector. "Come here, Mike. Look out the second port window and see."

Mike walked over to Melvin and peered out the port. The movie was still playing on the screen. Looking up at Melvin, he inquired, "How? Okay, Melvin, what's going on?"

"Come follow me, Mike." Melvin had moved over to the door and waved Mike over to him. Mike still saw spots from the bright light of the carbon rods as he walked out the door with Melvin leading the way to the outside port window. Pointing at the second port window, Melvin said, "Look up there at the port, Mike."

Looking up, Mike couldn't see anything different or odd about the window. "I don't see anything, Melvin."

"Come get next to the window, Mike." Pointing at the port, Melvin told him to take his hand and rub the window.

"Okay, I'll bite, Melvin." Mike placed his hand on the window. It was foamy and wet. Pulling his hand back, he brought it to his nose. It was Windex. *What?*

"Yeah, you thought the light went out," Ric said. "We could hear you outside trying to fix the problem. It took everything we had not to laugh too loud for you to hear us. We thought this would be a great beginner's prank on you."

"Well, it worked, you two got me good. Come on in, I need to get back in. The second projector is near its run. Got to switch over."

Back up the stairs, the door was closed. Reaching for the knob, Mike's hand felt this slimy, gooey stuff covering the knob. "What the?" he muttered.

Melvin laughed again. "Got you again. Ric covered the doorknob with grease when I brought you down here."

"Thanks again, you two finished with me?"

"You're welcome, Mike. Oh, maybe," Melvin replied with a smirk.

Entering inside the room, Ric was at the second projector preparing to switch over. Mike walked over to the table grabbing a rag to wipe off the grease on his hands. "Thanks for tending the projector, Ric."

"Thought you might need a hand there. It might be a little difficult with all that grease covering your hands. Hehehe."

Melvin said, "Mike, we noticed you drove here in an old car. When did you get a car?"

"Oh, my sister's boyfriend found this car and told me it was in good shape. I could buy it for little money. I bought it. It runs pretty good," Mike answered.

"When are you going to take us for a ride?"

"Ric, I'm not sure I want you two in my car. After all, you might blow it up as a joke."

"Mr. Deeks will be here in about fifteen minutes, Melvin. Is the new usher starting tonight?"

"Yeah, he will be with Rusty for the night shift. That leaves us to do some stuff. We figure in your new old car. You know, break it in, sort of."

"What you two got planned?" Mike asked.

"Well, depends on are you practicing tonight or off."

"I'm off. My master has to leave town for the week. What you got now?" Mike said with a leery tone.

"Didn't you tell us you knew how to make hydrogen gas to fill balloons?"

"Yeah, Ric, I do." Mike remembered back when he and Ron made some gas from lye and aluminum foil in a Coke bottle. It took several balloons to lift a small rocket. Mike wanted to test his theory of a rocket balloon launch. It almost worked if not for the rocket falling off the pad attached to the balloons.

Mike also remembered the fun the kids had following the balloons across the neighborhood once the rocket fell off. About eight kids, him and Ron included, chased those balloons all around the city. It kept rising and falling down to earth. Mike told them as the balloons got high, the gases cooled, and the balloons came down. Then the gases warmed up, and the balloons went back up in the sky. Never close enough for anyone to grab them. Eventually the balloons flew away, never to be seen again.

"Well, that's what we plan on doing." Both recalled Mike telling them about his homemade gas balloons. "Tonight, we launch operation radar blip. What do you want us to get?"

"We will need several soda bottles, some aluminum foil, and lye. Oh yes, plenty of balloons and string."

"We'll be on our way. Be back in thirty," Ric told Mike as he was walking out.

"See you two then." Mike waved them out the door.

Downstairs after Mr. Deeks arrived to relieve Mike, there was this kid waiting at the front door. A red-haired skinny kid wearing black-rimmed glasses walked up to him. "Hi, my name is Gerry."

"Hi, I'm Mike. You the new guy?"

"Yes."

"Well, I'm the doorman, and you will be working as an usher. As the doorman, I am in charge of the ushers and their operations. Come on in. Tad is not here at the moment. I will show you around, if you like."

"That will be great," the redheaded kid answered.

"Come then, I will give you the grand tour, Gerry. This is the same tour I got from Tad when I first started at the Rama."

"Hey, Mike, where does that door lead to you came out of?"

"Oh, that is the balcony and where the projectors are. I'll show you that after the downstairs tour is over."

Walking across the lobby, Mike and Gerry arrived at the candy bar. "These girls will call you to get supplies and to help customers with their orders. You need to be nice to them, Gerry. That is, if you expect not to get poisoned. This is Debbie, and this girl is Anne."

Gerry shook both their hands. Lindsey poked her head out the ticket booth door.

"Oh, that is Lindsey, the lead girl."

"Hello, Gerry, I run the ticket booth, and another girl, Connie, works in here when I am off. After the last show, you will escort me up to the office if you work at night." Lindsey offered a sweet smile at Gerry.

"Hey, Lindsey, I haven't told him any terrible things to expect from you as of yet. Gerry just started."

"Well, Mike, you best not say them."

"I know better than to do that, Lindsey." Mike gave a smile to her. "Gerry, any questions you have, talk to the doorman. Any problems with customers, see the doorman. You will be responsible for keeping the lobby swept and the movie aisle between shows. Hey, you thirsty, Gerry?"

"Sure."

"What'll you have?"

"I'll take an orange soda, Mike."

Tapping on the candy countertop, Anne turned away from the making of a new batch of popcorn. The popper was a large electric cooker. Every night after the last show, the candy bar girls had to lift it off the hinge it hung on. Sometimes when only one girl was working, she would ask one of the ushers or the doorman to assist her lifting it off its hinges. The usher would carry it to the sink where she would wash it. Then most times she would have the usher place it back on its hinges.

The candy counter had two large windows. One window faced the lobby, and the other was behind the popper and the soda fountain. Under the counter were shelves for all the assortments of candy.

"Gerry, the best candy I like are the chocolate almonds. They are the most expensive, twenty-five cents. Next to them are the twenty-five-cent assortments. All the other candy is ten cents."

"Mike, they might be the most expensive but not the best seller," Debbie interjected. Bending over, she reached behind the counter window where all the candies are visible to the patrons and pulled three boxes out, laying them on the countertop. "Now these are the most sold choices," remarked Debbie with a smile.

Gerry eyed the three boxes and noticed the one he often bought when going to the movies. "That one." He pointed to the Milk Duds. "That's what I buy." Gerry grabbed hold of the box and took a whiff from the box. "Hmmm I think I will buy it."

"That's on you, Gerry, any candy you buy."

"How much, Debbie?"

"That will be ten cents. Here you go." Debbie took the dime and turned to enter it into the change box. Turning back to Gerry, she watched him place the box in his shirt pocket. Seeing him do so, she asked, "You are not going to open them to eat?"

"No, Debbie, I'll wait later. I still got a box of popcorn to eat."

Anne removed a cup from the stack and placed it under the fountain then returned it full to Gerry.

"Thanks, Anne," he said. "How much?"

"It's on me, Gerry. Also, your first popcorn. After that, it is yours to get refills. You get all the Coke or popcorn refills you want free while working here. I would recommend you write your name on each of them. Only thing is, if you lose your box or cup, you will need to buy another," remarked Mike, remembering that Tad had done the same for him.

"Hey, thanks, Mike."

"Now come over here, I will show you where you sign in and out every shift." Mike and Gerry walked across the lobby to the stairs leading up to the projection room.

At the closet near the door, Mike pointed to the shelf where all ushers kept their cups and boxes. After showing Gerry the closet, he led him over to the first door leading inside the movie house. "When you enter, you will sit in the first seat on either side of the aisle. Try not to sit more than several seats down the aisle. Every once in a while, you make a walk around the movie. Look for anyone with their feet on the back of seats. Answer complaints and stop anyone causing trouble. If you think you might not be able to take care of a troublemaker, go get the doorman. Now to the stockroom, Gerry."

Inside the room, Mike grabbed hold of a red jacket.

"Here, Gerry." He handed it to him. "If this fits, it will be yours to wear while you are working. We each have our own jacket assigned to us with a name tag. In this room, we keep all the supplies for the candy bar and printed items to post outside. Over here is our letter box for the marquee. Please do me a favor and place all the letters in the correct slots. Some of the ushers just toss them back here, and it usually falls on the incoming shift to clean the mess they make.

"Right now, your first job is to begin sweeping the aisles and between the seats. In the auditorium are three rows of seats. The main row has fifteen to twenty seats across from the top just below the balcony to the front closest to the screen. On either side of the main row of seats are the aisle seating. Five seats across down to four at the front. The front row is where most of the kids love to sit." Mike pointed this out to Gerry.

"Saturday is kids' day, and at the front is the most troublesome. Popcorn fights, seat kicking, and chasing. All ushers have to make a lot of rounds to keep them from causing all kinds of trouble. On that day, we have two matinees. Once inside, the kids stay until the evening show. Around five thirty, all the ushers would round them up and shove them out the doors. We stay outside to maintain order and to keep them out of trouble until their parents arrive. Sometimes the parents show during the evening show. It's the Rama's policy to let the kids go in and watch the show free until the parents did arrive.

"Come, we'll go and get a broom, Gerry. I will help until Ric and Melvin come. Then I'm off. Rusty should be here to assist," Mike explained.

Both walked back up to the lobby, and Rusty hadn't signed in yet. They grabbed a broom and were about halfway down one side of the seats when Rusty arrived. Both Ric and Melvin came in at the same time.

Mike shouted up at them as they entered the auditorium. "Come on, you two, help out with the sweeping. This here is the new guy, Gerry."

Gerry waved to them.

Soon all had the place swept.

At the candy counter, Ric left all the stuff for the balloons. Anne asked, "What you going to do with all that stuff?"

Hearing that, Mike quickly answered back. "Anne, we are going to make gas balloons."

Ric piped in, "Yeah, we going to go behind the base and launch them."

"Why?" Anne asked.

"You know, to cause a blip on their radar. They think it will be a UFO. It'll be a hoot!" Ric cried out.

"Can I go?"

"Sure," Ric replied.

Lindsey poked her head out of the ticket booth. "I want to come too."

"You're working, aren't you, Lindsey?" Ric butted in.

"Well, can't you wait until I get off?" Lindsey tended to refer to Mike when wanting to go with them. From the past experiences, she often got a no from Ric or Melvin. Mike was easier.

Mike spoke up." This is Ric's plan. Ask him."

Before she had the chance, Ric answered her question. "No, we are not going to wait until you get off, Lindsey."

Soon everyone walking in wanted to go. Ric caved in. "If any of you want to go, then you need to help in making these balloons."

The three guys and Anne went to the side of the Rama behind a wall that had been erected months ago to begin making balloons. Mike showed each one how to make and fill a balloon, and then they started their balloon filling. Within thirty minutes, the three of them had twenty-two balloons floating.

"Mike, how you learn how to do this?" asked Anne. Anne was short, cute, and had long brown straight hair. Also, she had a face filled with tiny freckles.

Mike explained he had a chemistry set and learned some keen things.

Anne was often teased by all the ushers calling her plain Anne. She wasn't plain. She had a good, kind heart and was pretty. Most of the girls who worked at the Rama were pretty.

Before the halfway showing of the first evening picture, Tad stopped by. He parked his small four-door sedan he had been driving since the day he bought it in front of the entrance. Walking through the two three-sheet poster billboards, he stopped long enough to inspect the order in which they had been placed. Satisfied, he continued to walk to the doorman, greeting Rusty, who was sitting on his stool. Rusty was the only usher to wear a bowtie. Everyone else wore a clip-on tie. Some shared the same tie. Mike wore the only tie that needed to be tied. Rusty stood and asked Tad if he planned on remaining for the evening show.

"Not tonight, I got other plans. If you need me, I will be at the drive-in theater. Just call there and ask for me, Rusty."

He stayed long enough to check on the new boy. Tad was wearing his black suit and pants. Rarely was he ever seen any other attire. Looking around, he noticed Mike standing by the window near the ticket booth outside. Mike spotted Tad at the same time. Stopping what he was up to, Mike quickly turned to walk over to Tad.

Speaking first, Mike began with, "Good evening, Tad. I met the new man, Gerry. I spent some time when I got off breaking him in on his duties."

Mike and Tad together walked to the road in front of the marquee. Mike filled him in on what he taught Gerry.

"Is Rusty going to take care of the new movie to be posted on the marquee?"

"I hadn't had time to touch base with him on that matter, Tad. I made sure he knows what to do. If he needs assistance, I will be glad to stay and help out. I just finished with Gerry and was about to talk to Rusty," Mike hurriedly said.

"Sounds like you got a handle on what needs to be done. I didn't expect you to be here after you got off."

"I was going to leave until Gerry showed up early. Rusty hadn't arrived yet, and Randy had a date. He couldn't stay longer. So I did. I broke him in with sweeping down the aisles. He's a good worker."

Tad seemed satisfied. "Where is our new usher, Mike?"

"Oh, he's in the movie. I bought him a Coke and popcorn. Want me to get him?"

"No, I'll go and fetch him. I want to talk with him some. See if he needs anything for now. Thanks for staying." Tad walked over to the entrance door to the inside. After pulling Gerry out into the lobby for a short discussions, Tad shook Gerry's hand.

"Good evening, ladies, you are looking good. I see you got on fresh popcorn and all the shelves are stocked. Need anything?" Tad asked before he left.

"No, sir, we are fine," both girls responded back to his queries.

Tad didn't stay long and left shortly after talking to Gerry and the girls.

Both Rusty and Gerry kept coming over to see what was transpiring outside behind the wall. Both shows this night had few turnouts to watch the flick. Lindsey usually stayed in her booth, but the excitement of the balloons kept her coming out of her box to check on the four's progress filling balloons.

"This is so cool, Mike. How is this going to block the radar on base?" Anne inquired.

"Well, the strips of tinfoil will reflect the radar signal back at them," Mike attempted to explain when Ric blurted in.

"Just like a plane," Ric cited.

"Yeah, just like a plane, but there will be no planes, and the radar will see a blip looking like a UFO, or I think that will happen," Mike replied.

"I hope they won't send the police after us," Melvin cautiously mentioned.

"Ah, we will be long gone, Melvin. Remember what I told you."

"Ric, your plans tend to go awry," Melvin retorted back at him.

"Yeah, Ric, I agreed with Melvin. Besides, how are we going to get behind the base to launch these balloons, Ric? You got that in your plan?"

"Mike, I got this. I know where a dirt road behind the base is."

Melvin gave Mike a queer look after Ric told him about the dirt road. A funny feeling rose up in Mike stomach when Melvin gave him that look.

By the time the second feature began, the three had twenty-eight balloons filled and tied together. Ric unrolled the tinfoil. Melvin held the balloons while Mike tied them together.

"Ric?" Mike turned to ask him a question. "Do you still have any of the M-80s left?"

"Sure, why, Mike?"

"I got an idea. What if we tied several of those to some of the balloons as well? I will attach my cigarette fuse to delay the boom," cited Mike.

"Oh man, let's do it," Ric excitedly replied.

"Do what?" Anne asked.

"Anne, you hear about the rolling of the vice principal's home Ric, Mike, and Rusty did?" Melvin said while Ric and Mike were preparing two balloons for the M-80s.

"Who didn't?" she answered back. "Why you think I want to go with you guys?"

Lindsey had stepped outside the booth for the fifth time when the M-80s were brought up by Ric.

Turning to Lindsey, Mike asked, "Lindsey?"

Before he could finish, she responded, "I know, you need my cigarettes." Reaching into her purse, she pulled two from her pack and handed them over to Mike. "Now, tell me why you need them."

"Well, we are going to attach some of the balloons with these M-80s."

"No way," Lindsey said with a snort.

"Yes way," Ric answered back. "Here, give them to me, Mike. You need to go get your car. We need to put them in before everybody in town drops by," Ric quipped.

Apparently, people walking by stopped to watch what the group was making. The balloons towered over the wall they were behind. A small crowd grew. Each person in the crowd wanted to see the four's endeavor. Questions, questions were coming from everywhere.

"Mike, this isn't going to be much of a secret plan."

"I agree with you, Rusty."

Gerry walked over. "Hey guys, you're getting a crowd. You still going through with this idea?"

Ric had to admit, this plan might have to be cancelled, watching the crowd grow larger with every passing minute.

Lindsey hearing this had just finished the counting upstairs and walked out to see the crowd. Hearing Ric make that comment made her upset. "No way. You cannot stop this thing. We all are excited to do it. If you are not going to do this, Ric, then give us the balloons," Lindsey demanded.

"Okay, okay," Ric and Melvin agreed.

"It's up to you guys. I'm just the driver," Mike told them.

"Okay, then it's on," Ric remarked to all.

Mike had parked his new old car near the front door. Walking over to the door, he opened it. Ric and Melvin carried the balloons over to the door.

Whoops.

"Hey guys, guess what!" Mike shouted out. "These balloons are not going inside this car."

"What? Oh no!" Lindsey's face turned beet red.

Quickly, Mike responded before Lindsey hit the roof with a shout fest. She did have quite the temper when provoked. Mike felt that anger when her boyfriend happened by one afternoon. He made some remark that apparently set her off. He had to tell her boyfriend to leave while holding her door shut. That didn't stop her. She went into the candy bar area and tried to squeeze through the outside port window where patrons waiting in line could buy drinks or snacks.

"Well, Lindsey, we can put some balloons in, but that means some of you won't be able to get to ride in the car."

"Again, hell no!" came a shout from Lindsey.

Ric spoke up. "Some of you can ride with me and Melvin in our cars. Mike, you follow with whoever can fit into your car with them balloons."

"Ric, I got news for you, it is going to take several cars to take all of these balloons," Mike said.

"What about the rest of us?" Rusty, Gerry, and Anne all spoke up together.

"Well, if you can squeeze in my car with these balloons, get in."

Thus began the long succession of cars being led by Ric, Gerry, and Anne in the lead car, then by Mike's new old car with him and Rusty. The third car carried Melvin and Lindsey in her car and the remaining balloons.

When the movie was finally over, everyone was in cars and rolling out of the parking lot. Apparently, the onlookers didn't want to be left out of this caravan waiting along in the parking lot. Several of the crowd decided to follow the Rama convoy. By the time the Rama cars arrived at the Macon Airport, their convoy had ten cars behind Melvin's lead car.

The caravan turned onto the highway and went a short distance before turning on a road leading behind the base. Before reaching the next road that turned onto a dirt road putting them on a parallel drive to the base, the caravan stopped.

Getting out of the lead car, Ric's group walked over to Mike's car. Both Mike and Rusty open the door and exited. All three cars unloaded.

Ric began. "Guys, you do know we are not alone on this road?"

"Yeah, Ric, I think we all figured that out." Looking around, every light from the ten cars lit the night sky. Lindsey smirked.

Mike turned toward the cars. "Ric, Melvin, we need to get everybody together and discuss our plan."

"What plan?" Lindsey asked.

They all turned to Ric.

"Well, I didn't plan for this."

Melvin said, "Here we go again."

"Wait, I got an idea!" shouted Mike. He wave for everybody to get out of their cars to meet. Car engines went quiet, and the lights went out. Soon everyone turned their lights back on when it became obvious it was dark on this back road. A mass of people gathered around the seven Rama employees. Everyone stopped talking once they gathered around.

Mike spoke. "Okay, everyone, we hadn't counted on every one of you following us. So if you intend to follow, you need to do as we ask you. If not, we are not going to do anything. Do you agree?"

Everyone answered with a soft yes.

"First thing, there are way too many cars. Some of you need to ride together. If we go down this road with all these cars, we might not be able to turn around. I know I don't want to be stuck down this long, lonely, dark-as-hell dirt road," Mike quipped out to the crowd.

"We are going to follow the lead car. Only two cars will keep the lights on bright. We will go slow, but keep your distance. Once in a while turn your light on to help you keep your distance. Only a few of you need to keep your lights on. Too many beaming lights might look a bit suspicious, and we might have unwanted visitors coming to our little party.

"Remember to turn the lights on quick and back off quick. When we get to the launch site, the lead car will begin blinking his lights. That will be the signal to you we intend to stop," Mike instructed to all.

"It will be okay to turn on your lights at that time when we stop. One light, my car's, will remain on, and everybody will get out of their car and meet us at my car. We will discuss what to do next." Mike peered around to make sure everyone could hear him.

Finished, Mike signaled for the mass of followers to get back into their cars. That was when Mike saw this one person wearing a bandana around his head with a T-shirt. On his arms he could make out an array of tattoos. Mike watched him open the driver's door to his car. Two other guys also entered wearing similar attire and sporting many tattoos.

Taking note of their place in the caravan's line, Mike turned back to the lead car. Both sides of the dirt road were bound by a thick growth of trees. Mike hoped when they got near the launch site, Ric had a turn-around area for the cars. From the looks of the road, it was appearing this line of cars might be stuck down that road all night trying to turn around. Mike's worst thoughts began to appear to come true.

"Okay, let's do this!" Lindsey shouted out.

Mike got in his car. Ric and his group went to their car in the lead. Several people got in Melvin's car, and so it went down the line of cars. Only six cars left from that meeting followed the last car with the Rama team. Several cars remained parked off the road before turning down the dirt road.

Ric began at a slow and steady speed ahead of the caravan into the dark eerie night. If not for the remnants of his low beams flashing against the woods, his car would have disappeared before it went a few hundred feet. The road was bumpy the farther the caravan drove. It wasn't long that every car was making a *rat-a-tat* drumroll with every tire bouncing on washboard road ruts.

In front of Mike, a loud thump could be heard from the lead car. Up in the air, the front end of Ric's car went soaring. It quickly came back down with another loud thump. Ric came to a sudden halt.

Mike, seeing what happened to Ric's car, slammed on his brakes, just stopping short of rear-ending Ric's car. Everyone behind Mike slammed on their brakes. Luckily, everyone stopped short, preventing a slam-bam fender bender of epic portions.

Every light was on now. The woods on both sides of the road looked like a Hollywood premiere opening of a new movie. Not a person remained in their cars. The last car in the caravan with the three bandana guys went back into their car and immediately began to back up. After many back and forth with their car to get turned around on the dirt road, they succeeded. The two others who sought a ride with them were still watching them attempting a turnaround. Once they got turned facing the road back to the turnoff, they left. The two people were left standing without a ride back.

The two stranded individuals tried screaming to no avail to stop them. The bandana men drove on down the road. No taillights showing to allow their passengers to follow could be seen.

Ric was looking under the front end of his car. Melvin walked past Mike to where Ric and his passengers were milling around the car.

"Hey, Ric, what happened? Why'd you stop?"

"You didn't see what happened?" Ric retorted back. "I hit a ditch. Someone had dug this ditch across the road."

"Dang, Ric, is the car okay? Are you going to be able to drive back?"

"I'm not sure, Melvin." Looking back under the front of the car, he turned back to Melvin. "Get in the car and try to turn the steering wheel, Melvin."

After getting out of the second car along with Rusty, Mike stopped, allowing Melvin to walk to Ric's lead car. Lindsey was standing alone with Mike and Rusty near her side. "What happened, Mike?"

"Well, Lindsey, Ric ran into a ditch someone dug across the road. I slammed on the brakes just in time."

"Is everyone okay, Mike?"

"I'm not sure, Lindsey. I was about to walk over when you and Melvin came up," replied Mike.

"Should we go and check on Ric?"

"No, knowing him, he would probably be furious and begin shouting at anyone now."

"I'm going anyways, Mike," retorted Lindsey.

Mike, Rusty, and Lindsey met up with the others at Ric's car.

"Everyone okay?" Mike asked.

Speaking up first was Anne. "Yeah. Gerry hit his head on the back of Ric's seat. Other than that, we are fine."

"Melvin, you can stop turning the steering wheel. One of my tire rods is slightly bent."

"Hey, Ric, you got a hammer?" Mike yelled to Ric, who was still under his car.

"Sure," Ric answered back.

"Where is it, Ric?"

"Look in the glove compartment."

Mike thought Ric was kidding. Melvin pulled the hammer out and handed it to Mike. Crawling under the car beside Ric, he began to pound on the bent rod. After several good hits, the rod straightened.

"Mike, you saved my butt. My dad would have my hide if he had to come and get me this late at night."

"Let's get this show on the road, Ric." Mike was looking around with all these car lights shining. "This is a good a place as any. There are few trees just ahead. It looks like we are near an open field. We can set the balloons free without any worry of them snagging on the trees as they rise," Mike explained to a crowd watching.

"Good idea. We'll do it," Lindsey agreed.

"Going back up to the third car, Mike yelled to the crowd that unloaded from the cars. "Turn your lights off!"

Soon, every light was off. The darkness that shrouded the area was unbelievable.

Lindsey yelled out, "Mike, it's too dark! We can't see where to go!"

"Lindsey, with this darkness, it's like standing in a closet. You couldn't see your hand if you placed it in front of your eyes. Melvin, turn the lights on in Ric's car," Mike called out.

Several people from the other cars came forward to assist getting the car out of the ditch. As a team, they lifted the front end of Ric's car out of the ditch. Then with a mighty effort, they lifted the front end again and walked it around. The car made a perfect pivot on its rear wheels. Soon Ric's car was turned in the other direction.

The rest of the people picked up on the sight, and every car was soon facing the direction back out. Rusty and Mike started to unload the balloons. Hands fluttered about them as they pulled the balloons out of their car. Each hand groped for a balloon. Anne and Gary had most of the other balloons out of their car. Rusty and Mike held on to the last clump of balloons.

Mike handed his balloons over to Melvin. The Rama Rowdies proceeded walking to the middle of the open field. The field was knee high with tall grass. Some of the other caravan followers came along. The rest remained back by the two lead cars.

"Okay," Mike said, "we want everyone to take several balloons with the tinfoil and spread out across this field. On signal, we will let them go."

Walking over to Lindsey with three balloon sets of clumps of three, he handed them to her to hold.

"Okay, Lindsey, I need your lighter."

Taking the lighter, Mike lit up three cigarettes. Carefully he ran the fuses through the hole he prepared earlier.

"Now you take this set, Lindsey, and I will hold onto the one set." The last set he handed to Rusty.

There was a slight change to the payload on two of the rockets without tinfoil. Ric only had one M-80, so it was decided to attach some bottle rockets to several of the balloons. Mike had some left over from the night raid on the Boy Scout camp under the front seat of his car.

Walking out to an open spot, Mike stood waiting for the count-down. Gerry thought it would be a good idea with all these people to get them do a count before the grand release.

"Okay, Gerry, it was your idea for a countdown. You can start anytime," Ric told him.

Looking around in the open field with Ric's car lights on the crowd, they had little trouble watching the launch take place. With no trees to block the starlight, every balloon shone against the brightly lit sky.

Gerry began his countdown, starting at ten. Soon, the crowd began the countdown chant. "Six, five, four, three, two, one!"

On one, all the balloons started their slow ascent into the sky. The last three sets of three balloons rose slower than the others. The tinfoil flickered in the sky from the wind, making them swirl about. All those balloons remained in their close grouping. It did have a UFO appearance. The crowd made an "Oh wow" shout of glee.

Everyone was caught off guard when the first set of three went off. It was the set that had a cluster of bottle rockets. When the rockets took off, they went every which direction. One flew back toward the cars. It landed near the largest cluster of people standing. It hit the ground and swirled around. People were jumping like frogs in a hot frying pan before it went *pop!*

Then the second set ignited. It carried two packs of firecrackers. Most of the tinfoil balloon remained overhead and drifted just a little past where the cars were parked. They climbed to about two hundred feet before they started to drift toward the air strip. The firecracker set drifted a little. It never reached the same height as the tinfoil balloons. When it lit the firecracker's fuse, the firecracker bundle must have dislodged from the string holding them to the balloon set.

A girl in the crowd screamed out. "Look, something's falling from that balloon! It is exploding!"

Someone else yelled, "Run!"

The crowd went wild. A panic run to the cars unfolded. That didn't stop the rain of popping coming down all around the cars. By the time the crowd was safely in their cars, the second string of firecrackers barely attached to its string let go as the fuse got lit.

Ric yelled out to the group in the field. "Hey, Mike! You see that? You couldn't have ever planned for that to happen exactly like that on time."

"Cool!" Lindsey watched laughing at the mad scramble of those who followed in the caravan of cars. Rusty and Gerry were clapping their hands. Everyone started to clap. It became apparent, and it added to the racket intensity, increasing the panic. Those not clapping thought more firecrackers were raining from the sky onto them.

"Look, Ric!" Mike called out. "Look, they are leaving."

"Yeah," Gerry quipped, "even the ones we had in our car are leaving with the others."

Before the cars had a chance to begin moving up the road, the last set went off. It had the M-80. When that went off, it was such a loud sound, it provoked the drivers to step on the gas pedals. The effect was a high-squealing sound of tires against the dry dirt road. Dust rose up, creating a cloudy, blurry haze onto the road. The cars tore down the road bumper to bumper in a mad scramble.

Within minutes, only the nine in the field remained. One person remained in the field who was not a Rama Rowdy; he lost his ride. Standing near Rusty, he looked puzzled about being stranded.

"Hey, you guys, you're not leaving me out here by myself to walk home, are you?"

"What, of course not. You can ride with us," Rusty relayed to him.

"That was the coolest thing I've ever done," Gerry remarked. Watching the balloons fly out of sight, Gerry asked, "You guys do this kind of stuff all the time?"

"Yeah, Gerry, we do, that's why people at school refer to us at the Rama as the Rama Rowdies."

"Yeah, Ric, thanks to you telling everyone about our pranks," Mike reminds him.

"I'm surprise we haven't gotten in trouble with you blabbing it around," cited Melvin.

"Yeah, Ric," followed Lindsey with a curt snide remark at him. "Asshole."

"Well, this time it won't be me who tells anyone. I won't have to with all these people who followed us out here. Besides, you wouldn't be famous if it wasn't for me spreading our exploits. Duh," jokingly responded Ric.

"Hey guys, let's enjoy the sight. Look at them pretty glowing balloons fly toward the base. Tomorrow is plenty of time to find out the results of tonight. You all agree?" Mike asked.

After several minutes and all the balloons nearly out of sight, the group walked back to their cars.

"Thank god we turned these cars around before we let the balloons go," Rusty quipped.

"Yeah, we would have a hard time trying to turn these cars without all those people's help." Anne was quick to drive the point home.

"Hey guys, I had that all figured out. Just down this road is a place we could have turned around."

"Ric, aren't you forgetting one little fact? There is a ditch we will have to cross," Lindsey reminded Ric. "Duh."

"Who or when did someone dig this ditch?" questioned Gerry.

Ric replied, "There was no ditch here when I drove down this road four days ago."

"Maybe, Ric, that is the reason someone decided to dig it. They saw you driving down their road and wanted to keep others out," Mike answered.

Everyone got in the cars. Mike noticed the sole person who was with the followers standing by the road. Rolling down his window, he asked the person if he wanted a ride back to town. The sole survivor of the caravan wasn't sure which car Rusty told him to get in until Mike yelled at him. He quickly came running to Mike's car. He got in the car, and soon, a once ten-car convoy traveling down the road was now just a lonely three-car caravan returning back up the dark road. All headlights were on.

Arriving back at the Rama, all left the cars and drove home. The one person remaining was greeted by his friend standing near the marquee in front of the theater. The passenger in Rusty and Mike's car screamed to his friend, "Why'd you take off?"

His response was, "Everything got all mixed up obscured by the noise of everyone driving off. I never looked to make sure. I thought you might have been in another car. Sorry, my bad, buddy."

Several days passed before any news was known. In the local papers, there was a small article about some unknown blip appearing on a radar dish of the local airport and nothing reported by the air force. That was it. To everyone at the Rama, it was a great adventure and many talks followed by laughter for weeks to come. They met many people who said they had been at the launch that night. There did seem to be more of them telling the Rama group they had gone than those who had actually been there.

THE OBSTACLE COURSE

MIKE HAD STOPPED DRIVING HIS car to work for several weeks. Every day he was seen running up the main street or back streets to the Rama Theater. Gerry was the first to notice him running up the street when he was placing the new movie promo on the side marquee. Mike had run up to the corner road leading into the parking area. He turned to enter the lot, then leaped up onto a telephone pole, flipped off it onto the ground, then immediately hopped against the side of the office wall, doing a reverse backward flip to the ground. Finally, he jumped up over a small car doing a split with his legs as he planted both hands flat on the roof. It was smooth and done effortlessly.

To Gerry's astonishment, he landed on the ground with little impact as one would expect one to do when jumping off a high structure with a flop or thump. It was as if Mike was a feather slowly touching the ground, as if a light gust of wind blew him forward, skipping with each step across the surface of the street.

Gerry hailed to Mike. "Hey, Mike, great move."

Mike reacted by stopping his run. He waved back to Gerry then pointed out the spacing was off on the second line.

After school, Mike was not going to the Rama; he was back at the dojo. Sifu Cho began a new line of training.

"Mike, come with me," Sifu Cho called from the rear of the dojo exit door.

Mike just entered the dojo and bowed to the room and to his karate instructor. Mike earned his black belt early. He was Sensei's best fighter. His visiting sifu instructor, Mr. Cho, requested Sensei to have his students spar with Mike in groups of two, then groups of three. Sensei had to admit, Mike was far better at fighting skills than himself.

Passing through the rear door to the backyard, Mike saw what appeared to be an obstacle course. In the backyard of the dojo was a corner where two buildings met. Then a six-foot fence crossed the whole of the back facing the next street. On the third side was a wooden ten-foot-high wall. Within the yard were a series of short walls made of whatever lay nearby at various heights, followed by a long balance beam, then a longer slack rope line.

What really caught Mike's eye was two ten-foot or maybe taller buildings. Spanning across them to connect the two buildings was a long narrow board.

"Now, Mike, pay attention to my movements. You will learn to do the same," Sifu instructed.

Both eyes were glue to Sifu swiftly running, jumping over, flipping, and easily striding over the fence. Quickly Sifu returned back over the fence, up a corner between the two buildings, what seemed like him walking right up them. Then he did a most remarkable balancing act, running not walking across the top of the wooden fence tops. When he neared one of the two tall buildings, he covered his eyes with a cloth pulled from his blouse. Then walked across the thin narrow board that spanned between the two buildings. He halted midway, jumped high into the air, making a backflip, and back down to the narrow board without making the board bend the slightest.

"Now, Mike, you have witnessed the power that comes from training in my art. You will succeed in performing as I have done on the very same obstacle course. Now begin and continue until you have satisfied me," Sifu commanded Mike.

For two weeks, Mike practiced. Nothing else was taught him accept fighting before the course could be run. Always fighting was the main practice. He was exhausted at the beginning of his obstacle run.

Once this training begun, Mike quit driving his car to and from work or school, always he ran. Not a jog but a full-out run.

Sifu Cho added a backpack to his run. Of course, the backpack wasn't empty. Neither was it empty when he went to school or work. Most of the ushers at work thought it contained his shirt, tie, and shoe. If they had lifted the pack, then they would learn the truth.

Training had picked up. It seemed to Mike that Sifu was trying to rush his training. After each class, when the doors were closed to the dojo, Mike and Sifu would meditate for many minutes, which increased with time. On many of these after-school training meditations, Sifu would challenge Mike to sense his presence at different places in the dojo, using only his other senses and not sight. To aid in his sensitivity, Sifu would make his presence known when Mike assumed incorrectly. Usually, a sharp blow from a bamboo rod across his back, legs, or chest. Either place, it hurt.

When Mike developed an acceptable degree of awareness, Sifu took the training out to the obstacle course.

"Mike you are still developing the sense of awareness," Sifu said to him one night. "This exercise should constantly be your main object to acquire. Never not practice the ability to use all your senses. Even at work, practice senses everything about you. Know their sounds, scents, movements, and presence. In time a roach walking across the floor will sound like a lion's roar, the slightest breeze a hurricane, the aroma of scents will be like a menu of ingredients to your nose. Each item you smell, you will be able to discern their makeup. Now prepare for this night's practice."

Before Mike began his run, Sifu Cho had him put on leg and wrist weights along with his backpack. Then one hundred deep knee bends followed with two trips around the yard doing squatting hops. Once he had competed his hopping, both legs felt like mush.

Everything on the course was changed. The slack rope walk turned into forward flips and backflips. The wall climb bounce was repeated many times until he couldn't do any more. After rerunning the course many times, Sifu Cho had Mike do avoidance practicing. This time without the backpack. Mike had to avoid any strikes from a bo staff. He could jump, flip, roll, cartwheel, or spin but not block.

Quickly without advance warning came a series of swirling bo swings. Mike ducked, spun, shot up in the air, flipped, twisted, ducked again, cartwheeled, and so on for thirty minutes. The night ended with a sparring drill with three men in the dark.

MANY EYES IN THE NIGHT

After not training with Mike for a week, Sifu Cho returned. Entering the dojo, he greeted Mike as usual. Together they practiced punching and blocking. Six inches was what Mike was allowed to strike and block before.

"Extend your chi. Draw your strength from your center."

On some nights Mike would spend two hours just punching at a board six inches from him. Sifu would watch Mike's every move carefully. "Every movement from your feet, hips, waist, shoulder, elbow, wrist must be utilized. Breathe and strike. Timing of every movement into one masterful motion will increase the power of each punch and block. Remember, each move adds to your power." This was a constant reminder since he began training with Sifu Cho.

In the first week of this training, Mike's fists were bruised and bloody. Sifu continued to have him practice a set of strike blocks, block strikes with the same arm, then with the other. "Strike with the fist and block with the same fist. It is difficult to draw power from such a short distance, Mike. Through practicing your punching and blocking techniques, you will see the power come."

At a point when Sifu Cho felt satisfied with Mike, he began the same practice sets with circular movements. Sifu had multiple students during class strike at Mike. He had to counter with the block, strike, block, strike techniques and spin to meet the other opponents. Kicks were added later. Over time the complexities increased. Always before the end of each period and before the karate class ended, Mike had to return to the basic four techniques. Always returning to the basics was now expected after training.

When Sifu returned from his trip, they began where the two left off. After school, Mike always expected an encounter from Sifu with several students. On several such nights, Tad witnessed them.

On one night, another person witness the ongoing fight. Lindsey had stayed late upstairs with the boss. This sometimes occurred, especially if the Rama had a lot of patrons.

Mike had closed up. Most of the time the other ushers were allowed to leave early before closing up. This was the case on this night. The crowd leaving was huge. The parking lot was filled across the whole shopping center. The Rama was located at one end of the shopping center. It was amazing to see the cars leave quickly, emptying the whole parking center, Mike had noted to Tad witnessing for the first time this scene. One minute slap full, the next minute, totally emptied.

Leaving after the show, Mike went to the edge on the corner of the building. He donned his heavy backpack and walked into the street to begin his run home. After locking the doors to the theater, two men were waiting in the bushes under the side marquee. Mike became aware of their presence as soon as he stepped off the sidewalk and on to the street on that side.

Mike continued to walk, and Sifu watched from a car opposite to where he was spying on Mike, parked several rows of cars in front of the theater. Both men ran out from their hiding place. Lindsey just walked out the side door, leaving to the outside balcony.

Halfway up before the top of the stairs onto the balcony seats was a side opening aisle leading to the boss's office. The walk down the stairs was short, and she stood at the door to exit. Opening the door was a sight she had not expected. From her point of view, Mike was walking into the street. Suddenly, two figures emerged from around the building darting toward Mike.

It was too late to yell to Mike. All Lindsey could do was watch. What happened occurred too quickly for her to respond calling the police or running back up the stairs to inform the boss.

Mike turned quickly to his first assailant. His turns allowed him to pivot and block the first punch. Soon as the punch was blocked, a hard fist met the lower rib of his opponent. His opponent gave in to the pain where his floating rib rested. As the assailant gave way to the pain, Mike was able to direct his arm movement into an upward arc. It was a quick movement, and Mike's arm rammed under the armpit of his foe. His opponent began to rise off his feet. The arc upward assisted by the ramming arm allowed Mike to lead him into the next move. With a tuck and twist of Mike's hip, he pivoted, and this threw the foe high in the air and down into the other man who was fast approaching.

The oncoming man easily avoided the first man flying at him. Leaping into the air, he thrust out a side snap kick. Mike was still in the act of spinning when the kick was within striking range. Without a stop or hesitation in his flow of movement, Mike easily blocked and spun away from the kick. Continuing his spinning, Mike followed with a spinning back heel kick to his foe as the second man landed on the ground. Quickly his foe was barely able to prevent the hit. It grazed him on the shoulder, propelling him back off his feet. With his balance offset, Mike rushed forward with a barrage of kicks. The last kick made its mark. The second foe hit the ground. He remained there. The first attacker had now righted himself and prepared to return to the fight.

When the first assailant stood, he came within striking distance of Mike. Quickly, the first man shot out a kick, only to be blocked. Lindsey watched the man mysteriously bend over, reeling in pain from Mike's kick to his groin. Mike dropped to the ground, placing his foot kick halfway to its mark. Once Mike hit the ground, the kick closed the distance, finding its mark.

Lindsey saw Mike's incredible speed; his foot was at the assailant's groin the instant he touched on the ground. It was as if Mike knew in advance the other man was going to kick at him and fell to the ground waiting. With a rotating spin of his body, Mike was quickly back on his feet with both foes lying on the ground. The fight had ended.

Lindsey gasped at the sight of the attack, holding her hand to her mouth to keep quiet. She stood watching the scene unfold. Mike's speed was almost invisible to her eyes. At one point, it appeared the man fell down without Mike ever laying a hand on him.

Slowly a man emerged from a car across from the fight. This man was short and having a wiry appearance. He was dressed the same way as the two men attacking Mike. All wore black clothing. Walking over to Mike, Lindsey saw Mike turn to bow to him. The strange man stopped and returned a bow back to Mike.

The man suddenly disappeared. Mike picked up his backpack he put down when the two men ran out to attack him.

Lindsey stepped out from the nook near the ticket booth for patrons to buy drinks while waiting in line to get tickets. She stood there as Mike ran off. Never once did he look toward her direction. In reality, Mike was quite aware of her presence and decided not to let her know of his awareness for the present time. Lindsey walked to her car very shaken from what she saw. Before she unlocked the car, the strange man bowing to Mike suddenly appeared by her side.

The next day that followed, Mike was off duty. He went to class early. At the dojo, Sifu Cho met with him. This was typical after each night's escapades.

"Mike, we were not alone last night. Are you aware of that?"

"Yes, Sifu, I did have a feeling someone was watching me."

"Who do you think it was?" Sifu prodded.

Mike suggested, "Someone at the Rama must have stayed late."

"No, not the girl," Sifu responded. "I mean the other persons watching you."

"No, Sifu. Where were they?"

"Mike, I am afraid there are some players in our affairs you are not aware of."

Mike pondered what he wanted to say to Sifu. He did not want him involved with his troubles. Could it be that those gang members from Atlanta are still after him? He started thinking of the base trip with the balloons and earlier with the person asking questions at the ticket booth. *Hmm, maybe they are coming after me*, Mike began to wonder.

Sifu interrupted Mike's thought. "Do you know these other fellows I am talking about?"

After training with Sifu for several months, Mike became aware of Sifu's ability to see through any veil of deceit.

The dojo was a small room with many mirrors displayed on every wall except one. On that wall, racks of bo sticks and several bladed weapons were mounted. Along the front of the dojo was a row of chairs separated from the workout mat with a low rail.

Sifu and Mike found two seats in the corner to sit while they had a discussion on Mike's trouble. The sensei of the karate class worked with his other students while they talked.

"Okay, are you going to tell me who those two men watching you were, Mike?"

Well, Sifu Cho, I ran into some gang members while I traveled back home. I was helping this man. They were trying to rob him. He and I fought them off. I took off as soon as I helped him. They followed me to a wooded park. In the woods, I felt I had a chance to elude them, or if I had to fight, it gave me an advantage. Them being city boys and me, I been living off the land for nearly a year. I got to know some tricks, Sifu."

"I see. Go on, Mike."

"Well, they followed after me. What tricks I had learned came from the people I met on the way home. Many of them lived near or in the woods. I learned how to set snares, traps, bait fishing lines, start fire, clean water to drink, and track. I, as you might say, became woods smart," was Mike's reply.

Mike continues to explain. "I knew the plants to eat and the ones that are harmful. I even learned to avoid dangerous animals and to scare them off. I had several encounters with a few. I know what wild animals are capable of. I learned to survive in their world. Knowing the rules is important for survival."

"That is correct, Mike. In the city there are rules as well. To know those rules is as important for survival as those you learned in the woods."

"Yes, Sifu, I understand."

"What do you plan to do with them, these men who seemed to be trying to do you harm?"

"I am working on that. Right now, training with you is part of that plan."

"Hmm, this is good." Sifu stares away for a moment. It was as if he wanted to tell his student something, then thought another.

Sifu sat quiet for a long time before speaking again. "I have some news I need to share with you, Mike. In a few weeks, I will have to leave. I am not sure the duration I will be gone. I wish I could stay and aid you in this trouble."

"Thanks, Sifu, I appreciate the offer. I want you to know I am very grateful for all your interests in me and your willingness to take me as your student. I hope in dealing with this trouble that may come my way, I will do your training and the art honor." A short pause, then Mike continued. He had some concerns as maybe Sifu had when he heard his story.

"Sifu, this trouble, well, it's my trouble, and I'd rather not have your assistance. I don't want anybody to get hurt helping me. This trouble may become theirs later."

Looking back at Mike, staring deeply into his eyes, Sifu spoke. "I see your point. You will do me and the art great honor. Mike, this is your trouble. You are my chosen student. Any trouble you have has now become mine. Never forget this, we are forever bonded in this art and in life. Do not take what I say as simply talk, it is a shared bond in life and into death. It is the way you and I have chosen as our path together."

For the rest of the week, Mike asked Tad to be off work. Mike asked Sifu if he could train with him as long as he was here. They trained for many hours each day and at night. Sifu had him practice entirely in the dark. During karate class hours, the two would go in the back of the studio outside and train. After hearing what Sifu had told him, Mike felt a sense of truly belonging to something or someone who somehow was forever going to change his life.

The end of the week came quick. Sifu and Mike didn't train on that last day. Together they talked for several hours, walking about the yard they practiced in. When not in class behind the dojo, they would discuss many things. The yard was well concealed from any eyes. A tall six-foot wooden fence surrounded it.

Sifu offered Mike some advice. "Mike, remember not to let any foe fight their fight. Take the fight from them. You choose the ground. It will be your advantage over them. Choose the time. Separate them. Smaller groups are more manageable. Try to divide them. Fear and the unknown can cause much dissention among them. Don't be afraid to ask for help. Above all, set your traps for them ahead of any encounter. Always have an escape plan, then another escape plan."

Sifu Cho hammered home these concepts as if Mike was his own son.

"My last advice is to have several alternate plans. Remember this above all else."

"What is that, Sifu?"

"They intend to kill you. Strike first and hard. No second chances. No second chances." Sifu Cho knew Mike felt something with his last advice.

"Yes, Sifu, I think that lesson was well hammered into me. I surely won't forget that lesson."

"Good. I will let you know where you may contact me. Could be a while, Mike. Now, go and practice. I want cartwheels with a forward flip then a tuck and roll. Give me five laps then thirty minutes of six-inch punches. To end the session, finger jabs into that board until it breaks."

"With pleasure, Sifu Cho."

Mike immediately began his session.

Sifu watched for a few minutes then slid into the darkness. Mike finished his sessions. Sifu Cho had left.

HIDDEN PLANS

TAD WAS STANDING AT THE front door at the Rama. It was nearly six, and the afternoon show was still playing. A small man pulled into a parking spot in front of the theater riding on a large chopper-style bike. His bike was loud and had short forks. The man sitting on top of it caught Tad's attention. Wearing only a vest, his arms were covered with tattoos. Standing up, he removed his German-style helmet. It was shining like chrome. Before he turned around, he lay the helmet on the seat. As soon as he turned, Tad recognized him.

The familiar man slowly walked across the street and headed straight to Tad. Tad, seeing him approach, walked to him. They met at the curve. Tad extended his hand out. The man took hold, and together they greeted each other with a smile.

Speaking up first, Tad remarked to this familiar person, "I would never have thought you were the type to be riding a chopper. My name is Tad, and I am the assistant manager at the Rama Theater. What I can I do for you?"

"Glad to meet you, Tad. My name is Cho. I had explained a bit when we first had our discussion. I am a master of the lost art my father taught of a deadly martial art. Mike is my protégé and therefore of great interest to me. He has been selected to learn my art. Plans are set in motion to teach him far beyond any who have been taught this art. He is a very valuable person to me. When I saw you on that night, I didn't want to make it known at the time I noticed you.

"The other time you approached me, I had little choice. When the time was right, I had every intention of seeking you out. We need to have a serious conversation about Mike."

"Mike is running the projector at the moment. The picture will end in about ten minutes. He will be relieved by the evening projectionist. Would you like Mike to be present while we have this talk?"

"I prefer not to."

"Okay, why don't you walk up the stairs over by the ticket booth?" Tad pointed to where the door was. "Halfway up, turn into the aisle, and at the end is a door." Reaching into his pocket, Tad removed a ring of keys. Sorting through the key ring, he handed the key to Mr. Cho. "When I finish with this movie, Mike will come on for the evening shift. First, he will go home and change then eat, and by seven, he should return. Will that be enough time for this discussion, Mr. Cho?"

"More than enough time, Tad."

Before Mr. Cho walked to the door, Tad asked him if he would like a soda while he waited in the office.

"Sure."

Before he completed his sentence, Tad called over an usher. Gerry came over. Turning back to Mr. Cho, Tad asked him what he would like to drink. Cho said anything.

"Gerry, how about getting a large Coke for my friend, please."

"Yes, sir." Gerry went to the candy counter and asked Debbie for a large Coke. "Tad said he will pay."

Pretty Debbie handed the Coke to him.

Returning, Tad gave Gerry a quarter and a thanks. He hands it to Mr. Cho, who takes a drink then walks over to the side door.

Once he went through the door, Lindsey in the booth tried to get Tad's attention. She poked her hand out of the port hole where she received money for tickets to the show.

Seeing a hand waving at him, Tad walked over to the booth. "What you need, Lindsey?"

"Tad, who is that man?"

"He is a friend."

"A friend! Do you know what he did to Mike a few weeks past?"

Puzzled by her remarks, Tad asked, "What happened to Mike? When?"

"Well, I had to stay late. It was one of those nights when we had a huge crowd. I walked down the stairs, and before I walked through the door, I saw two men running toward Mike. I was about to yell at him to watch out. Before I could, Mike…Mike…he…he did this thing. The man tried to kick him."

Lindsey paused for a second, not sure if she should tell Tad. She was doubting he would believe what she was about to explain happened on that night. She kept quiet, not sure how or who she could tell. It upset her for many weeks. Seeing that man gave her the courage to address Tad.

Tad seemed to have known this man. Tad she trusted. She knew him for years.

"Go on, finish what you are going to tell me, Lindsey."

"Well, Tad, Mike seemed not to move. I finally realized later, he did move. It was the fastest thing I ever saw. He threw that man across the parking lot. He must have gone twenty feet in the air before he hit the ground. Then this other guy attacked. He hit that guy a million times, and that guy never laid a hand on him, except he tried to do so, but couldn't. After what he done to those two guys, this man, the same man you bought a Coke and gave the key to the office, he went over to Mike. He attacked Mike. Why'd you let him upstairs? Tad, you want me to call the police?"

"Lindsey, wait a second." Tad raised his arm to motion he was coming into the booth. He walked inside the lobby and knocked on her door.

Opening the door, Lindsey gave Tad a nasty look as he entered. Closing the door behind him, Tad puts his finger to his lips. "Lindsey, keep your voice down. What I am going to tell you must not be repeated to anyone. I mean no one must hear what I will tell you."

"Okay, Tad, I can do that. What's up?"

Tad stood looking at Lindsey sitting on her chair for a brief few seconds to determine how he should approach this matter to discuss with her.

"I talked to Mike a while back. I saw what you had seen. Mike had introduced that man to me on the second time I witnessed his fighting. He is Mike's karate teacher. What you witnessed Mike doing was part of his training."

"What's so secretive about that, Tad?"

"Well, from what Mike had told me, he is receiving this special training to prepare him for what is to come."

"Prepare him for what?" Lindsey was getting a bit upset with Tad's flimsy explanations. Her voice got a little louder with each question she posed to Tad. "That still doesn't explain to me about preparing him to do what, Tad?"

"That, Lindsey, I am not privileged to tell anyone at the moment. That is why I am asking you to say nothing to Mike if you see him. I will be upstairs talking to Mr. Cho. When I get down, I will tell you as much as I can from our discussion. That okay with you?"

"I guess that will have to do, Tad."

Tad walked out of the ticket booth at the time the movie let out. When most of the patrons were out the door, he called Gerry over. Gerry quickly came when called. Gerry always walked quickly, whether he was told to do something or was just going from one place to another. He moved about as his red flaming hair might predict he would, walking on fire.

Looking at this wiry kid before him, Tad had learned to rely on him. Gerry worked hard and was dependable. "Take the door. When you see Mike get down, tell him to go home and change. Have him come back at seven for the evening shows. I have important business to discuss with a person. Do not have anyone disturb me while I am upstairs, please."

"Will do, Tad."

Tad proceeded up the stairs to the office. Inside sat Mr. Cho in front of his desk. No sooner than Tad sat, Mr. Cho started to tell him a story about Mike.

"Tad, what I am going to tell you is important. The reasons for this secret to be kept will become evident to you. Mike, as I believe you to be aware of, is quite a young man. He works hard and is good at his job."

"Yes, he is. I gave him the doorman position because of his dependability and work ethic."

"Good, that is good, and this is why I will tell you what I am to reveal to you. How much do you know of Mike and his family?"

"Really not much. I do know he has two sisters and a mom. His dad died serving our country. They moved to Georgia to be near his mom's family."

"Let me fill you in on some of the things you don't know. His mom was nearly killed in an auto accident. He ran away from home. He did that because prior to the accident, he and his sisters had been placed in a foster home. He left believing they would have been sent to another foster home. After watching the auto hit his mom, another car ran over her. Then another car half ran over her again. All three kids felt that she was going to die. The mom's boyfriend took them and dumped them off in front of their home. For three days they remained in their home without anyone aware of the accident.

"One family next door discovered this from his sister. They took the sisters into their home. Mike, feeling this was a prelude to going to a foster home, took off. He lived on the beach eating any food left by swimmers. He slept under the pier at night. When it got too cold, he covered himself with sand to bear the freezing winds coming off the ocean at night.

"Later, he somewhat got adopted by the carnie people. He did odd jobs for food. Walking around the town, he discovered a martial school. Watching the class, he would practice for hours on the beach. One day, the sensei of the school became aware of him spying. Impressed with his skill, he offered to train him. Mike worked hard around the dojo. Soon, this sensei provided special training before class and after class.

"One night, as Mike had told me, Sensei found him sleeping in the back of his school. He offered Mike a place to sleep. He did so, knowing if he did otherwise, Mike would take off.

"Apparently, the police stopped by one day to inquire if he knew of any boy alone on the street. Mike witnessed this meeting. Believing his sensei had called the police, Mike took off. He left a short note behind. Unable to find Mike, Sensei got very worried for the boy.

"Mike went back to his home to see if his family was still there or to find out if any of his friends knew anything. That was when he discovered his mom was alive. He was afraid to go to the police, still feeling they might put him into a foster home. All he knew was his mom left, and nothing about his sisters was mentioned."

Tad was about to ask a question.

Mr. Cho raised his hand. "Tad, allow me to finish this story. Did you ever read a story about a year ago concerning a kid walking home from Virginia to Georgia?"

Tad nodded. "I think I remember a story on that. Wasn't that kid attacked by a bear and bitten by a poisonous snake? I think it mentioned some other horrible things that happened to him before he finally reached home."

"Exactly, but there is more to that story you were not told in the article."

"Wait a minute, are you telling me Mike was that kid, Mr. Cho?"

"Mr. Cho nodded back in agreement."

"My god, that boy was clawed by a bear and had these deep wounds as scars for a reminder. Wasn't there something about being lashed by a whip?"

"Yes, Tad."

"Oh yes, that monster alligator he killed and eating worms and bugs."

"Yes, all those things happened. He learned to live off the land from people he met on his journey. How to catch fish with his hands, make and set traps, identify plants he could eat and to avoid. He traveled through the woods and learned how to evade pursuers and trap animals. When he entered a town, he would scavenge trash cans for food, collect soda bottles to sell to buy food. He always went behind restaurants or fast-food joints to get work or dig in the dumpsters. Do you know what he told me many of the people did when he asked for work to eat, Tad?"

"What?"

"Some of the young people that work at these fast-food places found it funny to spike Mike's food with food that fell on the floor. Some even dip the food they gave him in a commode or spit on it.

Those were our so-called good Christians kids you find in a small town. They were bored and entertained themselves with silly pranks. Mike knew this because they often would tell him when they started laughing while he ate the food offered him for work he'd done. He told me this, Tad, he ate the food knowing what they did."

Tad's face became distorted from the thought of anyone eating food that had been trashed.

"He ate the food because he was too hungry not to eat it. He went in towns when he got pretty hungry. Tad, that kid, Mike, he survived. Instead of filling himself with hate, he learned to love. It was because of all those other people who was there for him. When he was whipped, a family took him in, nursing him back to health. When he was attacked by a bear, he did that to save a man he just met from being killed. That man took him into his home. The townspeople treated him like a hero. The townspeople were all black folks. A woman nursed him after a snakebite. She later taught him to hunt and work on a farm while he stayed there.

"Tad, there many stories I can tell you about Mike. These are but a few, and what I am going to tell you is the thing not written down or maybe what Mike has never told anyone but a few people."

Tad sat there thinking about Mike's adventures and how little he knew about him. His eyes stared at Mr. Cho. Never an eye blinking was seen looking at Tad face. He was so entranced from the story Mr. Cho was telling him to blink.

Speaking softly, Mr. Cho startled Tad back to the conversation. Mr. Cho began the story of what was not told.

"Tad, this is the reason I need you to keep quiet about it. Mike is a strong person. You know understand how strong. He is also a very caring person. He cares so much, he remained and took care of her. A total stranger she was to him. She was very much alone in her home. Her children rarely visited her. She was very old. Tad, she was dying. She had weeks to live. She knew that. She didn't want to die alone. Mike felt this without her saying a word to him.

"A neighbor came by one day telling Mike about her condition. He could have left and not remain there. He been through the agony of his father's death and what he believed to be his mom's death. Death is painful to the ones having to go through with loved ones.

"He chose to remain by her side. He held her hand as she lay in bed. She called him by her dead husband's name. He stayed there holding her hand. A smile crossing her lips, she passed in peace as her last breath left her. He was holding her hand. Mike cried after her passing. He loved her. Her children were called days before her final passing. They arrived two days later.

"Mike saved the life of that newspaper man as you were told. What you might not know is that the gang that attacked them followed after Mike. Throughout Atlanta they trailed after him. He led them into a wooded park. By nightfall, they were on his trail leading into the park.

"Mike learned many skills, I recounted to you. He set some traps and false trails to lead them through. He lay waiting for three big men to come get him. Did you know he had a fractured ankle? With an injured foot he waited. They came.

"He had begun a fire for them to spot. They did. They followed his false trail into the woods. It was night and dark in the woods. The fire was about the only thing those three gang members could see. The trail led them through briars and poison ivy. After fighting through the tangled mass of plant, they were scratched from head to toe. Seeing the fire was their only relief as they neared. Silently in the dark of night, they crawled up the hill.

"Before they reached the summit, a cloud of smoke had descended from the hilltop. Soon eerie sounds were heard. Animal sounds. Bear sounds. Mike wore a jacket with a bear head. It was the skin of that bear he killed. He wore gloves made from the claws of that bear. He howled loud like a bear. They screamed, afraid of it being a bear coming at them. They believed it was truly a bear attacking them. In a way, it was, Tad."

Tad sat there totally mesmerized by Mr. Cho's story. It had been nearly half an hour past the time Tad sat down.

"Mike attacked, clawing at the first of his pursuers. He screamed and was thrown back into the others. This went on with each of the gang members. They left those woods screaming about a monster bear attacking them. That was in the police report the officer recanted, placing them into custody leaving the park.

"Those three gang members broke loose from the officer before he had time to take them to jail. Those three returned last year to this town. They were looking for Mike."

Tad's face spoke volumes of all the questions that he wanted answering. He sat there in his seat as Cho requested and remained silent.

"Yes, Tad, they located him. They tracked him back to his home. They were about to break into his home. His mom was at work, but his two sisters were there. They carried knives and guns. It was their intentions to slay all in Mike's family. Him too, if he was there.

"Mike was with members of our group. They were passing through town at the same time those three came to your town. They met up with Mike on the corner street from his home. Our leader was taking him to his home.

"He told our leader to stop seeing those three trying to break into his home. Leaping off the bike, charging at the leader man of the gang. He had his knife drawn. With a leap, Mike landed on the leader man's back, driving his knife into his arm. Struggling with Mike and unable to throw him off, he pulls a gun. Our leader just finished off the second gang member and returned to where Mike was fighting with the leader man.

"The gun went off, and the bullet meant for Mike wounded our leader's girlfriend. If it wasn't for Mike's quick reaction, she would have been killed. Mike removed his knife from the gang's leader man's arm, then quickly drove it into his foot. He saw the leader man aim his gun at our leader knowing that the gang member's attention would turn back to him. This left Mike at a great disadvantage. In removing the knife, the gang leader man could swivel and aim his gun at Mike. He did just that. Our leader got there quick before the trigger was pulled a second time. The gang leader man swirled to shoot at him, missing our leader.

"I was asked to come here by my leader. I came to check this boy out. I was impressed right off. I knew seeing him, he was the exact person I was seeking to train. My leader told me what to expect.

"Tad, Mike and his family are poor. They are made poorer by his mom's drinking. They have little food in the house. Mike worked to help bring money in to buy food. This family has very little but pride to sustain them.

"I learned from Bell, my leader's girlfriend, that they often go hungry. Mike rarely eats food in the home. He gives what food to his sisters."

"Hmm, that explains his devouring boxes of popcorn. I figured Mike would burn out like others after the first few weeks eating popcorn."

"I was sent by our leader to help train Mike to defend himself. Just in case the gang from Atlanta decided to return. We sent them a message, and we soon realized they didn't get our message to cease attack on Mike. They ignored it and by our recon was going ahead with what they intended to do, whether or not what we told them would happen to them if they did continue their attack on him.

"When I was training Mike, on the fourth engagement after work here at the Rama, I became aware of two individuals watching Mike. It happened again, and this time Mike became aware of their presence.

"Part of his training is to make his senses more acute. He can sense things and people when most people cannot even become aware. His speed and power I have been developing. He is stronger than most his age, probably more so than those larger and older. Many of his fighting skills are from a secret art rarely known in the west.

"When I came to this country as a youth, my father was a master in this little-known art. Before my father was killed, I became a master. I avenged his death. In doing so, I went to jail. Getting out of jail, I went into the service. I met many of the bikers in Nam. It was this gang leader asking me to join their club. They have become like family to me. Mike has been adopted into my family. Therefore, we will protect him. The problem is we are currently experiencing some problems that need to be dealt with. I will not be here for him."

Sifu Cho paused. Tad saw he had more to tell him. Something he decided was not the time.

"Mike will not want my help, as you are now aware of how he feels. His friends are important to him. He will protect them. If dangers come to him, he will leave here before anyone gets involved or hurt. This is a true thing. This place is like a family to him. While he is here, I feel he will be safe. They would never attack him while he is here, but if he leaves here and they can get him alone, well…that."

"Yeah, I understand. What about his family?" Tad asked.

"I hope they won't attack them. I feel they are not out of this danger. They want Mike bad, Tad."

"Does Mike know this?"

"Like I said, Tad, Mike has all his senses developed beyond a normal person's senses. He knows."

"What can I do?"

"I'm glad you asked me what you can do and not what you want me to do. That shows me I can depend on you, Tad. Now, before you make the decision to help, I must tell you one thing. Mike's uncle was slain. A young punk shot him in the front yard. We believe strongly that the punk was given a contract to kill Mike's uncle. This gang means business. Mike does not know of this. I believe he suspects much he has not said to me."

Ted remembered reading in the paper of a man he knew, Dat. Hearing this from Master Cho was another shock to him. After a short pause, Tad gave Cho his response. "Anything, Mr. Cho."

"If Mike should leave quick without telling you, something is going down. Mike will not tell you this. You must be able to see the signs. When they happen, call us. If we are near, we will help. If not, call the law. Get them to his home fast. Anything unusual could be a sign of trouble. I guess it is not necessary for me to tell you not to say a word to him?"

Tad nodded to this acknowledgment. "I will need to let a few people know to contact you when I am not here. They will be sworn to not mention any of this to anyone."

"Then we have an understanding, Tad."

"We do, Mr. Cho."

Mr. Cho, satisfied with talking to Tad and given his assurances, got up to leave. Tad stood as well, and they shook hands.

Walking down the stairs out the side door, Mr. Cho walked over to his bike. Starting it up, he placed his helmet on his head and, with a roar from the bike, drove across the parking lot, then down the street to nowhere.

Tad stood there as Mr. Cho rode off. The theater was empty. Gerry was heard sweeping the aisles. Vic arrived and got a broom and said hello to Tad and the girls coming in to replace the girls from the previous shift.

Lindsey stood by the open ticket booth waiting for Tad to enter. "Okay, now, what's the story? What is going on, Tad?"

"Lindsey, you need to promise me. I mean, a person might get hurt, really hurt if you tell anyone." Tad stood looking hard at Lindsey. Worry, fear, and hurt filled his face.

"Dang, Tad, how bad is this?"

"You need to promise me or forget this. Which will it be?"

Lindsey took a long pause. Speaking softly, Lindsey asked Tad, "If you tell me this, will I get hurt?"

"No, I don't believe that could happen. But you will know what I tell you, if you agree to promise me never to say a word to anyone. It can help save a person from great harm. Lindsey, if you must know, then I need your promise."

"Tad, that makes me scared."

"Then, Lindsey, don't ask. But know this, I will need to inform someone to assist me."

Lindsey hesitated, but then steeled herself. "Okay, I promise, Tad."

"You sure now? This is a great responsibility you will have. I mean, no one is to know. You sure you are fine with that?"

"Yes."

"Lindsey, why not think on this for a day or two."

"No, I won't need to do that, Tad. I spent weeks with this thought of the fight I saw, and it has made me worried not telling someone. Now that I know, it feels good, and I want to help, really, Tad."

Tad spent the next twenty minutes retelling a brief part of the story Mr. Cho had told him.

Mike came in the front door.

"Are you telling me Mike, our Mike, has this special training from this master of some ancient martial arts? He can do all those amazing things I saw him do and more, Tad? That explains all the bruising I've seen on his hands. I asked him why they were bruised. He said he was practicing and got hit a lot."

"Yes, Lindsey, more. This Mr. Cho has also taught him some weapon skills. Mike already had a good background in the martial arts.

He has excelled in this specialized art. His training has been extremely rough on his mind and body. His training is far from over, but it will continue. Mike has achieved an ability to use all his senses beyond any normal persons.

"Mr. Cho explained to me that Mike can hear, smell, feel, taste, and see more keener than any person. His senses allow him to know what is all around him. He hears things people whisper softly far off. He can taste without putting food in his mouth. His sense of smell allows him to smell living creatures approach. Mike has become more than anything we can comprehend."

"If Mike can sense all these things, won't he tell if we are aware of his skills?"

"Lindsey, he might or will know of our involvement. If he doesn't, then he will surely suspects something. Mike, I was assured, will not pry into our involvement because he wants us not to know.

"Lindsey, Mr. Cho told me Mike considers us like part of his family. He has an extremely strong nurturing attitude. He will do anything to protect us from danger. One day if danger comes, he will disappear quickly to draw that danger away from the Rama."

"What kind of danger are you talking about, Tad?"

"Lindsey, I will tell you this, and you must not tell anyone. Mike apparently made enemies of some gang in Atlanta. They have been after him for a year. Before he started to work here, his family was attacked by this gang. Mike stopped the attack along with some of Mr. Cho's members. Mike stabbed the leader. He is the one who has it in for him. He promised to kill Mike. This isn't something said out of being mad. He really intends to kill Mike."

"Tad, what do those gang members from Atlanta look like?"

"Lindsey, they wear a bandana and have tattoos covering their arms. Usually, a red or blue T-shirt. Every one of them will have their hair cut short, even the girls."

"Tad." Lindsey paused, then she repeated, "Tad," pausing again. Finally, she blurted out, "Tad, I saw two of those gang members when Mike, I mean, when I saw Mike fight. But, Tad, that wasn't the first time I saw them."

"Huh, when?"

"Well, it had been a while back, I told Mike about someone asking about him. I…I'm pretty sure from your description that was them."

"Mr. Cho said they had been aware of them keeping tabs on Mike. Like he told me, all we can do for now is to keep an eye open. If we cannot get into contact with Mr. Cho, he mentioned someone will take his place until he can return. Mr. Cho told me he would tell that person to drop by and introduce himself to us. He might dress different than Mr. Cho.

"So, Lindsey, if someone wants to talk to me, it might be that man. I will have him meet with you as well."

"Tad, do you know when?"

"No, Lindsey, I don't. Soon is all I can tell you at the moment."

CREEPY CRAWLY
THING IN BED

O NE WEEK PASSED BY, AND no one dropped by the Rama. Mike came to work as usual. He greeted the doorman, which was either Gerry or Rusty. A new usher was hired. He was tall and rather good-looking. Rusty broke him in.

Mike entered the lobby and walked over to the candy counter to get his mixed soda with a tad of orange soda splashed on top. He would always ask the girl behind the candy bar to mix extra oil in the popcorn. The extra oil made for a more buttery popcorn.

Rusty and Mike would often talk by the ticket can. This night, both of them were discussing their night before frolicking.

"Hey, Mike, when you came by my house to get me the other night for that little raid at the bowling alley, my mom thought you were very good-looking. My sister did too. You made a good impression on the both of them."

"Gee, thanks, Rusty. How is it going with that girl you like so much at school?"

"Well, Mike…" Rusty turned his head down to not tell Mike about why he hadn't asked the girl out.

"I see, you still haven't asked her to go out on a date, huh?"

"Well, I was, but…"

"But, but, but, Rusty. Look, you got nothing to lose by asking. The only thing she could say is no. You get your feelings hurt. Then you cry a lot. Curse me for getting you to ask her, then kill yourself. So get it over with. I'm getting tired of you moping about her."

"Yeah, you're right, I'll do it, Mike."

"Good, the next time I see you, you better not tell me you chickened out. I'll make you wish you had."

"What are you gonna do?" Rusty curiously inquired Mike.

"You'll know, Rusty, when you show up and not ask her.

"Ahh, come on, man."

"Sorry, put up or shut up, Rusty."

Vic came out the auditorium door and saw Rusty and some other guy. Rusty heard a door open and the movie playing turns and spies. Vic was coming from the inside.

"Mike, here comes the new guy."

Turning, Mike saw a tall guy walk over to him.

"Vic, this is the doorman, Mike."

"Rusty, I thought you were the doorman?"

"Only when Tad or Mike is not here. Mike's head doorman and in charge."

Mike turned to face Vic. "Rusty, you break him in?" inquired Mike, extending his hand to Vic. "Will you be working with me tonight, Vic?"

"Mike, I took him around showing him all the stuff. He may need some further instructions," answered Rusty.

"Only for a half hour, then I'm off," replied Vic to Mike's question.

"You know any good jokes, Vic? We about ran through all the ones we had. The girls love it when we tell jokes during the slow days."

Vic replied, "I got a few."

"Good," Mike answered.

He walked Vic over to the counter. Debbie was behind it along with a new girl. Mike introduced Debbie to Vic. "Vic, this is Debbie, the prettiest girl at your school, and this girl is Marcie, the prettiest at my school."

"Yes, I met them," Vic answered quickly.

"Vic tells me he has some jokes to share with us."

"Good, I'm tired of those old jokes everybody repeats all the time," remarked Debbie.

"I don't feel comfortable telling dirty jokes being new on the job," replied Vic.

"Oh," Debbie sighed. "Come on, Vic, just one." Debbie could smile her way into a yes from any boy.

"That's okay, Vic, wait till I tell them what happened last night to me. It was the scariest thing that ever happened to me."

"Really, Mike?" Marcie asked.

Lindsey heard Mike say that to the candy bar girls and opened her door to listen in.

"Hey, I want to hear this myself, Mike. Wait for me to finish up with this man at the door," called Rusty. Rusty went to the ticket box, taking the patron's ticket, then waved to Mike to start telling his scary story.

Since the time Lindsey and Tad had their discussion about Mr. Cho, two new girls were hired. Marcie was the girl working with Rusty when the other new girl came walking in.

"Hi, everybody."

Everybody turned to see who said hi, and they all watched this thin, short, feisty red-haired girl stroll through the main door.

"Welcome to the Rama," all three boys said simultaneously. Mike, Rusty, and Vic walked over to her by the door. She walked through the door after the two patrons entered and Rusty had walked to the candy bar counter to listen to Mike's scary story. She stopped as they approached.

Mike spoke first. "Hi, my name is Mike, I'm the doorman. While you are working, anything you need, just let me know."

"Thanks, Mike."

"Hey, I'm Vic. I' m new here. I am the new usher."

Rusty was last. He just offered her his hand to shake.

The girl looked at the three young men who impatiently approached her and smiled to all three of them. "Hi, my name is Wanda." Looking around, she asked Mike if Tad was going to be at the Rama that night.

"Sorry, Wanda, you are stuck with me. I'm in charge. What can I help you with?"

"Oh." Looking at Mike, she echoed, "You are in charge?"

"Yes," Mike replied.

"Nothing, I thought he was going to introduce me around."

"I'll be doing that tonight. Right now, you are in the middle of the first show ending and a shift change. Go get behind the candy bar. Debbie will show you what needs to be done. The rest of you need to tend the doors. Rusty, you're going to stay and lend a hand in the auditorium."

Rusty replied, "I got nothing to do, Mike."

The movie ended with about twenty people walking out. Once the movie house emptied, Mike closed the two main doors. Lindsey took the money upstairs. The girls cleaned the popper and countertops. Any restock Mike took care of, and Rusty helped Vic sweep the aisles.

Ronald walked in. He was the other new usher hired a week ago. He was the tallest usher Rama had working. Thin as a rail, wearing horn-rimmed glasses. His hair had a Beatles-style cut. He was shy and rarely was seen out of the auditorium when he came to work.

Mike motioned to Ronald to grab a broom and go to the aisles. After refilling the stock for the candy bar girls, it was time to reopen the main doors. Lindsey was down within minutes from upstairs. Donna took her place behind the ticket booth.

Lately, the Rama went through a string of new people coming and going. Sometimes this was the case. Only Mike, Melvin, Ric, Gerry, and Rusty, were the old hats still there. Lindsey was a permanent fixture. Debbie and Anne remained. Connie, Marcie, and Wanda were the new girls.

Ric hadn't the opportunity to ply his antics on them as of late. Mike got one of the new girls a week ago with a prank. She was a good sport about the prank and quickly learned from the other girls how to get even. She hadn't the chance of late. This night was her first opportunity to get even with Mike. This night might offer Mike another opportunity to break in the second new girl before Ric had the chance. Everything was set for some comeuppance to fall.

Once the main door was opened, two people were in line. Rusty stood near Vic and Ronald, having walked over to where they were waiting for the ticket buyers to enter. "You guys need to watch this," Rusty told Vic and Ronald.

The two people handed Mike their tickets. With one hand, he tore the tickets in half. The young man took his two stubs and asked Mike how he did that with one hand.

"See?" Rusty yipped out to the other ushers watching. "Mike can tear the two tickets together with one hand."

"It takes a lot of practice," Mike answered the patron.

Not happy with that answer, they walked on in, stopping at the candy bar counter. Turning around, the boy asked when the show starts.

Mike remarked back, "In about ten minutes."

He turned and ordered popcorn and two sodas before entering the auditorium.

Vic hurried over to where Mike stood. He was curious how he could tear the two tickets with one hand.

Rusty walked over. "I see, Mike, you got a new devotee to teach how to tear tickets with one hand."

Vic, impatient to see Mike repeat what he saw earlier, butted in on Rusty's sniping at him. "Hey, Mike, let me try that?" Vic asked.

"Sure, Vic," Mike replied. Mike put his hand in the torn ticket can and retrieved several torn ticket stubs. "Here, Vic." He handed him two stubs.

Vic tried but was unable to tear one stub. Mike had four stubs in his hand. Taking the four stubs, he placed them between the crook of his middle finger and thumb, easily tearing all four. Then he went through the ticket can, handing Vic another stub, showing Vic his technique.

"Go ahead and try all you want, Vic, no one has been able to do it."

"I will," Vic responded to Rusty's jiving.

"I'm leaving Mike," Rusty told him.

Before Rusty left, Mike reminded him of the story he was going to share with them of the scariest thing that happened to him last night.

"Dang, I forgot about that."

Looking out the door, no patrons were coming. Mike walked over to the candy counter. Lindsey stayed as well. Vic quit after several tries and walked over to the counter along with Rusty.

Mike, seeing the disappointment on Vic's face, told him, "Vic, give it a break, I will show you later. You can practice anytime, okay?"

"Okay, Mike, I will hold you to that promise."

"Okay, Mike, we all stayed to hear this scary story, so tell us," Lindsey smartly demanded.

"Hey, no one's forcing you to stay. I'll tell it to you another day if you are in such a hurry to go."

"No, no, I'm not. Go ahead and tell us, Mike.

All the girls were at the countertop along with all the ushers remaining.

"Okay, last night when I went to bed, my dog Boo usually sleeps on my chest. Everything normal this night. I quickly fell into a deep sleep. Nothing happening. Suddenly, I was woken by this tapping on my head. Well, at first, I thought it was a dream. You all had a dream when suddenly you woke up? Something caused you to wake?"

"Get on with it, Mike," Anne retorted.

"Okay," replied Mike. "If you're going to tell a story, one has got to take their time. The details are important. If I leave them out, it causes you to miss some important facts. Now listen carefully. What I am about to tell you, I will drop some hints. Those hints will give you clues. See if you can figure out what happened. I didn't until my sister told me later that day what she witnessed. It scared the heck out of her when she removed everything on my bed."

"Okay, Mike, get on with it."

"Okay, Lindsey, you are so impatient."

Now Lindsey's face was clearly getting a bit upset with Mike slowly prodding along. The popper was going full blast popping corn.

"Let me see, where was I? Oh yeah, as I was saying." Mike continued at a slightly faster pace. "Boo, my dog, was still lying on my chest. Apparently, he wasn't disturbed from whatever hit me on the head. I shut my eyes thinking it was my imagination or a dream. No sooner than I was near fully asleep, it happened again. This time it was a much harder hit on my head."

Looking at all of them listening to him, Mike knew he had them hooked. Mike slowed down a bit, knowing full well Lindsey would soon be biting at the bit again to urge him along. "Whatever it was that hit me the second time, I sat up in bed immediately. I reached around the dark room, feeling for anything in the bed with me. Boo was a tiny bit upset being woken from his sleep a second time.

"I pulled my pillow around and held it up, shaking it back and forth. I reached inside the pillowcase, nothing. Satisfied nothing was in my bed with me, I lay back down, covering myself with my blanket. I lay in bed with both my eyes wide open, staring into the night at my ceiling. It took me several minutes before I was asleep again.

"You know when you try to keep your eyes open in the dark, not wanting to close them to sleep? Well, the more you try to keep them open, the more they just want to close on you. Hey guys, remember that when you have a hard time trying to sleep. Just lie in bed trying to keep your eyes open, they will shut in no time," Mike explained.

Lindsey was getting beet red when Mike looked at her.

Before Mike could continue, someone was at the ticket booth. Connie went into the booth.

"Well, continue, Mike." Lindsey nudged him.

"Wait a second, I got to take their tickets," replied Mike.

Four people came in, and after Mike tore their tickets, they marched over to the candy counter. Ronald ran over to the auditorium door, holding it open while they walked through.

Mike motioned to Ronald to walk in with them to light their way to their seats. Mike could see his "Aw, shucks" look across his face. Calling back to him, Mike told Ronald he would wait for him. It didn't take long for him to return.

"Wanda, fill me a box of that hot popcorn, please."

Wanda quickly filled Mike's box that he hadn't had the chance to fill since coming to work. "Here. Now, any other thing you need so we can hear your story?" asked the candy girls clearly biting to hear Mike's story.

Mike shook his head. "No, nothing else," he said, shoving popcorn in his mouth. Still chewing on the first gulp of popcorn, he was interrupted.

"Tell us your story," Wanda demanded.

Mike swallows his partly chewed popcorn before continuing. "Okay, now I was sleeping for the third time, and it happened a third time. Each time it felt, whatever it was, was hitting me harder. Apparently, I didn't get the message whatever it was trying to tell me."

"What? What happened next, Mike?" Rusty and Pretty Debbie were now getting frustrated with him delaying the story.

"Dang, where was I," Mike quipped out after their outburst. "Oh, I screamed out to my mom. The third time when it hit me, I was ready. I reached up and grabbed my head when it hit. I could feel it under my hand moving around. I had it. Mom, hearing me scream, rushed in my bedroom. 'Quick, Mom!' I told her to turn on the lights."

Everyone was glued listening to the story.

Mike paused for a minute to eat more popcorn. Munching on his second handful, he raised his drink and took a swallow along with his last mouthful of corn.

"There I was." Mike began anew, "sitting on my bed with this thing under my hand, wiggling. My mom stood by my bed looking down at me with a question written across her face. 'What is it?' she cried. 'Why did you scream?'

"All I could tell my mom was, 'I got it, I got it.' Mom asked, 'Got what, Mike?' 'I got that thing that kept hitting my head tonight.' I can tell you this, she was getting upset that there was something in our house attacking me in my bed," Mike explained to his now growing more frustrated audience.

"Of course, my mom wanted to see what I had under my hand, so I slowly and carefully slid my hand down off my head." Mike had now begun to demonstrate with his hands his actions in bed. Mike slowly slid his hands down and slammed them both on the countertop.

Everyone jumped back. One of the candy girls shrieked from the suddenness of his quick motion and the loud thunderous smack of his hand on the countertop. He got the intended reaction he was looking for. Everyone jumped and some screamed. Then everyone took a deep breath.

Looking back up to the listeners, Mike continued, "I was pretty sure it didn't get away. I could still feel it wiggling. Even Boo was curious and had jumped off the bed due to my hands slamming down on my bed, and he now had jumped back on. Boo sniffed around my hand.

"'Okay,' I told my mom, 'be prepared in case it jumps up at us.' She slowly nods back." Mike looked at the listeners and asked, "Do you know what it was?"

There came a string of nos.

"No, dang it." Lindsey was the third no from those who spoke up and clearly upset with the pace of the story being told.

"When I raised my hand, under it was a finger."

A puzzlement swept the faces of everyone standing around Mike.

"A what?" cried out Connie, still sitting in the booth.

Lindsey replied, "He said it was his finger."

"Your finger hit you?" remarked Rusty. "Is that all?"

"No, no," Mike replied. "Remember what I told you all at the beginning that my sister was scared silly when she cleaned my bed? She saw what it really was. After that finger in my hand I was holding onto, I realized my arm must have went to sleep and jerked, hitting my head. I fell back to sleep.

"The next day my older sister went into my room after hearing what my mom and I told her. She pulled everything off the bed. Not until the bed had nothing left on it did she see the thing. It crawled up from the headboard. She screamed when it suddenly popped up. She had her hand near where it appeared. She ripped the mattress sheets off, throwing them to floor."

"What was it? Come on tell us, please tell me, Mike."

All were in Mike's grip. He had them at his mercy. Should he eat another mouthful of popcorn or tell them before they kill him?

Looking at their faces, he decided to tell them quickly. He had strung them along long enough.

"My sister jerked her hand back, falling back against the wall. We ran into the room to see her frozen with fear. She pointed down on the bed. We turned and looked down. That thing wasn't afraid. It just lay there on that box spring staring at the three of us.

"It was the biggest one I ever saw. Thinking about that night lying there in my bed, darkness all around, and that creature coming out below my bed hitting me on my head. Not once or twice, but three times. Thinking that was in my bedroom all this time. It caused me to think twice before I ever want to sleep in my bed again," Mike said with a shudder to his listeners.

At this moment, Mike looked into the eyes of his fellow workers. He could see the rage rising up in each of them. Mike knew he better tell them soon. He enjoyed running a story along, dragging out the climax.

"It was ugly, long, nasty looking. Just thinking that was in my bed with me gave me the creeps," Mike conveyed to all of them. "When you go to sleep, I will advise each of you to double-check your beds because that was the biggest, I mean the *biggest*, roach have I ever seen."

"Roach? Roach? It was a roach?" screamed Lindsey.

Connie called out, "What was it?"

Lindsey screamed back to her, "It was a giant roach!"

Rusty shrugged, making a queasy sound. Most of the girls gasped.

"Where did it come from?" Vic asked.

"Well, the only place I thought of it coming from was my window. I leave it cracked open. One of those palmetto roaches crawled into the window when I left it opened. I closed the window in the morning. Well, it got stuck in my room," Mike explained. "It had to be ten inches at least, I believe."

"I'm leaving on that," Rusty said, walking out the door.

"Me too," followed Lindsey, leaving.

"I am not ever going to sleep at night," Wanda remarked.

"Me too," said Connie.

Mike couldn't help but tell all of them, "Don't let the bedbugs bite."

* * *

Next time Mike saw Rusty, the first question he asked him was, "Did you ask her out?"

Rusty stood and looked right at Mike. A smile came across his face. Not one word was said.

"You did, and she accepted to go out with you! See, I told you, Rusty."

"My first date is this Friday, Mike."

"Yeah, Rusty! Where you taking her?"

"Here, where else, Mike?"

"Fantastic, we will finally get to see this girl you been tied into knots by." Walking over to the ticket booth, Mike poked his head in to tell Lindsey the news. She in turn opened the door leading into the candy counter and informed the girls working.

Rusty looked at Mike. He turned to see Rusty looking at him. "Why'd you go and tell them for?"

"Hey man, I'm proud of you, Rusty."

"I guess it's okay, Mike. I just didn't want to listen to all the stuff they're going to ask me."

"What are friends for, my man?"

"Hey, Mike, you know the bowling arena incident we went on a few days ago?"

"Yeah, Rusty, that almost got us put into jail. I haven't told anyone about that. Especially big-mouth Ric. He would have loved being part of that prank. Too bad he was off that night."

"It's all around the school what happened. Somehow our names have been mentioned concerning what happened."

"Really, how? Oh, I guess all those people who came outside to watch the explosion must have passed what happened to others, and they passed it on to their friends."

Vic showed up and heard part of the conversation. "Mike, Rusty, you mean that it was you two that did that."

People were lining up to enter the show. It was a good movie showing, and the line started early. It reached nearly halfway up the sidewalk of the shopping center. Tad was by the road doing a walking count with his counter.

"Shh, Vic, we need to be careful talking about that prank."

"Why? Everyone at school is talking about it."

"Well, we nearly were thrown into jail, Vic," Rusty explained.

"Not to worry, if they were going to, then they would have. They got no evidence. Yeah, we got rid of what was left," replied Mike. "The police searched our car but couldn't enter without a permit. Since nothing was visible on inspection, they let us go, Vic."

"Yeah, I was scared silly, Vic," Rusty responded after what Mike said.

"So was I, Rusty. That was too close," Mike retorted.

"Okay, okay, we can talk later. Now, we need to get ready for the onslaught. Rusty, you and Vic be ready to aid people with their drinks and corn to their seats. I got the door to man. Hey girls, you got everything you need?"

Connie, Wanda, and Marcie had the candy bar for the showing. Connie called out, "Mike, we can use some extra Coke. One of the dispensers has a lot of CO_2 coming out instead of cola."

Pointing to Vic, Mike called to him to get some Coke from the back room. Vic rushed to the storeroom and grabbed a carton, taking it to the counter.

"Vic, take it inside and dump it in the fountain for the girls. They are pretty busy with boxing popcorn and filling drinks," commanded Mike.

Lindsey, working the ticket booth, poked her head out the door. "Mike, they are forming a line at the soda counter outside. Tell the girls they need to open the window and begin selling drinks before we begin selling tickets."

Going over to the counter, Mike told them to open the window and take orders.

Wanda asked Mike, "I didn't know we sell drinks out the window."

Mike replied, "You mean no one told you we do that?"

"Nope."

"Me neither," cited the other girls.

Responding to their query, Mike told them, "Girls, we do, and one of you will need to tend the window. So choose one between yourselves. I'll go outside and have them form a line."

"We surely don't need a pileup. Makes it a bit confusing selling tickets and tending to their hands full of drinks," Lindsey told the girls, poking her head out of the ticket booth into the candy counter.

Tad returned to the main door. Mike met him under the marquee. "Mike, we are going to have to open the balcony."

"Tad," Mike responded back, "we only have two ushers. Can you call for another? Wait." Mike thought of another still at the Rama. "Gerry hasn't left yet, Tad. He went upstairs to talk to Melvin. I'll go up and ask him to stay on. You fine with that, Tad?"

"Go get him," replied Tad.

Mike was up the stairs like a shot. Gerry agreed to stay the night. Returning downstairs, Mike walked over to Tad. "He will work the balcony."

"Good."

"Anytime you ready Tad, I am," Mike told him.

Tad opened the main door. All the people who bought a ticket were standing in one line, and those not having a ticket in a second line. A third line was at the candy window outside. This was the time when the lobby can get pretty crowded. The ushers were on their toes. Each usher quickly assisted customers with their purchases into the auditorium seats, returning to assist others.

Mike was busy tearing tickets with both hands. He could move the people into the theater faster than any other. Often Tad would call him over to back him up prior to him becoming the doorman.

Ric dropped by to discuss some outing. He was quickly put to work. It was going to be like that for the next couple of weeks with this movie.

One night when the crowds were getting smaller, they still had most of the ushers and girls working.

After the last show began, Mike came up with an idea. "Hey guys, since we are all here, why don't we get together at the new Pizza Hut that came to town? We all can pitch in for the pizzas. Any drinks each person pays for. What you all say?"

It was almost everyone agreeing except for one of the newbie girls. Her parents wanted her home once she got off.

After the show, everyone stuffed into two cars. Tad stood by the main doors as everyone walked to the cars.

Mike turned back. "Hey, Tad, aren't you coming along?"

"Sure, I thought you guys meant yourselves, not the management."

"You are one of the guys," Mike told Tad.

"Mike, I'll meet you over there. I will drive my car and follow." Looking at the others, Tad made a suggestion. "I think some of you need to ride in my car. I don't think all of you will fit in two cars."

"You are kidding, Tad? Watch this." Mike walked over to his car. It was one of the few nights he drove. He didn't want to be sweaty with all the people attending the shows. "Hey guys," he addressed all the ushers and girls. "Tad says we can't get all of us in our two cars. I said watch and see. If anybody wants to ride with Tad, he's over there waiting."

Two girls walked over to Tad's car.

Five people managed to fit in Mike's car and four in Melvin's small car. That was tight fitting in his car. Mike's car was tight, but he had a bigger car.

When the cars pulled into the parking lot at Pizza Hut, Mike got out first. He had to open the other doors. The trip caused the riders to reshuffle and were packed tighter. So tight no one could open the doors. When the doors finally were opened, it looked like a river overflowing its banks. Everyone fell and rolled out onto the street, laughing. Mike helped the girl up off the ground, receiving a slight smile for his gallantry.

Tad had the other two girls and was at the door to enter the Pizza Hut. Melvin finally located a spot to park. Everybody except for Melvin and the riders he was carrying had gone in and stood at the counter. Tad arranged with the night manager to gather several tables together for their party.

Everyone found a seat they preferred. Tad spoke up, saying, "Does everyone agree four large pizzas should do the trick feeding us?"

Mike remarked that he was not much of a pizza eater and only wanted a slice or two. Everyone besides Mike agreed.

"Now what do we order to drink?" the waiter requested while most of the crew were deciding on the type of pizza.

Tad spoke up. "We will have four large pies. Two will be cheese, one with sausage, another with pepperoni."

Rusty spoke, "I want a beer."

"Yeah, let's order beers!" most of the guys shouted back.

The waiter said to everybody, "If you buy pitchers of draft beer, it is cheaper."

"Okay, then it will be pitchers."

Soon the pitchers were placed on the table and Cokes for those not inclined to drink beer. All the guys filled a glass and began drinking their beers quickly, and all but Mike had refilled their glasses.

Pizza came before anyone started on the second glass. Every hand was grabbing for a slice. Some had two or three slices on their plate. Laughing and a good time followed. Working all night for two weeks had given this meal together an opportunity for all to kick back and enjoy each other's company.

The pizza was eaten, and most were finishing their drinks. Tad spoke up, offering to pay the bill.

Mike retorted, "No way, Tad, we agreed to everyone paying their part."

"Well, at least allow me to buy the drinks."

"No," Melvin backed Mike.

"Okay, then I am going to leave the tip."

This time no one objected. They left one hour after arriving, meeting back at the Rama.

Mike was off the next night, one of the few nights or days he had taken off during this epic movie.

* * *

At the dojo, Mike practiced after his regular workout with his sensei. Sifu Cho was still off and had not yet returned. A stranger sat in the corner with an overtly keen eye pegged on watching Mike.

After the lesson, the sensei ended class, handing Mike the key to lock up when he completed his training in the backyard. The stranger waited until Sensei walked out the door before walking over to Mike.

This didn't go unnoticed by Mike. "Sir, everyone is required to leave."

"You Mike, right?"

Mike didn't have an uneasy feeling toward this stranger the way he had with others he encountered that meant harm to him. So without preparing his guard for an attack, he remained at ease, but prepared. Mike walked about the room putting up the mats and turning some of the lights off. He turned the rear door light on and opened the back door.

The stranger was by his side. "Excuse me, Mike. I was asked to check in on you by Sifu Cho."

Standing partly in the dojo and partly in the backyard, Mike bowed to the stranger. The stranger returned the bow.

"How is Sifu doing?" Mike knew better than to inquire into Sifu's business, but he asked out of politeness.

"Sifu informed me of your progress and that you had begun the obstacle course training. Well, let's see how far you have gotten."

Within seconds, Mike had completed the beam walking then jumping over the rails and was over the fence and back inside. Next came the various kick off walls, post flipping, and twisting. The final hurdle prior to the ten-foot walk blindfolded on the board was the walking up the two-cornered wall to the top.

Mike failed to make the top on the first, second, and third tries. Returning back to his starting point for the fourth attempt, the stranger called Mike over to him.

Mike walked up to the stranger who had his head bent down. With a little shuffle, he looked back up at Mike. "I see you are still having trouble getting up that wall."

Mike remained silent, not because the stranger was correct but because the stranger knew this obstacle had been a bane to him. Was the stranger somehow spying on him?

"Mind if I give you some advice on getting up that wall?" the stranger politely asked Mike.

"Sure, any help getting up it sure would be a blessing. I've been having a hard time trying to figure out why it is so difficult."

"Oh, I see, then Sifu hasn't gone over the fine details of this course to you. Well, from what I've seen, you have done quite well. Far better than Sifu thought you might have with it, without his being here. He would have instructed you on various methods to help allow you to learn the skills to master this course. As you know, he had to leave suddenly. Sifu would be very pleased to hear how well you have succeeded without being here. Let me help you with this corner. I am aware he showed you how to run the course one time. I will run the wall. You watch and see if you can spot the method I employ reaching the top of the wall."

The stranger kicked off his shoes then runs at the course wall at a slight offset angle. Nearing the wall, he leaped into the air. He bounced off the first wall and rose to the corner wall, alighting shortly, then twisted inward to the corner again. The last leap put him on top of the wall.

Mike yelled back to him, "I think I saw my mistakes. Let me see if I can do what you did before you show me again."

"Very good, go for it, Mike."

Mike aligned himself the same as the stranger and ran at the wall, leaping onto the first wall when he was close enough. From the first wall he successfully launched off and onto the second wall. This he had done but usually never could make the twist. This time Mike made the twist and neatly landed on the ledge next to the stranger.

Both jumped off the rooftop to the ground below.

"Mike, you made it. I see you figured out your problem. Good. Let me give you a bit of advice. When you make your first jump, land with your feet bent, become like a sponge. Allow your legs to collect the energy from the leap to spring up and out to the second wall. The second wall you use the same methods, but make sure both of your hands make contact. Use your hands to propel the twisting action. You want to turn inward and not out and away from the second wall. When you spring off the wall, you should be in your twist and in an upward motion. Your twist was too soon on that attempt. Now try it again, Mike."

The next attempt Mike succeeded with a better result. The third, fourth, and fifth attempts were successful. Mike conquered the wall.

"Mike, I want to spar with you. Will that be okay?" asked the stranger.

Mike stood from the fifth attempt and faced the stranger. They both bowed, and a furious fight ensued. Twenty minutes later, they bowed to each other. Neither landed a blow on the other.

"Sifu Cho will be happy, Mike."

"Thank you, sir. Are you going to stay until Sifu returns?"

"Yes, until Sifu returns. Tomorrow there will be a new course for you to master."

The next night after Mike's afternoon shift at the Rama, he stopped by his home before going to the dojo. He was anxious to begin this new training but made it a point to always stop by home to check on his family.

Dodie's new boyfriend was there when he got home. Walking in the door, this tall blond-haired stout young man faced Mike.

"Hi, this is my home, and you are?" Mike asked the stranger.

Seeing Mike walk through the door, the new boyfriend of Dodie prepared to meet Mike. "Hi." He extended his hand to shake. "Hi, I am your sister Dodie's boyfriend. Hasn't she mentioned me?"

"Yes, she had," Mike answered.

It was an awkward moment as both felt unassured how to respond.

"My name is Mitch."

"I'm Mike."

"I heard some stories about you from your sister's friends where we first met."

"Oh, where was that? I mean, where you two met?"

"We met dancing many Saturdays ago at the rec center."

"Dodie and Sharon been at me to go," responded Mike.

"Mike, you should. You can meet a few girls there."

"Thanks, Mitch. I work, and there are a lot of girls there."

"Where is that, Mike?"

"At the Rama Theater."

"Oh yes, Dodie mentioned that you worked there."

Dodie walked in from the kitchen. Seeing her brother was a bit unsuspected. Generally, he wasn't home. "Hey Mike." Turning to Mitch, she said, "This is my boyfriend, Mitch is his name."

"Yeah, we just introduced ourselves to each other."

Mom was sitting at the couch with a cigarette. Surprisingly, no beer was on the table. Most of the time, the house was hot. But the manager installed an air conditioner recently in all the duplexes. They got one of the first. Mom was dressed in her shorts and a loose-fitting shirt. Her usual garb.

"Mike, you know, Mitch is taking karate lessons too."

"Really?" Mike responded. Mike never told his sisters nor his mom of his training. He felt they might ask too many questions, especially after the attack last year from those gang members.

Mitch was tall and, from his body shape, strong. Mike had begun to size up the people he ran into. He never knew what their intentions might be. Lately, he was pretty good at all his assessments of people he met or happened to notice.

"Here, Mike, let me show you a few things."

"Sure," Mike responded back.

Mitch took a stance. Immediately Mike determined his strengths and weaknesses from that stance. Upon that, he correctly accessed he could easily take him in a fight. It was almost a reflex reaction to size up each person he encountered.

So it was for Mitch. "Now, Mike, this is one of my favorite moves." With a quick rocking of his forearm, like swatting at flies, Mitch shot forward with his flapping forearm. Then with the other arm, he shot out a reverse punch at Mike's face.

Mike stood motionless, never blinked or moved. Mike being rock solid, unflinching, and motionless, standing his ground, startled Mitch.

Mitch had a queer feeling toward Mike's unnatural reaction. It was like he knew he was going to attack him in that way and had no concern for being hit. Most of his opponents were caught by surprise with that move. They always backed up to avoid this unorthodox charge.

"I score a lot of points with that fake," Mitch commented to Mike, expecting some awe. "Most guys react by blocking it away. This leaves them open for my reverse punch. You want to give it a try, Mike?"

"Sure, Mitch."

Mitch stood, waiting for Mike to strike at him. He felt pretty sure of his abilities. Mike was smaller and looked weaker. If he had some trouble with Dodie's brother, he felt capable of dealing with this squirt.

"Go on, Mike, I'm ready." Mitch stood facing Mike about six feet away. This gave him a sense that he could see the attack coming and easily block Mike's advance. This would demonstrate to the kid Mitch's power and not to mess with him.

Before Mitch had finished his thoughts, Mike had attacked. Mitch blinked as the kid stood inches away with a punch at his face. Mitch didn't even have time to make a second blink. Once the action was completed, Mitch fell backward several steps, then blocked empty air.

"Mitch, did I perform it right?"

Mitch looked surprised from the suddenness of the attack, and not once did he see Mike move until his vision was blinded by Mike's fist. Then he lost control of his stance and felt like he was pushed back. Neither was the case. Mitch never encountered a force like Mike. Mike never laid a hand upon him, but the force of the attack felt as if Mike had struck him hard. The fact was Mike's chi energy was so great, the act of the attack caused it to be extended into Mitch. Chi was the internal energy everyone possessed, and in the martial arts, one is trained to apply it. Few really master chi energy' only a small amount of it is usually what many students experience. Seldom does one ever feel the force of the chi physically.

"Yeah, Mike, that was done really good." Mitch stood there reevaluating this kid facing him.

"Thanks, Mitch. I will remember that move."

Mitch was still standing in that place when Dodie spoke up and placed her hand on his shoulder. Her hand startled Mitch, causing him to come out of his wondering.

Dodie spoke once she saw what her brother had done. "Well, Mike, we will see you later. We are off to the movies tonight."

"Dodie, if you two come while I am working, I will get you in free. Rusty is working tonight. Tell him you are my sister, and I told him to let you two in free."

"Thanks, Mike," Mitch said, "but we are going to the other theater in town."

"Okay, next time, Mitch."

"Thanks, Mike," Dodie replied back as they walked out the door.

"Hi, Mom, anything happening around here?"

"Not really. While you are going in the kitchen, bring me a beer."

"Sure. Where's Sharon, Mom?"

"She is working now at that new hamburger joint. She should be home soon. I told her to bring some burgers for supper."

"Thanks, Mom, but I am going to be working at a friend's home most of the night. Still got a lot of work to do finishing his back porch."

Soon after returning with his mom's beer, Mike went out the door. Leaving his car in the front yard, Mike ran to the dojo. The stranger was at the front entrance to the dojo.

"Hi there, Mike." He was waving to him rounding the corner.

Mike lifted his eyes to see the stranger waiting for him. Coming to a halt by the door, Mike looked at the stranger with a puzzled glance.

The stranger pointed to his car. "Come get in."

"Where are we going?"

"That, Mike, will be your new obstacle course I set up for you. Lean back, this will take about twenty minutes to get to our new training site."

Turning off the highway onto a dirt road, the two of them drove for another ten minutes. Soon the car slowed. Looking out the window, there was nothing but trees. No houses nor any other buildings. Night was fast approaching.

"Come on, get out," the stranger called to Mike, stepping out of the car and onto a dirt road next to a clearing. The stranger exited his side of the car, waiting for Mike on the other side.

Turning to face the stranger while viewing his surroundings, Mike turned, and the stranger was gone. Just like that, the stranger disappeared.

Mike looked back in the car. The keys were with the stranger.

Night was upon him. Sounds all about, eerie sounds. Crickets began their harmonies. An owl was heard hooting far off. Movement seemed to rustle bushes around the parked car.

He was thinking to himself, *Well, that surely brings back old memories.* Mike moved over to a tree stump and sat. Soon he was able to sense the location of the stranger. He was near a clump of tall bushes observing him. Mike allowed him to sit there for thirty minutes. After enjoying the starry night sky and reminiscing the sounds he forgot, Mike called to the stranger.

"Hey, you going to sit among those bushes all night watching me, or are we going to train?"

"Sifu told me you had a strong chi. I can see now why he said what he said to me."

"Oh, I hope it was something kind," Mike responded.

"Hmm," the stranger answered. Walking over to where Mike was sitting, the stranger said, "This is your new course. How do you like it? I know it is a little scary being out in the woods at night. Most people are terrified not knowing what they cannot see. All these sounds can throw people off their game."

"Oh, well, I'm fine with it."

"Oh, how so, Mike?"

"I guess Sifu never mentioned my past to you?"

"No, not much."

"Well, I walked from Virginia to Georgia living off the land. I met many people who taught me how to survive in the woods. I am quite familiar with being all alone in swamps and forest areas."

"Oh, then this should be something you can learn to adapt to quickly. Are you aware of camouflage and moving silently?"

"Yes, sir!"

"Good, then I will show you things you don't know. First lesson to learn, animals when confronted, usually animals that are not predators, will freeze in place. Any movement will tell the predator of their position. Animals that flee get chased by a predator. Looking at prey versus hunted animals' faces, one can see the differences.

"Predator animal eyes are close together to focus their eyes ahead and on their victim. Their prey, eyes are on their side. This is to see around, to observe a 270-degree of viewing. So if you are seen, you can be dinner. The trick is not to be seen.

"Look over there near those bushes Mike." He pointed to an area that was darker than the surrounding areas on either side. "Look between the two larger bushes, see those tiny yellow eyes?"

"Yes, sir."

"Good, he is our prey. We are the hunters. He hides in the darkness. Where there is light, you can see. Light is all about him. Yet he cannot be seen. His eyes give him away. Notice, Mike, he stands away from any of the bushes. He is in the open area and not among the shrubs. Yet you cannot see him but for those tiny yellow eyes. His color matches the night. Darkness is his cover. He uses his color to blend in with the night.

"Darkness is a shield from those who try to observe you. If you use the night darkness correctly, it can be camouflage. Any darkened area light is not present, you can hide in. Wearing dark clothes matches the darkness.

"Quick, look!" He pointed to where the unseen spectator was standing, a flicker from his eyes and a small sound, then a slight movement near a bush gave them a clear picture of what their guest was.

"See, Mike, when he moved, we heard and saw change, that change pointed him out. Being silent is not only being quiet but remaining still. Your movement can make sound. It can make you seen. Even your heartbeat can be heard. Some animals have ears that are keen to the slightest noise. Our ears will never be as keen as animals. Ours eyes won't see as far or well as theirs either.

"Think about animals and all their adaptations for survival. Their paws are padded to muffle sound walking among the trees. Why? Everything about all wild creatures have prepared them for survival. This course is to teach you those lessons. To be successful at hunting, you must learn from being hunted.

"Tonight, Mike. Hide from me, hide well. If I find you within two hours, you won't get a ride home. Just in case you don't understand, you will have a long walk ahead of you if you fail and I find you."

"No, no misunderstanding there," Mike answered.

"Good, now I will give you a fifteen-minute start on your first night. Off you go. See you soon." The stranger waved Mike off into the night.

Mike followed a path to the stream. He entered the water and stepped back out. Softly Mike walked downstream and reentered the water for several steps. Then downstream again. Again, he retraced his steps to the second exit from the stream and jumped to the other side. Mike walked several feet downstream and backtracked his footsteps. Then he entered the stream again. Down the stream he walked to the point he last left the water. All this took fifteen minutes.

From that place, Mike leaped into a tree and swung using his hands from one tree to another, similar to a monkey. Next, he climbed up the last tree before a clearing, perching on the highest limb where he surrounded himself with the tree limbs torn loose climbing up the tree.

Feeling sure the stranger had been lost and he was in a tree covered with limbs making him totally unseen assured Mike he wasn't walking home this night.

"Hey, Mike, you up in that tree? You can come down now."

Mike heard the stranger yell up into the tree, and it gave him a shock. He had found him so quickly! *Can't be*, Mike thought to himself.

As he descended the tree, the stranger became more and more visible to him.

Jumping down the last few feet, Mike landed near the stranger.

"Well, my boy, enjoy your long walk home."

Mike called out to the stranger walking away, "Wait!"

"What?" he called back. "Let me guess, how did I find you so quick, right?"

"Yeah," Mike answered back with astonishment.

"Remember, I told you the darkness will hide you. Stay in the dark."

"I did," Mike answered back.

"Well, you did, but you forgot the light from the night sky was above you. You were a black cutout silhouette against the light color of the night sky. This night had many lights shining, and I looked up, *bam*, right there. Have a nice walk. I mean run."

One hour later, Mike was running down Main Street. When Mike neared his dojo, the stranger was standing by his car. "Mike, next time you keep me waiting more than an hour, I will take you much farther out."

"Yes, sir."

"Are you ready?"

"Ready? Ready for what?"

"Mike, you didn't think that was the end of your training section this night, did you?"

Pausing to determine what he should say was taking too long.

"Hey, if you are going to take all night finding an answer to my question, you might as well be running. It will help in thinking. Give me five laps around the block. You got fifteen minutes or five more laps."

Twelve minutes later, five laps was completed.

"Good, I knew you could do better. Now, my boy, on to the second lesson. To recap the first, tell me what you learned, Mike?"

"Well, I learned the darkness is a shield if certain rules are applied. Never move unless spotted. If spotted, never bolt. Move slow and remain in the dark. Any movement is always seen by others. Others could be passersby or those looking for you. The farther you appear from those looking, the harder it is to be spotted. Always keep a small figure and stay low to the ground."

"Good. Next lesson is always run with the pack. Alone, and you have no support. Alone you stand out. Blend in with the surroundings. With people, follow their path, walk like them, try to wear what they wear. Think if you look at ten people in a row, all wearing a white shirt and a tie, except one has a bowtie. Where will your eyes go?

"Don't walk into the crowd or opposite of the direction they travel. Everyone will part to allow you through, either that or make a noticeable attention-getting response to your wrong direction. Never walk faster or slower than the group. You drive your car too fast, the police will notice you. Do it slower, and they will notice you. Drive like the others, and you pass them by, unnoticed.

"Tonight, we go to the mall. Your aim is to not be found by me. One rule is you cannot go and hide in a closet or store compartment. You need to hide in plain sight. You can use your first lesson to hide from me."

The mall was around the block. The parking lot was full of cars. The stranger remained in the car. "Okay, Mike, you have ten minutes to get inside and hide from me. I will have thirty minutes once I enter the mall to locate you."

Mike walked to the main entrance and looked back. The stranger could be seen standing by his car. Mike could easily spot him. It was then that Mike took note of his towering height. He could spot the stranger before he could spot him in all the people walking in the center.

Good, this will be easier this time. There must be hundreds of people inside. Opening the door, Mike entered. True to his thinking, the mall was filled top to bottom with patrons.

People milled about; some stood looking in windows or standing in store entrances, trying to decide whether to enter or not. Others were walking one direction to a store along the aisle and the other aisle going in the opposite direction with their people. There were several benches stationed at strategic points on either aisle for those to sit and rest. A large central food court with a multitude of people standing to place orders or sitting eating their food looked to be a perfect place to hide.

I got a lot of options, Mike thought as he panned. Both eyes fixated on a place to blend in. Minutes remained before the stranger came to hunt him down. He walked over to the food court, choosing the longest line to stand in. After removing his shirt, he stuffed it in a trash can near the line. Wearing only a T-shirt, Mike pulled it out of his pants, stepping in line. Now came the wait as the line moved slowly forward.

The stranger walked in the mall and immediately followed the line in the direction Mike chose. Quickly, he arrived at the food court. After spying each store carefully, he proceeded along the mall. At the mall central, he stood watching people in lines. Standing there motionless, eyeing the people moving to and fro around him. Soon people began to stare at him. The stranger stood standing on one leg with his hand on top of his head. He apparently had the intentions of drawing people to look at him.

Thinking out loud but not too loud to be heard, unless you stood close to the stranger, one could make out what he said. "Hmm, now that I got everyone's attention, who is not looking?"

Everyone in Mike's line turned to see what was happening except him. Mike knew if he would turn around, he would be identified. If he would not to turn around, he will be noticed. *I got it!* Mike exclaimed to himself. Slowly he turned with his head slightly concealed by the person behind him.

The stranger eyed every face, finding no one he was looking for.

It worked, it worked, Mike said silently, moving his eyes, following the stranger walking away. Everyone turned back to what they were previously doing. Mike kept his eyes on the stranger. The stranger turned around a corner out of visual sight. Mike stepped out of line and walked to the trash can, relieved he was not spotted.

Suddenly, the stranger reappeared at the corner. Too late, Mike was out of line and moving against the flow of traffic. *Dang, he got me again.*

The stranger walked over to Mike. "By the way, Mike, remember what I said. There are always eyes watching you. When I went around the corner, I was viewing the food mall from a reflection on a store window."

"Really, so you didn't see me?"

"Not until you stepped out of line. Why would you wait in a long line, then step out before you got served? You went across what was normal. Before you pay me, I will give you a second chance. I'll wait here, you have five minutes. Oh, that T-shirt sticking out of your pants, I quickly spotted. I assumed it was you from that small mistake. Remember not to stand out from the crowd with this final chance."

This time, Mike figured to use the first lesson to evade the stranger. Walking down the aisle, Mike kept a keen eye on all window reflections. He noticed a small nook between two stores. A poster board was set near the nook, and behind it was a dark area. A shopper stepped out from that nook readjusting her blouse. Only when she appeared did Mike see her.

Good, that will be a great place to hide.

No sooner had Mike stepped behind the poster, the stranger came around the corner. The stranger walked right to where Mike was hiding. "Come on out, Mike."

"Man, what gave me away? I mean, I didn't even know about this until some lady walked out from behind this poster."

"Oh, I noticed the poster right off when I came around the corner. Many stores set them out to get notice for advertisement. My eyes were drawn to it. So I simply walked over. When I got close, I saw a nook it concealed. The nook was dark. Dark, I thought, hmm, maybe. I called out your name. You answered me back. If you said nothing, I thought about walking away."

"Should have kept silent," Mike replied.

"One new lesson for you to ponder on, Mike. Each of these ventures you neglected to apply all your senses. I felt your presence getting closer to you. I could smell the fear of detection surrounding you, that and your odor. You been doing a lot of sweating.

"Okay, enough for the first night, enjoy your run home. You got twenty minutes, try not to be tardy this time."

"Yes, sir."

Mike was about to begin his run when the stranger put a quirk in his run. "Mike, before you begin, don't just run home. Apply your first obstacle course training along the run."

Both Mike and the stranger walked out the mall to his car.

"Oh," came a murmur. The stranger was nearly bending down to enter his car when he suddenly stood back up, looking at Mike." Don't be seen."

Down the road, Mike hopped over anything in his path. Then he worked his way behind houses. Most of the homes had various heights of fences. Some Mike jumped with split legs, some he straddled. With tall metal fences, he gripped hold of the mesh, swinging sideways over the top. Any pole or corner between two buildings offered an opportunity to practice the two-step twist and up. Most were too high, and Mike made a good effort.

On a street that needed crossing was the first time Mike became aware of two guys shadowing him. Mike remained in the shadows running low along the hedges. Every once in a while, he stopped and paused, looking around for any evidence that his suspicions might prove correct. He arrived home within the allotted time the stranger set for him. Across the street from his home was a parked car. It was the stranger.

Every day hence, the same occurred. Mike would run home having a sense he was shadowed. Finally proving to the stranger he could prevent him from detecting his presence in the woods and in the city, it was time to begin another phase.

BIKERS CLUBHOUSE

"**G**OOD DAY, CHOPPER." A MAN rode up, sitting on his bike outside the club. Most of the gang just got off their bikes to enter the clubhouse. Chopper sat alone until every man entered the club.

The clubhouse was large with a run-down unkempt side. Surrounding the house was a tall wooden fence. Some places could use repair with pickets broken free of the rail, and generally, all needed paint. Rot had crept into the wood.

The house was off the street sheltered beneath trees and two smaller buildings adjoining the road entering the driveway. It was painted all white and needed a repaint. Bikes were parked everywhere there was a space. One place was reserved for the leaders.

Loud noise pervaded the house continuously. Hence, the distance from the road and nearby homes. Still, the police usually made a surprise appearance.

Inside, beer was the choice of drink. Vodka and whiskey bottles were littered across the shelves. In a small corner was an entrance to the kitchen and from there a hall leading to the bathroom and room with a bed. Usually, the back door led to the outside latrine. A nearby bush. It grew very tall over the years. It was much quicker and had no wait time.

Both Chopper and Razor saw Mr. Cho stop. Bell had walked into the house. Razor was entering the bar when he heard the last biker come to a halt. Two others entered. The screen door slammed shut behind them. Over at a table reserved for the leaders, three beers waited. After taking their seats, a fourth beer arrived for Cho, and they sat quietly listening to the blaring music.

Music was playing, but it ceased as soon as the conversation begun. Everyone gathered around the table. Some pulled up a chair, many stood. All were interested in what Cho had to say.

Chopper spoke first. "Glad to see you, Cho. We have a serious problem, and your specialty will greatly be needed."

"Not to worry, I sent Stephen to begin Mike's other training. He took several of his team along."

"So before I begin with our problem, let's here about our young hellcat, Mike, Cho."

"Chopper, that young kid is good. He's fast, strong, and powerful. He has a sense of awareness far beyond any ten-year student or almost equal to mine."

"Well, that's saying something, Cho." Chopper looked about the room to convey his approvable to his members.

They looked at each other as to nod to their teammates a "happy to hear that."

"I have him fighting multiple fighters. Seldom has any man landed a blow on him. He has dispatched them all. I began attacks at nights at the most unassuming times and places. He senses their presence and proves to be a remarkable fighter. I left him beginning the first obstacle course training."

"Yes, Stephen has reported that to me."

"Yes, he made contact with me, Chopper. He has mastered the wall."

"Really, Cho, that quick?"

"Yes, I told you, he is a most unusual student. He will make me proud."

"Great."

Everybody began clapping from the good news.

Chopper turned to Razor. "I see everyone has taken a keen friend-ship with our hellcat."

Razor responded with a yes. "After the Bell shooting and Mike preventing you from being shot, Mike has earned a dear spot in the hearts of all the bikers."

Not everyone was present when Chopper, Razor, Bell, and Cho walked into the house. Bone Breaker walked just as Cho ended with "a most unusual student." He made a quick path to the four seated, parting the bikers like the Red Sea. "What, what, is that about Mike?"

Standing tall, looming over the table like a giant redwood tree, causing a shadow blocking the overhead light, he planted both his fists down on the table. As soon as the table returned back to the floor and all the four leaders regained their seats, except Cho, all looked up at Bone Breaker.

"Now, Bone Breaker, Mike is doing fine," Cho interjected. "In fact, Bone Breaker, he is an excellent student. He has exceeded my expectations."

Feeling relaxed, Bone Breaker let out a breath then stood erect. "Good, that is good," he repeated. "When you gonna let me go and be with him, Chopper?"

Chopper turned back to Cho. "You can see Bone Breaker has taken a real shine to our hellcat. As have I."

"As have I," Cho repeated.

"Well, everyone has," Chopper replied back to his main man. "Okay, now that we are assured of how well Mike is doing, now it is time for our new concerns. This is why I had you return, Cho. We got some new people trying to move in our area. We plan on going to have a discussion with them. They may or may not be aware of our presence. Either way, we will make it known to them. Our first appearance must be strong and catch them totally off guard. I have let it be known to them where we are to meet."

Razor took over. "We have given them the time and location on purpose. When we meet, we will do so with the full understanding they will be prepared."

Chopper turned back to Cho after viewing his men. "I want them to be shocked and overwhelmed when we meet. The suddenness and power on their terms will portray our power. It will scare them and hopefully cause them to realize our power.

"They think they will have the upper hand, when in fact, we will destroy that illusion. Cho, get your crew prepared. Jackknife is at the site with men set. Razor will be in charge of the second team. I want this to go down smooth and clean. All weapons removed from every one of them. I want them to feel powerless. This will send out a strong message who we are."

"They should already know," a biker yipped out.

Razor looked at the biker who spoke. "Yeah, they should. Remember this, being the big fish in a pond, there is always someone who wants to replace you."

Bells made her point. "We want to do this without violence. But if it happens, then no holds barred. Total elimination. No one better get hurt on our side. You all got that?"

Chopper reached for Bell's hand to hold. "That goes for me too. Be safe and do what you need to do. Protect the club and your comrades. That is to be my final say on this," commanded Chopper. "Now, everyone, drink up to our plan! Cho, stay after we have our get-together party."

Everyone raised their drink, and a multiple chorus of clinking resounded throughout the house.

TRAINING JUST
TURNED REAL

SUMMER WAS TO BE A vacation time from school, but instead, Mike found himself studying and practicing more than he ever had. Often, Mike got home late from the Rama before leaving again to train. Recently, he was coming in later, just before midnight. Usually, his mom was up sitting at the coffee table, drinking beer and smoking. Boo sat next to her.

Mike was spending less and less time with Boo. Boo had a strong attachment with his mom. By now, Boo rarely left the comfort of the couch beside Mom when Mike came home. Mike would walk over and sit near Boo, picking him up. Boo still kissed Mike. A bond was created; he was always Mike's dog. Just a new attachment made to help him adjust to the long period of Mike being away.

All too often, those walks outside with Boo were fewer and fewer. Only when Mike came early, before midnight, did they still take their walks. Most often Mike and Boo would play on the couch beside Mom. When time to go to bed, Mike would take him out to pee, then lift him up, carrying him to bed.

In the morning, Boo was let out to pee with Mike's mom. Mom always was up before sunrise.

On one day, Mike got up early, going out the front door to train. Turning around at the door, he called for Boo. Boo came running. Both were out the door lickety-split. Once around the block Mike ran with

Boo doing his best to keep up. Several times Mike stopped to allow Boo to catch up. After the third stop, he picked Boo up.

Not long after picking Boo off the ground, Mike felt a strong presence shadowing them. Boo began to growl. Calming Boo with his hand across his mouth, he continued his run.

Cutting across to the other neighborhood with houses not duplex but double rental buildings, he applied his stealth training. Running near a hedge bent low, weaving in and out, he lost that feeling, arriving home quicker.

Putting Boo in the house, he continues his run. This time, Mike was aware of his shadows again. Whoever it was, they were not the ones who normally shadowed him. Something wasn't right about their intentions. It seemed their auras wanted harm for him.

Mike led them on a merry run throughout the other neighborhood. Arriving near the school, he kept near a fence. When Mike felt they could see him, he went over the fence, showing a great difficulty doing so. When he landed on the other side, he feinted a leg injury.

Two men came out from across the road doing a sloppy job of staying unseen. Mike allowed them to close the distance between them. He wanted to find out what he felt was what they had intentions to do. Soon, they caught up to where Mike propelled himself over the fence. Not as quick nor with skill, they scrambled up the fence, only to hang on the top, trying to determine the best way down. One jumped, and the other tried to climb down; he got partway down then fell the rest. His partner lent him a hand up.

Mike was about a hundred feet away looking back as they were climbing the fence. Once they were over, he yelled to them, "Hey, you two clumsy dips! Need any help."

Suddenly realizing they were spotted, one of them returned the yell. "Hey, kid, you got a smarty mouth! You want us to shut that mouth?"

"You two couldn't shut a door." Mike returned his taunt.

Both of his shadows took that as an insult, which it was.

"How about we come and kick your butt, big mouth?" Then they started to walk toward Mike. To their dismay, Mike stood waiting for them.

"If you two are going to kick my butt, what is taking you so long? You're not afraid of a small kid half your age? Mike flung a thumb from the nose sign at them.

Both of them didn't need permission. It was always understood among the gang no one but on one disrespects them. They charged at full speed toward the kid standing still in front of their path. It was plain as day he was injured from jumping over the fence. They felt less worried knowing Mike was hurt.

Suddenly without the slightest indication, the kid leaped into the air. A leg snapped out into the face of the first. Landing after the kick stopped on the nose of the first shadow, the second shadow had enough time to see his friend flung backward, passing him as he continued his forward movement.

He was swiftly at the kid just as his partner touched the ground from that flying kick. Swinging with a hook punch at the kid, he felt only air. The punch just missed its mark, the kid's jaw. The second shadow was propelled forward by his run and compounded the forward motion with a punch flung at the kid. He couldn't stop, having no choice but to continue his forward motion, unable to prevent what Mike had set up to do.

Mike twisted and turned as his shadow fell forward facedown from the near hit he attempted. Mike kept taunting the second shadow by laughing at him. The second shadow scrambled back to his feet. Meanwhile, the first shadow remained where he dropped from the flying kick.

Second shadow spoke up, angered by Mike's taunting and laughing. He was considered one of the best fighters in his gang. That was the reason he was sent, just in case some fighting might be required. He was told not to start any fight but to avoid it. Leader man made it clear, he didn't want anybody to know what they had been up to until it was time. Now, the two shadows knew they screwed up.

"Keep laughing, kid. That's all I want you to remember when you are lying flat on your face gnawing road tar. I is going to put on that skinny body of yours more pain you ever got." Second man decided if he was going to pay for this screwup, he was going to get some paybacks from this kid.

Both faced each other. Clearly the second shadow was not impressed with the smaller kid standing in front of him.

"Kid, you are about to get the whipping of your life," shadow man spoke, conveying to Mike he had no chance.

Mike laughed at his threat. "You are obviously afraid of me. You need to inflate yourself with platitudes to bolster your courage."

"What you say? It don't make no sense. You keep laughing while I bust you open, kid."

This was the final insult to the second shadow. This thin short kid standing there laughing at him only made him madder.

"Hey, big man, if that is how you going to beat me up, please, please make it quick. I sure don't want to suffer much longer at your stupid mouth yakking. The sound is driving me crazy." Mike, seeing this shadow man fuming to get at him, thought, *Good, just the way I like them to be. Go on, get mad as heck at me. The madder the better. You are going to attack without control. I have control over you. We'll see who kicks whose butt.* Mike watched his foe grow angrier at him.

Mike spoke loud for the shadow man to hear him. He said to him, "Go ahead, kick my skinny butt, you moron. I hate to send you back to your leader man crying like a baby standing in front of him."

Filled with rage, shadow man let loose with a shattering left punch, surely capable of killing a man if it hit its mark.

Without effort, Mike simply blocked the punch with a powerful two-finger strike at the crux of his elbow and forearm joint. The shadow man felt the blow being deflected and also felt the pain that followed. The block felt like the skinny kid had broken his arm.

Holding back a yell of pain, he was crazy with anger, wanting to hit that brat before he went back to Atlanta. With his other hand, he shot a straight shot to Mike face.

Mike, thinking, *Predictable*, blocked the second punch with the same force, this time using a crane wrist block strike under the oncoming blow. The blow impacted on the second man's center of the forearm. That blow made a slight cracking sound, followed by a great pain of grimace sweeping over shadow man's face. With both arms reeling in pain from each block, the shadow man realized for the first time, he could not punch at him. He was helpless.

Fear entered into his mind for the first time. Something he never felt before. Usually, he put the fear of God into his foes who had the misfortune to irk him or to those he was told to eliminate. The shoe was now on the other foot. Fear gripped at him.

He quickly looked for a way to escape. He expected the same for his enemies. It was what he would often see anyone he fought attempt. Fear of dying was now very much alive in him. Fear, fear, made him wet his pants. What strength he had vanished.

Mike walked to one side of shadow man. "See what happens to someone when they get overly confident with their foe. You felt I was easy to beat. You gave up your control and made serious mistakes. I will not bandy words with you. You want me dead, my family, and my friends. I won't kill you, but you will never walk again or see again."

The shadow man pondered the words this skinny kid made to him. Words came out of his mouth without him stopping the words. "Please, I beg of you, don't kill me." Words that crushed his soul and power he once held to cripple any and all of his foes who stood up to him. He was a killer and enjoyed his work. Never once did he ever think of the pain and fear he instilled in others. That was his great love, love to hear them beg for mercy.

Only a few seconds elapsed. He had little time to ponder any more on the words uttered by the kid: never walk or see again.

Mike grabbed him from behind on his shoulders. With a quick tug downward, he took the shadow down and across his knee. The shadow man's knees were not able to resist the downward pull and gave way easily.

The last sound the shadow man heard was a snap then a little pain as two lower vertebrates separated. Next, his sight was about to become dark. Mike hesitated to jab his fingers into the two orb receptacles that once stored his eyeballs. *Not necessary*, he thought. He released the second shadow man falling to the ground into a jumbled mass of jelly.

Walking over to the first shadow man, Mike was planning to plant a side kick into the pit of his lower back. Upon seeing his body lying facedown, the first shadow man's head had a disturbing crook. Remembering back to his flying kick, Mike felt the depth his foot had entered the throat, and the neck went caving in. He pulled back to stop short of a fatal strike but realized with the running force of shadow man coming at him, he may have miscalculated the thrust of his foot.

A fear of having killed him started to ebb into Mike's mind. Slowly, he stooped down, placing two fingers at the base of shadow man one's throat. A pulsating throb was felt flowing through the vein. Shadow man one was alive. His neck might be broken. If not, he will have one heck of a pain in the neck.

Mike stood back up. Silently, Mike disappeared into the brush and over a fence.

Later that day, two men were found lying in a backyard. Both were rushed to the hospital. Both lived. Both never went back to Atlanta. Nonetheless, the reports got back to leader man. Two of his best soldiers got hurt—and hurt bad. No one had witnessed the act.

Good, Mike thought.

That night at his dojo, Mike reported the incident to the stranger. Speaking to Mike, he asked him, "No one saw this? You are sure of that?" The stranger had not doubted Mike about anyone seeing what transpired, but what had concerned him was the attack made on him. "Hmm, it seems we may have to increase your training and surveillance," the stranger confided to Mike.

Mike responded, "What surveillance?"

Mike turned to look directly in his eyes.

"You going to tell me you never once felt someone was watching or following you?" replied a stunned stranger.

"No, I just thought they did that when I was training, Sifu."

"When you went home, did you feel or sense a presence?"

"Well, maybe I did. I let my guard down while at home."

"Hmm. From now on, Mike, never let your guard down anywhere or anytime. You understand?"

"Yes, Sifu," Mike responded to the stranger with curiosity. Mike suspected much and knew little of what was going on. Most of what he suspected, he passed off to Sifu's Cho training.

"Sifu. Hmm, I guess I am a Sifu to you. Thanks for the acknowledgment, Mike. You honor me." Sifu stranger bowed to Mike, and Mike returned the bow. "Mike, please call me by my name, Stephen. Sifu Stephen will suffice."

Every day since then, Mike trained either in the woods or the city. Sifu Stephen waited for Mike to arrive. When he drove his car to the assigned place, Mike walked over to where his new Sifu was often seen sitting.

"Sit, Mike," came a simple command, forceful and to the point. Reaching from behind the stump Sifu Stephen was perched upon, he pulled a net up from behind his back and over his lap. He held it up for Mike's viewing.

Looking at the net brought to Mike's mind a million questions. Knowing better, he waited for the explanation from Sifu Stephen.

"Mike, this is known as a ghillie suit. Snipers in the military use this to camouflage their movement. Being seen means death." Picking up twigs and leaves, Sifu began to weave the material in and out of the mesh. Sifu Stephen begansinstructing Mike while he worked. "Every terrain requires different materials. If done correct, it will almost keep you from being seen. Here, take this extra net and begin to weave what you think will be the best to use for today's practice."

Looking around the area, Mike gathered the local materials that would offer him the best concealment.

"Good, you happy with your suit, Mike?"

"Yep."

"Good. Get into the car."

"What? I thought this was where we were going to practice?"

"Mike, where did you ever get that idea?"

A short drive and across the other side of the highway was a field of tall grasses. Several patches or islands of small trees spotted the field. Stopping the car, Sifu let Mike out. Pointing to the field, he said, "I'll be back in fifteen minutes. Go find a spot. Your task is to spot me and make your way to my car unseen. The lesson today is to know your terrain to properly prepare. My best advice is to get prepared." Grabbing the door, Sifu Stephen shut it with a bang then drove down the road until out of sight.

Quickly, Mike started tearing all the limbs and leaves off his ghillie suit. While walking into the fields, he plucked grasses and other materials lying about. Mike came to a gully cutting the field into half.

Remembering other past lessons, he determined it was too obvious, and besides, Sifu surely had traversed the field before he took him there.

Mike sat down by the gully and waddled across the tall grass. *This will make a good distraction for Sifu. When he spots this grass lying bent over, he should, hopefully, focus on it as a place I might be stationed.*

Now looking about, Mike spotted a better place. It was normal and didn't stand out. *Here, this will do well.* Looking to where Sifu might park his car or perch himself for a good scan of the field, a depression was spotted running up to the road. *No, no, too well known. Looks like an animal trail*, Mike thought.

A car came quickly up the road. It never slowed down and drove past. Then another car and another drove past. Looking up the road, peering just high enough to get a better look, Mike could not see nor hear cars either way approaching.

A small crack then what sounded like a rustle of grass came from the direction Sifu had drove his car. *Could it be a small animal approaching?* Mike thought. Slowly Mike lowered his head.

Soon the sounds were easily discernible. It was footsteps approaching him. Then the sound stopped. Mike felt tempted to raise his head. *Movement, any movement, no matter how slight, can be seen, Mike, keep your head down. Let the sound tell you where it is. Follow the noise. Let the noise move and reveal itself.*

So it did. Each step was a signpost pointing to where it was. Then it happened.

A foot stopped short of stepping on his head. It paused; Mike could see the foot twist another direction. It lifted and stepped in the direction it pointed to. The shoe was not that of Sifu's. It was another foot. Within a second, the thought occurred to Mike. Sifu had others in the field. He was trying to draw him out.

Mike's theory soon came true. Another movement came from behind him. It followed close to the edge of the gully he came upon. *Good thing I didn't station myself there, glad I chose another place to hide*, he thought.

Mike took a bold move. Knowing that two men passed him without spotting him, he figured Sifu had his eyes fixed on them. Slowly Mike edged along, moving grass stalks with the slightest movement.

A breeze was blowing; he noticed the direction the wind came from and to where it was blowing. Taking a note how the bend in the grass swayed by the wind, he followed the same direction of the grass. After several minutes working close to the road, Sifu Stephen was spotted. Sure enough, he was focused on his two companions. Mike was glad he was correct.

Sifu stood just several feet from him on his left. *Just two more feet, and I'll scare the heck out of him*, Mike thought. Slowly Mike crept closer to Sifu. Now he was one foot from him. Suddenly Sifu stepped away several feet. *Damn*, Mike thought.

Then came a scary happening. Sifu turned back looking down at the spot he once stood. Mike hadn't move since Sifu took those several steps from him. *Whew*, Mike thought. *If I took that one move to close the gap, he would surely have seen me.*

Sifu turned back to one of his assistants. He was waving and pointing down at a place he thought Mike might be. Good, just enough of a distraction. With one small crawl forward, Mike got within being able to touch of Sifu. Reaching out slowly, he tapped Sifu on his foot.

Sifu quickly looked down.

Mike smiled and waved.

Next day at the Rama Theater, Mike walked inside, spotting two new ushers trying on red jackets. Tad introduce each one to Mike. "Mike, come and let me get you acquainted with Ronald and Bob."

"Glad to meet you Bob, Ronald." He shook both their hands.

Tad noticed the "what, who quit?" look across Mike's face. "Ric, he has given his two weeks' notice, Mike."

"Really?" was Mike's response. "Why?"

"Ric enlisted into the army, didn't he tell you, Mike?"

"No, Tad, he hasn't."

Ric had become one of Mike's closest friends at the Rama.

"Well, he will, Mike. Ric asked me if you were working tonight. Besides that, you got these two to break in tonight."

"Thanks, Tad."

Bob was tall and so was Ronald, but side by side, they were as different as day and night. As soon as Tad walked out the door, Bob approached Mike.

"Bob, right?"

"Yeah," responded Bob with a slurry tone.

"I need you and Ronald to sweep the lobby and check the bathrooms. Make sure they are clean, toilets flushed, and have plenty of paper. Did Tad show you two about?"

Ronald spoke first. "He gave us a short tour, Mike."

"Okay, I'll start you off once you get the bathrooms in order. We got twenty minutes before the next show."

Bob was standing still while Ronald began to work his way to the first bathroom, sweeping the floor.

Mike turned to Bob. "Yes, Bob, is there something you don't understand?"

No response came from him.

"Okay, Bob, you can start with the other bathroom."

"Who made you in charge, Mike?" Bob stood there as if he was not going to do a thing Mike told him to do.

"What do you mean by that, Bob?"

Bob answered with a slurry tone, "I mean, who put you in charge?"

"Okay, Bob, first I have seniority over you; second, I am the doorman; third, I am your boss."

"Is that so," Bob retorted.

"Yes, that is so."

"I heard of you, Mike."

"What did you hear that makes you think I wasn't in charge?"

"I heard you are some kind of a karate expert. You think you can tell anybody what to do."

"I don't know who you been talking to, Bob, but at this theater, you start at the bottom and work your way up. Anybody on the door has the seniority over ushers. That's the way it is, Bob."

"Well, I don't take orders from someone who thinks he's my boss. Tad hired me, he's my boss."

"Good, you take that up with him when he is here. For the time being, I'm in charge, Bob."

"You think you can kick my hat off my head like that guy in the movie?"

Mike had just turned his back to Bob when he made that remark to him. Turning around, Mike saw a hat on Bob's head.

Mike stepped up into Bob's face. "Bob, I don't know you, and from your attitude, I am glad. Do yourself a favor, and me, and do your job, please."

Staring back down at Mike, Bob returned with, "Let me see if you can do that."

Mike shook his head back and forth. "Let me get this straight, you want me to kick your hat off your head? If I make a mistake, you might be eating from a straw, Bob."

"I'll take that chance, Mike." Bob pulled his hat off and flipped it up and back in his hand then on top of his head.

Boy. Mike shook his head.

Connie and the two girls stopped what they were tending to. All three girls watched. They knew Bob was in the wrong. He was the type to cause trouble.

Ronald walked out of the restroom to get a bucket. He stopped when he heard Bob challenge Mike.

"Okay, Bob, if you are that stupid, so be it."

Bob snarled from the stupid remark. Still, he checked his hat was squarely on top of his head. As soon as the hat was placed on top of his head, it came flying off high into the air, stopping when it hit the ceiling.

Everyone cheered behind the candy bar counter. Bob watched his hat fly up then caught it on its descent.

Bob was upset, and he feinted a punch at Mike. Before his arm moved more than a few inches, Mike quickly sidestepped and tapped him on his head. Bob turned. Mike sidestepped again as Bob was turning and tapped him on the other side of his head. Turning again, Bob missed Mike sliding back to his first place and tapped Bob on the head a third time.

Cheers went up a second time behind the candy bar counter. Lindsey was working and heard the cheers. She poked her nose out of the door leading into the candy counter. She saw Mike sidestepping the new usher. Lindsey knew how fast Mike was. She hoped he wouldn't hurt the new usher.

Bob spun around to face Mike. After he turned to face Mike, he was a bit unsteady from his rapid turn. Mike gave him a slight nudge. Bob fell back, only to have his hand grabbed by Mike's hand, steadying him. "Now, Bob, if you want a further demonstration and need the urge to prove you are a man, we can step around the Rama after the show. Either that or get to work." That was the first time Mike had done any martial arts at the Rama. Bob pushed and pushed until Mike was provoked.

After that, Bob did his job. Tad set him straight later that night when he returned. Lindsey told Tad what took place. Of course, Bob believed Mike told on him. They never got along much after that first night.

By the next shift, the story got around the Rama. It got around the schools as well. What was secret soon became public. Every once in a while, when Mike was at the door, there would be some school jerk wanting to see what Mike could do. One guy threatened him. Mike had to take him to the side of the Rama. Nothing happened. He was all talk and wanted to make a statement to his friends standing by.

THE GANGS ALL GATHER

THE SECOND NIGHT CAME QUICK. The meeting was still on. Razor had his spies keep track of the new people trying to take over. As Chopper said, they were setting a trap for his group. The meeting place was in the industrial part of town. Many large and empty warehouses were littered about, abandoned and overgrown with vegetation. Easy to hide and plan for an ambush.

Razor counted twenty in this new gang. They carried guns. Some guns were planted near the sit-down. When the signal was given, it appeared they would draw their hidden guns and shoot for the kill. These guys meant business.

Reporting back at the clubhouse, Chopper reminded his men to refrain from shooting. "If it comes to that, so be it. The plan is to take them down quietly. Forget being nice! They want us dead. Dead it will be!" Chopper yelled out from the bar.

One biker did not want to play nicey-nice when he heard the first report from Razor. No response came from Chopper; it wasn't needed. After this report, the orders were to take them down.

Two hours before the meet. The new gang had men scattered into four groups. Each corner had a group. Each group of four split into smaller groups. Each person picked a spot to hide. Razor watched and took notes. Easy, just too damned easy. *This will be over before it even begins*, Razor envisioned.

Five men took their places. Each man had but one job to do. They were to get the others through the opening to their sit-down place. When the time came, it would be over within seconds. Chopper's men sneaked around to the different entry points. Quietly but with speed, they set themselves. Each had one or two preys to secure. The first victim needed securing quick, meaning kill. The weapon of choice was either a crowbar or noose or a knife, knife being optional.

A quick whack with a crowbar made a quick, quiet, easy method. A noose, maybe some kicking and struggle. With a knife, it had to be accurate; a messy knife could give away their surprise with the man screaming. A gun was too loud.

Noon came when the sun was directly overhead. Hot and dry. Four men stood just outside the tall warehouse. Both doors were shut. The four men walked together as if in formation before the two closed doors. Each stopped on cue. One advanced to the doors.

Two doors opened. Four bikers walked inside the warehouse. Inside was cool, and a marked difference in temperature was evident. Sweat was beading on each of the biker's heads. Not one swiped at the sweat to keep it from sliding down to their eyes. The intent was to stay focused. Four men were inside just several feet in front of the four bikers. Each noticed the sweat beads on the brow of the bikers. Each also took note not one of the men approaching them swiped the sweat away.

Four men greeted the bikers. "Good day, I see it is a hot one," came a half-joking remark from the second man waiting inside. His remarks drew little response from either of the four bikers standing stoically in front of them. The third man reached out to shake hands with Chopper. Chopper made no attempt to return his hand for a shake. Each of the hosts gave a quick glance at the others to their side. Then, without a word, all four of the hosts turned to walk to chairs set around a table. The table had four guns taped to the bottom on the host side. On the guest side was four glasses with a pitcher of water centered on the table. Either side of the pitcher were several bottles of whiskey. The host had four glasses as well.

The temperature was cool inside, but the atmosphere around the eight men was definitely boiling hot. The hosts became worried looking at the four huge men standing, not saying a word, staring at them with intent. What intent they hoped was their stupidity on their faces realizing they was going to die when they grabbed hold of their hidden pistols.

Chopper and the other three men accompanying him stood by their chairs. Bone Breaker stood staring with the intent of chewing on the bones of the other people. The four hosts looked like they might have to change their plans when they saw the height and size of Bone Breaker. They only hoped when the shooting began, someone would take that giant down quickly.

The host leader signaled for all to sit. The hosts all sat down. Chopper's group remained standing.

Each host members' hands were on the tabletop. The signal was given by the leader host. The signal wasn't anything special and was quickly seen by Chopper and his men. They stood waiting for the host to give his signal before they attempted anything unfriendly. If no signal, then maybe the hosts were sincere, wanting a peaceful resolution to the territorial claims of both parties. The host placed one hand under the table. Nothing happened. They froze before tearing the pistol from the tape.

Chopper and the three had their own guns drawn. Each host saw the pull and froze. No sound, nothing. Chopper stared at the host leader. Then spoke. "Nice and quiet. I like quiet."

He turned to his three men, and they agreed. "Quiet, that's good, Chopper."

Bone Breaker spoke last. "Hey, Chopper, should we tell them their guns are empty, or do you want them to pull them, and we shoot them?"

All four of the hosts looked at the other host. One man pulled his gun. *Click*. Nothing. Then another out of reaction to the first who pulled had his gun out. *Click*. The other two removed their guns and placed them on the table gently.

Chopper gently placed a handful of bullets on the table in front of the four men sitting. "Well, I see this wasn't a friendly get-together to iron out our differences. Such a shame. Right, Razor?"

"Yes, it looks that way. This all could have been avoided."

"Yes, Razor, you're right. These boneheads never learn," Chopper quipped with a bit of disappointment.

"Hey, man, we can still talk. Let this be a misunderstanding between friends. What you say, huh?" said the leader of the hosts.

"Yeah, I can see your point. Let me ask you this, if it was us sitting with our thumbs up our asses and staring at four guns, would you want to give us a second chance?"

"Hey, look, we get it. Let us go, and we won't be back. You the top gang here. We see that now."

Razor looked at Bone Breaker, and Bone Breaker signaled the others. Several boxes were kicked, others shoved. Each parting of boxes opened by hard kicks revealed each corner had four men lying dead on the floor. Each had two to three of Chopper's men by them. No guns, just crowbars and rope. Also, a knife or two.

Not a sound was heard. It was if they appeared and killed the host's men that were going to ambush Chopper's party. Dealing with the hidden men was over by the time all four hosts sat down in their chairs.

Cho had been watching from the ceiling, viewing their plans unfold. It was late at night when this new gang member bosses completed their instructions to their men. Each man was put into a corner group of two or three men. Each group had the same signal to step out of their hidden cubbies and begin the terrible slaughter of Chopper and his lieutenants.

When they walked out the warehouse that night, Razor and Cho's specially trained scouts put their plans into action. Nearly six bells or 3:00 a.m., each of Cho's black-suited special-trained team slid down silently from the ceiling to each of the four corners. Ropes were lowered, and a man slid down headfirst. A specialist was looming inches above the head of a hidden killer to take out. In each arm of the specialist was held a heavy crowbar at the strike position, ready to do just that on signal.

The other specialist made their way down various steps, over rails unto boxes to the ground in the pitch-darkness. Not one sound or inkling of motion could be heard or seen. Cho trained them well. The guards were replaced one by one. The first to be taken out was completed with a crowbar slap to their heads. Night became a bit darker for each one of them. As they were dropped to the floor, the other specialist was hanging inches above their man upside down, ready to make their strike. Each specialist was acutely aware of his other member's place, and together they dispatched all hidden gang members in their corners.

One specialist noted to his fellow members that he stood inches away from the face of his first man to take out. It was so dark, that man never knew he was facing him until he felt the whack across the top of his head. "I do believe he felt the floor slapping him on the jaw when he went down," he jokingly told his friends later.

The specialist he was talking to asked him, "How you figure that guy knew he hit the floor? That whack should have finished him before he hit the deck, pal."

"Yeah, you're right about that, except he made a low murmur when he hit. He must have been still thinking. I checked to make sure he was finished, just in case. It would seem that guy had an especially hard head."

"You think?" said the other specialist.

"Yeah, that's why I gave him a second whack to help him on his way."

Cho had one man especially placed to open the two large doors for the host to enter. Then he left his men as replacements to guard the warehouse until the meeting time. The replacement of Cho and Razor's men took less than half an hour. Morning was coming fast. A glint of sunlight prodded its way through the upper windows Cho's men left opened to enter the warehouse. Neither man slept, waiting in the cool darkness. Each remained vigilant through the night. No words passed their lips.

Morning came, and before 8:00 a.m., four men were standing at the warehouse doors to enter. One of the four rapped on the door to signal the man at the door to unlock and let them in. Leaders from the other gang were too busy discussing the plan to notice the guards were not theirs.

"Wish I had breakfast," one guard cited to his fellow guards.

"This ain't the time to eat when we got this kind of business to do. You gits plenty of time to eat after this is done with."

"Yeah, we don't need you puking before the deed is done," quipped another of the replacement guards, walking in front of the large door to the warehouse.

"Speak for yourself," he replied.

They all took their places near the front door. Each stood facing away from the door, waiting for Chopper and his men to arrive.

Within minutes of their entry into the warehouse, Chopper and the three men were seen walking to the doors.

Sitting before Chopper were the four men who plotted the demise of him and his fellow leaders, a nasty death, pleading for mercy. Each man changed from a strong, confident, bloodthirsty leader to a whimpering pile of sissies.

Chopper spoke. "Easy to give orders to your men to do your bidding without fear, until it came to you having to face what you often requested from your lackeys to do."

What you plan to do with us?" asked one of the four leaders facing Chopper and his lieutenants. The host along with his other leaders stood looking at the silent death that occurred under their noses. The four guns had been lifted off the table. They put them there when they realized there were no bullets in them to shoot. One bullet was placed inside the chamber of each gun by Razor. The four guns were put back on the table. Next to the four guns was a rope with a knot tied in the center.

"Either the rope or the gun. If it was left up to me, I would use the gun," Razor remarked. "The garrote can be slow and a nasty way to go. Bone Breaker hopes you will choose the rope. He likes the rope. The sound of a person making gurgling sound is music to his ears. Choose the rope if not for me, at least for Bone Breaker. Look, he is happy. He's smiling, choose the rope."

Each man opposite the table of Chopper stared at the grinding face of Bone Breaker. Each man made his choice. It was swift the way they all came to the same decision.

Bang, bang, bang, bang.

All four chose the gun. With a swift grab at their gun, each chose a different place to fire the killing shot. Two at the temples, one in his mouth, the fourth actually shook so bad, he missed the temple. All four made a mess. The fourth man wiggled around for a while, then stopped.

Razor turned back to Chopper. "Look, Bone Breaker isn't smiling." Looking around, he saw the bodies being dragged out of the hideaways of his men. "Well, get these bodies dumped, and then clean this mess up," commanded Razor.

Chopper waved to his men, telling them they did a good job. Turning to Razor, he asked, "Any of ours got hurt or killed?"

"Not a one," Razor said. It was clean.

Bone Breaker stood silent.

Razor asked, "Why so quiet?"

"Razor, they never attempted to take that last shot at us. They could have done us all in. Why you think they didn't think of that?"

"Bone, maybe they realized that if we could take all their men down at one time, then if they attempted that one chance and missed, well, you had your garrote ready."

"That's what I was thinking. I could have done them in if they weren't so smart figuring that out."

"Maybe next time, buddy," Razor quipped.

Cho turned to walk out of the warehouse.

Chopper called to him. "Hey, Cho, where you going?"

"I have been away too long."

"Remain for another day, Cho. Bell and Laura have been constantly on my back about what you been up to with Mike. Stay and fill them in. I would be grateful for that."

BOO IS A FUNNY DOG

ANY A TIMES, MIKE WOULD go home, and Boo would be waiting up for him. Boo constantly reminded him that he was first dog and should be treated like a first dog. That first dog was loyal, loving Mike no matter how he was treated by Mike. This wasn't going to happen with Boo. Mike decided to spend a good half hour playing with him every day. Many times, he took him out in the night for a walk around the neighborhood. When he came home from school, before going to the Rama, he spent time with Boo. Mike reflected often how Boo stayed along his side, protecting him.

Sometimes when Mike was off work and wasn't practicing, Boo rode on the bike wherever he went. Only on long adventures did he make him stay home. During practicing kung fu at home, Boo constantly tried to join in. Mike taught Boo dog kung fu to help him defend himself.

On the couch, Boo sat with Mom all day. Mike walked in early one day, and Boo was lying beside her. She started to feed him candy, and Mike noticed his weight grow. He didn't have the heart to tell Mom not to feed Boo chocolate. He was gone for long periods of time. Guilty feeling swept into his mind watching Boo as he left home every day.

Boo had seemed lazier when Mike came home. He never knew his age, assuming he was a pup when he found him tied to a tree half starved. He definitely looked like a puppy. He never realized how old he truly was. Mike's thoughts never considered Boo was getting older, but now, he saw Boo for the first time differently.

Every night, Boo would sleep on Mike's chest as he had done on the road. In the morning, Boo was still on his chest. Recently, he stayed on the couch. Usually, Mike had to return to fetch him off the couch. Picking Boo up and carrying him to bed was now becoming a routine. He never left the bed to go to the bathroom. In the morning, Mike lifted Boo from his bed to the floor. Boo had stopped jumping down from the bed one day. Mike had walked out of the bedroom hearing a whimper come from his room. Returning, Boo was limping. After that, Mike gently lifted him to the floor, then walked Boo to the back door. He seemed fine.

Another day coming home after school entering his house, Boo remained on the couch. This confused Mike. Boo never once did not run greeting him at the door, jumping up and down just yipping. He only stopped once Mike picked him up.

"Mom, is Boo okay? I thought he tired himself out waiting for me to come home. Does he lay around a lot while I am gone?" Mike questioned.

Mom answered back with her usual, "Boo has nothing to do. So he sleeps. As far as I can see, he is fine."

Mike replied with skepticism, "Usually, Mom, Boo will run to the door to greet me. I kind of feel worried about him."

"Don't be, he's fine," replied Mom, lifting her beer for a drink. Placing the beer can on the table near her ashtray, she picked up her card deck to play solitaire. Between each play of a card came either a drink of beer or a puff on a cigarette. That was her routine for the day, to play cards, watch TV, smoke, and drink beer.

Mike walked over to Boo and lifted him off the couch. "Come, boy, we are going out the back and practice." Outside, Boo acted like his old self. Quickly, he entered into the kung fu play.

At work, Mike often talked about Boo's antics around the house. On one telling at the Rama, Mike just started his shift, quickly going to the candy counter full of excitement. Everyone stayed to hear after learning he had a great story to tell.

"A funny thing occurred this morning," Mike began. "Boo was in the backyard by the fence. Mom called me over to the kitchen window when I got up. I just put Boo out of bed and went to the bathroom. Hearing my mom call to me, I went to the kitchen. She pointed out the window. Looking out the window, I saw Boo appearing to take a pee. His rear leg was hiked up near a fence post.

"My mom got the family a pet rooster," Mike said to all gathered in a cluster around the candy bar. "He was mean. I would bet he was as tall as any turkey compared to."

Mike had often cited to his friends about the rooster in his backyard.

"I have seen some big roosters and even had chickens when we were younger. Nothing as big as this bird got to be. He was as black as coal with a small sliver of red streak running from his comb down his neck. He was a good-looking bird. He strutted about like a prima donna," Mike explained with a sense of pride.

"If you walked out back, that bird would chase you down then jump up, attempting to spur you. Those spurs had to be at least two inches in length and deadly," Mike added. "That rooster thought he owned the backyard. He did. Even cats and other dogs passing through our yard gave way to his fierce demeanor. That was one tough bird." Mike often remarked about this coming to work. Boo seemed to be forgotten when it came to that rooster.

Mike continued, "I would practice my karate staff katas in the backyard. When that monster of a bird came at me, I would fight with him. He'd usually run after I got the better of him. He was getting better with time. He rarely ran from me. He would hold his ground instead of fleeing. I kept my eye on him even when I finished to go inside. I knew that bird wanted payback.

"Well, I looked out the window, that rooster was about ten feet from Boo. His head was down, staring hard at him. If, I didn't know better, it looked like he was going to head-butt Boo like a charging bull. Boo stayed near the fence with his leg up. I could see him eyeing that bird." Mike imitated the rooster's demeanor.

Mike hesitated. This he did for the effect. Every time he told a story, people listening were anxious to have him continue. After a short well-timed pause, Mike would start back up.

"That bird made up his mind and charged at Boo. You should have seen that bird. You ever see a bull fight? The bull would lower its head, snort, then kick out his leg? Well, that rooster must have been part bull. That is exactly how he stood, watching my Boo.

"Boo remained calm. He knew that rooster was hooked. He had him and was going to relish the time, teasing him. When the rooster couldn't take any more of Boo's disrespecting him, he let go with a shrieking charge. When that rooster got within a foot or so of Boo, he, with no thought or worry, lowered his leg. Boo was in control. It was all that dog kung fu I taught him," Mike said with a chuckle.

"Then, to my utter surprise and Mom's as well, that rooster kept charging toward Boo. Boo took one step away from the fence post just as the rooster came close enough to make impact. Watching that bird's fierce charge, there was no way he could stop or had time to stop. Boo planned it perfectly.

"The next second, pow!" Mike slammed his hand on the candy counter. The girls screamed. "That rooster ran smack into the fence post Boo had his leg held up against. Mom and I both gasped. That bird hit that fence post hard. He stopped his charge just like that, then stood up from the whack he received on his head. Then he staggered a foot or two and fell over, out like a light."

Mike once again acted out the rooster's charge and sudden halt after whacking the fence post. He staggered around the lobby floor and fell to the carpet. Everyone roared with laughter watching Mike pretend to be his rooster.

Mike paused to giggle about the memory he was recalling. It still had a titillating effect on him. Quickly, Mike rose from the carpet.

"What happened next was a real shocker," Mike went on to explain. "Boo turns, walks up to that rooster, made a circle around that fallen bird. The rooster fell knocked out, not knowing Boo was circling him. Standing near the bird's head, Boo...Boo...I still find it hard to believe," Mike remarked to his listeners. "Hahaha!"

"Hey, are you going to tell us, or are you just going to keep laughing, Mike? Dang, Mike, get on with it!" Connie carped from the ticket booth.

Everyone stood anticipating the climax to come. None had any idea of what Boo did.

Mike responded to her demand. "Okay, okay, give me a second to get my composure back. It was seriously funny and just as funny retelling what I saw, okay?

"Boo, lifting his leg, begins to pee all over the head of that rooster. The bird immediately woke. That rooster woke from dreamland with a snap to his feet. It stood shaking off the pee. Feathers on the rooster flew out around his neck. He would twist once then several times. Not one instant I believed he was capable of slinging all the pee off. We just laughed and laughed." Mike demonstrated the rooster's swinging his head back and forth.

"Boo nonchalantly walks over to the back door. That big bad rooster stepped aside quickly to allow Boo a clear path. I opened the door, congratulating him for a job well done. He looked up at me, wagging his tail, yipping. I was prouder than I'd ever been with Boo's cleverness and courage. Everyone clapped.

"I had many great times with my Boo," Mike often told his friends. One thing about him was his smartness. I could teach Boo any trick I thought of. I had him learn to sit, stay, lay, roll over—all the basic dog tricks in one day. Some that impressed me, Mom, and both my sisters was how quick he learned. One trick was Boo would hop on my back when I walked on all fours. Then, I would walk about the room, him standing on my back. Surfboarding was one of the many proud achievements," Mike expressed to his friends concerning Boo.

"Boo loved playing ping-pong and keep away. Usually, I offer him a reward. I had a box of milk bones. He especially like the colored small bite-size varieties. One trick that shocked and amazed all was he learned to unscrew the canning jar I kept his milk bones in. Boo sat on my lap, I loosened the jar lid, and with his paw, Boo pulled on the lid, making it unscrew. After about five to six twists of the lid, it would fall off. Boo would stick his nose in the jar and grab himself a milk bone.

"Boo loved showing off. Anytime someone visited our home, he was quick to show them his tricks. Of course, I wanted to show him off. I was proud of Boo. Most of all, I loved him," Mike shared with everyone.

PLANS AND IDEAS
FOR THE BIG EVENT

Two Months Before

"MR. HOWELL, WE GOT THE animatronic beast completed. We tested it, and it's a go."

"Good, how long to load it up and truck it to the site?"

"Twenty-four hours and another to get it on site. That is, if there are no mistakes."

"That is why I pay you to make sure there will be no mistakes. What about the tracks?"

"They are already in place. One question about the screen. It is long, and in that woody area with the small driveway, we might have to do some clearing to prevent any damage to it."

"That won't be necessary. I thought up a better way to set them up. In fact, I think this new way will work out even better than my first ideas for it."

"How so, sir?"

"By breaking the screen into several sections, we can use the trees and shrubs to mask any of the supports. Also, you need to elevate each screen to add to the distraction of supports."

"That is brilliant, sir."

A third man was in the room watching Mr. Howell discuss with the prop master the project. He stood there wearing his two-thousand-dollar suit and silk tie. Prim and proper was his mannerism.

Mr. Howell turned to ask him a question. "Mr. Peabody, the house, is it ready? And if it is, have you begun with the storyline to the press? That is the key to this being successful. We sell this to the public, the movie will go ballistic."

"By all means, Mr. Howell. The storyline will be on your desk first thing in the morning. My men have laid out a wonderful way to get the public interested in this movie. About the house being ready, our end of this project is set to fly."

Quickly Mr. Howell turned back to the prop master. "Good, you heard what Peabody said, Dennis, just tell me the house is set up with all the tricks to fool even the best investigators. I want the best, and the best is what I better get."

"You got it, boss. All the mirrors work fine, fog generators are super, some of the trapdoors and floors are being placed as we talk. We even got the graveyard set with a few surprises."

"What kind of surprises?"

"Boss, we want you to experience them when you come down."

"A surprise, Dennis?"

"Yes, sir. The boys love this project, and they wanted to add a few extras for you."

"How much are those extras going to cost me?"

"Very little, sir. They know how cost conscious you can be. We used that magazine article on that haunted house as an example. Even I got scared just checking some of the props in place."

"Good, good. So I might assume we are a go in several weeks?"

"That's a fact, boss."

Mr. Peabody nodded in agreement. "I figure the movie should come to its final phase in one week. Just need to go to the cutting room after that."

"Good, good, everything is going as planned. Just hope we won't run into any new snags. I planned for a few, nevertheless, it would be good not to run into a few this close to finishing." Mr. Howell turned, walked back to his desk, and sat down. Grabbing hold of his ledger, he waved his hand for his two men to leave.

Walking out of the room, Mr. Peabody could hear a soft comment coming from him.

"I wish, I knew who that young kid was and where he is now."

Together, Peabody and Dennis walked out of the office. Once the doors closed, Dennis slapped Peabody on the back.

"Please, you know, Dennis, how I hate your informality," Peabody said without missing a step nor turning to look at Dennis.

"Okay, Peabody, I got the message. So what's the line on the kid?"

"I will tell you the same as what I told Mr. Howell. That lad is like a ghost. He appears and disappears. He'll show up in one place, and poof, like a wisp of smoke, he is gone. In every case, he is described the same. A boy around thirteen or fourteen. Standing about five foot eight, maybe ten inches tall, and close to a hundred and twenty pounds. Brown hair and eyes and nice looking. About the only thing else is what he is wearing, most people tend to fixate on."

"What's so special with what he is wearing that people remember him?"

"Nothing of note, just some old worn-out boots, dirty pants worn and tattered, and a coat."

"That's it?"

"Well, the coat is the main feature people tend to fixate on."

"How so?"

"It seems to be made from the fur of an animal. Most encounters with the lad believe it to be a bear's fur. There is the face of the bear across the front. When he closes the coat, the two halves of the face come together, making the head. The last item I located was a news article that tells a story of a lad named Mike who made a trek from Virginia walking all the way to Georgia, alone. The lad seems to have been in many places. There is little to tie him to those other places. Some places are many of the same areas that agree with the magazine article. The only problem, and the main problem, is we haven't his full name. We are in the process of making contact with the newspaper editor to follow up on the story he wrote."

"Okay, then it sounds to me you have your lad."

"Yes, you would think that, but the editor doesn't want to disclose the lad's name. He is underage. There seems to be some kind of trouble the lad has been put into. Revealing his name may lead to him and probably his family put in danger."

"Peabody, what's up with this kid?"

"I am endeavoring to find that out. I will be taking a plane to Georgia as I part with you."

"I bet the boss was not pleased from that report you gave him."

"No, not at all."

Dennis looked perplexed with Peabody's reply.

Peabody hesitated long enough to irritate Dennis. He often enjoyed his little taunts to him. "I left out a few facts."

"Which facts?"

"If you must know, the one that the editor said he could not tell because of the age of this kid. I am leaving this very day to fly to Atlanta to talk to the editor."

"Hmm, good luck." Dennis smiled a tad, knowing Peabody was going to get in hot water if he couldn't get what he wanted from that editor.

A RETURN TO NOT AGAIN

A 1958 CHEVY TRUCK COMES TO an abrupt stop in front of the theater. Mike recognized it almost immediately. It was Ric's dad's truck he sometimes used. It was that same truck Ric took Mike on a fast romp down a dirt road to practice shooting their rifles. Mike had been down that road by himself doing the same thing target practicing with his .22 cal. Browning rifle many times.

Swinging the truck door open with gusto, Ric was not too concerned about damaging the door. That was Ric, act first, think later. He was wild, and being around him brought out the wildness in Mike.

Mike liked Ric; they were fast friends upon first meeting. Ric was a year older and about the same size and build. Having sandy blond hair and blue eyes only enhanced his pretty boy looks to the girls.

Ric came running up from his truck. He stopped suddenly by the front door where Mike was taking tickets from a couple. Excitedly, he barked out, "Mike, did you read this?"

"Wait a minute, Rick, I'm busy at the moment." Mike put his hand up to stop Ric from intruding upon his duty.

"Can't wait, you got to read this about the house."

"What house, and why is that so important?"

"Just read it." Rick thrust the paper into Mike's hands.

He read the title story. "House Angeles may be the most important discovery since the first reported haunted house was discovered two years ago by Dr. Strange and his assistants." The story continues retelling all the events of the house discovery. How a young boy who only was given the name Mike led the team to the house deep within the swamps. Many unknown occurrences happened to this boy prior to Dr. Strange's arrival at the house.

The boy disappeared while traveling back to the college. Later that night, the team recording various places inside the house and later outside by a separate team observed many strange things happened.

Several unexplained and horrifying occurrences led to several of the crew members leaving traumatized. One was severely hurt, not fatal, but an ambulance was called to the scene.

"Didn't you tell me you were at a haunted house traveling back home, Mike? Is that the house?"

Mike wanted that kept secret and hesitantly responded to Ric's question. "Well, I'm pretty sure that…huh, maybe. There was a Dr. Strange I met, Ric."

"One more thing." Ric took the paper out of Mike's hand and perused through it until he arrived at another page. Reading a few lines to make sure it was what he wanted Mike to read, he handed it back to Mike. "Now, Mike, read this."

"Ric, can this wait? Some people are coming up to purchase tickets for the show."

"Okay, okay, hurry it up. You got to read this. I showed it to Dinky, Victor, and Melvin, and they want to go. You got to go with us."

"Us? Where, Ric?"

"Read it and say yes."

After taking the tickets, with one hand, Mike snapped the ticket in two halves.

Ric watched him do that, remarking, "I can't see how you do that with one hand. No matter how hard I try, I still can't tear even one ticket, and you can do that with two to five tickets together with one hand."

"Practice, Ric. I did a lot of practicing."

"Why you want to do that in the first place, Mike?"

"I told you, Ric, ever since Tad told me about some guy doing this he saw at one of the theaters he checks on, I decided to see if I could." Taking the paper from Ric for the second time, Mike reads the article.

"Okay, some scientists are going to investigate this house called Angeles. What's the big deal, Ric?"

"Mike, don't you get it? They are setting up all kinds of experiments. They are going to invite the public to a viewing after running through their test. We got to go there before all this happens."

"Why is that important, and when will it happen?"

"No date has been set. It does say it will be several weeks before they get all the written approvals signed and permission from the owners."

"I thought that place was on government land, Ric? Where is this house, or is that even the same place we know about?"

"I've been there during the day and stopped in the drive, Mike. It's an old house. Two stories type, and it has a graveyard. Just like the one you said you fell into. Don't you remember the time we took Ronnie out there to give him a scare? You know, to initiate him when he started to work at the Rama. We nearly finished off that pint of liquor down the road from where we dropped him off."

"Yeah, we walked halfway up to the house with our flashlights along that dirt drive. I only saw a small part of the house with my light shining on it. When you grabbed my arm to turn and run, Ronnie was still staring at the building when we started running back to the car. Only when we got in the car did Ronnie hear the engine turn and ran back to the car."

"Remember the look on his face when we locked the doors, Mike?"

"Yeah, Ric, he was scared, and we drove off, leaving him standing in the pitch-black of night."

"Yeah, up to a point, then I turned off the lights. After that, we never knew how much farther he chased after us. We coasted for a while. I remember it was so dark outside on that road, you couldn't see your hand in front of your face. We only went a short distance down the road and stopped. We turned the engine off. Mike, we weren't going to leave him out there long."

"I remember only for a minute. Then we backed up. Good thing I decided to stop. He was frozen stiff in the middle of the road. I still think about how close we came to running over him, Ric."

"Well, we didn't."

I know, rolling the window down, we called for him to get in the car. I pulled out my floodlight, and there he was. Standing dead still behind my car. That light might have scared him more than the darkness."

"Mike, I remember that. He told us when that light came on, it scared the heck out of him. He thought we were long gone down that road."

"Oh yeah, you're right. He did say that he thought it was somebody else on the road. Finally, we had to get out and almost drag him in my car. He sat there staring at us. I thought we traumatized him, Ric."

"Yeah, that was a weird stare he had. After a few swallows of that pint, he came around, Mike. That story spread all about the Rama. Everyone still talks about that scare."

"Yes, they do, and the other stories as well. I still have memories of the Boy Scout camp that you and Melvin dumped me off at, Ric."

"We had to come up with another way of getting you to go into the woods. We wanted to take you snipe hunting. When we mentioned going, you said you knew what snipe hunting was and weren't going to fall for that trick. Hence, the Boy Scout camp story, Mike."

"Ric, I didn't fall for that story, I still had some reservations it was a story to get me to come along. The fireworks you brought did make me think you might not be tricking me. When you dropped me off while you two stayed in the car, that gave me second thoughts."

"We did have you believe we were going to another place to get out of the car to place the rest of the firecrackers, huh."

"Well, I went through the woods fighting every limb that slapped me in my face away. Once I broke through the woods, it was easy going. Tall grass and small bushes made for a quick advance to the campsite. I could see their dying campfires once I left the tree area into the grass. I really thought about just walking through their camp when I noticed there was no sentry. Then I thought about how you two might leave me, and I wasn't sure where I was.

"I put out three bottle rocket launchers with five to six rockets in each launcher and one pack of firecrackers to go off. I wanted to get back to the road to make sure you guys didn't leave stranding me."

"That was so cool. That homemade timer worked pretty good. That adventure will go down in the Rama Rowdies' history as one of the greatest pranks ever. Everyone still talks about that adventure, Mike."

"Yeah, they do. Gerry never lets me forget that either."

"Why, Mike?"

"Oh, you don't know him too well, do you, Ric? He is a Boy Scout, and when he heard that tale, he asked who was behind that. The girls told him about us."

"What he says about it?"

"I told him what we did. He replied that he and the rest of the scouts, upon hearing the racket of fireworks, went about the camp looking for the persons responsible. What made them most madder was they kept going off at different times. I told you those timers I made would work. Timing may be different. Apparently, it worked to our benefit and gave them a bad night.

"After a while, later, he told me it was all the talk among the scouts for a long time after the campout. I even asked him if he was game to go out with us to repeat it."

"What did he say?"

"No. He went further to say he would let them know it was us and warn them if we tried."

"See, me made history. I guess he's out for the Angeles trip."

"I didn't ask him, Ric. Besides, Ric, that scout prank, it would have been a lot cooler if you and Melvin followed through with the other fireworks. You two chickened out."

"Well, we didn't think you really would set them out. This will be so much cooler, Mike."

"Yeah, Ric, I heard that before. Besides, what happened to me in that haunted house wasn't so cool. In fact, I still have dreams of that night. I'm not so sure I want to relive that experience again."

"It'll be all right, there will be the five of us. If anything happens, we won't be on foot. We got a car. Yours."

"Wait a minute, that car is old. I don't know how well it is. Where is this house again?"

"Not far. We go down Highway 96 a few miles and turn off past the railroad tracks. About five miles down that road, and we are there.

We got lights and flares. Also, I will bring along my M-80 firecrackers if we need more firepower, Mike."

"If I go, this ain't no dropping me off like the Boy Scout raid you and Melvin did to me?"

"No, man, this isn't going to be an initiation."

"What about the candy bar girls? Anyone ask them if they wanted to come along? Remember the M and T Drive Inn. They were with us. We laughed so hard at that movie with Paul Newman. Charlie the manager had to make us move the car to the rear of the concession stand because we were so loud."

"I know, I laughed so hard, I fell out of the car."

"You and me both did, Ric."

"We can ask them."

"I am not sure how many people we want to pack in my car."

"All heck, that old car can easily hold at least six people. Besides, the way Melvin is talking, I think he is going to back out. That will give us another empty seat to fill."

"What if the car breaks down on that long dirt road? We might be there all night with those girls scared out of their minds."

"Yeah, I thought of that, Mike."

"One thing you forgetting, Ric, the last time we used my car to go on one of your adventures, we ended up in jail. Remember? You didn't say that was private property, right?"

"Yes, but we won't be long, and it will be night. No one every goes there at night. Besides, we only got caught because you ran up to the car and told me to move over for you to drive. I was ready to leave when you came in. You were running scared that night."

"Well, Ric, you would have been a bit scared if someone was shooting at you. It was you who told those two girls you were going to visit them when we got off work. You and Dinky just wanted to impress those girls."

"They were pretty, weren't they? I did visit them as I told them I would."

"No, you stayed in the car and wouldn't walk up to the door of the trailer. I wasn't going to drive all the way out in the boondocks and not go and see them. When I got to the front door, they met me in their pajamas. If only I walked back to the car and not to the side windows where they asked me to go. I climbed up the trailer hook and talked to them. They wondered why you didn't come to the window. I kind of wondered that myself."

"Okay, I admit, I chickened out. I almost did go up to the window though. I saw her father and some other men walk out the door of the trailer next door. They were having a party. When I saw those guns, I changed my mind."

"Wish you had told me sooner."

"I was waving to you to hurry up. I didn't want to let them know. I thought they didn't see you at first, Mike?"

"Well, Ric, after the first gunshot, I think they knew. I dropped to the ground looking around to where the shot came. That was the only time I heard you or Dinky call out to me."

"Yeah, we were trying to get you to run."

"By that time, Ric, I didn't need to be told to run. I saw you at the driving wheel. I was afraid because of the car's peculiarities that it might stall. That's why I yelled for you to move over."

"Well, it stalled."

"Yeah, I know, and sometimes I wished I hadn't told you to move over."

"We didn't get to far down the road before the car stopped running. We coasted a hundred feet or so to a stop. I sure am glad Dinky was with us. That old car of yours is big and heavy, Mike. We barely were able to turn down that side road pushing it."

"It didn't do much good, did it, Ric."

Both of them giggled.

"Yeah, that was some night. Mike, what do you think that man must have thought when you went up to his door and knocked on it about two in the morning?"

"Ric, there was no guessing what he thought. Did I tell you when he came to the door, he also had a gun in his hand?"

"No. I was too worried those men following after us to listen if you did tell me. Hahaha!"

"They did. And by the way, it was me again who had to confront those two drunken men in their car when they drove up."

"Well, it was your car."

"Yes, and your idea. When I got to their car door, looking inside between both of their legs was a rifle. The one man had a pistol in his hand. The other guy had a pistol lying on the dash. Both of them had beers in their hands. Both of them were drunk as skunks, Ric."

"Well, you did good."

"Drunk, Ric. What, you expect me to argue with them, Ric? That one man, the driver, was those girls' dad. He gave me a nasty look after asking me if we came up the road along their home. I knew telling them the truth was going to be a bad idea. The way he spoke to me said redneck. Better tread carefully."

"I was thinking the same thing when I heard him talk to you. Dinky wanted to run. He gave me a nudge, pointing to the road for us to scat. I motioned back to stay with you."

"Dang sporting of you two. If you did, I can tell you I would have told everybody about you two running out on me. I thank god the man in the trailer door I knocked on came to the car when he did.

"After telling daddy we came from the other direction then him asking again if we saw another car. Well, you almost blew it, Ric, when you spoke up. Telling him we didn't see any other car on the road. That man coming from the trailer saved our butts that night. If it wasn't for him telling those two drunks, we'd been parked in front of his house for more than an hour, no telling what might happened."

"If only your sister was able to come and get us sooner, we would need not have gone to jail."

"But it happened, and now that is part of the Rama Rowdies' history. We got a lot to be thankful for. If not for Tad and Mr. Bill and the two girls'' mother, we would have been charges as peeping toms."

"Looking back, Mike, I will tell you this: I was more afraid when the police showed up."

"Me too, Ric."

"Yeah, when that officer had us line next to your car with our hands up, I nearly lost it. After he walked around looking at the tires, I was a bit puzzled why he did that."

"I was too, when he said our tire threads matched the ones in the girls' driveway, I knew he had us. Remember, Ric, the road was wet from the rain earlier that day. We would have gotten away if not for them wet roads."

"Sure would have. Know what makes me laugh at that today?"

"No, Ric."

"When that police officer asked each of us if we were the one driving the car away from the girls' home. He pointed at me, I replied, 'No, sir.' Then he pointed at Dinky, and he said, 'No, sir.' It was when he pointed at you, and you said, 'No, sir,' then he walked past you and turned quickly back to you, pointing his finger in your face. 'It was you, kid.' You squealed like a baby, 'Yes sir, yes sir,' you kept repeating."

The both began laughing again at that incident.

Dinky stopped by while they were in that last bit of laughing. "Hey, guys, what's so funny?"

Ric spoke up, "We talking about that night on Shot Gun Road."

"Huh?"

"You know, when we got arrested, and those two men wanted to press charges against us. If not for their mother, we might have gone to jail."

"Oh, that night. Hey, Mike, did Ric tell you about the house?"

"Yes."

" Well, you going, aren't you?"

"Dinky, he hasn't told me he will yet."

Both Dinky and Ric looked at Mike, waiting for him to tell them yes. So he said yes. Thinking on it later, Mike prayed that the car wouldn't die again.

"By the way, Ric, I hear you plan on going into the army. Thanks for not telling me."

"Mike, I kind of wanted to leave unnoticed."

"Why, Ric? Don't tell me you expected me and the others to cry?"

"Nah, I didn't want to tell why I am going in the army a million times."

"Well, Ric, one time to me would have been nice. I could have told the rest. When is it planned to go to this haunted house, Ric?"

"Well, the best I can figure would be in a week. That should give everybody a chance to decide if they want to come."

"I hope we don't end up going by ourselves."

"Are you kidding, Mike? Who wouldn't not want to go? This is going to the biggest event yet. All those other things we did, well, that's all most everybody talks about. They wish they could have been asked to go or been there. Heck, we might have to say no. It could be like the balloon blimps behind the base. Remember the car caravan following us?"

"A week is a bit off, yeah, Ric. By the time this gets around, we might just have to beat them off with a stick, either that or they change their minds when they start to think about all the weird stuff happening out there. I'll see you tomorrow, Ric, I have practice."

"Yeah, see you tomorrow, and I am going to hold you to that yes!" Ric shouted to Mike as he began his run home.

Running along the back roads made it easier for Mike to apply his training routines, jumping fences, flipping off telephone poles, and jumping hedges. Mike kept near hedges and close to wooden fences to keep himself concealed and to spot would-be followers he had felt dogging him lately.

One of the many tricks Mike was taught and developed into a skill was climbing trees. He applied it jumping on poles, backflipping to propel himself upward. When he came to a tree, he would jump onto the trunk, bounce off upward to a branch, then swung up on top of the branch in one fluid motion. Once on the branch, he would quickly hop off to the ground, sometimes rolling and back up to his feet running.

CHO RETURNS

A T THE CLUBHOUSE SITTING IN a corner was the normal scene happening. Since the warehouse incident, nothing changed. Beers were still delivered to the four leaders. Chopper and Bell were just putting the beers down when Cho walked over to their table.

"Hey, Cho, great job, have a beer."

"Thanks, Chopper, but I prefer to get going back to Mike."

"What's the rush? Stephen told me Mike was doing great. Now he is working on the gillie suit. You know what Mike had done on his first attempt sneaking up on Stephen. He got right under his feet. Hahaha!" Chopper started to giggle telling this to Cho. "Mike, he tapped Stephen on his foot. When Stephen looked down, Mike waved to him. Can you beat that? It ain't ever happened before. Someone got the sneak on him, and it was a kid. Hahaha!"

I heard from Bone Breaker. Seems everybody was told before me."

"Hey, you ain't jealous? If you were, I would have told you first. I just got the news. I know everybody is hankering to hear anything what's going on with him."

"Ah, I—"

"Yeah, he got under your skin, Cho. He does that. In fact, he done that to all of us. That's why I didn't wait to tell you. Don't be mad. We all care."

Razor butt in. "Look, Cho, we all been to hell fighting. We all fought for this country, we put our lives on the line in service. We are all brothers. We are Americans, not African, German, Mexican, Asian, Italians, etc., just Americans. We are only Americans. Americans come first, all them other things, well, they are our heritage and not who we are. We are not like the rest, we don't have dual citizenship. We have one culture, and that is American. We earned that right. All others, they…they just plain citizens. They looking to belong. We belong."

"Cho, we all know this. We did the talk and then did the walk. That is why we are here. This is our group." Chopper continued to talk and stood to be heard. His voice commanded silence from the others in the club. They all turned to hear his words.

"Men and women who served. Each and every one of these sons a bitches are Special Forces. Green Beret, SEALs, Rangers, hell, even some Tigers and Israeli Special Forces who we allowed in this group. We all know the measure of the other, and we will fight and die for each other. Mike, he may not be Special Forces, but his dad died for this country, and he can fight. He has what it takes. He is a good man and will stand by all of his brothers, just like you and me. He ain't alone no more."

Everybody cheered.

"Beers all around!" cried Chopper. Turning back to Cho, he said, "Now have a beer. You can leave in the morning."

* * *

Later that same day, Mike arrived at the training site Sifu Stephen had set up. Seeing Mike rounding the hill into the wooded area, he signaled his companions to seek a hidden site. Mike stopped just short of Sifu not even breathing hard. It was as if Mike drove here and just got out of his car, and not just finishing a five-mile run. Then with a spurt of effortlessness, Mike bounded up onto a tree limb with a single leap.

"Nice flip up into that tree, and not even a rollout onto your feet. You hit the ground, what, ten, twelve feet from the tree branch, Mike?"

"That felt about right, Sifu."

"I guess you are wondering what the lesson is for today. Well, look around, what do you see, Mike?"

"Sifu, it appears to be a small campsite. Is this where you live now?"

"No, no, Mike. This is a campsite. You noticed the size, good. Remember, when you enter the woods, any sounds you make, animals hear. Any movement, animals hear and see. Any change has a reaction. The bigger the change, the bigger the reaction. Hence, a large camp, large change. One person compared to several persons.

"Mike, changes can help or harm you. The smaller the campsite could mean less distance to travel looking for game to feed yourself. Predators and prey each have certain behaviors you can learn from.

"You look at a predator, what you notice is their eyes are forward and not on the side. Prey, their ears are larger and move to detect noise. Every animal has traits allowing them to hide to avoid being caught or to aid in catching prey.

"Keep your camp small. Fires hidden, smoke little to none. Find a shelter that is part of the terrain. Don't try to change the land. Every animal like a human knows their home. You move things, they notice the move. Put things back when you leave.

"If someone is tracking you, every little change can be a trail to where you are or going. Your scent is noticeable to animals. Do you think any hunter worth a hoot would wear cologne on a hunt? I don't thinks so, unless he's looking for a mate."

"I get the point, Sifu. I was traveling in the woods for a year getting home."

"I am aware of your background, Mike. There are things you might know, and things you think you know, and things you don't know. So listen and relearn the lessons you learned, and the lessons you think you learned, and the lessons you haven't, I will teach to you."

"Yes, Sifu."

"Good, this exercise begins now. There are three campsites within a few hundred feet. Go and find them. Once you have correctly spotted the campsites, then I will teach you some new ways to setting up camp."

One campsite was well hidden in a treetop. Mike walked past it twice. Sifu offered a hint. "Mike, every camp is not always seen on the ground." It wasn't. Above the branches, a rope was strung between two trees. A hammock bed with leaves could barely be made out. Mike soon spotted quickly.

Each campsite became more difficult, and some hints were offered on each to aid locating by Mike. The second was inside a hollow tree. The entrance was limbs woven together. Inside the hollow was a fireplace with a snug bed of tree boughs. Sitting on the floor, a person could see out into the wooded area. Outside, one could not see in.

The third campsite was the hardest of the three sites to find. Only after several hours of scouring the area, many times the same site two or three times, nothing revealed the whereabouts of the third site. Only when Sifu and Mike returned to where Sifu was sitting did Mike tell Sifu, "I give up, I can't find the third one."

Sifu laughed. "Mike, you did find it, you are standing in it. This place is the third campsite."

"You said there were three camps. I thought you meant three different camps, not yours."

Looking around, there were telltale signs reconfirming Sifu camp. His log revealed a bedroll in its hollow. A small firepit was neatly concealed near a depression of many such depressions that littered the open space. Except his depression was among those least likely to pose a place to inspect. Over by the trees that bordered the site, Mike gazed up to the upper levels. There among many branches was a faint shape of a bag. Most likely a stash lofted up away from hungry animals looking for a quick and easy snack.

Sifu was correct, this was his campsite—well hidden but surely in plain sight. Too obvious for most people to view as a camp that has an occupant.

"I said there were three campsites. Mike, sometimes what you are looking for is right in front of you. Anytime you get into a situation, stop. Rethink the questions. Are their hidden meanings? Clues you missed, or are you overthinking? We can get into a real horrible mindset trying to find solutions to problems. These mind games can eat at you. They can break you down, causing you to quit or let your guard down. Just stop and allow your brain time to figure it out. Sleep allows your brain time to filter through all the crap you went through.

"It is just like a campsite. Too big, and your food travels farther away. Too much crap, the longer it takes for the brain to find a solution. I always see a thing as simply as possible. This keeps the solution simple.

The madder you get, the greater the lack of attention. Think about your campsite for all things. Little fear, little threat, little hurt, less time to heal, etc.

"Now run and evade. Once you leave, you will have followers. Mike, this time, be prepared for a fight if they catch you."

Mike could see the change in Sifu tone when he spoke. *This training session has changed. The threat is bigger, the harm is greater*, Mike realized.

Mike started to run through the twisted limbs of low-lying tree branches and bushes. Thinking, Mike said to himself, *If they want me, they're going to work for that hard.* Not once did Mike leave the brush; he remained in them throughout his long run home. Across a snaky river. Up to and in some cases well above his head were places he deliberately waded through. Emerging from the water wet and dripping, still he ran. Then up into a tree. He swung up into and leaped from one branch of one tree to a second branch of another tree. He deliberately ran through as many places a rabbit or squirrel would give second thoughts about going through.

In the treetops, both pursuers never once took care to view. Most of their trackings they had been led on by Mike usually was on the ground. Needless to say, they forgot some key aspects of their own training. Over time, they became accustomed to Mike's usual patterns of evasive running.

Never continue a routine, Stephen said many times. Over time, it will reveal itself to your pursuers. Apparently, that lesson was forgotten by his followers.

Mike set a trail for them to follow, just not the one they had expected. It led the two followers through a part of the woods with all kinds of thickets, briars, and swamp. The ground gave little evidence of any trail to spot. Too swampy with water constantly removing any traces of footprints.

By the time the two discovered the ruse, Mike was well on his way home by another easier route.

One hour later, Mike arrived home, still panting from the most difficult run he ever done. Standing in the backyard, bent over trying to regain his wind, he met his first attacker. Mike felt the pressure wave sweep across his face. Then came the stillness of his foe tensing to make his strike.

From a bush, he leaped out. The kick to Mike's head almost caught him squarely. Being bent over offered Mike a chance to tuck and roll. The kicker followed through with his kick, only to make contact with empty air, and his spinning hook kick threw him off balance. The kick happened before the attacker could adjust to Mike's tuck and roll. The hook kick breezed over the kid's head.

Luckily, Mike was within striking distance. His foe pivoted on his leg to follow up with another kick. He had not advanced much forward from the second kick. Before the third consecutive kick was readied, Mike simply spun with a low sweeping kick. The attacker hit the ground hard. Mike jumped up; he was going to punch him in his jaw, just enough to let him know he was stopped.

Mike didn't have the time to evaluate the intent of his adversary and presumed he was another of Sifu's followers. It seemed he forgot one of Sifu's lessons to never assume anything.

While Mike was coming down to finish the fight, he realized the attacker was not one of Sifu's followers. At the same time, he heard a scream coming from the front of the house. The attacker had both arms covered with tattoos. What was to be a tap turned into a jaw-shattering impact that left his attacker out, like a light lying beneath Mike's two spread legs. Boo was yapping loudly. It was apparent there was more than one attacker. Their intent was sensed. They wanted to do harm to him and his family.

Getting up, Mike dashed to the front. His older sister was being held by another tattooed man. A third man was in a car. Mitch, Dodie's boyfriend, saw Mike turn the corner to the front of the house. Mitch was about to get out of his car to aid Mike's sister until he saw Mike at the corner. Mike was on the tattooed man. Mitch saw the third man opening his car door. Mitch was out of his car faster.

Before the third man had his door opened to get out, Mitch was at the door. Mitch took one swing. His fist shattered the window. The glass flew into the third man's face along with his fist. Both glass and fist left a bloody featureless pulp of a face remaining. Turning to aid

Mike, Mitch was stopped. What he witnessed from Mike was cause for him to pause.

The tattooed second man swung to face Mike. He heard his shout to let his sister go. Dodie twisted on the hold of the second tattooed man's grip. This caused an imbalance in the second man's stance. A slight swipe and a strike to the forearm weakened his grip on Dodie. Dodie screamed and tore free of her attacker. Later, Mitch was given credit for teaching her that technique.

The second man with his free hand had hold of a knife. None too soon it appeared to Mike. He was taking his sister by force. Why? Mike remembered the leader man's promise. He was going to kill Mike and his family. *Why now?* Mike thought briefly. Dodie was about to enter their home. The front door was ajar. Boo was jumping up and down yapping. *Where was Mom?*

No time to ponder the obvious. Mike saw the flashing blade in the tattooed man's opposite hand. It was fast approaching in his direction, leveling out for a direct thrust into Mike's guts. It was clear the knife had a purpose—it was to kill him.

Again, Mike slapped at the wrist. The force of the slap dislodged the blade. Tattoo's wrist bent back. A slight grimace swept his face from the distorted angle his wrist had drooped. Soon a shallow "Oh shit" followed his words spoken with a grimaced look. Rapidly, tattoo man twisted to throw a punch at Mike.

The second man was no slouch; he immediately shot out a punch. Mike was quicker and blocked the punch, then followed it with a strike to his floating rib. The second man flinched. Mike took the second man's arm. Sweeping the arm behind the second man, he stood with the arm held in an unnatural height above the second man's back.

A quick forward thrust with a knife hand to a pressure point, the tattooed man bent to one knee. The next movement was painful to look at. Mike stepped over the second man's shoulder, holding the arm high, then with a twist, Mike followed through with his spinning, making the elbow angled to drive the arm forward in an arc. He extended his chi, directing the internal force down through the tattooed man arm. Mike had thus put his entire weight onto the shoulder joint. To the eye, it only appeared he was pushing on the arm. The results were the arm becoming removed from its socket. What followed was the elbow becoming separated, then the wrist with a gut-wrenching twist made a nasty sickening sound. It was completed with a beautiful spinning motion like a dance by Mike.

Every joint in that arm was separated. Tattooed man's arm was completely useless. He didn't have long to suffer.

Mitch turned his head when he saw what action Mike was attempting to do next.

Mike grabbed hold of the second man's neck. With a quick twist, another and final snap was made. Mike let the body fall to the porch. It lay there like a pair of dirty pants thrown across a chair, only to slide onto the floor. Two of the three were dead. The third man was alive. Upon visual appearance of the hit Mitch had given him most likely made the third man wish he was dead. Later, his wish was granted. Not by Mike nor his friends.

Mitch reached for Dodie jumping off the porch, running to the car with the broken window. Dodie grabbed Mitch's arms and embraced him. Then she saw the third man sitting, not slouching across the front seat, face up. Blood was oozing from his nose. Cuts scattered across his distorted face. His nose was present, just bent to one side, flat against his cheek. She held back a scream of horror.

Mitch pulled her closer to him. He could sense the fear rise up inside her, knowing she was about to scream. After Mitch pulled her head to his, Dodie saw his fist that broke the window and the third man's face. Mitch's fist was bloodied, and two of his knuckles appeared to have separated. He broke his fist.

"Oh my, Mitch, look at your hand!" she exclaimed. Dodie grabbed his hand, pulling it from her face. Extending his fist out, Mitch saw his fist. He hadn't felt or considered any pain from the window breaking. His attention was quickly diverted to Mike's actions. Only when Dodie grabbed his hand and presented it to him to see did he begin to feel the pain.

Mike walked down the three steps over where the two cars were. Dodie was showing Mitch his hand. Mitch began to show his pain. A tiny murmur was heard from the inside of the car. The third man was beginning to come to.

"Mike, what did you do? How…how did you, I mean, that was unbelievable!" Mitch could only fumble with the words he thought, unable to put into speech. Stuttering and having a dumbfounded expression were the only thing he could express. Slowly the words formed in his mind, making it out of his mouth with clarity. "You killed that man, didn't you? He is dead, right?"

"Yes, Mitch, he is dead, and so is the first tattooed man on the side of our house. There were three, Mitch. I don't think you saw the third man. He was the first that attacked me," Mike said in a coldhearted fashion.

"You killed two men in the face of a minute, maybe less time. How did you learn how to fight like that? Why did they attack you and Dodie? Was it necessary to kill them?"

"Mitch, if someone was attacking you and threating your family, what would you do? He had a knife and was going to use it on my sister."

"The law, it is against the law."

"Mitch, what law, where are they? Did you have time to go get the law? How many would be dead when they got here?"

"It is wrong to kill," Mitch reiterated.

"Why, Mitch? Animals kill to protect their home, their babies, to eat. The rich have laws to protect them against the poor. Are the laws the same for the rich and the poor? No, Mitch, they are not. That is why we have laws to protect them and their wealth. To keep us in line with laws and religious ethics. God created man. He created nature. The law of nature is to kill for food, defend oneself and their home. Why is God's law different for humans? We are animals. Yes, we think. But also, animals think and feel. You hit a dog, it barks in pain. You keep hitting that dog, and you cow it. Look at the eyes of a cowed dog. It is afraid, shows sadness, and is unhappy looking. Why?

"Don't humans act the same? Don't humans hunt and raise animals to kill and eat? Why is it correct for a rich man to take your land and money? He has the law to back him up. His family will never go hungry. Do you think that rich man would offer you or your family food? No, he won't. Look how the Irish was treated during the potato famine by the English. They begged for food. What they got was imprisonment, spit on, and deported. They shot them down for sport. This is not the only time people treat others like that, Mitch. It goes on now and will continue.

"I will fight for my family just like any living thing will. I will obey the laws as long as they are fair to all. When comes an imbalance in the law, then we have no choice. You have God's law on you. That is nature's law of survival. In nature, you are not punished for killing to provide for food nor to defend yourself. Killing is wrong, and it is wrong for the rich and the poor. To steal is wrong, whether the law is used to steal what you rightfully earned or not. Stealing is wrong by law. Man's law, not nature's law.

"Mitch, if my family is starving, is it right to let them starve to death? What law says that is right? I will take bread or steal to get food. If people have food and care for only themselves, why is that right when others can't eat the food they that have hoarded? Right and wrong has different meaning to different people. One country has certain laws. They may or may be the same laws in another country. What makes that country's law superior to the others? It is their power, wealth they wield, Mitch."

A loud noise was coming up the road. Two men ran from behind Mike's house. Both of them stopped short to inspect the first dead man. One of the two reached for the neck. Looking up, he signaled to the second runner that the man lying on the ground was dead. Quickly the runner stood, and both quickly ran around the corner of the house. Two cars were parked next to each other, and three people stood by the closest car to the house.

The noise rose as the two runners walked silently to the three standing. The noise began to ease as all three people and the two runners meet.

"Mike," the first runner said, "you killed the man on the side of your house. Why?"

"Yes, also the one lying on the porch." Mike pointed to the slain tattooed man lying wadded up on the porch.

The second runner walked over to confirm what he already knew. After reassuring himself, he signaled back to the first runner.

Dodie began to cry. "What about the one in the car?"

The noise had stopped. A tall slender man unsaddled from a black bike. All in black, and not any other color was evident. Mike knew immediately it was Sifu Stephen.

He parked his bike between the large bushes Chopper had when the first tattooed men came to his home. Sifu walked over to all five gathered at the car. Pointing to the two runners, he commanded them to take the bodies to the house next door. "The back door is unlocked. Go now, hurry before this scene gets noticed."

"Sifu, how did you know about the other house?" Mike was a bit dumbfounded he was aware of the house and its history, of three tattooed men from before who were held in it.

The police never checked the place out when they came by. This time, there was very little ruckus. Dodie was the only noise being created to maybe attract someone's notice. Mitch hushed her with his hands around her head. Softly, he began to calm her with soothing words of assurances.

"Mike, I was one of the men Chopper sent to remove those three gangsters to a safer place."

Mike kept quiet hearing Sifu Stephen's remarks.

Looking in the car, Sifu took note of the tattoos dressing up and down the arms of bent-nose man.

Speaking with a soft voice looking at Mike, Sifu declared, "Well, this is a bit early and unexpected. Are you all right, Mike? Are the rest of you okay?" Sifu took a glance at Mitch's hand as he spoke those words. "Here, Mitch, give me your hand."

Mitch had a question expressed over his face when Sifu called him by name. So did Mike, for that same reason, especially the black leathers he sported and the bike he was riding.

Sifu was aware of the questioning looks he was receiving from the two. "Mike, why the curious look? Remember what Chopper said to you?"

Now Mike was puzzled. *How does he know Chopper?* he thought.

"Chopper sent me after Cho left you. Mitch, relax, the pain will end soon," commanded Sifu Stephen. Sifu Stephen pressed on a point on Mitch's arm. The pain ended.

"Cho too?" Mike asked Sifu. "Why didn't you two tell me?"

"We felt it wasn't necessary at the time. No need having you worry for nothing. We were sent to train you. Everybody that is with Chopper are ex-Special Forces. We come from the best this country has ever put into harm's way. We even have some members join from other countries. Your training is coming from the best. Now enough. We are not alone. We need to keep some things private for the time being."

Mitch turned to Sifu. "What the hell are you teaching Mike?" Mitch was getting a bit heated from what went down. "Why are these men trying to kill him and his family?" Mitch took Dodie, placing her behind him. Mike sensed he was shielding her from impending danger Sifu might inflict on both of them.

"Calm down, young man. We are here to help. Mike is our dear friend. We are here to teach and prepare him for what's to come," Sifu Stephen said to Mitch.

"What's to come? What is coming, mister?" Mitch demanded back to Stephen.

Sifu asked Mitch and Mike to step away from the car. "Let Dodie go inside, Mitch." Looking at Dodie, this strange man wanted her to go inside. Dodie was about to object to this stranger's demand until he commanded her to do so. Dodie went in the house.

Dodie walked up the steps into the house. Boo came out as she went in. Boo quickly was by Mike's side, jumping up and down. Mike reached down, taking hold of Boo. Boo licked and licked Mike's face. Mike just hugged him. It was plain as day to all that Boo and Mike were more than master and dog. They went through much in their travels. Each shared scars from their adventure that bonded them forever.

Mom was inside, passed out. She was drinking hard liquor. Sleep often followed or one hell of a yell fest. Luckily, she went to sleep. Sharon wasn't home; she worked at night. Dodie went to the kitchen table and sat, then sobbed. She never was brave. Anything or anywhere she wanted to do or go, she had Sharon go with her. Mitch continued aiding her when Sharon began work.

"Mitch, Mike," Sifu began, "your first three friends you encountered resulting in saving Bell's and Chopper's life were left along the road miles from anywhere. They made it safely to a doctor. Then back to Atlanta." Turning to Mitch, Sifu looked him straight eye to eye. "Mitch,

Mike made a few enemies when he was walking back home. In Atlanta, he saved a man's life. Doing that made him enemies of the gang that attacked the man he saved. They chase after Mike throughout the city.

"Mike confronted three of the gang members chasing him. The same three that attacked him and his family months before you met Dodie. We dealt with them. Mike knifed the leader man. He swore to kill him and his family.

"These men are from Atlanta. I am afraid this is the start of the payback." He turned back to Mike. "You are ready. Rest assured we have been preparing for them of late. We have them watched. I was coming to tell you Cho is on his way back."

Mike's face lit up. Stephen realized the connection Mike had for Cho. Like himself and other students learning from a master, they developed a strong connection. Cho had an attachment for this young man. So did Stephen now.

"Mitch, we will take care of this. You are part of this. You will answer to the law, as will Mike. I intend to prevent that. Mitch, you have two choices. One is agree with us, and we will help you, or do what you think is necessary. Remember this before you choose. There are four of us to give evidence and one of you. Never mind Dodie, she will do as she is told. Trust me, we will make this go away."

Mitch didn't take any time to make his decision. "I'm in, how can I help?"

"Good, good, Mitch. I hoped you would be the kind of man I first thought you were."

"One thing that puzzles me, uh…?"

"Stephen, Stephen is my name." He sensed Mitch was fumbling to think how to ask what his name was. "Sorry, I hadn't mentioned who I was. I've been training Mike while Cho, his other teacher, has been called to our clubhouse.

"Mitch, I will ask one thing from you. It will be dangerous. I hope that you will not need to deal with any other attempts to Mike's family. Trust me, you will be shadowed, and if any threat is visible, it will be acted upon. Here, take this card." Stephen pulled a card from his pants pocket. On the card was two telephone numbers. "Call either number anytime. Help will be here as soon as possible."

Turning to Mike, Sifu pointed him to a backyard empty area. "Wait there, Mike. Mitch, I am going to give you a safe house to take this family. If for any reasons, go there. Then call either number again. First call the numbers. I will have some of our members contact you soon. Now go and tend to Mike's sister inside."

Mitch offered Sifu his hand and thanks.

THE CHOSEN

WALKING OVER TO WHERE MIKE stood holding onto Boo, Sifu waved for him to sit. Looking around, the only place to sit was the ground. Mike sat on the ground. The two followers of Sifu were told before Sifu sat to take the driver and secure him in the empty house, then call for members to come and clean the area. With a wave of his arm, they left.

"Mike, I am going to tell you a story. This story may sound like a far-fetched fairy tale. It is hundreds of years old. In Chinese and Japanese lore, this story is told and retold. You have been given by Sifu Cho several pictures to study. Both of the pictures show a human with many lines traveling along the body. Each line has key points of energy.

"You asked Sifu why you needed to study the pages, learn where every line led, and where major conjunctions were. That chart was an acupuncture chart. Vital organs can be affected and controlled using pressure on nerves the Chinese refer to as lifelines. Penetrating these lifelines may cure pains in your body. If these points can be used to heal, they may also be used to harm a man.

"Many Sifu masters are highly trained in acupuncture. So true is Master Cho. Mainly the teaching of acupuncture is for the purpose to heal people."

"Is that why you asked Mitch to give you his hand?"

"Yes, I stopped the pain, but it still needs some medical attention. This story I am about to tell you begins with a bandit attempting to rob an old man walking on a path. After the attack, the bandit begins to die. Returning to his lair, he starts to shake and sweat. Several of his co-bandits went for a priest to aid their leader. Upon examination, the priest turns to them. He relays to the bandit's men, 'I had hoped the master's hand was less gentle and might have shown this bandit the error of his ways. Instead, the master was not gentle and the force great and will soon be to your leader's regret.'

"'What regret did they have?' the followers asked the priest?

"The priest replied, 'You fools, do you think a man appearing old and weak that struck your leader with little force was helpless? This was Master Lin, the most venerable Sifu in all the land. He has surpassed any level to use physical force on a foe. He transmitted his chi, life force, into your leader, now working to destroy your leader. He will die, slowly and fearfully. He was touched by Master Lin the Touch of Death.'

"This Master had the Dim Mak. It is believed many martial artists steeped in the arts achieved the mysterious inner force that allows them to transmit the power of their minds, soul, their very being into a fearful destructive force entering unseen into a body. This unseen force or power causes unbelievable pain, crippling persons or bringing death to them.

"This is not a blow of force such as a strong punch. Instead, this power is done with the slightest of force, a gentle touch. Some believe the Delayed Death Touch by past masters were secret poisons applied to the hands.

"Many Chinese artists today admit to poisons, often applied to the hands prior to delivering the Death Touch. An artist would have special ointments to protect his hands and arms, coating them before applying the touch, then immediately wash his hands. The delay was introduced through the skin. Each person would have different reactions to the administered poison. Hence, the delay of death.

"To develop their lorgoon or chi, they would begin a terrible training practice. First was lighting a stick of incense at their chest level below their nose, then enter into a deep trance while inhaling the scent.

"One of the most important training activities was to refrain from elimination of all bodily waste. A student every morning would take a deep stance, remaining in that stance shaking, sweating his waste from his body rather than the normal means of using the restroom. Most of the waste would be sweated out, leaving certain poisonous acids to remain in the body.

"Another practice was to refrain from sex, which drained the body of another vital ingredient. Then breathing exercises, followed by various herbal medicines. Many believe that the technique involved a vibrating palm, transmitting the chi into the internal organs.

"Cho's father once demonstrated to Cho the power of the vibrating palm. He laid his hand onto a pile of tiles. His touch was ever so light, but the tiles crumbled before Cho's eyes.

"Most of Dim Mak blows are delivered to the chest area, meant for the heart, not the lungs. Some blows can be delivered to the skull's seam or a baby's soft spot.

"Once a person has been targeted, he would wake the next day with bruises at the site of the touch. This usually causes great pain when they try to move. The impact from a Dim Mak touch varied. A single finger was believed to be employed for pinpoint accurate pressure to specific targets inside the body. Hence, the connection to acupuncture.

"It had been mentioned by Sifu Cho his own father's death may have been from such a blow. The blow may have been from the iron palm being applied."

"Iron palm? Is that Dim Mak, Sifu?"

"It is an easier of the techniques to master, Mike. The flat palm rests lightly on the chest over the heart. The fingers rested lightly down to the base of the palm. The palm was an inch away. Suddenly with a snap from the wrist to the palm, a great thrust forward. The force would generate over a broader area than the finger and not kill outright. Instead, the target might feel like someone tripping into you with a slight bump.

"There are three kung fu powers: the Iron Palm, the Poison Hand, and the Delayed Death Touch. The Iron Palm is the baby of the three. The power of the Iron Palm depends greatly on the user's practicing, herbs, and sometimes heat. The hands are dipped into this herb medicine, first warming the hands. The deathliness of the Iron Palm is on sheer strength.

"The second, Poison Hand, uses herbs, mixing them together with the hands. It takes a very long time for the student to achieve, to absorb the poison. Students allow their fingernails to grow long, changing color to a smoky gray over time. The nails now have absorbed the poison, becoming hard as steel. When scratched, the poison enters the skin. Some poisons require medicine to prevent killing the student. When the student has allowed the poison to build an immunity in his body, the antidote is no longer required.

"The third power was the Den Mur or the Death Touch. The Den, meaning the point of the fingers. Mur meant the blood causing a surge or wave to build and flow dangerously to the heart. Mike, feel your pulse."

Mike applied two fingers to his wrist. A steady flow and ebb coursed through the vein.

"Think about this as I continue my story. What happens if the pulse has stopped? You die. What happens when the pulse is delayed? A buildup, like a river being dam occurs. When a dam is breached, the wave of water will cascade down into the valley, destroying everything in its path. Knowing the exact points in your body and the time of a person's pulse, one can conceivably cause a blockage. Applying a force at the moment of the heart pulse could delay the blood's flow, and when released, a wave would flow through the body. A tsunami inside the arteries. If the waves entered the lungs, brain, heart, or other vital areas, the result could mean disabling or death.

"Master Cho, when he returns, will have a conversation with you, Mike. He has informed me to begin your indoctrination before he arrives back. This is some of the information I was to share with you."

"You mean I am to be taught this by Sifu Cho? Why would he train me in this deadly art? I just killed two men. I am not worthy of being his student. For him to share that knowledge with me. It is a powerful thing to learn. It can harm others if misused. I just misused what I have been taught with these two deaths."

"Mike, all I can tell you is killing is wrong. To kill has its consequences. But death is part of this world. We kill to survive, to eat, to protect ourselves and loved ones. Killing is justified every day by the churches around the world. Christianity, Islam, Buddhism—every religion one time or the other has sanctioned killing to spread its beliefs or to justify some wrong. What is right and wrong is in each person's soul to answer. Why is one person's life more important than any others? We are all the same, humans, created by our God, to serve him, to obey his laws, not man's law.

"Sifu Cho has spoken to me. He has told few of this. You are worthy, and he desires to pass his knowledge to you. This is a great honor to have been presented to you. Trust Master Cho's decision, Mike. He does so because he knows your heart."

"I do trust Master Cho. I…I feel ashamed of my actions."

"Mike, you should, and again, this is in your heart. It should remind you every time that this hurt is from doing a terrible act. It says you care. Your hearts feels the pain, and for this reason is why you will be worthy of this knowledge Master Cho will teach you.

"I teach you, and others will too, that will follow. You will be a great force of good. Do us proud when the training ends. Honor what we share with you by doing what is right…always." Sifu Stephen patted Mike on the back.

Mike returned the gesture with a hug. Tears filled his eyes. They sat on the ground until the night fully replaced the light of day.

Standing, Mike and Sifu Stephen walked to the front porch. Boo had settled into a comfy position in Mike's arms. He remained so into the house.

"Mike, continue your regular course of daily routines. Wait until I get further information from our club. We have eyes on their warehouse. This was a possible attack. Stay alert. We will keep you informed. Training as usual. In fact, more so than ever. Good dog you have there, Mike." Stephen patted Boo on his head.

Boo accepted the pat.

"Now rest, we will continue this later. Right now we need to take care of our guest." Sifu Stephen turned around to go to his bike. "Mike, study your maps. Practice your short strike techniques. Get faster and more accurate. Tomorrow, I will give you a target sheet to practice your finger strikes. It was the same board Cho gave me."

"I will, I promise."

Sifu walked to his bike and resaddled. With a quick kick, a loud roar bellowed from the black bike. A puff of smoke followed as the bike rode down the street. A long wave Mike kept up until Sifu Stephen reached the end of his street.

Boo wanted down. Mike put him down, and Boo walked over to his favorite spot and took a long pee. Then he followed Mike into the house.

Mitch was beside Dodie. She stopped her crying. Looking up at her brother walking in, she pointed to Mom on the couch. Not a hint of waking. When Mom got drunk from hard liquor, she often snored. She was snoring hard. A bottle emptied lay fallen on the end of the small table where her cards also lay. A cigarette was still burning.

Mike stopped at the table and snuffed out the cigarette.

"Mike!" Dodie cried out. "They're dead. You are going to jail. You got to leave."

"Dodie, calm yourself, this will be taken care of, as was the others that attacked us."

"They're never going to stop trying until they kill us all. You got to go, if you don't, they will kill us. I don't want to die. It's all your fault. If you never came home, we wouldn't have them trying to kill us. You got to leave."

That remark was like a dagger thrust into Mike's heart. Mike always felt that he and his sisters had a strong bond. After the foster home, they all promised to look after each one. Now that bond was replaced by fear, and Dodie wanted him gone. She never was brave but always was the one to take care of them. That was her strength, taking the place of mom. She was the strength keeping the family intact. Her strength was never to face adversity or danger. That was his and Sharon's contribution to the family.

"Dodie, I intend to leave." Mike calmly tried to explain the situation to her. "I know how you feel. I can't leave now. Don't you understand, whether I stay or leave, they will come for you. They will get you, my family, just to get at me. You will be unprotected if I leave. Soon as I am informed of the situation happening, Chopper will contact me. They have us protected for now. When the time comes, it will be over. There will be no more threat. I will leave then. Mitch will be here to assist me in protecting you, Sharon, and Mom."

"You…you…you're just a kid, Mike." Mitch turned Dodie to have her look at him. "Dodie, didn't you see what happened on the front porch? Your brother, he fought the man that had a knife held on you. He took that man out faster than I could blink. You didn't see that? What were you looking at when all that went down?"

"I don't remember seeing him do any of that. When that horrible man let me go, I ran to you. I didn't see my brother."

"How do you think you got free of him? Mike knocked his hand away from you, then punched that man and then twisted, tearing his arm almost off. It was the most incredible thing I ever saw. You didn't see any of that?"

"No."

"Well, if you had seen it, you wouldn't be afraid. Your brother scares the hell out of me. Anybody that can do that, I wouldn't want no part of."

"I don't care, he needs to go."

Mike stood there looking at his sister, then Mitch. Mitch held her, consoling her. He shook his head. "Mike, she is upset. She will change her mind after she gets over this experience. It comes as a shock to her. Also to me. I still am having trouble wrapping my head around all of this."

"Mitch, you do not need to involve yourself in this."

"Mike, it's a bit too late. I am involved, and I care about your sister a great deal."

When Mitch said that, Mike suddenly realized Mitch was in love with Dodie. Mike nodded his head. He understood a great deal this day.

PLAN GOES ASTRAY

NIGHT WAS ALONG THE ROADS that led into the old warehouse district. Nearly eleven at night, a man walked through the double large doors. One was kept slightly ajar to let members inside. Opening the doors just a little resulted in a loud squealing racket. It was best to leave one of them slightly open. Besides, leader man got really annoyed with the constant in and out of traffic coming and going.

Slowly, the stranger made his way across the huge expanse to a small corner. Most of the gang hung out in that dingy-lit pantry of men. There was a second floor with stairs leading to an office above the bottom floor. This was the leader man's main domain. Usually, he was found sitting in the office. After the fight at the kid's home, he preferred this second-floor room.

One of the gang members scrambled up the stairs to leader man's office. This time, he was pacing the floor, not sitting. Leader man turned when his guard posted outside the door reported that the limping man wanted to see him.

Leader man had little time to wait when the guard went down the stairs. He heard the uneven steps coming from the stairs made by this limping man's hobble and a tapping sound. He turned to meet this limping man entering his room. The overhead light cast a shadow across the man's face as he entered the office. Leader man was set back by the obscure distortion of the nose placement to a familiar face he knew.

The strange man before leader man stood bent, crooked, and appeared shorter than he recalled. There was a lack of fire or meanness within the eyes he knew so well about this shadow of a man he once knew.

"Whare iss the oathers I sens with yoo, Billy bop?" asked leader man. He still had trouble speaking, and without his friend nearby to interpret, others would have to piece each word to make sense from his patter.

Billy boy only stared down. He knsew the response that followed failure, especially failure to not follow leader man's orders. His only consolation was that he was not in charge. The gang member in charge was lying on the porch of the assignment with a broken neck and arm distinctly malformed—something limping man worried about when he got sent home to deliver a message given to him.

"Huh, I was, we tried to, but—"

"Bot what, Billy boy? Speek what hippened? Yoo wern't to be bick here ontil I colled yous back."

"I…we had a problem."

"Yees, I con seee thot."

"Well, Carrot decided to act when he saw Mike's sister go into the house. He decided to take her as hostage. We were told by him if we brought her back here, you would be pleased. We didn't plan on her boyfriend acting so brave like."

"Wait, yoo teeling me heer boyfriend dig thit to yoo. Okay, dig yoo toke core of him, end wheer is Mike's siser? Yoo ore ewore I seid do nothing but wotch. So, where is the siser? By thee woy, thit wos a good ideo. So, where is his siser? I don't seee no siser wolking in? Tell me she is outside woiting to be brout in. Yes?"

"Well, you see, there was a little problem, leader man."

"Yoo ore not going to tell me, she isn't outside, ore yoo? Please don't leet my ears heor thot. They oren't going to hear thot, ore they, Billy bop?"

"No, sir, I mean, she isn't outside, but I am not going to tell you that. I obey orders. It wasn't our fault. Carrot, he and Zero were killed by Mike."

"And yoo, why ore you olive? Why ore yoo stonding here elive? How did yoo get free? Please, tell me yo didn't escope and thot he ollowed yoo to go free?"

Billy Boy just figured what leader man was attempting to convey. If he was let go, why? It suddenly dawned on him that Mike and the other men let him go to follow him back to the warehouse.

The shot rang throughout the warehouse. It kept ringing after Billy Boy hit facedown from a gunshot in the back of his head. No one could tell him he didn't know what the leader man was going to do. He knew. He died knowing that.

Yelling at the top of his voice's limits, leader man told them Billy Boy had led the bikers to their warehouse. "Prepare to clean and move to the second site!" Turning to repeat man, who was entering the office upon hearing the shot, he commanded him to set the traps for the bikers.

"If they show, I want them to git a surprise. Two con ploy this gome."

"You got it, leader man," replied repeater man, hobbling down the stairs.

THE GAMES AFOOT

THIS NIGHT FELT DIFFERENT THAN most nights at home. For one reason, Mike's sister flatly told him to leave home. "Go away before you get all of us killed" still rang in his hears. That still haunted him days after it was said.

Sitting on the edge of his bed with Boo at his side, Mike reached under his bed. With the door closed, he removed his backpack. The shoes he wore were still under the bed.

Seeing Mike pick up his shoes, Boo yipped. Looking at Boo, Mike spoke softly. "Yeah, I guess you liked the road, probably wouldn't mind being on it. It was some good times, huh, boy." Patting Boo on his head, Mike picked him up, giving him hugs for several minutes. "Boo, I didn't think coming home would be like this. No. No, I really didn't. Maybe she is right. I need to leave. They would be better off without me. Mom, she can still collect government money, just one less mouth to feed. I mean, two less mouths to feed, huh, Boo."

Boo seemed pleased with the correction to the one being changed to two mouths to be fed. He wagged his tail, staring up at two eyes dripping with tears.

Both boots Mike lifted to his knees. "Hmm, they do need some polish, you think, Boo?"

"Yip, yip!" he replied.

Turning the boot over to inspect it, Mike noticed the loose heel. "My god!" Mike exclaimed. "I forgot about the heel." Quickly Mike twisted the heel. An opening Mike had forgotten suddenly revealed a wonderful find. Under the heel was money, not just a few hundred dollars, but thousands of dollars.

A vision entered his mind, one of Jacob the ginseng hunter and his wife, Ms. Debbie. *He took my boot and put some money inside.* He saw the amount, and it wasn't but a few hundred dollars, not all this. A flash of insight came quickly in his mind. *Ms. Debbie told me they had a surprise for me. Not to remove the heel unless I desperately needed it.* Under the money was a small note.

> Dear Mike,
>
> This is the money we thought you actually should have. We kept it from you to keep you from worrying about the amount. That root you handed Jacob is worth more than this small amount in your heel. We are going to place some money in the local bank in your name, just call or drop by. Enclosed is a phone number and our address.

"Oh my, look at this, Boo. If I give this to Mom, it would be gone soon. Can't do that. Maybe I will show Sharon and Dodie, and if they need it, they will have it for an emergency. Yes, that will be the best way."

Mike took the money and divided it into three parts. His part was the smallest. It was for his leaving to be used on the road. The other two halves were equal.

"Now let me check my pack. I need to prep it for our journey, Boo."

Boo's tail was beating like mad.

"You really are looking forward to this trip."

Boo stood and jumped about.

Mike opened the pack. At the bottom was a small pistol Sam handed him. It had accumulated some rust. "Well, this needs to be taken care of soon." By the pistol was his boot knife. Removing it from the handmade sheath, it still proved to be sharp. Mike ran his finger across the edge, and a small incision appeared on his fingertip. His shoulder knife with the sling was still in place. *I wish I didn't put these back in my bag. Now rust is beginning. Need to clean before we leave*, Mike thought. Lifting it out of the bag, he threw the sling around his neck.

"Well, boy, I will be carrying you around again soon." A water bottle and an axe was also left in the bag. In the pockets were matches, petroleum jelly for a fire starter fuel, and his flashlight. Both batteries needed replacing and some old food. In the last pocket was his fishing gear, hooks, line, and a roll of wire used for traps and snares.

"Well, after some upgrades, Boo, we can be on our way. Just got to figure the best time. I guess I will wait until Sifu Cho gets back. Him and Stephen might have some good ideas."

Next day before 11:00 a.m., Mike finished off a bowl of cereal. Sharon came home and went straight to bed. Dodie remained quiet at the table. Mike's mom woke up and was thirsty. Soon after her first cigarette, she arose from the couch where she slept throughout the night. It became her second bed.

"Dodie, I guess you still don't want to talk about what happened last night. Okay, so be it. Please keep from telling Mom about what I am going to show you. She would only get drunker. I'm going to the Rama. Say hi to Mitch when he comes over. Bye." Before rising from the table, Mike slid a package toward his sister.

Mike took his car to work. Some days he drove, most days he ran. It kept Mike unpredictable. At the Rama, he waited at the front doors, Mr. Cox arrived and opened the doors. He greeted Mike with his usual smile and went up the stairs to his office.

Going inside, Mike immediately pulled the candy counter board off the bar and returned it to the backroom. Then he checked all the restrooms for any items needing refreshing. Once the restrooms were checked, he went into the auditorium and made a walk around to the other side. Everything looked fine, thinking to himself before the walk back to the lobby.

Once back in the lobby, Vic, Wanda, Connie, and Randy walked in. They met outside and walked in at the same time. The day began as usual. The movie began to play, and telling jokes ensued after three patrons bought tickets.

Before the ads ended, there were nearly fort-five patrons for the first show. Quickly appearing, most of them arrived late to pay. All the ushers and candy bar girls were not in their busy mode when all the people decided to see the show.

Cleanup was quick after the first show. Randy was off, and Wanda and Connie were finishing up. Lindsey had the evening shows, and Donna and Debbie took over the candy counter. Vic stayed, and Rusty replaced Randy. Melvin walked in and immediately went upstairs. He had the projectionist slot. Mike went up after he had met with Rusty.

Melvin was first to ask him. "Hey, Mike, are you going to the house with us?"

"Yeah, Melvin, I told Ric and Rusty several days ago. From what I gather, there will be several of us going. You going?"

"Sure."

"Good. That means Vic, Connie, Lindsey, maybe Debbie, Rusty, Ric, maybe Gerry, me, and you."

"Mike, we might have Bob and Marcie going. Depends."

"Depends on what, Melvin?"

"Okay, unless we pick up a few more, it looks like we are going to have a huge group keeping each company."

"What about Dinky? He was to be here, Melvin."

"Haven't heard from him for some time. Besides, if he doesn't show, we ain't staying waiting for him to show."

About eight, Ric drove up to the curve. Getting out, he walked over to Mike. Vic and Rusty were in the lobby getting drinks and chatting with the girls.

Ric greeted Mike at the door. "Mike, I see we got a good-size group going."

"Better than that, Ric. We got several more that wants in. We might have to take three cars. Heh."

Mike and Ric both gave in to a chuckle.

"Sounds like the convoy is on the go again."

"This time, Ric, the more the merrier. Going to a haunted house down a long dirt road at midnight, more cars the better. I sure don't want to break down on that road," quipped Mike.

"Me neither, Mike. Me neither. Hahaha!"

"Yeah, Ric, haha."

"Hey, Ric!" Vic called to him.

Everyone got together at the candy bar discussing the new adventure and making plans throughout the night.

After the last show, Ric wanted to cruise around town. "Mike, you coming along?"

"No, Ric, I can't. You guys can tell me what you did tomorrow."

Mike went to his car and drove to practice. This night Sifu said they were going to practice blocking and countering. It was never fast enough for Sifu Stephen. He was pushing Mike as hard as he could. Then came the accurate striking on his board perforated with various-size holes to jab his finger into. Every miss meant ten more tries.

Mike didn't finish until three the next morning. Sifu told Mike to run home. His car would be waiting when he arrived.

Each of Mike's fingers became insensitive to feeling. The constant banging on the board was toughening them. On one night, Sifu had him strike a board. He struck it with a thumb. The board broke in two pieces. Them again with his fingers. He broke several boards easily. Mike constantly practiced at home and work. Many times during a slow show, he would practice striking the concrete wall off to one side of the theater.

This came to a surprise to Mike's Sifu. He developed his fingers harder, faster than expected. He was pleased, but not once did he let Mike know. Sifu Cho was told the next day. He was more than pleased.

PLANS REMAIN THE SAME

A T THE WAREHOUSE, LEADER MAN was walking using his cane. He spoke with less of a lisp. The second man or repeater man walked along his side. A smell from the cargo that was kept there before was still lingering in the air. No matter the ventilation and keeping the doors wide open, it never got rid of the warehouse's odor. Various fifty-gallon oil cans and diesel fuels were the main purpose of this warehouse. It would serve until after the possible attack pending from Billy Boy's report, thought leader man.

The third man who made it back from their first encounter with Mike that turned disastrous of the three surviving was away. This new attack would not give him an opportunity to get his revenge. He had plenty to take out on that kid. He always saw himself as a ladies' man, up until that time. Now all he can do was remember his past conquests. Conquests that bring horror from the knife cut he received from them bikers. Also, the eye patch now covering his face where two eyes once were. Not much to look at or anything a woman wanted from a man after that incident. The taunts and jokes made the loss of his eye worse. He was constantly referred to as One Eye.

Leader man continued his walk. Others were readily unloading a truck laden with some of their things and quickly gathered to take to their secondary residence, leaving only the basic items to fool their would-be attackers. Preparations were nearly completed for the big surprise waiting the foreboding assault. Leader man just paced back and forth.

Finally, repeater man spoke. "What's the problem? You acting like you are scared. We got them where we want them now."

"That's the problem, this whole motter has a stink to it. If Billy Boy was followed, then it mokes since, they think we would think of thit. And by chence made plons counting on that foct. If they did, then we are the ones set up. It going to be our gooses cooked."

"Hey, you always overthink things. This time we got them. Yeah, they may well have followed Billy Boy to find our location, but even them ain't that smart to figure we figured their plans out. If we over-think this thing, we be giving them suspicions, then they will go and change their plans."

Stopping his pacing, leader man turned to repeater man, nodding and slapping his friend, his second in command, on his back. "You're right, I do tend to overthink. What yoo say mokes good sense."

Both men turned, walking back to the corner where his members prepared a makeshift office.

* * *

Every day since the fight and the two dead men taken away from Mike's duplex home, Sifu Stephen having their bodies quickly disposed of gave him concern, as well as having the third man, Billy Boy, taken to a special campsite for two days. After Billy Boy readily gave him all the answers to his questions, they prepped him. Unknown to Billy Boy, Stephen placed a tracking device to his car and to his jacket collar, then called Chopper.

Jack Knife answered the phone.

"Jack Knife, Mike was attacked a second time. This time, Mike killed two of the three men from our leader man out of Atlanta."

"Dang, wasn't expecting this to happen this soon. We just finished dealing with this new problem, and now this."

"New problem? I wasn't told about any new problems. What was it about, Jack Knife?"

"Chopper said to leave you out of this. He wanted you to stay with Mike in case this went south. He knew you would jump on your bike and get here. It went down real easy. It would have been a waste of your time. Besides, Mike's training still comes first."

"Since the fight, Jack Knife, I been busting his balls. Every training session he practiced one or two techniques only. One tiny mistake, and he ended up repeating the exercise five more times."

"Dang, Stephen, you going to kill him at that pace."

"Heck, no less than what Cho put me through. Besides, after this last encounter, he needs as much training as I can shove down his mouth. On the first training, I had him striking a board with his finger. Every time I thought he softened his blow, he did it a hundred times again. If he missed the circle with his strike, he did it a hundred times. His finger on both hands were bloody. That kid doesn't know the word for quit. He went at that board harder every time. Cho is going to be proud.

"The next day, Jack, not one word or complaint came out of his mouth. Listen, Jack Knife, he knows his family and friends are on that hit list. I wouldn't want to be on his list when he goes after them. The second night, tell Cho Mike spent practicing the whole time with his drop-down spinning sweeps. After he did two to three hours practicing full-contact fighting using only one technique.

"He got tough, Jack. The boys won't fight him unless they wear padding. Each punch, kick, or block is as powerful as Cho's. He nearly broke Jason's arm with a block and actually fractured Fat Foot's leg below his ankle with that same sweep he practiced for hours every day."

"Sounds to me he can take care of himself, Stephen."

"Yep, he can do that. Still, I have him practice drills with three men. Mike can throw you so fast as soon as anyone tries to grab hold of him. He becomes as one with throwing as he is to walking. Never, and I mean *never*, try to grab hold of him, Jack Knife. You'll be looking at the stars before you could blink."

"I'll make sure I'll let Bone Breaker know about that. You know how he loves to give that kid a hug."

"Don't you dare tell him. I want to be there when he tries. I can see it now. Hahaha. Yes sir, that is going to be a sight to see."

"Stephen, it's your neck if Bone found out you knew this and let him get thrown."

"Hey, don't tell me you wouldn't. That would be a hoot seeing Bone Breaker get his butt busted on the floor."

"Hell yes. I'm just afraid of what Bone Breaker's going to do when he ends up staring at them stars."

"You going to fill me in on the problem or not, Jack Knife?"

"Last week, after getting word off the streets, we heard a new club was moving in. Chopper sent out a squad. They ran into this new club at one of the speakeasies. Three of our men walked in. You know, not expecting trouble, just walked in for a beer. One waited outside. Jeremy took a gander at the bikes parked in front those men rode. Real pretty, they were. Had all the bling you could want in a bike. Big money, my guess. He kind of worked a bit on their bikes while the other three went in for a beer.

"Inside the joint, there was six of them. Four standing at the bar, two at the pool table. Once they saw with their peepers our jackets, it went south. Hey man, at least you'd think they wait until someone smarted off to them. They didn't."

"You mean to tell me they came at our men without even saying nothing to them? Hmm, that tells me they were looking and ready to start some shit."

"Yeah, me, Chopper, and Razor came to that same conclusion. We thought about calling you in. You know, this being your specialty and all that. Before we decided on that, we sent a team to track them. Razor led that team. Good thing he had. They saw one of their members driving past our clubhouse as they were leaving. Razor decided to drive that car he loves with the three guys tagging along."

"You mean that old Mustang?"

"Yep, the very one, Stephen. Well, to continue with this, that biker didn't recognize the car. Razor thought if he was spotted, he wouldn't be figuring one of us were riding our bikes in hot pursuit. He led Razor and the three of our men straight to where they had set up shop. It was an old warehouse.

"Razor and the three got on the roof. They had some special equipment along. That worked out well also. On the roof they lowered a wire. They heard every word to their plan. Stephen, it was going to be an ambush. They intended to slaughter everybody that showed up for the meeting. They even stayed and watched them set the stage.

"Stephen, this plan was meant to go down soon. Even if we wanted to get you here, it was going to be late. Razor watched them position each corner of the warehouse with their boys. They took a table and taped four guns under it. Eight chairs positioned with four on one side and four on the opposite side. Each leader would face the other leader. It was to be a sign of friendship. Except they had candles to blow out on their cake.

"When the two sides met after the warehouse was prepped, a time was established the next day. That was okay by us. When they left the warehouse, Razor sent word back for extra men. Within the hour, after most of them left, Cho had his men on site.

"Stephen, it was so sweet. Three of our guys walked in the front door. Two of theirs came out of hiding. Six men on the roof had opened a window and were climbing down ropes to the upstairs office. One man was atop the roof with a rifle and scope. He was taken out before the front door was opened enough to walk through. Once inside, all six guards were on the floor. When the two new guys on the block got to where our guys waited for them to walk to, all seven in each corner were dropped. Either by a rope or crowbar. Mainly a crowbar. You know how some of the guys like to make home runs? Instead of crowbars they decided to use baseball bats.

"One of our men got a little sloppy, and a sound was heard. Both guys went for their guns. Both guys better yet tried to reach for their guns. Reach is the operative word. Pulling out the knife from each of their throats made more noise than all the seven getting a home run with a crowbar. Except for that one.

"When Chopper, Razor, Bone, and me got to the warehouse the next day, we knew the place was secured. We just opened the door and walked over to the table. They offered seats for us to sit in. Oh, did I mention the table and the four guns taped to the bottom?"

"Nope."

"Oh, after our guys made home runs, they took each gun from under the table. The bullets, they replaced them with empty shells and repositioned them back under the table."

"Three words, maybe a few more said, then they reached for their guns. Before they had their guns out, our guys stood out from their hiding places. We all watched two pull the triggers to their gun. It was funny seeing them squeeze empty pistols. Everybody started to laugh. I mean, I wish I had a camera. Their faces, Stephen, the look on their faces.

"You know what Chopper did? He placed four bullets on the table. Bone Breaker pulled his favorite toy out. Razor gave them a choice. Either make Bone Breaker happy or sad. He begged for the four of them to keep Bone Breaker happy. They chose to make him sad. Bang, bang, bang, bang. That was it, problem solved. Sorry you missed it."

"No, no, you told the story good. I could visualize the whole scene."

HOLLYWOOD
ON THE MOVE

"AHEM, MR. DENNIS, WOULD YOU mind coming over here and take a look at this?" Sargent called out.

In midstep from another site on the property, Dennis heard Sargent's call. Before responding, he commanded two men to clean up the area they had completed construction on. "Mr. Howell wants this to appear that no one has ever been here. When the public comes, they will only see what we want them to see."

"You got it, boss."

After a few minutes, Dennis went over to where he was summoned. "Okay, Sargent, what is so important that I had to drop what I was doing to scramble over here?"

Holding up a shear pin the size of a rolling pin, Sargent said, "Look at this. Do you know what this is?"

"No, why would I, Sargent?" replied Dennis in a matter-of-fact response.

"Look at the size of it. Notice it has a piece broken off. This machine is out of order until we replace it with a new pin."

Looking at the piece then taking it from Sargent's outreached hand, Dennis fondled over the shape and saw the end had been cut in two. "Okay, get a new one, Sargent."

"That is the reason I called you over here, Dennis. That was a special piece. Machined specifically for this machine. It's one of a kind."

"Well, you got to ask me how to get one. Just go to a machine shop and get one made. Mr. Howell will be here in a day or two. You want to explain to him you don't know how to have a machine shop make this pin? Just go and get it made. Pay extra, don't come back without it. This will be up and running before he gets here, you got that, Sargent?"

"Yes, sir."

"Hello, oh, Peabody." Dennis heard the new phone just installed from his small operational post set up near the house. Luckily, he was at that spot when the phone rang. Generally, it went unanswered. Most of the controls were in the cellar. Dennis rarely stayed there. He was constantly having to chase down small problems preparing the house before Mr. Howell got there.

"Dennis, is everything set to go?"

"Almost ready, some small problems as expected arose. Should be set for the visit. Is that the reason for the call, Peabody?"

"No, I have some information on that kid. The one Mr. Howell was so insistent on finding. His name is Mike. Guess what I was able to find out?"

"Look, Peabody, I got plenty of things to finish up before the visit. The one thing I haven't got time for is to play guessing games with you. You got something to tell me, please, make it quick. Got the point?" Dennis retorted with a snappy curt tone.

"Mike, the kid, he lives nearby. He was walking to his family in the swamp and happened to meet up with Dr. Strange and his crew. They stopped to ask where this house was located. That fits the magazine article to a tee. I'll be down this evening. I got to get to him to meet Mr. Howell. Have someone meet me at the airport. I need to make sure that kid will meet the boss man Mr. Howell before this show gets started."

"Will do. Tell the boss we are nearly there. By tomorrow, we will be rolling."

"Good, see you soon, Dennis."

Turning to two men working on the machine, Dennis asked them if it was going to be ready.

One man replied, "It's ready now, Mr. Dennis."

"I thought Sargent said it needed a shear pin?"

"Yes, sir, it does, but it can run now. The shear pin is for the engagement of the carriage. The carriage is for moving around the heavy stuff. Most of that is in place."

"So let me get this straight. We are a go?"

"Yep, sir."

"Good, good, that is the best news yet. Well, let's give it a try, boys. Everybody at your stations. We are going to showtime."

Within minutes, everyone below the first floor of the basement were busy preparing for the test. The basement had two rooms; one to walk down had only a water heater. The other room was hidden from the public. Inside was all the equipment to run the show. One control panel was for the animatronics. Two machines each had one operator when on manual control. One automatic one was only needed. The house needed two operators on the monitors just to spy on different groups of visitors if they split off.

Outside, two generators were in the back behind the house. Both were camouflaged to appear as large moss-covered boulders. Each could run the show. The only reason for the second was as a backup. Various lights positioned in treetops were used in case of an accident. Everything was thought out for any and all contingencies to happen. Well, that was the idea behind Dennis's planning.

"Okay, boys," Dennis spoke, "let the show begin."

Two men were left outside to walk through the stages visiting the house, unsuspecting and innocent players to experience the show. They stood near the graveyard waiting for the signal to begin. The signal was given. They began walking past the graveyards up to the front steps, then stopped. Two microphones were fitted to each man's ear. Every command Dennis called out to them was to be done. No adlibbing allowed; none was done.

"First step, okay," one man called out. Next, the second man took a step. A squeal was heard. The second man was startled from a prop he didn't expect to pop out unexpectedly.

"Good," Dennis spoke. "Continue."

At the front door, both men stopped. First door opened, then the other. Squealing sounds were heard when activated. Each door opened on its own and closed by command. Slamming each door by remote worked, which was done by the first house controller.

"Good," replied Dennis. "That is another to check off. The double parlor doors now."

The same test, the same success on both doors. At the fireplace, the fire burst forth on signal and went out on cue. A large rat crawled back into its hole. Some real rats let loose. Trained of course to return to their homemade containers. Dennis was pleased when the rats went back to their cages.

Cobweb nets dropped down and raised back up. Cold chilling air entered the room. Windows flew open and shutters slammed shut. The stairs had a loose board. Anyone walking up could easily find themselves slipping down the stairs activated by remote control to release. At the bottom was a fake rubber floor. A special vacuum pump inflated the floor to create hardness to walk on or deflate it enough to soften a fall. A trigger device activated a ghost image from a projector to appear at several points located throughout the house. Also there were fog generators.

To add to the thrill, double mirrors were arranged to multiply images like that in the Orson Welles movie *Citizen Kane*. One bedroom door was inflated to expand, the bedpost to lower, the blankets to rise or be yanked off. Most of the furniture in the house had multiple purposes. Triggers were installed to activate all the effects from the control panels. Hidden walls to track and even pull persons into. Every conceivable horror was put into this house. Floating lamps, moving pictures on the walls. Each picture had three sides rotating to a different portrait when commanded by the control center. The two men went after each trick and tested them within the house. Two windows at the attic even looked like their shutters moved to blink when the lights went out.

Into the yard they journeyed back. Each grave was rigged with a zombie to rise, either a hand, head, or the whole body. One area marked off-limits was a liquid pit filled with a mud pool of slime. A remote control panel would slide open for any unwary visitor to fall in. Some of the trees were motorized to be relocated along the road. The road had two ways to enter. The trees directed the entrance to the house and away from the house. That was necessary to keep unwanted visitors away.

What really set this house off from the normal house on Dennis's haunted hill was the giant monster. Four screens were positioned to rise and lower. Each would display a movie of the creature, giving it the appearance of moving. A rail system was created to allow the mechanical part of the movie monster to move in and out from the screen and across the road. In a secondary road, rails were laid. When in use, the secondary road would be closed to traffic. Several flying ghosts and other nightmarish creatures were activated as needed.

The first trial was successful, and the control room lit up with applause.

"One more test, boys!" Dennis shouted out. "When the boss man gets here is the real test. So get some sleep. When he arrives, make sure you check everything twice. So when he comes, it will work. No boo-boos after tonight.

"Now, I need two men to drive to the airport and pick up Peabody. Oh, while you're at it, you two can pick up dinner for everybody for this evening. No one's going home tonight. My treat. So eat good, men."

Dennis called for a driver. He was in the car departing as Sargent returned from town. It was just after 10:00 p.m. as both cars drove past. Dennis was going to the airport to get a plane ticket to fly back to his office after Mr. Howell came. He was not allowed to fly on his plane. No one was.

* * *

At the Rama, Mike was outside by the small six-foot concrete wall erected to prevent passersby from walking to the rear of the theater. It still had a small opening near the building, so it really offered little resistance to anyone wanting to walk around the building.

Lately, Mike was seen standing by the wall, jabbing his fingertip into the concrete. It was a bit silly watching him at that wall stabbing it with his finger. It was apparent to some who got to know Mike that he was troubled.

Lindsey, before entering the Rama arriving to work, walked over to him. Putting her hands around his waist, she gave him a little hug.

"Mike, Tad and I had a talk. You know, he met your teacher months ago. What you don't know is your teacher had a talk with me."

"What?" a shocked look crossed Mike's face as he swiftly spun around to face Lindsey.

"Lindsey quickly explained why. "Mike, I saw you being attacked one night. I had trouble dealing with what I saw. I had to speak to someone. I saw Tad a while back and asked him to talk with me about you. Tad pulled me to one side, and I told him about the fight. He told me about your training. Mr. Cho had a talk with us before he left for business and Stephen's arrival. We are to help keep an eye out for any strangers and let you and him know. He explained your feeling for our safety. We do this to help you. We care about you, Mike."

"Then you know why I don't want you to be involved, Lindsey."

"Yes, Mike, but it is too late. Mr. Cho acknowledged that. We were in, and it was out of his and your control."

"I…I…don't know what to say, Lindsey."

"Don't say nothing, Mike. Now, was that what was worrying you?"

"Some of it, Lindsey, some of it."

"I'll be in the ticket booth if you want to talk, Mike."

"I know, and thanks a heap, Lindsey."

Lindsey was just entering the two front doors, and Mike began again with his finger jabbing the concrete wall. Several chips of stone were flying from the wall with every strike. A small depression had been dug.

Bob arrived, the same Bob who had a purpose to give Mike nasty snubs. Mike really didn't need his presence at that moment.

Bob spotted Mike standing at the concrete wall and quickly made a beeline straight to him. "Hey, I see you are still trying to prove you are a badass? Think that poking your finger into that concrete wall impresses anyone?"

"Good afternoon, Bob. I see you still like to mess with me. Please, for this one time, could you let me be for some time? I will be in soon."

"Sure, but first tell me when this haunted house business is going down. It seems no one let me on to it, Mike."

"Sorry, I felt sure Melvin or Rusty had told you. But if you want to come, you are more than welcome."

"Sure, yeah, sure," Bob replied as if Mike was yanking his chain and not really desiring him to come.

"No, I mean it, Bob. You can come."

Seeing the expression on Bob's face, it was apparent Bob still had doubts and was going to stay and pester him until he was satisfied it was a go to the haunted house.

Mike turned to Bob, remarking, "Well, I guess I best go inside."

"What? Mike, you ain't going to stick your finger in the wall for me?" Bob walked over to the area Mike had been striking with his finger. Looking carefully, he noticed a small circle, and inside the circle was a depression. Bob took his hand, rubbing over the depression left in the concrete. "Hey, what's the circle for, Mike?"

"Oh, that circle you have your hand over? It is for me to focus on that spot. I try to strike in that circle. You know, for accurate pinpoint hits."

"Really, and this little hole was made by you?" replied Bob with a nasty snarl.

Suddenly Mike turned with blinding speed. Bob's hand was barely away from the depression. Mike shot out his index finger, striking between the two open fingers of Bob's hand, barely revealing the slightest depression the rest of his hand had kept covered. Mike made a pinpointed strike onto that spot. Chips of concrete flew between Bob's fingers. A small shard slammed against his cheek. Bob turned to see a finger being pulled out from between his two fingers.

Awe creased across Bob's face. A sudden chill went up his spine. It was quick, so quick he never had a chance to see the motion of Mike's arm. He heard the impact, felt the shard slam his cheek, before he understood what just occurred.

Mike turned and walked to the front doors.

Bob slowly removed his hand stuck to the concrete wall. Still a tiny bit shaken, Bob remained standing at that place, looking at his hand. He was thinking if Mike didn't miss his fingers, they might have been that shard hitting him on his cheek. Removing his shaking hand off the place, behind his hand revealed a larger hole between his fingers. The hole slowly got bigger the more he moved his hand. Once his hand was safely back beside him intact, he saw the entire hole. A hole twice the size before the strike was now present on the wall.

Bob reached up to his cheek and brushed off the shard slightly indenting his cheek. Not so deep to cause bleeding, just enough to irritate him if not removed. Bob turned to the front door and walked past Mike sitting on his stool.

"Nice trick, Mike. You almost had me fooled." Bob never dropped a step walking to the candy bar.

Anne and Marcie were behind the counter. "What was that all about?" quipped Marcie.

"Oh, Mike tried to impress me with some trick."

"Yeah, what trick was that?" asked Marcie.

"Oh, he thought he could impress me with stabbing the concrete wall outside with his finger. There was this small hole he was trying to make me think he made hitting the wall with his finger. Nobody can do that. He probably had the hole fixed to crumble when he hit it. I saw through that trick really quick. He thinks he is such a bad ass."

"What makes you think he wants you to think he is a badass? Really, Bob, from where we sit, you are the only one working here that thinks that. Mike has always been nice," replied Marcie.

"Well, at school, people think he is some tough guy. I don't. He can't scare me. I ain't afraid of anybody, especially him."

Listening to the banter Bob was making from the ticket booth, Lindsey turned and poked her head out the door leading into the candy bar. Usually, the door was shut except on days with little attendance. "Hey, Bob, do us a favor, will you?"

"Sure, Lindsey," he replied.

"Shut up. You got no idea what Mike can do. Just stop with all your mouthing off. No one cares to hear your shit." Lindsey turned back and closed her booth door with a slam.

Hearing Lindsey's remarks, Mike was about to stand and stop her from continuing and maybe say something she shouldn't. At least not now was a good time. With something coming down soon, Mike began to ponder. Sifu Stephen has constantly been reminding him after every training session to tell him or Tad where he goes. Now, he has to make sure Lindsey knows as well. It seemed he was being mothered by too many people lately.

At the last training session, Teddy Bear and Mandy told me they were going to be keeping close to me. Both told me one will be at the theater every day and night. Stephen had his other team members return to the club. Cho would bring his men upon arrival. I reminded Teddy Bear and Mandy to come when he was on the door. He will get them in free, Mike thought, sitting on his stool in heavy thought on his strong feelings of impending doom. *If I am not there, Tad will let them in or leave notice to the working doorman. Now, I will have to tell them to check with Lindsey. Oops, that reminds me.* A sudden thought entered Mike's head. Standing, Mike knocked on Lindsey door.

Opening her door, Lindsey poked her head out. She saw Mike with a queer look on his face. "What's the problem?"

"No problem, Lindsey, I just got to let you know one of two men will come by every day to watch a movie. They are friends of mine. Tad told me it was okay to give them a pass to enter. I will let you know who they are when they show."

"Okay, sure, anything else?"

"Nah. Thanks, Lindsey."

Not long after the doors were opened for the show, Teddy Bear arrived on his bike. Parking near the front, he waddled up to Mike standing in front of the double entrance doors. Mike stood watching this huge mountain walk from the parking lot. How a man that big, hence his name coming from his burly look and massive size, could move fast still had Mike amazed.

"Over here!" Mike called to him. Teddy Bear walked to where Mike stood. Lindsey recognized the bike and figured this was one of Mike's friends.

"Lindsey, this is Teddy Bear." Next to Teddy Bear, Mike looked like a tiny ten-year-old.

Bear extended his hand to shake Lindsey's hand. His hand was massive. He tried to poke it through the ticket window. The hole was a bit too small. Lindsey put her hand through the hole, and they shook hands, or it seemed Teddy Bear's hand was moving up and down, appearing to be shaking her hand.

Mike told Bear, "Come on in, see the movie."

Entering inside, Bear noticed the candy bar. The smell of fresh hot popcorn would make anyone entering immediately yearn for some. With Bear, no aroma in the air was needed. He had a way of locating any food nearby. That you could count on. Mike had to call Bob over to assist Bear with carrying his three boxes of popcorn, a large Coke, and two boxes of chocolate-covered almonds into the movie.

Bob, hearing Mike call him to aid Bear, couldn't stop himself making a nasty remark at Mike when he went to assist Bear. "Jerk."

Bear took note. He heard the remark.

"Hey, he's your friend, you help him. I told you, I don't take orders from you, Mike." Then Bob followed it with a smug undertone name-calling that he thought Bear would be unable to hear. Tubby.

Mike was too far and learned to ignore his banter. He heard the remark coming from Bob, nonetheless. He hoped Bear would ignore the remark.

Bear didn't ignore the remark. Once inside the auditorium, the movie just began. Two patrons sat on the opposite side of the large room. It was dark. Bob flashed his light down the aisle. Just entering the second row of seats, Bear stopped and motioned to Bob the place he intended to sit.

Bear put down his popcorn and large drink in the holder and the next seat adjacent to his. Bob placed the other two boxes of popcorn and both boxes of almond candy in the seat. Bob was still bent over next to where Bear was about to sit. Before Bear sat, Bob felt the huge hand of Bear pat him on his back side. Bob soon realized he was facedown on the sticky floor between the seat rows.

Lifting himself off the sticky floor, Bob again felt another slap of Bear on his back side. For the second time, Bob raised up off the floor. For a third time, he received a slap. Down on the floor he went again. This time Bear asked him to lie there on the floor. Bear planted a foot on Bob's back. Bob was about to make a serious second comment to Bear. The first was to Mike. This was to Bear.

Bear politely asked Bob to rise a little for his feet to be elevated to a more comfortable height. Bob made his comment. "Look, tubby, that foot better move if you want to keep it!" Bob had a hard head as Mike learned and decided to just ignore him.

Bear did not ignore Bob's remark. Half a large glass of Coke trickled down on Bob's head. His hair was soaked from the drink. Then his face felt the hand of the jolly green giant shove his face into the floor, just enough that Bob realized he could only comply with Bear's forceful hand.

Bear bent down and asked Bob, "Have I made my point, or do you prefer to remain there with your face in that goo keeping my legs elevated until the movie ends?"

Bob decided the right course of action. Bear allowed him to stand. Bob left as soon as he stood up. Walking out of the auditorium, Mike spotted Bob. Both the girls and Mike looked with horror at Bob walking out of the movie with his hair wet and dripping. Bob hurried to the men's restroom behind the concession stand.

Teddy Bear walked out shortly. With a large Coke cup in his hand, he walked over to the candy counter. "May I get a refill? I seemed to have spilt my Coke." He handed the half-empty cup for a refill.

Marcie took the cup and refilled it to the top. Bear thanked her and reentered the auditorium.

Both girls covered their mouths to keep from making a loud laughing sound. Bob walked out of the restroom. His shirt was partly covered with some sticky goo, probably old Coke not mopped up. He immediately walked over to the cleaning closet and looked for the Windex. Windex cleaner was used for everything. It worked well on clothes from spills a patron might accidentally splash on an usher assisting them to their seats in the dark.

Mike walked over to him. "Hey, Bob, I am truly sorry for Bear's actions. Can I help you?"

Turning to face Mike, Mike could see his face become red. He was humiliated from what had occurred and tried to keep it hidden.

"Bob," Mike said, "go back to the storeroom, I will bring you some stuff to clean up with."

Bob simply turned, and before he left, he thanked Mike. Then he quickly walked to the storeroom.

After leaving Bob to clean himself, Mike went over to the candy bar. Both girls were still giggling. They stopped when Bob came out of the restroom. When he turned to walk back to the storeroom, they saw him up close. They held off laughing until he entered the storeroom, shutting the door with a bam.

Mike asked the candy bar girls to get over it. "Hey, girls," Mike replied, "he fell between the aisles apparently making that big guy spill his Coke. Bob may have bumped into him."

"Sure, Mike, Bob tripped over the big guy."

Returning to the stockroom, Mike knocked on the door to enter. Bob opened the door. "Bob, I told the girls that you tripped trying to get around the big guy. Unless you tell them something else, well, that's your business. Now, I know the truth, and I will advise you of this. Some friends of mine tend to be a bit sensitive to any remarks you make to me. Please take this advice as friendly. The next person I know will not be as polite as Bear was."

Bob gave Mike a funny look. "That was polite?"

"Yes, Bob, compared to how Mandy would have treated your bad manners, yes, that was polite."

"Just how many of these types of friends do you have, Mike?"

"Look, Bob, you got a nasty attitude, and trust me when I tell you this. Learn some manners, or someone will teach you some."

The first show ended. Bear reemerged, refilled his drink, and got more popcorn. After checking the parking lot, he walked back in.

Ric arrived as Bear patted Mike on the back, walking to the auditorium door.

"What was that?" commented Ric, seeing Bear squeak through the two doors into the auditorium.

Bob was standing by Mike and heard Ric's remark. Quickly Bob addressed the remark. "Hey, Ric, don't let that man hear you say that."

"Huh." Ric could hardly believe Bob told him that. Bob had gotten the reputation of badmouthing people, and this rebuked startled him.

Turning back to Mike, Ric spoke up. "Tomorrow's the night. Make sure everybody planning to go gets the word."

"I took care of that, Ric," Mike answered.

"Just don't want to leave anybody out."

"Yeah, me too. By the way, Bob said he wants to go."

Ric stared at Mike with a queer look. "Hey, Mike, you good with that?" Ric inquired.

Bob turned to Mike when hearing Ric's rebuke. His face revealed his being upset he might not be included in this foray. This was the first time he realized Mike was behind the planning, deciding with Ric who goes and who don't.

"Sure, Ric. Bob can go. We could use all the men on this adventure."

Bob let out an exhale. "Thanks, guys."

Mike turned to Bob. "Remember, Bob, it is tomorrow. We are leaving after the last show. Be here. We are not planning to wait around for any who comes late."

Next day, all the players going were either coming to work or getting off. Mike mentioned to them to be there around nine thirty.

Nine thirty came quick. Lindsey was up and back down from the office ahead of her normal time it took to go over the ticket sales and money.

Waiting downstairs was Tad. He was asked if he could remain at the theater by Mike and Melvin until the show ended. There weren't many patrons for the last show. Tad agreed.

Tad started to have suspicions to why he was to remain at the Rama. Tad took Mike to one side and asked, "What is happening tonight? Remember, you need to keep me informed."

"Sorry, Tad, I thought you were told by Lindsey. The lot of us are going down Highway 96 leading to a haunted house, Angeles. I wanted to check with you to see if you want in on this."

"Thanks, Mike, no."

"Okay, when everybody arrives, you mind if we leave early?"

"Go ahead. I hadn't heard anything from your teachers, Mr. Stephen or Mr. Cho."

Vic arrived driving in his small Fiat. It was a tiny four-door car. Melvin was already there, and Ric just pulled in. Both Marcie and Anne were working and had planned on going. Another two girls arrived, Connie and Debbie, pretty Debbie. Then Rusty and his girl drove up. Rusty walked over with his girl. "Hey, guys, my girl wanted to come too."

All the girls gathered in a group to discuss the big event. Rusty, Melvin, Ric, Vic, and soon to follow came Bob. Mike turned to Ric and Vic. "I figured he was asking but not coming. I guess I made a mistake."

"Wish you did," replied Vic. He had a low opinion of Bob. Vic almost got into it with Bob the second night they worked together. Mike only prevented a fight that still was brooding inside the both of them. Since then, they never got along. Bob and Mike made peace since Teddy Bear made a point to show him the error of his thinking.

Gerry said no also as he was running the movie. Randall and Ronald never showed. Twelve was the final count. Now to see who was driving and who was riding. Mike told everyone his car may break down. If they were willing, he will take his car. No one was willing, and Mike's car stayed parked in the parking lot.

It was decided that Ric would lead. He had been to the house more than the rest of the group. Riding in Ric's car was Melvin, Connie, and Anne. Rusty volunteered to drive. His girl Diane, Mike, and Lindsey rode with him. At the last minute, Bob requested to ride with Rusty. Apparently, Vic drove the last car. Debbie, Marcie, and him took the last place in the second convoy. Bob's last-minute change didn't work out. Mike decided to ride with Vic and the other girls.

Mike only thought about Mandy when they were driving out of the parking lot. His thoughts were on the venture the whole night. Mandy was to be at the Rama on this night. It was decided between Bear and him to switch each night to be at the Rama. Something, Mike thought, got changed. Nothing to worry himself. They will tell him if there was. Several ushers arrived late after the convoy departed.

Three cars started up. Before they left, Mike had to go and get the last remaining cooked popcorn left bagged to go. He asked the two working girls to bag what was left to take along earlier. The convoy drove out of the parking lot, making a stop at a store Ric turned into.

Getting out of the car, Ric yelled to the rest parked and anxious to get going to wait. In the store he bought a fifth of vodka and a six-pack of Cokes.

Ten thirty and on the highway heading east were three cars fully packed. Ten miles down the road, the cars crossed the railroad tracks. Just a mile ahead was the turnoff. At the turnoff, Ric pulled over a second time. All cars pulled up to his. Mike had his cigarette-charged spotlight, and with all the ushers' flashlights, those pulled over lit up like a football stadium.

Mike got out of the car first, shining that huge beam of light of his floodlight around the empty road. Then everybody feeling safe was out. Ric and Mike looked around. Mike spoke first. "Look, guys and girls, this seemed like a great idea, and it is. But this is a long winding dirt road. It gets pretty dark in the woods at night. Some of you never been in this kind of darkness. It can get pretty scary down a long dark dirt road with very few places to turn around if you should change your minds. Once on this road, you will need to go to the house before we get to any place big enough to turn cars around."

"Everybody turned and looked at each other. Who would be the first to chicken out?

"Okay," Mike said, "we're going down this road. Anyone wanting to change cars needs to before we begin. If not, then you are stuck with your riders."

Only two riders swapped, Mike and Bob. Rusty wanted Mike to ride with him.

"If any of you get scared, remember, you are not alone. Don't take off and leave your riders. If you do, you will be driving back down this road alone to fetch them." This was the last thing said by Mike. Ric stood beside him giving an approving nod.

Each car was filled for the third time, the last time until they all got to the house. One by one, each car turned down the dirt road. With each mile, the night grew darker. The road seemed to close in the farther the convoy drove. There were bumps along the winding road. None was as bad as the darkness shrouding the cars. Every bump added to the haunting, eerie darkness. Everyone's nerves were wearing thin, and it could take a small unexpected event to make everyone change their minds.

Mike shone his floodlight all about. This calmed all the riders in Rusty's car. Rusty wasn't the bravest, but with his girl and Mike along, he was given a renewed sense of bravery. Up ahead in the other cars, fears were growing with each bump. They could see the light shoot from the rear car. The light seemed to reassure each of the other riders in the cars that everyone was together, and no one had deserted the rest.

Rusty hit a bump, and Mike was thrown up just enough for him to jerk the cigarette plug to his light out of the socket. Rusty's girl, Diane, fumbled for what seemed like minutes, trying to feel around in the dark for the plug. Once she found it to refit it in the lighter, the car ahead had stopped. Rusty barely stopped before a rear-end collision was caused. Vic squealed his tires, just stopping before an impact into Rusty car.

Getting out of the car, Vic hurried over to Rusty's car, screaming aloud. "Why in the hell did you stop?"

"I didn't, the car ahead of me stopped. I barely stopped from hitting Ric's car!" Rusty yelled back at Vic.

Ric walked back to where Vic was screaming.

"Sorry, guys, the girls in my car got scared when the floodlight went out. They shouted for me to stop the car."

"Dang, Ric, you nearly caused an accident."

"Damn right you did," Vic added his two cents.

"Okay, I promise not to do that again," replied Ric.

"I hope so," Rusty quipped.

Ric brought out the bottle from his back pocket. With a twist and a crack from the seal, the bottle was opened. "Here," he said, handing it to Rusty, "take a swig."

Rusty took the bottle and heaved it up to his lips.

"A swig," retorted Ric, "not the whole damn bottle."

"Sorry, Ric, that stop shook me up."

"Here, give me that bottle," Vic told Rusty. Next came the girls in Rusty's car. Soon others seeing the drinking decided they wanted their share.

Soon, the bottle was nearly empty by the time it got back to Ric. Two swallows, maybe three, remained at the bottom of the bottle. Mike was the only one not to take a swig. Once each person felt their courage return, back in the cars they went. Everyone was fortified with courage, roaring to go. The final stop was to be the last stop, it was decided. It took longer than Ric had expected, and everyone felt a bit upset.

In Rusty's car, the girls' courage was beginning to wane, making them want to quit. It was taking too long.

Ten minutes passed, and still no road leading to the house. When it seemed they might have turned down the wrong road, appearing ahead was a road going off in the direction of Angeles. Ric honked his horn. Then Rusty honked his, and finally, Vic honked horns. All three cars made the turn down the road.

Up ahead was a tall house looming in the darkness. Every car stopped. Ric got out of the lead car. Walking over to each car, he told the drivers to make their turnaround. Within minutes, all the cars had turned around, ready to leave when the time came.

THE NIGHT OF THE NIGHT

Peabody at the Airport

A T THE AIRPORT, PEABODY WALKED off the private jet. Below waiting was two men from the house. "Good evening, sir," each spoke out.

Peabody waved his cane to acknowledge their address to him. On the ground, the lead man extended his hand to greet Peabody. "Sir, this way." The other man reached for Peabody's luggage consisting of two large bags made of rich red leather adorned with brass trimmings.

Both the first man and Peabody walked to the car. Peabody stood waiting for the second man to catch up, standing, thumping his cane on the ground. Clearly, he was in a hurry to get to his destination to arrive at the theater before closing time.

Peabody wore a rich silk suit and a bowtie. The bowtie had a large diamond stickpin squarely in the middle of the knot. It wasn't a required necessity, just a decoration to further his status. His cane had a gold knob.

The car was small, so once both suitcases were placed inside, there was only room for Peabody and the driver. The second man was left standing on the tarmac.

"Driver, take me to the Rama Theater," Peabody first commanded.

"Sir, I was told to take you directly to the house."

"Yes, yes, of course. But right now, I want to go to the theater."

"Yes, sir."

It was nearly 11:00 p.m. when they got into their car. By the time they arrived at the theater, everyone had left. Tad was about to leave when a car pulled up to the marquee. Stopping near Tad, one man stepped out from the driver's side then walked around to the other side of the car. He opened that door; a stranger exited the small car. To Tad's surprise, the stranger getting out looked totally different from the car stopped in front of him. A mismatch as any Tad had seen. This tall skinny person wore a thousand-dollar silk suit. Staring at the bow-tie, Tad was amazed of the size of the diamond attached to it. Then Peabody tapped the ground with his cane to make his appearance and title be known to this commoner standing in front of him. Tad got the point. Still, he couldn't believe the differences of the car to the man in front of him.

"Sir?" Tad spoke politely.

"Yes," Peabody responded similarly.

Tad restated his first response. "Sir, can I help you?"

"By all means, yes. Do you employ a young man named Mike?"

Tad responded with some trepidation. "Why would you like to know this, sir? We are not accustomed to telling people we're not familiar with the names of our employees, sir."

"Quite understandable, sir. I commend you on such actions. Let me introduce myself to you. My name is Peabody, and I am employed by a Mr. Howell out of Hollywood. You have heard of Mr. Howell?"

Tad stood there not sure of what he heard. Tad did take a notice to the name; it had a familiar ring to it. *It couldn't be the producer's name of the blockbuster movie that was now playing at the Rama*, Tad thought.

TAD AND PEABODY WITH CHO AT THE RAMA

BEFORE TAD COULD REPLY TO Mr. Peabody's question, a loud sound turned into the parking lot. Four bikers stopped by the car. Three huge men unsaddled from their bikes. The fourth man Tad immediately recognized; it was Master Cho. Turning to address these bikers, Tad left Mr. Peabody feeling dismayed by the abrupt ignoring of his personage.

"Hmm, this commoner surely doesn't know to whom he just turned away from," Peabody murmured through pursed lips.

Mr. Cho spotted this prim and proper man near Tad as he walked up to him. Tad watched as Mr. Cho stopped and peered at this dandy and his seemingly snub stance. Quickly, he had a nasty feeling for this man after he heard the snobbish offhanded remark by Peabody meant at Tad.

"Hmmph" was the only remark Mr. Cho said to Peabody, then he turned to ask Tad about the whereabouts of his protégé. "Good evening, Tad. A pleasure seeing you again."

"The pleasure is mine, Mr. Cho."

"Hmmph," came a loud response from Peabody being ignored by some biker trash. The biker trash remarks were meant to be a silent thought but managed to eke itself out from Peabody's lips. Not loud enough for most persons to have heard or even notice the murmur.

Cho wasn't a normal man. He was trained his whole life; all his senses were greater than any man's. It was almost to the point of being considered a super being level by his biker brothers.

Mr. Cho received the message and turned back to Peabody. With a quick flip of his wrist to a place along an acupuncture line, Peabody suddenly stopped talking, taking on a pallor of ashen paleness to his face. Unable to move, Peabody stood there. One could see the pain that crossed his face.

Tad watched. He was aware of this small man and familiar with only the slightest aspect of his skills. Seeing Mike practice and watching him practice striking the concrete wall on the side of the theater with his finger made him appreciate Mr. Cho's training.

The first man driving Peabody to the theater was about to act. Seeing what just happened to Peabody made him think otherwise. Besides, he kind of was glad it happened to that smug dandy that continuously made demands as if he was some royal person.

"Tad," Mr. Cho spoke, "where is Mike? I need to get to him as quickly as possible."

Tad was caught off guard by this sudden rush to locate Mike.

Peabody's face changed when he heard the name Mike. His pain was temporarily lost as he tried to listen in on the conversation. The only problem with every slight movement he attempted, unbelievable pain coursed through his body. Tad kept looking back at this Peabody person, frozen stiff.

"What is the problem? Is Mike in danger, Mr. Cho? Is that man okay? He hasn't moved since you did what you did to him?"

"Yes and yes, he will be fine, and yes, Mike is in the worst kind of danger, Tad."

"Oh my," Tad responded. "If it's that bad, you need to get to him as quick as possible. He left from here, Mr. Cho, only about thirty minutes ago. He wasn't alone though."

Mr. Cho was thinking the worse. Mike was being followed. "It might be too late," Cho pondered upon hearing Tad's reply.

Tad quickly explained, seeing the dread on Mr. Cho's face. "He is with most of the ushers and several of the girl working here. They planned on going to some haunted house off the highway. Some house they called Angeles."

"Quick, where is this so-called house? Time is running out. This can be a real nasty situation if we don't get to him and the others soon, Tad."

"Mr. Peabody quickly realized the house they were speaking of was their house. They were on their way to the house. Trying hard to speak was nearly impossible with his pain, but he made a sound. It was a slight murmur barely high enough for Tad nearest him to think it wasn't a small buzzing insect. Cho heard the silent scream eke out the lips of Peabody. Peabody was able to get Mr. Cho's attention.

Stepping to one side of Tad, who had placed himself between Mr. Cho and this fancy man, Peabody's face strained to speak. Looking at this dandy, Cho sensed a great urgency on his face. Sifu held as much contempt for this frivolous creature before him as Peabody had for him. The only difference was Peabody learned quickly his mistake, and Sifu was yet to learn Peabody regretted his mistake. With a quick tap to another line along the median on Peabody's back, his face turned red, unstiffened. Blood was quickly returning to Peabody's face, but not his whole body still racked with pain.

"You have something that necessitates my releasing you, I hope," Cho demanded.

After some panting and a readjustment of his bowtie, Peabody spoke. "Sir." Peabody quickly realized this was a peasant; he had to be careful with what he says. "Please, sir, let me illuminate both of you. I am here to arrange a serious meeting between my boss, a producer from Hollywood, with Mike. Our next picture will be made from the article printed in a magazine that caught the eye of my boss. He has begun to make a movie about Mike's adventure."

A hand was raised in Peabody's face. He stopped talking.

Mr. Cho remarked, "Make this quick unless you prefer me quieting that useless yapping continuously erupting out of your pie hole like trash being dumped words with little meaning. Do you have something to say or not? If you hold back any info whatsoever, I can assure you, this will be just a tiny pain as to what will follow. So speak!"

Stephen walked over to where the three stood under the marquee and whispered something to Mr. Cho.

Mr. Cho responded, "Where is Mandy now?" Turning to Peabody and Tad, Mr. Cho excused himself. Together, Stephen and Cho quickly paced to the other two riders still waiting by the bikes. After several minutes, both returned to where Tad and Peabody stood watching the scene unfold.

"Tad," Stephen called over to him.

Mr. Cho walked to where Peabody was left standing alone. "You were about to tell me quickly where this house is? Please continue."

Peabody cleared his throat, then began his shortened version of explaining where the house was located. As usual, for Peabody, nothing was said simply. Mr. Cho put his hand on Peabody's shoulder as he had earlier. Peabody sped up. Quickly, Cho decided this was a waste of time. Peabody began with a soliloquy as was his normal chore to impress a person he was trying to entertain or motivate to his will.

Turning to Peabody's driver, Cho commanded him to lead them to this house. Tad returned after talking to Stephen. Both stood next to Peabody, waiting for Stephen to complete his business. Peabody was still talking. Cho's patience was wearing thin.

Cho looked at Tad. "I think Mr. Peabody will be joining me to where this house is."

Tad stared at Peabody, deciding he too wanted to go with the group. "I feel I need to go along with you gentlemen," Tad responded.

Mr. Cho reminded Tad about his earlier conversation. "Tad, remember the people I had discussed with you. These are the ones we need to stop. They mean business. This could be serious, so serious you need to reconsider the consequences before you come with us."

"Ahem," sounded Peabody to get the attention of the two people who never considered that he was standing there and were making all the decisions without his consent nor his advice. "May I remind the two of you, this is my property, and any decisions about some kind of violence on this property, you will be held responsible."

Cho turned to Peabody and returned his hand, applying the touch as he had done earlier. Peabody returned to his previous frozen state of pain coursing through his frame. His face returned to that ashen appearance once again.

Tad had decided and restated his demand. Cho stood there looking at this overweight man. He had a kindness about him. Cho liked Tad the first time he met him. Now, he added respect for him. He was about to enter into a field of danger with open eyes. He thought to himself, *He will do fine.* Cho nodded in agreement to Tad. Then he turned his gaze to Peabody.

"Now, this excuse for a man, if not for his knowledge to get us there, I would leave him this way until we got back. So be it," Cho spoke up. With his hand, Cho unfroze Peabody for the second time. "Mr. Peabody, let me assure you the next time I ask something of you, be aware, I will, and I promise you this, you will remain in that state until the next day. You best hope I can return alive to undo that state I will leave you in from this venture."

Peabody nodded his head and absolutely repeated several times, "Yes, yes, yes, anything you want, I will get you. Also, please accept my apologies for inferring that you and Mr. Tad would be held accountable for any damages to the property. I understand absolutely the danger this man and his friends are in and will assist you in whatever ways you would require of me. Please just ask and watch how fast and efficiently the request will be granted. And let me continue."

Cho turned back to Peabody with a menacing look. No words were necessarily needed to be said. It was for Peabody to stop his ranting. It was becoming annoying. The ranting ceased.

Stephen returned from the inside of the theater. Walking over to where Tad and Cho stood, he began his report.

Peabody, not to be left out, leaned close to pick up any of the conversation he was so evidently left out of by the three men. He still was able to gather some tidbits. Not much to get a whole picture, but enough that gave him concern.

"I called Chopper. Apparently, that gang found out about this little trip to the haunted house. The Atlanta boss ordered a team to meet them at the site by whatever means needed. Take Mike and return him to Atlanta," Stephen told Cho hurriedly about his phone call.

"Hmm." Cho pondered Stephen's words.

Tad suddenly had a sense of fear well up inside of him. "If what Stephen said is true, then all my employees and friends, they could be killed?"

Cho asked Stephen one question. "Did Chopper tell you what was said to do to anyone with Mike?"

"Yes, Cho, dispose of any witnesses. It seemed this has taken a new turn."

"Tad." Cho put his hand out and grabbed Tad's hand. He looked deep into his eyes. He saw a great concern. "Tad, when we arrive, you need to remain behind. Before you say anything, know this. I sense a great courage in you. This is not a fight you can be involved in. You will serve best as to stand guard, waiting for any of your people to run out of this area. Getting them to safety will be your job and a most important one.

"Tad, look at me when I tell you this. There is to be killing done there. I need skilled men to deal with this. Your skills are not what is needed. You will need to keep the others calm and secure. That is your one and only job. Do not enter the area. Your life will surely be forfeit if you do."

Looking around the parking lot, Teddy Bear noticed a bike by the side of the building. Walking over to the bike to his horror, he realized it was Mandy's. Quickly, he studied the bike and the place it was moved. It was to be parked where he had his bike last night. Why was Mandy's bike in this place? His bike was placed as if to keep it hidden. *Hidden.* Teddy Bear's eyes lit up. *This can only mean one thing.*

Teddy Bear frantically pushed the bushes aside, then removed Mandy's bike. Looking the bike over with his big burly hand, he swiped something wet on Mandy's handlebars. Pulling his hand back, he saw the ghastly color of red. Then he touched the red liquid to his lips. It was as he believed and dreaded—blood.

Walking up and down the side of the building, he saw no sign of Mandy. Puzzled to this riddle, he quickly turned and walked to the front of the Rama. Seeing both Stephen and Cho under the marquee, he hurried to them.

Both Stephen and Cho turned to see this huge man running to them; his large belly looked like a bowl of jelly with each step. Stephen was about to ridicule him running but noticed his face. It expressed a dread of fear.

Teddy Bear came short of bowling the two of them over from his speed. Stopping usually was a problem. Cho planted a palm squarely on Teddy Bear's chest. He stopped. Panting from the run, Teddy Bear said two words: "Mandy's bike."

Stephen, seeing the place Bear ran from, took off with the speed of a bullet. Mandy, like Teddy Bear, was one of his first students and had been with him on all training assignments. They became the best of friends. Mandy's loss would bring Stephen great pain. He only prayed he lay hurt and not dead.

At the bike, Stephen saw nothing, just the bike and the blood. He saw how Teddy Bear had cleared the area for any signs of Mandy. Then came the scream. When Stephen got to the point of the scream, a lady stood near her car. A body was next to the car. Black boots were under the car's rear end.

From her appearance, she looked to be a nurse. She must be getting off duty out at this hour. Also, the uniform helped him get to this conclusion. Rushing over to the body, he knelt down. With one hand, he grabbed hold of the boot leg. Slowly he pulled the body from under the car. It was facedown. The jacket on the body made it clear. It was Mandy.

Both Tad and Cho quickly came to his side. No words were spoken. Both stared at the body. Blood was still oozing slowly from his body. Cho bent down to examine Mandy's body. Rolling him over, Mandy was looking up at them, smiling. "Took you long enough. What does someone have to do around here to get help? Die?"

A long sigh followed from his three friends looking at him, smiling.

"Quick, nurse, look at him," commanded Stephen.

The nurse pulled open the shirt and saw a wound near his side. Looking up to Stephen, she said, "He's one lucky man. His wound just missed being fatal."

ATLANTA GANG WAREHOUSE

Before the Arrival at the Rama

THREE MEN WERE STANDING NEAR a desk. Leader man and repeater man were discussing a most important subject to another member. "Why in the hell am I getting info now? You were told to get any news back here on the double." Clearly leader man was angry. His voice reached three levels higher with each poorly spoken explanation or excuse given him.

"If one more etcuse is told me, someone will poy."

The man shut up.

"Okay the damage is done. Now, how to fix this? I want that kid in this warehouse by morning." He wa yelling across the warehouse for all to hear. "If this kid is not here by morning, hell hath no mercy for you! I want a team ready to leave now! screamed repeater man.

Within minutes, twenty men gather about leader man. "You." He pointed to someone. "Take four more men and get down there."

"Boss." The pointed man stared with an apprehension born from the terror leader man had been putting the gang through ever since his return. Meanness and revenge ate at him. Every wound he had was a constant reminder of how much he hated that kid. Every member of the gang had heard nothing else. Same yelling and ranting day in and day out. The same was true at night, never-ending ranting. It got to the

361

point any assignment was better than staying around the warehouse listening to the boss yelling constantly.

"Whot, you don't know whot, I meent. Are you some dummy or something?"

The man tried to ask leader man a question but was berated with every word be had begun to speak. Finally, leader man remained quiet.

"Boss, all I want to know is what if he isn't alone? You want us to sneak in and get him or do it the faster way? That could mean it will get nasty."

Leader man stood there staring at this guy with a cruel, menacing look.

"Got it, boss." He suddenly got the message before leader man had to tell him. Turning around, he chose the four best members before him. "You, you, you, and you, get your gear. You got five minutes."

The leader of the team removed his gun from his back pocket, pointing at each of the four chosen.

"Five minutes, and I mean five minutes." Then he cocked his gun. "Anyone late will be replaced."

Six minutes later, all five were in a car heading south. Leader man turned to repeater man. "Get ready when they get back. All hell is going to break loose. See to it. I want this done quick and easy. We take those bikers out as soon as they come for the kid."

"I hope that messenger was right about that haunted house."

"Yeah, he better be," snarled the leader man. "From what I heard, that biker gang has that kid watched day and night. If they know about the house, they might be prepared for any attack on him by us."

Repeater man said, "You are now worrying too much. I got this figured out. That shadow on the kid's butt is at the theater he works at. I told the boys to drop by before they leave and visit the shadow. He won't know what hit him. That kid won't have his babysitter with him. This time, they can't help."

On the rooftop of the warehouse, Razor's man heard what went down. Both he and his partner were taking turns watching and listening to what was going on for days. Two more men were stationed at the old warehouse, and Chopper was made aware of their move. That plan was almost perfect and could very well have meant doom for their men tending the gang. Luckily they had the warehouse watched when a gang member was spotted leaving it. One of his men had the good sense to follow him. Good thing he did.

Reaching over to his companion, he slapped him on his leg. "Get up, something just went down, get back to Chopper as fast you can. Tell him they are after Mike. They are leaving now to his town. Somehow, they heard he was heading to a house in the woods. They are to return him back to the warehouse before morning. Anyone with him is dead."

RETURN TO BIKERS CLUBHOUSE

INSIDE THEIR CLUBHOUSE, CHOPPER WAS sitting beside Jack Knife drinking a beer. Razor was off finishing on the final solution. A man came running inside. Both the screen door and the main doors were thrown opened. Once inside the home with a bar or the bar with a home (either was appropriate to its title), he spotted Chopper with a beer to his lips. Rushing over, be bent over to get a full breath. A few seconds elapsed before Chopper set his beer down.

"What's the rush?" Jack Knife spoke to this panting young member.

Standing tall and almost ready to lend a salute, he hesitated and lowered his hand. "Sir, reporting valuable intel from the second rooftop of the new headquarters of the Atlanta gang."

"Okay, what is it?" replied Chopper, somewhat annoyed he had to put his beer down.

"I just received a phone call from one of the men stationed there. He reported the leader man has just sent a five-man team to capture Mike. They plan to take out his shadow and apprehend Mike at some haunted house. If he has anyone with him, they are to be taken out. They want the kid, I mean Mike, by the morning, sir."

"Easy, lad." Chopper sat up. "Now say that again and a bit slower. Where is this haunted house? Did they say?"

"No, sir."

"Get on the phone now, get to Stephen, let him know, *now!*" Looking at Jack Knife, a worried looked appeared on his face. "I hope he is on to this haunted house jazz. If not, they better react quick. This is going down fast."

"I'll get Cho."

"No need, he left earlier with one of his men, Baby Face."

"Do you think he can get there fast before this has a chance to go down?"

"I don't know. The Atlanta gang has a two-hour drive, and we are just a little under an hour and forty-five minutes. Hopefully that will give us the opportunity to reach Mike."

Razor called Stephen. His phone rang many times. Before Razor hung up the phone, he heard Teddy Bear's voice.

"Yeah?"

"Stephen, I mean Bear, this is Razor. Mike will have company at a house in the woods. We believe he will have his friends with him. They are going to a haunted house named Angeles. Check at the theater. Make sure one of you men tell Mike about five gang members going to the house. Keep him there until Cho arrives at the theater."

BEFORE THE RAMA THEATER AT THE TRAINING SITE

RUNNING OVER TO STEPHEN, TEDDY Bear called to him fifty feet away. "Stephen, we got a problem. We got a real problem. They're on the move."

"Who is on the move, Bear?"

"The Atlanta gang sent five men to fetch Mike. They plan on nabbing him tonight."

"What? How did you find this out?"

"It came by phone. Chopper sent word to get to Mike."

"Where is he?"

"He should be at the Rama tonight."

Looking at his watch, it read ten thirty. "He is working tonight, isn't he," Stephen asked, turning to Bear for a good answer back.

"Yeah, Mandy has his back."

"Good. How fast can we get there, Bear?"

"Fifteen minutes or twenty tops, Stephen."

"Well, get your bike."

"Wait a minute, Stephen, aren't you forgetting Cho? Cho, he's coming here. He should be here soon. If we leave, we could miss him. If this is going down, then we could sure use him. Besides, if he comes and we aren't here, and this goes down and Mike is taken, I don't want to face him. Do you?"

"You got a point there, Bear. If we leave someone behind, we would be shorthanded. Did Chopper say how many?"

"At least five from Atlanta driving in a car."

"That leaves you and me against five. Seems fair. Let's wait until we get Mike. Cho should be here by then. Is he bringing Baby Face with him?"

"He always does," replied Bear.

Ten minutes later and no sign of Cho. "Dang it!" Stephen angrily slapped his bike's fender. "Get on, Bear, we got to leave, to hell with waiting. Mike's going to need us. Cho, he'll have to deal with my decision later."

Before they reached the rode, two bike engines were heard approaching the intersection. Stephen put his hand out to signal Bear to hold still. Soon the two bikes pulled up to Bear and Stephen. Hailing to the riders as they slowed to stop next to them, Cho pulled alongside Stephen.

"Thanks for the parade, Stephen. I wasn't expecting any."

"Hold a sec, Cho. This ain't no escort. We got problems. Mike has five Atlanta men about to kidnap him tonight. Word got down to me and to let you know. They want him in Atlanta by the morning. Nothing is to stand in their way."

"Where are you heading now, Stephen?"

"We on our way to the Rama. We might get to him before he leaves."

"Who's with him tonight?" Cho asked.

"Mandy," Bear returned the answer.

"Does he know?"

"No, Cho, he doesn't. The more the urgency it is."

Both feared the answer they were thinking. Both sensed this was news too late in coming.

RAMA THEATER AT THE PARKING LOT

"WHO IS THIS MAN, AND why is he stabbed and lying under my car?" the nurse stammered out. Clearly, she was upset and scared.

"Calm yourself, miss," Cho said. "This is a friend. We are at loss as to why he is stabbed as you are. Can you please get him some medical attention?"

"Oh, dear me, wait here, I will be back within minutes." Quickly she began to run to the nearby hospital across the street. Within a minute, she spanned the distance and was through the doors. Soon a siren was heard, and true to her saying, medical aid was at the car.

Once Mandy was safely attended to, Cho and Stephen rushed back to their bikes. Peabody was in his car and nearly half out of the parking lot. "Damn his hide!" Stephen shouted at the speeding car.

"Tad, get in your car or hop on back!" Cho called over to him.

"I'll get my car."

"Hurry then, that SOB ain't getting away!" Stephen yelled to Cho as he gunned his bike. Before Peabody's car had a chance to turn after first stopping at the main road, Stephen had his bike pulled in his path.

Stephen jumped off his bike and within seconds had the back door torn off its hinges. Both Peabody and the driver looked terrified, and rightly so. If not for Cho, Stephen, who was holding that dandy by the crook of his neck, would have made sure Peabody, turning his second shade of blue, might not have made the trip to the haunted house.

"I should have took a picture of him through the rearview window," sniped the driver of the car.

Cho grabbed Stephen's arm, gently pulling it down until the dandy's feet felt the firm ground. Still, he allowed Stephen to retain his grip around Peabody's neck. Slowly the blue faded to a pinker tone on his face. Peabody wanted to talk, but Cho wasn't in the mood to listen to any of his ranting and excuses. He was clearly leaving without them. The evidence for that was still dripping from Peabody's trousers. A small puddle formed along with an odor. Too bad for the suit; it still had to be worn by Peabody.

Cho for the third time tapped Peabody on his shoulder, but not before he had him give them the directions. Placing the frozen body of Peabody on the back seat of Stephen's bike, they left the parking lot. The driver led the way with four bikes following. Tad took up the last position. It turned out it wasn't necessary for unfreezing Peabody. Just the same, they made it a point to unfreeze him to check the accuracy of his driver.

The driver seemed to be overly pleased to have his boss in this frozen state Cho was placing him in. He led them on a false trail so Peabody would suffer longer. It took three more times of untapping and retapping Peabody before they got to the correct turnoff onto a dirt road leading to the house. The driver drove true, but it seemed he did like his boss frozen.

THE HAUNTED HOUSE

ONCE ALL THE CARS WERE turned around to make a quick get-away if needed, then all the occupants crawled out of each car. Twelve people stood staring at the old house in front of them. The darkness shrouded the house with an eerie fog. Fear slowly ebbed into each one. Mike felt this fear before and had no reason to go through that experience again. Once was enough.

Each girl stood between a boy. Each girl chose her protector. Only one among the group of twelve knew the real person who, if danger arrived, had any chance to ward it off. Lindsey was the first to choose Mike's side. Debbie was second. Rusty had his girl, and she had second thoughts, but nonetheless remained by his side. He looked as scared as she was. Vic and Ric both had girls by their side. Melvin standing near Ric had the honor of being by a girl he chose. Bob was at the end of the long line, and his girl was what was left. It wasn't her choice and became apparent once he tried to grab her hand. She pulled free and got behind Mike.

All the boys had their flashlights out shining. Mike handed his to Lindsey. Not to be outdone, Vic and Ric handed theirs to one of the girls. Mike took the first step forward. Not too far from where they stood looking at the house was a pole. Bob was the closest and noticed the pole first. Mike noticed it, but only took note of it as a landmark in the darkness that overwhelmed each person.

"Hey, guys, there's this pole over here. It might be some kind of a switch box!" Bob called out.

Mike spoke softly back to Bob's yell, only a bit quieter. "Well, open it and look."

"Not me," Bob called back to him.

"Why? It might be a power box for the house."

"Yeah, and it might have spiders inside."

"Dang it!" Mike called back at him. "All you got to do is brush them away." Mike walked past where Bob was standing.

Bob pointed to where the box was hanging.

At the pole, Mike flipped the lid and brushed the webbing out. Lindsey stood by him and held the light. "Thanks, Lindsey." Grabbing the switch, Mike pushed it up. The pole with the box had a light, and it suddenly came flashing on. Everybody applauded. Bob got a few snickered looks from the girls.

WHAT THE HELL
CONTROL ROOM

"**H**EY!" CAME A SHOUT. "SOMEONE just turned on the outside panel box. The whole front yard has lit up."

Sargent replied, "Not to worry, it's probably Peabody coming in." Sargent had returned back to the house only for Dennis to leave shortly after his arrival. He left directions for him to follow to a tee. Those directions were going to have to be modified before the night ended. Not one thing on Dennis's list was going to be obeyed this night.

"The driver was told to turn the lights on when he arrives. Everybody gets ready. Showtime will be starting when Peabody enters the control room."

Walking about hurriedly, Sargent checked everyone's station. First, the power to the house, it was on; all switches in the on position. Next, the house operations. Each person's desk was up and prepared. Next was the outside operations. Then came the one thing no one had expected. The cameras were to be on with each site having a view overlapping the other sites. Not one entry into the driveway would go unnoticed. Even the road leading to the drive was monitored for half a mile from the turnoff.

Not one camera was ever on to keep a constant vigilance on the road leading to their house. Mistake one. This was a priority; it was unsecured and off. Yelling to the top of his lungs, Sargent screeched out, "Who the hell turned off the road cameras? This was to remain on always!" Sargent snapped out for all in the room to hear.

No one turned to acknowledge the foul-up. All Sargent could see was the three cars parked in the driveway. Ten maybe twelve young people emerged from the cars walking to the house.

"Okay, okay, this is going to be one shit hole if you don't get them out of here before Peabody arrives. You all got that! Get them the hell out of here now!" Sargent ordered.

One man turned to say, "Boss, if we go out and tell them to leave, won't they leave and tell everybody what they saw? It could ruin this whole game." Mistake two.

Thinking of what the man said, Sargent then countermanded his first order and told his crew to begin the thrills. "We'll scare them so much, they will do all the work of informing the media for us. Get the spook show rolling, boys. This is going to be fun. They'll be gone before they even get through the front door."

Mike and Ric led the way to the front steps. Suddenly, an eerie sound was heard near the edge of the side yard. It sounded like stomping footsteps. Then a low moan followed. Everyone froze in place. Suddenly, every head turned in unison to the side of the house. Some bushes were seen moving. Whatever it was, it moved a lot of bushes, and it gave the impression it was massive to all staring into the shadows.

In the command center, Sargent and his station man were watching the kids freeze. Now, everyone wanted to stand by the monitor to see them react when the monster revealed itself. Sargent motioned to his animatronics controller to give the creature a quick and sudden jolt of movement. "That should do. When they see that movement, that should have them running to their cars, boys," quipped Sargent. "When they get to their cars, Jerry, ease out the creature just enough to give them a peek. That should finish the trick."

"Quick, everybody into the house. We will never make it back to the cars. It's moving too fast and to our cars. Hurry!" Mike called to them.

Melvin and Vic grabbed hold of Connie and Debbie, assisting them to the porch. Most of the girls froze in place and had to be prodded by the boys nearest to them.

Lindsey and Marcie needed no prodding; they moved before the order was given. Rusty was nearly to his car with his girl before he realized the distance was too far to reach with that sudden jolt the creature made. His girl was the first to realize they would never make it. She halted, and Rusty was thrown back by her hasty stop.

"What the hell just happened?" Sargent turned to everyone looking over his shoulder.

"Boss, they are coming into the house. They ain't running to the cars." Mistake three.

"Really, smart guy? When did that occur to you?" Sargent snipped. "Okay, everybody, to your stations. This has to be corrected before Peabody gets here."

The front of the house was old-looking with each step the twelve made approaching it. Arriving quickly to the porch, everyone ran as fast as everyone could before the creature was upon them. Everyone stopped short of advancing up the steps. Mike led the way. The porch boards creaked. Melvin followed Mike. One step, *snap*! Melvin slid back to the ground. This stopped the rest trying to get on the porch. Anne was behind Melvin, aiding him to his feet when the head of the creature poked its head from a bush.

Rusty and his girlfriend were running back and unable to see how close they were to the creature's mouth. If they could turn to see, it would be the creature's mouth opening a few feet to their rear. Everyone was on the porch yelling at them to run. "Run, Rusty! Rusty, hurry, hurry, it's about on top of you!"

Ric and Mike were trying to get the door open. Everyone managed to get to the porch except for Rusty and Diane. The doors were stuck and couldn't be budged an inch. Rusty and his girl jumped to the top of the porch. Everyone was standing looking down the driveway as the creature poked its head back into the bush.

Everyone was screaming at both Mike and Ric to get the door opened. Vic told everyone to back away. He found a small log as he was running to the steps. "Stand back, I'll smash the door open with this log."

Backing up, Vic heaved the log back to swing at the doors. Then the doors opened with a creaking sound. Vic stood with his log, watching them creak open as if by command. Vic dropped the log. Every girl had someone's arm to hold on to out of fear. They were just about to enter a house that wanted them to come in.

A cold breeze swept across all their faces, then a musty mist followed it. The smell that followed the mist was old and stale like rotten paper. Mike took the first step through the door. His light lit the way. Rusty dropped his on the run back to the house. Melvin lost his when he fell.

"Hey!" Melvin yelped out. "My flashlight, I dropped it when I fell. I need to go and get it. Someone come with me?"

No one volunteered, and Melvin chose not to go back for the light.

Each person walked through the doors with trepidation.

"Okay, everybody, they are in the house. Start the fires, let's get this over this time," Sargent barked out new orders. "So far nothing has gone right."

Mike turned to Ric. "Hey, this is the exact same type of house I was in, in the swamps. I tell you this is the same house. Look there." He pointed to the double doors leading into a larger room. "Look, if that opens into a fireplace room, this is the same type of house, Ric."

"Mike, you're just imagining this."

"No, I am not, Ric. Go open those doors. See if I am imagining things."

Ric walked up to the two doors and tried to pry them open.

"See, stuck just like they did in that swamp house I was in."

"Hey, Jerry, turn the sound up. Did you hear what I heard? That kid, his name is Mike. He was in this house before. Hey!" Sargent turned to one of his controllers. "Is that the name of the kid Peabody has been wanting to find? He said this kid lived in this area. This can't be the same kid. What are the chances of that?"

"I don't know about the chances, but his name was Mike, boss."

"Keep your ears on for any more info he might give us."

Jerry called Sargent over to convey to him the new information.

"Mike, these doors are stuck. We aren't getting through them."

"Step back, Ric," Mike told him.

Everybody stood watching the doors. Slowly they opened just like Mike said they would.

Looking at Ric with his astonished blank stare watching both doors opening by themselves, Mike replied, "You can't open them, Ric, they will do that when they get ready."

All mouths dropped open as the doors slowly creaked open—all but Mike's.

" How did…did you know they would do that?" Melvin asked.

Ric spoke. "He never told you about him being in a haunted house in the swamp, Melvin?"

"I guess so, Ric."

"Tell him, Mike, tell them all what happened in the house."

Before Mike could begin, Ric started to tell them Mike's story.

"See, he was in this house, and it was just like this one. Two doors that opened themselves. When he walked through them, the room was full of giant spiderwebs, and there was this huge rat in a corner."

"Ric, I thought you wanted me to tell the story?"

"I do, Mike, continue."

Everyone was waiting for Mike to continue where Ric stopped. But with the doors wide open, Ric decided to walk through them. Once in, he ran smack into a giant cobweb. He let out a small scream. "Hey, it's just like your house, Mike." He turned around to wave the others through the doors. Everyone got a face full of web entering the room.

Suddenly, a loud "Eek!" and then a "Yeow!" bellowed out from two girls. A third girl yelled when she turned her head to look where the first two girls were looking. In the corner of the room was a giant rat, bigger than the largest cat anyone had ever seen. Its eyes were red as beets. The rat stared back at its intruders then suddenly turned, entering a hole in the wall. It had a most unusual turn of its body. It almost looked like it had pivoted on its belly. His tail whipped around. Before the tail could finish its full snap, the rat scurried back into the big hole in the wall, dragging its long convoluting tail.

Anne, Rusty's girl, Diane, Connie, and Debbie were nearly turned around and out the two doors when they spotted the giant rat. One thing prevented their leaving—both doors had closed silently when the last person entered the room. Another eek soon followed the realization they were trapped in this room with a big rat. The doors locked with a click at night, and it was cold. The final thoughts of "Get the heck out of our way!" came when the flashlights started to fade.

In one motion, the twelve began a slow backward walk toward the fireplace. Looking at the doors being closed without anyone doing that sent a shiver up each person's spine. Mike called out, "Stop!"

Everyone halted on cue.

"What?" both Vic and Melvin asked Mike.

"The fireplace, Ric. What about the fireplace?"

"Quick, Jerry, ignite the fireplace. We got them with this scare."

"Boss, they are a bit too close, the fire, it might burn them."

"Duh, lower the flame, Jerry. Do I have to tell you how to do everything around here? Turn it down, now do it!"

Jerry adjusted the control knob for a small burst of flame.

In the room, everyone turned around to view the fireplace. Mike's and Ric's flashlights lit the mantle up. On each side was a lion's face, and above the mantle was a large picture of a person. Ric raised his light, and the portrait was illuminated. It was that of a woman dressed in a gown. She had long flowing hair. She was quite beautiful but eerie looking.

"Her eyes, her eyes are shining!" screamed one of the girls.

Mike quickly noticed a fuel scent from the fireplace. Quickly, everyone back up!" he yelled to them. Mike began to shove at the two people standing closet to the mantle. Not to soon, a fire leaped out of it. The flames came within inches of Lindsey's and Vic's faces.

Two of the guys, Bob and Rusty, had wandered over to where the hole was in the wall. Rusty's girlfriend tagged along, holding dearly to his arm. The rear of the group that was closest to the double doors turned to try again to open them.

"See, I told you that fireplace was going to do the trick," smirked Sargent when the kids tried to open the doors to leave.

Meanwhile at the control room, one of the monitors was doing a good job watching the main dirt road. Another car drove up the entrance and stopped. Turning, he called Sargent over. "Hey, boss, there's another car at the drive. They stopped."

Sargent turned from watching the group of kids being scared to walk over to the road monitor. Sargent was about to give the signal to open the door and let them go when he heard the call. Mistake four.

Speaking to the man who called him over to his monitor, he asked, "Why did they stop? Is the road blocked? You need—" Then a sudden realization came to him. "Oh no, it's Peabody. Damn, we got to get these kids out of there."

Before Sargent had time, Jerry called to him. "Boss, that kid they call Mike, he just mentioned a Dr. Strange he met at the house in the swamp. Ain't he the same Dr. Strange Peabody had read about in that magazine and flew up to talk to?"

"Yeah, that's the same Dr. Strange, Jerry. He said that he knew a Dr. Strange?"

"Yep," Jerry answered back again.

"Quick, someone call Mr. Howell ASAP. Now, damn it!" Sargent turned and saw two men jump out of their chairs and scramble to the phone hanging on the wall.

"Boss, why you calling, Mr. Howell?"

"Hell, that Peabody's going to cause us all some kinds of trouble. At least we can say we got hold of the kid he's been searching for all these months. We'll beat him to the buzzer."

"Yeah, that's good thinking, boss."

Within seconds, the phone was ringing in Hollywood. A secretary answered the phone. This is Mr. Howell's office, may I assist you?"

"Nancy, Peggy, or Sue, or whatever your name is, this is Sargent at the house. Get Mr. Howell on the phone, quick."

"Sir, Mr. Howell is with a client now and—"

"Just do it, he wants this information ASAP, and I mean, *now!*"

"Well!"

"Well hell, get him on the phone! This is of the most utmost importance, please!" excitedly screamed Sargent.

After a long minute, a loud and anxious voice came over the phone. "This better be good, Sargent."

"It is. Guess what we have here in this house right now?"

"Sargent, do you think I want to play twenty questions with you? If so, begin to look for another employer."

"Mr. Howell, Mike the kid is in the house."

"What?"

"Yes, sir, right now, him and a bunch of other kids are here."

"Why, how? Where is Peabody? Is he there?"

This was what Sargent wanted to here. "No, sir," he responded with a sense of finally a chance for revenge against that SOB.

"Whatever you do, don't let that boy get away. I'll be on the next plane. See you in three hours."

Click.

"But sir, sir, sir! Dang, he hung up." Turning to Jerry, Sargent instructed, "Don't open those doors. We need to keep them here until Mr. Howell gets here." Mistake five.

"Boss, that could be kidnapping."

"No, no, turn on the lights. We will go and have a talk with them."

"Okay, you're the boss."

"Boss, boss, stop!" the road monitor called out to Sargent with urgency.

"What?" Sargent turned quickly around, but not before he waved to Jerry to not turn on the lights. It was close. Jerry was just about to raise the lights.

"What?" Sargent screamed. "What is it now?"

"That car that stopped, well, the people coming out of the car don't exactly fit the bill for Peabody and our men."

"What? Who the hell is it now?" Sargent was clearly getting upset with all the people popping up at his house unexpectedly. Mistake six.

Looking at the screen, five men with T-shirts on, heavily tattooed, and wearing bandanas were standing by the car that stopped.

"Who the hell are they?" Sargent asked.

"Beats the heck out of me," answered the watcher. "Want me to turn the lights off?"

"Yeah, that might detour them from going to the house," responded Sargent.

THE MEETING OF
FIVE PARTIES

FIVE MEN WALKED OUT OF a car and down the road. Their car blocked the road when they saw the other three cars turned facing the direction of leaving.

"No one is to leave is the order, boys. Got that? Any questions to that order?"

No one said a thing to their leader. Approaching the first car, one man jabbed his knife into the tire. The squeal of air made it clear he flattened the tire. The second car got the same treatment. Only the third car was spared.

When the five walked near the third car, the leader halted the attempt to stab the tires. Grabbing the knife hand of the man who was in the motion of doing that, he told the rest of his men, "We might be needing this car. Think about the bodies needing disposing of later." He made this joke followed by a chuckle.

They all saw the logic and nodded with agreement and also to his leadership. Seems no one gave that a thought.

The lights went off, and the darkness was total. The lights going off did little to halt the five men advancing to the house. Barely able to walk down the road in the dark was almost impossible until they got near the house. A small light shined from the windows. Then a flickering of lights from the front doors guided them in the dark, looming with a mist shrouding their way.

One man pointed and said, "It must be them kids with some flashlights. See that flickering? Them is lights."

"Good, they can give them to us when we get there." He chuckled.

Inside the house, Ric began telling the story about the house Mike had spent the night in the swamps. "Yeah, this Dr. Strange took Mike back to that house where all these things happened. Just like in the magazine story."

"Yeah, I remember that story! My mom told me about it," Rusty spoke up excitedly.

"So did my mom," all the girls spoke, saying the same thing.

Vic mentioned, "I do remember something like that my brother was talking about at school."

All eyes turned to Mike.

Anne was the first to pose the question Mike knew was coming. "You mean you were that same kid who stayed in that house in the magazine?"

Silence held for a minute, then Marcie, who had said very little even when every girl was screaming at the rat, finally spoke. Looking at Mike with a quizzical stare, she asked him point-blank, "You were the boy in the boat too?"

Now everybody turned to face Marcie.

"What boat?" asked Anne and Debbie with one voice.

Marcie began her story about Mike in the boat. "In that same magazine, it tells a story about a kid killing this giant alligator. A boy named Mike with two others went into this swamp to look for this monster they had named. He was the biggest alligator known to exist in that swamp. Mike fell in the water and nearly got eaten alive. That monster alligator bit the boat in half. There was several pictures of the boat and the alligator. One picture showed the boy, Mike, and the other two men. One man was badly hurt." Marcie had put two and two together hearing Ric talk about the haunted house in the swamps. She always thought Mike seemed familiar, and now everything became clear.

"That man was the Old Man, Jethro's dad." Mike finished her sentence. "They saved my life. Both he and his dad nearly lost their lives saving mine."

Everybody now had their eyes glued to Mike. Something like awe had eased over them. Mike seemed different for the first time.

Back in the control room, Sargent listened in, slapping his leg. "If I wasn't sure of him, then I am now."

"Sargent, come here!" a man called to him from across the control room.

"What now?"

"The lights ain't making them turn around. Also, they just stabbed two car tires with a knife. I don't think they are going to be sightseers. Some of them have clubs and tire crowbars in their hands. They are coming straight to the house." Mistake seven.

* * *

"Hey, you driving this car, wait a second!" Stephen called out to him as they came to a stop before entering on the dirt road off the highway.

Peabody's driver poked his head out the door of his car. "Yes, sir," he replied.

"Wait right there," Stephen commanded to him. Stephen got off his bike and walked over to Cho's bike. "Cho, that dandy has nearly soaked me with his pissing. Those pants are dripping on my seat. I'm going to get chaffed from all that piss. You got to unthaw him."

Taking a good whiff of the air that surrounded the big man Stephen, Cho understood his concern. "Well, that should have been a good lesson for him." Unsaddling from his bike, Cho walked over to where Stephen was yanking Peabody off his bike. Peabody was placed seated on the highway edge on top of a sand pile.

"That should work," he said to Cho. "I got him sitting on a litter box."

Cho tapped him on his shoulder a third time. Looking down at the darkened face of this dandy, Cho reminded him of another interruption without permission and the consequences to follow. Peabody barely heard a word Cho said. His concern was on the smell and his suit. Either way, he was assisted by his driver. Stephen had motioned for him to pick up his boss. Holding Peabody at a distance, he assisted the man to the car. Being frozen in pain had made Peabody's legs slightly stiff. The driver had the rear door open and laid him across the seat. Then hhe quickly lowered all four windows.

Tad motioned to Cho and Stephen while Bear remained in the lead. At the car, Tad handed them each a flashlight he kept in his car. "Just in case you might need it in this dark."

Cho took the light. "Thanks, Tad, but this is of little use to me. I'll give it to Bear up front."

Stephen was about to hand his back for the same reasons but decided not to, thinking it was a good thought of kindness and no need to disrespect Tad. *It makes him think he is of some help.*

Soon, the three bikes and two cars were speeding down the dirt road to the house.

* * *

At the front of the house, the gang leader sent one of his men to the window where the light was seen blinking on and off through the cracks. Listening with his ear pegged to the glass, he could hear voices. He was able to make out some of their conversations. It seemed they were talking about some giant monster.

He walked back to the leader. "Hey man, them kids are scared stiff. They are talking about some monsters they think they see. Hahaha!" he laughed.

The leader quickly shoved his hand in the man's face to quiet his loud laughter.

Too late, one of the girls nearest the window heard the laughter outside. It was no mistaking, it was laughter. "Shh." She motioned with her hands to Ric, who was about to talk again.

Mike just explained what the monster was. He told them it was an alligator nearly twenty feet long. It took one bite and almost severed the boat in half. He went on to explain they caught five other gators, and if that boat sank, he and the others would never have gotten out of the swamps alive. Then explaining to his friends, Mike said, "With all that blood and dead meat in the water, it was a dinner bell to all the gators to come and eat."

Walking over to the center of the group, Rusty's girlfriend softly told everyone that she heard someone laugh outside by the window. All eyes turned toward the window.

By the front door, the five men stood. Slowly, the leader man turned the knob. It wasn't opening. Harder he tried, and still it did not turn. Then he pushed on the door, and it did not open. Then all four men leaned against the door, giving a heave-ho with all their might.

Back in the control room, Sargent was beginning to feel fear. Seeing those five men, those five tattooed men, of a dangerous persuasion, with not nice thoughts, and bent on getting into this house was not helping him any.

Thinking out loud, Sargent said, "We can't let them in. If they get in and the kids are present, this could get nasty. We are dealing with some dangerous people. Quick, call for the police."

Reaching for the phone, one of the men who attempted the phone call to Mr. Howell now was dialing for the police. Listening for a pickup sound, he soon realized there was no sound coming through the receiver. Looking back to Sargent, he said, "Hey, boss, the phone is out."

Running to the phone, Sargent yanked it from his hand. True, no sound. The phone was dead. Mistake eight.

"Boss!" Calling him was Jerry. "Boss, you need to see this." Back at the monitor, Sargent and Jerry saw a horrifying sight. To their dismay and astonishment, the four men slammed against the front doors, and the two doors gave way to the impact. Now they were five. A fifth man returned as they crashed through the doors.

"The phones are out, boss. I found the phone line on the side of the house. I cut them. No one's calling for help, boss. But...but I need to tell you—"

He was stopped before he could tell the leader man what he saw in the bushes.

Leader man stopped short of sending his men upstairs to search when he heard the slightest sound emerge from the double doors to one side. Leader man waved to his men to stop on the ascent of the stairs. Then he waved to them to open the doors going into the fireplace room. The fifth man tapped him on his arm again. Leader man, turning curtly, asked him, "What's the problem? I'm busy right now, so what's so damn important now? We got the kid. He ain't leaving. The door is locked. That kid ain't getting away, not again," leader man said.

The fifth man was persistent. He tapped leader man on the back a third time.

"What?" leader man again asked him.

"Boss, when I was cutting the phone lines, something was in the trees behind me. It was big."

"Well, what was it?"

"Boss, I don't know. All I do know is we better have our guns out if we go back outside."

"Why?"

"It stuck its head out of the bushes, boss."

"Sargent, I moved the creature back to its cave. Then when I heard that those guys broke down the door, I positioned the creature by the side of the building. It's ready when you are."

Sargent turned to his animal control robot operator smiling up at him from his desk. "Did you say, it was by the side of the house? Was that the side where the phone lines are?"

"Yep."

"Do you think that guy who cut the lines saw the creature?"

"I sure hope he did. I made every intention for him to see it, boss."

Damn good job." Sargent slapped him on his back.

"What are we going to do?" someone said within the group of twelve behind the door.

A loud voice came from the other side of the double doors. "Hey, Mike, if you can hear me, come out. If you don't, anybody with you is gonna get hurt. All we wants is you."

Ric yelled back, "Who are you?"

"Are you Mike?" came a response.

"No."

"Then shut your mouth, boy!" leader man yelled back.

Everybody was getting scared again. After the story, most of all the scary stuff happening in the room seemed to stop. Then some laughter and most of the group thought they might be part of some joke. Now this threat and the fear rose back up.

Mike quickly began to talk. "Listen, if these are the men I think they are, everyone here is in danger."

Lindsey broke in. "Mike is telling the truth, listen to him."

Ric and Bob both turned to her. "How do you know this?"

"I just do."

"She is right, guys," Mike answered back to their question they posed to her. "You got to listen to me."

"Why should we?" Bob answered with a stern and mad response.

"Look, Bob, I can see why you might be upset with me. These men are after me, and you are here, and your lives are in danger."

"The hell you say?" was Bob's quick reply.

"Listen, Bob, if you open that door, every one of you are not leaving here alive."

"Damn, Mike!" Bob yelled at him.

The girls began to cry except for Lindsey.

"Look, we need to work together to survive," responded Mike to all in the room.

"Hell no," Bob said. "You are the one they want, not us. Why do we have to get hurt or killed?" Bob looked around for any support from the others. No one said a thing.

Lindsey spoke again. "Listen to him, I saw what he can do. Mike can save us."

"What can he do?" asked Bob.

"Yeah, Lindsey, what can Mike do that can save us?" spoke Melvin, Ric, and Vic. Rusty was the only one not to respond. He held on to his girl.

"Listen, I know you all are aware of his martial arts training. It is more than what you think it is. What I saw him do to those two grown men put a shiver up my spine," answered Lindsey.

Everyone turned their eyes back to Mike. Ric was the first to speak, and what he said was what every person wanted to say. "Mike, is anything what Lindsey says true at all?"

Mike stood there alone in the near darkness and nodded his head in agreement.

"Oh my," someone said in the room.

"Listen to me now, please. When they break through that door, we need to ram into them. We all have to work as a team. You girls need to run out to the cars. Rusty, Ric, and Melvin, give the girls your keys. Guys, we need to buy them time. There are six of us. Pair up and take two at once. Drive them into the corners of the room and into each other. Then run out of this room," Mike finished.

"They will quickly catch up to us," one of the girls remarked.

It was still dark in the room, and Mike reminded them of that. "Look, everybody, they can't see us, and they don't know how many they are in this room. Not if we let them in, and they can't break the doors down. We rush them before they can react. We can close the doors behind us once they rush inside. That should give you time to make it to the cars."

"Mike, who is going to close the doors when we run out of here?" somebody inquired.

"I will, you guys just make sure everyone gets out of this room, okay?"

Ric and Bob paired up and took one side of the double doors. Melvin and Vic took the other side. Each stood near the door, ready to ram their man against the back wall. Rusty was with the girls, and they stood near Mike by the fireplace.

In the control room, Sargent was listening to every word spoken. He had his team slowly raise the lights. This lit the room enough for the control room to spy on both groups. Hopefully the group didn't notice the lights getting brighter.

Mike noticed the lights' slight elevation and wondered who was controlling them.

Back in the control room, Sargent gave the order to begin the ghost protocol on the stairs. Quickly, a mist formed at the top of the stairs. A cold breeze traveled down to the main floor. The first gang member to notice the cold was the first man to look up at the stairs where the cold breeze seemed to have originated.

What he saw made him fear God for the first time in his wicked life. No time had he ever entered a church since the time his pa left him and his mom home alone. He never came back that night. He slapped his wife after they argued over the same old thing, money.

Now, before him, coming down the stairs was a spirit of death. He believed one was never going to visit him. His eyes grew in size as the ghost floated down the stairs. It was coming to him. If it touched him, he believed death was to follow soon after.

His friend standing near him gave him a slight nudge to get ready for the rush at the doors, like the front door to smash through. Only when he didn't respond did he turn to see why his friend wasn't responding.

The spirit was next to his friend, and when he shined the flashlight, he found at the foot of the stairs illuminating the two doors to his friend's face, it was as white as snow. Standing some feet away was a woman, a beautiful woman wearing a white flowing dress. Her hair was as black as soot. Those eyes of her were staring through his soul. His friend stood watching. She reached out to touch him on his face with her thin bony fingers. Before she touched him, the leader man gave the order to charge at the door.

Inside the room, Mike yelled at his group to prepare for the onslaught. Mike sensed the charge before the leader man gave the order. Bob hesitated and stood too close to the door on his side.

The door bulged with the weight of four men pressing against it. In the control room, Sargent gave the order to let the doors open. Then he turned to the controller who had the monitor to be prepared with the fireplace. He nodded back in response and kept his hand on the knob, ready for the order.

Everyone in the control room quickly became aware of the dangers when the gang members pulled out weapons as they started entering the house. The leader held a gun. It was evident as the man holding the flashlight shined it on the leader man. It also revealed the other weapons the rest of the gang had removed from their pants. Mistake nine.

At first, no one suspected they were there to attack this first group. When the leader called out Mike's name, something was up. Then his demand for Mike to come out of the room. They knew he was in the room. How, was the question. Why was concerning Sargent. His next move may result in getting these kids killed. Mistake ten.

"Damn, the count of mistakes, there's just too many to count, and the way it appears, the count is only going to get bigger. Damn, damn, and damn," spouted Sargent of this mess he was in.

Mike looked up at a small glass protrusion in two corners of the room they were in. Sargent stood staring at him looking at the lenses installed in every room, monitoring any who walked in. *How in the heck does that kid know he was looking at a camera? Maybe he thinks it is some kind of a hole in the corner. He can't know it is a camera. No way*, thought Sargent.

With a wave to his throat, Mike had signaled the person viewing him to cut the lights. Sargent responded immediately to his signal. *That is just weird. How can the kid know about him and to tell him to cut the lights?* Sargent and the controller watched as the room became dark. Bending down, he told the man to get ready. "When that kid tells you to light the room with the fireplace, you light it up."

The controller looked up at Sargent. "What do you mean when the kid tells me to? How is he gonna do that? He doesn't even know we are watching him."

"Just do it, watch him and only him. He knows. I don't know how he does, but he knows."

"Sure, boss, will do."

The doors flew open, slamming into Bob. He went flying into his partner, and both of them were thrown away from the door. Neither was in place to charge at the intruders.

Vic and Melvin did as they had prepared to do. They hit the first two men to enter the room. All four were propelled to the outer wall away from the entrance. Mike sensed the other three men running into the room. He shoved Rusty and the girls ahead. Didn't matter at all if the plan fell apart; the girls had to leave.

Bob recovered just in time to push off the wall and run at the center of the three men entering the room unrestrained. Rick was not far behind. Between the two, they hit two of the men, and all of them went flying across the room into the other gang members. Vic and Melvin, after shoving their men into the wall, was in the act of following the girls out of the room.

Bob did the most shocking thing that night. He took a swing at one of the men he pushed to the wall. He hit him, and before he could take another swing at the other man, he got hit by one of the three men with a club. It flung him back at Ric. Ric grabbed hold of Bob. It didn't stop them from falling to the floor.

Mike was standing, watching the action unfold. He noticed Vic and Melvin were out the door behind the girls. Two of the girls fell in the hallway, and Melvin tripped over one of them. She let out a scream.

The leader man had an unencumbered path straight at Mike. Even Ric and Bob falling in front of him did not deter his path. They simply kept rolling to one side. Both soon were on their feet. Bob was a bit woozy from the hit. Ric kept hold of him, guiding both of them through the doorway. Neither could see what was happening. They only heard several men yelling at each other to get off.

Mike was now alone. The double doors were still opened.

Sargent, seeing the doors still wide open, ordered them close. A yell came from the controller in charge back to him. What he said caused fear to fill Sargent's soul. He thought with the kid knowing they were viewing them, he had it under control. Now with the doors jammed open and they couldn't be closed, he started to panic.

"Close them doors now! Someone is going to get killed. Close the doors!"

"We can't!" he kept coming back. "We can't!"

Leader man lifted his gun, pointing at Mike or at least in the general direction he was faintly able to determine. The flashlight was dislodged from the man holding it. It lay on the floor with the beam aimed to one side. Still enough of the light had given the leader man enough of an image to make out Mike's place.

"Hey, I sure hope you are Mike! I sure hate to shoot you and the others to get to the right one."

Mike knew he had to answer his request. If he didn't, then everyone who got out of the room will be in danger. This was going to reaffirm to the leader man his position and limit his chances to get out alive. No matter. It had to be done. His friends were out.

Thinking quickly, Mike tried to determine his best options. He knew the doors were opened, and leader man might send his men out for the others. One chance he had. He hoped whoever was watching would get the message.

Mike looked up at the glass lens in the corner and nodded his head, then he moved to one side away from the fireplace. Within seconds of that nod, the order was given.

In the command room, the controller saw the nod. He looked at the kid nodding at the lens. *It can't be? It is, he is telling me to light it up.*

Sargent yelled out, "The kid nodded for the fireplace! What are you waiting for, do it, damn it!"

Both he and Sargent saw the kid move away from the fireplace. Others in the control room stood and walked over to the controller and Sargent. All were watching the action unfold. The fire bellowed out of the hearth straight at the leader man. He screamed when the flames struck him on his face. The gun pointed at Mike went off.

In the control room, what happened next was unbelievable to everyone viewing the action in the room. All the other men in the room saw the flame and stood in amazement at the sudden eruption of fire coming out of the chimney. They watched as their leader was nearly lit up with fire as the flames flew into his face. The gun went off.

Mike was prepared for the flames and to the gun's possibility of firing at him. Mike sensed the flame and felt the air rush from the hearth. Within seconds of the fire, sure to follow was the gust of air, and he knew leader man would shoot at him. Not because he wanted to, but because he had the gun out and trigger pulled back. His reaction from the flames would surely cause him to squeeze the trigger.

To all the men in the command room watching the monitor, to them it appeared he moved faster than a bullet. A bang of the gun was loud in the room. Outside, the girls and most of the other guys were nearing the cars. Upon hearing the loud bang of a gun, they froze in place. Everyone stopped their mad run to the cars and turned.

Lindsey screamed at the loud bang. It was a gunshot to all that heard the sound; there was no mistaking the sound. Only one person was left in the house. Only one person wasn't outside with them. It was the same person responsible for closing the door and making sure they were bolted, preventing the gang from following.

It was Mike.

All eyes stared back toward the house. Each person hoped the front doors would once more open. Open to reveal Mike had bolted the doors and left. Mike had left them trapped in the room. Maybe in frustration, the shot was them trying to shoot the doors open.

The front doors did not open, and Mike did not come out.

Lindsey yelled, "It's Mike, they shot Mike!" The other girls held her. Lindsey almost collapsed. Vic and Ric started to return to the house. Melvin grabbed Ric's arm. "Stop, you two! If that was Mike being shot, going back won't help. He gave his life for us to get away."

Rusty's girlfriend grabbed hold of him, and the other girls grabbed hold of the nearest person for comfort. Some cried; some just held tight to one other. They all walked to the cars.

"Hey, Sargent, the kids are at the cars now."

"Good," he replied. "Turn on the outside light."

With a quick flip of a switch, the front yard lit up.

To all, it was weird. Why did they come on? In front of the group, they saw two cars with a tire flat as a pancake. Only one car had all four tires inflated.

Turning to Ric, everyone or several asked him what they were going to do. Ric looked puzzled. He was clueless. Rusty was the first to suggest they change tires. He also mentioned the girls to get into the one car with good tires. "Everyone who can get in that car should do so. The rest of us will stay and get the tires changed."

To the credit of all the Rama crew, they all agreed to stay together. "No one leaving unless we all go." Every girl nodded in response to Lindsey request. The boys were somewhat upset. They went along with her suggestion rather than to argue with the girls; the tires wouldn't get changed if they did.

Inside the room, the leader man screamed once, then twice from the pain from the burns he received to his face. With those burns covering his face, a fury lit inside of him. He was mad, and he was going to take it out on someone.

Mike, seeing the leader man grab at his face, quickly charged at him with a side skip kick to his guts. Leader man was too busy with his pain to notice Mike charging at him. He took the complete force of the kick. That caused another scream.

Outside they heard screaming. At first, they thought the screams was that of Mike being shot. "He might be alive," Lindsey called out to the group.

Leader man went flying backward down on the ground. His gun went off a second time. This time Mike was in the clear from the get-go. The other four men saw where Mike was standing after the second shot flash. The light on the floor aided them as well.

One man called out to the group to spread out. "Everyone," he said, "form a loop. He can't get through us."

They were wrong. Mike had no intentions of leaving. At least not while he still hadn't heard the sound of cars starting up.

The room quickly returned back to the darkness it had before the fire. The flashlight was losing its battery strength. Before the four had a chance to close in on him, Mike ran at the center and, with a jump into the air, flung his body up with two front kicks to the faces of the two men holding the center line.

One man went flying back into the hallway. The other got a glancing blow and stepped back a few steps. One man in the line took a wild swing with his fist at Mike. Mike saw the fist coming at him. Quickly blocking the fist, he followed with a kick under the chin of his face. The gang member's head rocked back with a snap. He dropped straight to the floor. The other man who hadn't been hit drew his knife and swiped at Mike. It missed. Leader man got off the floor and was pointing his gun around, looking for his target.

"Sargent!" controller called out. "That kid, he kicked that one guy's head nearly off his shoulders. Should I turn the lights up?"

"No, no, keep using infrared lenses to watch. Don't turn on the lights. That's probably the only thing keeping that kid alive, the darkness."

Outside, one tire was changed. Rusty turned to the others. "Hey, guys, do you hear all that ruckus inside the house?"

"Yeah, it sounds like all hell is breaking out," responded Ric.

"Someone is trying hard to break out of that room!" shouted Melvin.

"Ric, you and Vic get the tires changed. We need to get out of here soon. I think they are about to get out of the house," Bob demanded to all.

"We are nearly there, Bob. Shut up, Bob, let them work," Anne said.

Bob turned back to the house, watching.

"Okay, kid, I was told to bring you back alive. That ain't going to happen now. We're taking you back, that's a promise, but dead. You hear that, kid? Dead."

Outside, everybody heard what leader man said as well.

"Mike! He's alive!" Lindsey shouted at the girls watching the house; now all knew this for sure.

The man with the knife swiped again at Mike. This time Mike was focused on the leader man and his gun. He was caught off guard.

Stupid, just stupid of me, Mike thought as the knife sliced through his shirt, cutting a deep gash in his arm. *No time to worry about a little scratch*, Mike thought to himself. He turned to the knife wielder as he was about to take a third swipe, Mike caught the arm. With a circular movement on his arm, the man felt his feet leaving the ground. Mike had, with one movement, continued his grab and twirled the man around, pulling his knife arm with the momentum in an upward arc. The knife man felt the pain and had little choice. He allowed the force to drag him along to keep the pain from overwhelming him.

It hadn't eased the pain. He screamed as he felt his shoulder disconnect from the arm socket. Again, the scream was heard outside.

Mike brought the arm down and around the knife man's back. The knife man had no choice but to bend down from the force. It was too little too late for the knife man. Mike suddenly reversed the flow of movement, and again a man went flying through the air. Down he came hard on the floor. A loud slam followed the descent.

With the slam to the floor, the leader man turned to Mike. Mike saw the turn and ducked. Again, the gunshot missed him.

At the control monitor, all saw the movement, only to behave the same as they had from the first shot. It wasn't possible.

He moved again as that leader man fired his gun at the kid. The bullet hit the mantle and ricocheted.

Sargent stood up and put his hand to his head, a reaction to what he saw. "Who is this kid?"

A swooshing sound was barely audible, but there it was coming down from the overhead toward Mike's heads. Mike had just enough time to swerve his body. With a twist, he was able to manage just enough clearance to the head. Passing along a line down the front of his torso, Mike felt the metal rod brush across his chest and stop on his upper thigh. The pain ran up from the area to Mike's brain, setting it ablaze with agony.

Mike knew if he yelled out—and he wanted to yell from the force of that impact and reeling, searing pain flooding his mind—it would alert the leader man with the gun to his whereabouts. Forcing himself to subdue the urge to yell, he knew the man with the metal rod was raising that rod for another swipe.

Metal rod man yelled out to his companions, "I hit him, I hit the kid with my tire iron! He's hurt, I got him."

Mike's leg buckled as he attempted to move out of the next incoming blow he knew was shortly following the first swing. Instead of trying to stand, Mike gave way to the yielding weakness in his leg to give way.

Mike rolled onto his back on the floor as the second swing swiped the air above his head. Continuing the roll backward, Mike was able to rise from the rear motion and onto his feet. With a little backward motion still carrying him in that direction, he came into contact with the third man still in the room.

Mike could feel it was the man he kicked into the hallway. He returned, and Mike bumped into him. He reached out with both of his arms, grabbing hold with a viselike grip around Mike's torso. This man was strong. He held onto Mike to the point he was having trouble getting his breath.

Mike had no concern; it seemed everybody always tried and grabbed someone from behind. He thought to himself, *Don't they ever learn that anyone with some knowledge can easily break from that hold?* With his foot up, Mike shot it down on the instep of his grabber. Then he extended his hip out from the front and quickly reverse thrust them to the rear into his grabber's groin area. Needless to say, the man bent forward from the impact. All Mike needed was to slam his head backward into the face of his grabber. The force of his blow caused an explosion from the assailant's nose. Mike could feel the warm flow of blood down the back of his neck.

The grabber let go of his iron grip, grabbing at what was left of his nose. On his face he felt about the area, feeling the flatness left behind. The blow was so powerful, it totally flattened his nose. What he felt caused an overwhelming urge to scream. He yelled and stunned his fellow companions.

Once Mike felt the blood flow down his backside, he immediately spread his legs outward, then followed with both arms, breaking the hold of his bear-hugging companion. His entire body dropped down beyond the loose grip his grabber now had on him. Below his belt, Mike tucked and rolled between flat nose's legs and back behind his grabber. Not once did any part of Mike's body touch his grabber; he tucked tight and cleanly came up to his feet before the man finished checking for the whereabouts of his nose.

Suddenly the grabber man without a clue dropped to the ground like a rock. He collapsed in a pile of ruffled mass of mangled blob of a man. His body seemed to have fallen apart from the final blow Mike delivered.

Mike with his foot swung into a wide rotating arc upward. Some people describe the kick as an axe-style kick. It went up over the grabber's head and straight back down. It hit the top of the man's skull, an impact that squashed the neck like an accordion being squeezed to play a tune. Only thing was this was a dirge, his funeral tune. Two men left, Mike figured.

Mike received his fair share of the damage from his foes. He was still bleeding on his arm from the knife cut. His leg was nearly broken from the iron rod crashing into it. The pain was still there, and he had two men to deal with.

This time, Mike had moved from that last advance where he tangled. Luckily, he escaped both attempts that left him wounded but not out. He was by the double doors. If he could manage to keep them away from the doors, he still might be able to lock them in the room and make his escape.

In the command room, Sargent was busy trying to get the phones up. He had another line that led out on the other side of the house. One of his crew reminded him of the backup phone line. Sargent made sure every aspect of the house had a backup contingency. Soon he had Mr. Howell on the line.

"Sir, we have a little problem."

"Deal with it, Sargent. I should be landing in Macon soon."

"Sir?" Sargent asked him. "How is that possible? You were in Hollywood when I called you. It should take several hours from there to even get to Georgia."

"Sargent, I was in my plane and traveling this direction. I told my pilot to get this plane ready is what you heard. Ready to fly for Georgia. I don't see the reason to explain myself to you."

"No, sir, sorry. I was amazed at how quick you got to Macon."

"Now what about this problem you have? Am I needing to deal with this problem, or are you capable of dealing with it?"

Knowing Mr. Howell's attitude toward people who cannot cope with changing problems as they arise, Sargent knew from previous experiences to take care of the problem. If not, then be prepared to look for another job. "No, sir, that problem is being taken care of. I just thought incorrectly, sir, you might want to be informed. My mistake."

"Good, Sargent, I have no need to hear every little problem that arises. See you soon."

"Yes, sir."

Click.

"Another mistake, damn." Turning around, Sargent spoke up, and all could hear his thoughts. Damn, damn, damn, where is Peabody? Wish he was here. This problem can be his problem and not mine."

"Sir, sir, come here."

"Damn, what now?" Sargent barked out.

Over at the monitor, Sargent watched Mike drop the third man to the floor with a wickedly high kick down to the head of the man who was once holding on to him. "Is he dead?"

The monitor man looked back at Sargent. "That makes three he killed, sir. Also, sir, he dodged three bullets."

Sargent again scratched his head. "Who is this kid?"

Before Mike could complete his plan of getting through the doors, the second man reached out for him with his knife. He just picked himself off the floor, finding his friend lying near where he had landed dead on the floor. Before he was able to stand, his other friend fell at his other side, dead. Blood covered the floor.

He stood and reached out. It was dark. He could hear but was barely able to see his hand in front of his face. It was a fortunate grab he made. Second man knew it had to be that kid. He was smaller than any of his companions.

Outside, sounds kept coming out of the house. One yell followed by another, then a lot of noise. Noise sounding like things were being thrown inside. Things crashing into walls, breaking apart at impact.

Mike felt the arm, then the knife. The knife slid off his other arm the second man was holding on to. The point of the tip just pierced his side above his belt on the right side, not too deep. Mike reacted before the point enter deep enough to cause serious harm. He tore loose from his grip. Mike's shirt was ripped from his shoulder, and the knife man fell away from his release on the hold. His feet could not keep their traction on the wet blood-saturated floor. It was enough to distract him.

Another cut, Mike thought. *What is Sifu going to say when he sees these cuts on me? He's going to think I am unworthy to be his student.* Mike began to fear. *Dang it*, he thought, *no more, I will not disgrace my Sifu with any more cuts to me.* Mike yelled to the two men remaining. "Gentlemen, you just got me pissed off!"

"Screw you, kid!" a voice yelled back to Mike.

"Bad move, asshole," Mike replied. Knowing from the yell, the second man with the knife revealed where he was standing. Mike, with a movement so fast, hit him squarely between his eyes even before the words he said had time to travel the distance to him. Both his eyes ran into each other from the impact of the blow between them. "One punch, fourth man down," Mike told the last man in the room, the leader holding the gun.

Leader man, fearing for his life, was on the ground and felt his comrades' dead cold bodies lying around him. Then his last man hit the ground on top of him.

Mike fell backward, slipping on the blood from the blow he delivered to the knife man. Leader man was able to quickly slide off his last dead man's body to his feet. He was quickly trying to see where this most dangerous and most unexpectedly skills this kid had gone to. With the failing light, he saw what appeared to be a kid moving to a corner. With his last two shots remaining in his pistol, he fired at the corner.

"Sargent, did you see that man? That makes four."

Then came the two final shots inside the room.

"Look, that man with the gun, he shot at the wall near the kid!"

"Move over, let me see," Sargent ordered the man at the monitor. "Damn, if that kid is shot…God, don't let that kid be shot."

Inside the command room, everyone was watching the same monitor. Each man stood with awe at this one kid's daring. One man remarked, "That kid got more guts than the Marine Corps."

"Quick, did you see the gunman? He's running out of the room. That kid scared the hell out of him. He scares the hell out of me," said one of the men watching.

Another man agreed.

"Quick!" Sargent barked out. "Turn up the lights. Is the kid still in the room, or did he chase after that guy?"

"I don't know, sir. I heard the shots and saw the gunman shoot at the corner where it looked the kid was in. I haven't seen any one move around since."

"Turn up the lights. How many times do I have to tell someone to do something?"

In the hallway, the gunman or leader man fled, running smack into the ghost protocol image still remaining. Her black hair was flowing. The dress was wispy and eyes icy cold staring right at the leader man. Both eyes met. A scream followed. Both of his eyes grew as big as baseballs. Then a shiver ran the length of his spine. A tiny tingle was felt in his hair. Out of terror, he tore at the image before him to no avail; the image remained. The cold air drifted over his steaming hot body from the fight he had been in. The cold chilled him to the bone. Death was coming to him. This was his thought as be broke free of her grip.

Outside, the front doors flew open. A man came running down the stairs. He fell when his foot touched the earth, falling face forward into the ground.

"You, animal control man, turn that creature on. Let's give that SOB a real good scare!" Sargent screamed.

The leader man jumped up off the ground. The creature was walking; the movie was playing. Sound was turned all the way up. Feeling the ground vibrating, leader man looked over to where the sound was coming from that was causing the ground to shake.

First thing his eyes saw was a slow moving of bushes, then two large legs, followed by a tail moving near the road. Close to him but not coming at him. Then the head appeared. A head that towered over the treetops. Its head turned. It turned and looked his way. Leader man saw the eyes looking down at him. The tail started to wag.

Everybody by the cars was about to enter their cars, but they turned when they heard the doors crash open from the house. They watched a man run out and trip, falling facedown to the ground. The lights made everything easy to see. They watched him lying there only for a few seconds. Then the loud shaking from stomping feet came, and they saw the same thing leader man was looking at. It was huge and moving their way. It stopped.

First, they heard the last two shots and was nearly in their cars, then the leader man came out, and now this giant creature appeared before them. All that made each and every one by the cars freeze. They couldn't help but stare at what was unfolding in front of them. It was totally bizarre. This couldn't be possible.

Ric spoke out first. "It's like Mike told me, it's just like that giant monster he fought in the swamps".

Inside the house, the lights were fully on. Mike was sitting in a corner, holding onto his side. It was apparent that he tried to chase after the leader man but only made a few steps. He was crying. He kept saying in a soft murmur, "I can't save them. He's going to get to them. Please, Lord, give me the strength to get up! I need to get to them before he does. They hadn't left, I didn't hear the cars start up. Why didn't they leave? They had enough time to go. What stopped them?"

One couldn't help to feel for this kid lying there, pleading to God to help him save his friends.

"Quick, you two get up top and see if he is okay. Check on the kid. You three come with me." He pointed to three men standing near the last monitor. They turned and followed after the boss. Before Sargent left the room, he gave one final order to the remaining men. "Keep at the controls. Light this place up."

Outside the house lit up like a Christmas tree. Every floor in the house was lit with light. Men came into view inside the house. One man then another crossed the window, going to one side of the room they were in.

Ric called to everyone to look at the house. "See the windows? Someone just walked past the window in the room we were in."

"To hell with the men in the window!" Bob cried out. "Look at that big-ass creature standing near the house. We got to get moving. I ain't going to be supper to that thing."

Most of the girls were in the cars. Rusty's girl had her car up and running. She revved up the engine to get Rusty's attention. He was focused on the house, as were the others, except for Bob.

"What the hell's going on in this place?" Ric inquired out loud.

Lindsey stood next to him and answered him. "I thought this place was abandoned? Why are all those people there and this house all lit up?"

Bob shouted to them, "Hey, guys, am I the only one who sees that big-ass creature standing there? We going to stay and meet this creature. Hey, glad to meet you, we here for the free meal. Guys, we gots to leave!"

"Look, Bob, that creature, it's not moving. It just stopped and not moved again."

"Well, that's good, but the guy with the gun, he up and running this way. He still got his gun, guys."

Before they could react to Bob's alarm, two bikes roared up to the road and stopped. Then a car followed by another bike and a car.

Two men hopped off their bikes. One man, the tallest, started to run toward them. The others larger around the belly followed. The first tall man flew past them, and the second man stopped. "Who made those gunshots? Was anyone shot?"

Everybody looked at this huge, overweight man standing before them. Bob had to be the first mouth to speak. "Who the hell are you, fat man?"

Lindsey looked at Bob then to Ric. "Won't that guy ever learn?"

"Nope," Ric replied.

Before Bob had a second chance to rephrase his first remark, he found a big hand slap him across his mouth. The slap knocked him back into the car. Holding onto the car fender, he slowly returned his eyes back toward the mistake he made. His eyes were still rolling around his head, giving him double vision. What words embarked from his mouth could be perceived as an apology of sorts. Either way, the big man made his point again. He turned to follow his companion to the house.

The gunman was back on his feet, running straight at the man who went past the Rama Rowdies. Gunman was trying to reload his pistol as he ran. He soon saw the taller man coming at him full bore. The last round entered the chamber, and the cylinder slammed closed.

On the floor lay Mike, blood still flowing out of his arm. The wound was being held closed by Mike's other hand. Blood still flowed out. Some blood could be seen on his side. A small circle of red spread out from the place the hole was made by the knife. The kid's leg was curled up under his other leg. As the two men tried to lay Mike out, they grabbed hold of the leg bent and pulled it straight.

A loud scream came from the house. Stephen running to the house heard the scream and recognized the sound. It was Mike's cry.

Sifu Cho was at the car with the Rowdies and Tad. He heard the scream. Not saying a word, he soon was on the heels of Teddy Bear and Stephen. Stephen saw the gun and remembered hearing the shots as they approached the road entering the house's driveway.

As the gun was raised, the leader man had it at the ready, fixing his aim. Before the trigger ever got pulled, Stephen was on him. Without stopping, he flew past him. Leader man felt shocked that he couldn't get the shot off fast enough drop the big guy. He turned and saw him continue running to the house.

Cho managed to pass Bear a few feet before Stephen passed the leader man. Cho continued his flight past leader man as well. Leader man barely returned his head back toward the direction he was heading. After Stephen passed him, he had to slow his run so as not to stumble on the road. Now, he was moving much slower, staring at the two men who had passed him. Then he heard a loud lumbering gait coming up behind, slower than the two before him. Turning back just in time to glimpse this huge mountain that blocked out the light from the pole overshadow him then shroud him in darkness again. What he saw was Teddy Bear, he didn't know who he was, neither did he know the other men who passed him by. It needn't concern him anymore.

Teddy Bear stopped. Leader man never did learn their names. He was happy to lie face up staring at the stars. He wondered at the flashing lights so high in the sky. In the city, one could never see them as pretty as they were in the woods. He closed his eyes, thinking about them stars so high in the sky.

Tad remained with his crew. He pondered as he looked at Bob. Bob seemed to have a queer look to his face and holding onto the car he was near. Lindsey notice Tad's apparent concern for Bob's appearance.

"Tad, he is all right. None of us got hurt, thanks to Mike staying behind."

"Where is Mike?" Tad began to scan the group for him.

Lindsey continued as Tad was still scanning the group. "He is still in the house. That scream we heard might be Mike's."

"What? He is still in the house? Why?"

Ric spoke up, telling Tad he remained to close the doors for the rest of them to flee to the cars. "He was supposed to follow us out."

Debbie jumped in to say, "He saved us. He shoved me, us, out the door. The leader man had a gun and was pointing it at us. We ran." Debbie began sobbing again.

Anne and Rusty and his girlfriend Diane continued what Debbie was trying to convey. "Bob hit one of the men, but another one hit him with some kind of a stick, and he went down. If not for Vic and Ric taking their men, jamming them into the corner as Mike told them to do, we might not have gotten out either."

"Yeah, we were the last two out of the room, and we expected Mike to follow us. Mike told us he was going to close the doors behind him. As we jumped off the front porch steps, that is when we heard the gunshot. We turned to go back for him, then another gunshot. Someone yelled out in pain. That's when we all figured Mike got shot and killed. We had to get the girls to safety as Mike told us to do. It was dark out here, and you couldn't see where anything was."

"That's right, Tad," Rusty interjected. "We didn't know if those guys were behind us or not. We were constantly tripping and falling down. We were busy picking each other off the ground. When we got to the car, some of us wanted to return to the house until we saw the tires were flattened by those guys after us."

"Why were they after you?" Tad asked.

"Well, we thought that at first, until Mike explained they were after him. The leader man wanted Mike."

"Yeah, Tad," Melvin added to what Rusty was telling him. "He told us to send Mike out, if not, he was going to kill everybody with him. Mike told us they were going to kill us whether he went out or not. They had no intentions of leaving witnesses."

"He was right," Tad replied after hearing the story his group was telling them.

Lindsey took her turn to fill Tad in with the rest of the story. "Tad, Mike came up with the plan for the guys to pair up against the men in the hall. We weren't sure of how many were out there trying to get in. When they finally broke through the doors, Ric and Bob were knocked clear by the door slamming into them. Melvin and Vic hit their two men, driving them to a corner in the room. That's when Bob was able to get on his feet and attacked one of the two men shoved into another corner. That was supposed to let the girls and Rusty through the doors. Bob hit one, and he got flattened by a bat, then Ric knocked that man down."

"Yeah, Tad, Mike shoved several people forward. Melvin and I bumped into two guys and knocked them backward, clearing the way out of the room."

"My god, it was plain lucky anyone got out alive. You all did a heroic job fighting off them men."

All the girls said to Tad, "They sure did. They helped save us."

Reaching the steps and before Stephen entered the front door, a man stood holding his hand out to prevent his entry. "Stop, this is private property," Sargent spoke to the tall man running up the stairs.

Stephen gave him a look that said, without speaking, he better move out of his way. Stephen offered him a shove, causing Sargent to fling back against the wall opposite that of the two double doors into the den. Before he could recover from the shove, another older shorter man also assisted with another shove back into the wall.

Inside the den were two men, and one was bent over a body. Blood was covering the floor. Four bodies lay scattered across the room. One man was twisted in a most unusual position facedown. To the right of him was another man squashed in a pile. It gave the impression someone took a dump in the middle of the floor. It surely looked like someone cleaning this mess up was going to use a whole lot of toilet paper.

The third man appeared to be sitting, holding his leg. The leg was broken. The third man was dead. The fourth man was half buried in a wall. Somebody threw him headfirst into it. It was obvious the fourth man's head was harder than the wall. Both of his feet were hanging like drapes on a curtain rod.

The second man kneeling alongside Mike was busy getting material out of a first aid box. They were focused on the task at hand. The person on the floor they were attending to was stretched out on the floor. He was crying, saying he disappointed his Sifu.

Cho quickly reached down to move the second man from his medical kit. When Cho put his hand on his shoulder, he almost jumped out of his skin. He fell backward and crawled several feet like a crab upon seeing this oriental man. Then he saw a much taller man by his side looking at him with a most menacing smile.

Cho spoke first. "What nonsense is this, Mike?"

Mike looked up and saw Sifu.

"Why do you speak as if I was disappointed in you? What you did made me proud and honored to have such a student as you."

Stephen followed with, "Now stop that crying. You are a student of us, and there is no need for such behavior. Every man is entitled to cry. This is not that time."

The man on his back that crawled from the two men realized after that remark that they were friends of this kid. "You two know this kid?"

Cho turned to look at the man sprawled upon the floor behind him. "Did I not just say that to my student? Are you hard of hearing?"

"You, man, move away from this kid."

The man doctoring Mike turned momentarily to look at the two men standing near the kid lying prone on the bloody floor. He scrambled back to Mike. Then he turned to administer to Mike. "This young man has a serious wound on his arm. One of those men lying on the floor ripped his arm open to the bone with a knife. He has lost a good deal of blood fighting these killers off. I don't know how he was able to do what he did."

"Move away from the boy," Cho repeated his demands to the man doctoring Mike.

"Are you crazy, old man? He is bleeding out. If you care one bit for this young man, you will allow me to finish closing his bleeding wound. I heard you were some kind of teacher to him? Whatever you taught this kid, he did things I never thought anyone could have done, much less a young man his age."

Cho almost lost his temper when the medic made that last comment to him. Cho reached down, grabbed the medic by his shirt collar, and with a flick of his arm, the medic came off the ground and on his feet. Then off the floor and into the air. He dangled there just enough to realize what he said was not what he should have said.

Quickly the medic began apologizing to this short man holding him off the floor with a single hand. Stephen lightly touched Cho on his shoulder. The man was gently set down on the floor.

Both Cho and Stephen bent down to examine the wound. Cho asked Stephen to hand him a cloth. With the cloth, Cho lay it on top of the blood-soaked dressing the medic had applied with little success.

Cho rubbed his hands together; after several fast strokes, he placed one hand over the wound. With another hand, he removed from his jacket a small box. He handed the box to Stephen. Stephen opened the box, revealing many small long needles. Lifting one of the needles, Stephen placed it into Cho hand. This occurred several times to the medic's eyes.

"What the hell are you sticking him with those needles?" he inquired the two tending to his patient.

Neither of them responded. Cho placed one last needle, and suddenly Mike stopped wincing in pain. The bleeding seemed to have ceased. The other man that lay sprawled behind both of the strange men was now standing, watching Cho and Stephen next to the other medic.

Tad and the group of Rama Rowdies were now making their way to the house. As they neared the house, they kept their eyes on this huge creature looking toward them. Tad stared in disbelief. He simply asked them, "Is that thing alive? I swear it looks like it is ready to attack us."

Lindsey remarked to Tad, "We thought the same thing when we saw it. Except it was moving at us. We—"

"What?" interrupted Tad. "That thing could move? Did it attack you?" Tad, after he got over the awe-inspiring sight, froze in place. "It moved, you say, Lindsey?"

As the group neared the house, the creature looked bigger. Everyone looked up at the creature. Some half expected it was playing dead to lure them in.

Bob came to his senses from Teddy Bear's slap, and he was being led to the house. Looking around, wondering why they were returning to the house, he saw the huge creature staring menacing down at him. He jerked at the arm holding his. Not breaking free of the grip two of his fellow ushers had on him, he screamed out, "Let me go, that thing is going to eat us! What are you doing? Run!"

Tad placed his hand on Bob's shoulder to settle him down. "Easy, Bob, you been out for a few minutes. Apparently, Teddy Bear had to teach you some manners and slapped you. You been a bit flighty since then."

"Who, what, how did you get here, Tad? Why are we going back to the house? We got to get away." He looked at the others walking alongside. "Didn't anyone tell you there is a guy with a gun? He shot Mike. He said he was going to kill all of us."

"Bob, it is all over. All the men are dead. The man with the gun is lying on the ground. He is ahead of us."

Bob saw a man lying face up on the ground as Tad said. Next to him was a gun. Tad reached down, picking the gun up. The man's hand wasn't going to let it go. Tad was insistent and twisted the gun free. The arm fell effortlessly back to the ground as they continued walking to the house.

Someone yelled behind the party of kids advancing to the house. He was calling to somebody named Peabody. "Peabody, wait here! Come back, it might not be safe. Wait until we can be sure!"

A twangy, nasal sound retorted with a huffy reply, "Nonsense, I am in charge of this place, and anything going on is my responsibility." With his cane tapping the ground with every step, Peabody walked straight to the house. When he reached the body lying on the ground face up, he paused. After viewing him, he was heard to make a remark. It was something about someone will be held responsible for this mess, then continued to the house.

All twelve friends of Mike with Tad walked up the steps. Sargent was about to make a second mistake but thought better of it. He saw these young people fight for their lives, and besides, there were way too many of them and so few of him to halt their advance. He stood near the wall he was placed by the short guy waving them into the den.

Tad was first to enter the large vacant room. The first sight was the same that of his group first witnessed. He saw the huge fireplace with the two heads. Then a movement alerted him to the two men standing near Cho and Stephen. Both stood watching Cho. Mike lay on the floor.

Lindsey then Anne, Debbie, Marcie, and finally Connie shrieked at the body lying on the floor in that order following after the one before them. One of the girls remarked of the strange odor that was present entering and not present earlier when they first entered the house. It had a rusty iron smell. Only then did one of the other girls see the blood.

Blood was everywhere they looked. They turned to what they believed was Mike dead on the floor. The floor was shiny bright with red blood. Most of the blood was coming from the four bodies of men lying all around the room. One then two girls ran from the sickening scene.

The boys tried to squeeze inside but forced to back up as several of the girls ran out the room. Outside, they all threw up on the ground. They remained outside the rest of the time. After the girls ran past did the boys enter the room. All they could see at first was all the people loitering near a person lying on the ground.

Ric spoke out. "It's…it's Mike."

The room grew quiet as he said his name. Everyone watched Cho apply his hands to Mike's cut. They saw Mike's legs move. They saw one leg twisted funny. They saw the blood coming out of his side where one man tried to stab him unsuccessfully. Blood had formed a small circle on his shirt. What shocked most of them was the amount of blood by this short man holding on to Mike's arm. It was coming from Mike.

Stephen stood, sensing the presence of the group entering the room. Turning to look at them, he spoke softly. "Mike is okay. He was stabbed, not shot. He is alive but lost a good bit of blood. Master Cho has stopped the blood flow. Mike is in no pain. Master Cho has rendered the pain away."

Several of the onlookers turned to each other after hearing the last remark this tall man said. "He rendered the pain away?" repeated one onlooker.

"What the heck does that mean?" asked another person watching the scene unfold.

"I don't know," said another.

Stephen, listening to all this banter, asked everyone to leave and to wait outside. "Mike needs to be tended to. All this excitement is totally unnecessary and can cause him further harm. Please, all of you step outside."

Everyone turned to leave except for Tad. Stephen saw Tad remained behind, nodding that it was his right to remain.

Tad bent down next to Cho. "Master Cho, how is he doing?"

Cho turned to his friend. "Tad, he is doing as best he can. His fight, a most magnificent battle, one worthy of the training I had consented to teach, was most heroic. To fight so many with a cut as serious as this is even beyond my understanding. He must truly have cared a great deal for those people to give as much as he did. I wouldn't have expected anything less of him," Cho said, looking squarely into the eyes of Tad.

Stephen walked about the room, inspecting each body. He returned to Cho's side at the same time Bear entered the room. Bear was shocked by the scene and the amount of blood. Stephen waved to him to come close.

Bear walked over to where Stephen stood. "He did all this, Stephen?"

"Yes. He is hurt bad, but will survive with Cho's attention. I need you to take this info I dug out of the pockets of these men. See if any of that info has some useful information we can use."

"Got it," Bear replied.

Everyone was walking out the hall; some had made it to the steps leading down the porch when Peabody walked up. An odor was following, or should be said led him. Each person who Peabody passed parted like the Red Sea in the movie *The Ten Commandments*. One person went so far as to make it known to everyone the awful smell he gave off. Peabody pretended not to hear the snide remarks.

At the top of the porch, Sargent smelled him coming. He knew it was Peabody by the tapping of that damn cane he carriedand also his nasal sound he evoked when he spoke.

"You move, you get out of my way, and you stop that disrespectful behavior of holding your nose."

Peabody finally arrived. A bit too late but here. Good, now he is in charge of this mess. He can take the blame. Good. Boy, will he be surprised when Mr. Howell gets here. A snicker crossed Sargent's lips as Peabody broke through the crowd. He looked as if he was in a fight. He had tried to tidy up; it was plain to see. It didn't change the fact he was a mess. *I sure hope he still looks like that when Mr. Howell shows up*, Sargent thought to himself.

Looking at Sargent's face upon entry into the house, Peabody quickly reminded him who was in charge. "What have you done here, Sargent? Why are all these kids here, and who is that dead man in the road, Sargent?"

Sargent thought Peabody said his name to emphasize he was the boss and to all in earshot. "Mr. Peabody, you are in charge. I was told you were here to inspect the site. I am only following your orders to prepare the house. I figured you sent these kids to test the effectiveness of the tricks. Aren't they here for that reason, sir?"

"Don't be silly, I never sent these kids here, and never would I allow a dead man to be lying in the middle of the driveway. And yes, I am in charge. So if you mind, while I get cleaned up, get this place in the proper order. And get these kids off this property. Now!"

Peabody abruptly turned to enter the den, then unexpectedly turned back to Sargent.

"Oh, do get me a man to show me where I can bathe and get these rags changed. My luggage is in the car. Have them sent to where I will be taking a bath." No sooner than Peabody entered the den, his driver was walking up the steps with two of the four bags in the car. Sargent pointed in the direction Peabody went to his driver.

Inside the den, Peabody halted. Looking down at the blood covering the floor, he yelled to Sargent. "Sargent, I hope you think I am not walking across this blood wearing my very expensive Italian hand-made shoes! Either have me escorted another direction, or get some of your staff here to aid me over this bloody floor."

Not once did Peabody take a look or a glance at the men tending to a boy lying on the floor; neither did he note the other dead bodies lying around the room. He simply pretended to think of other things. Looking at the ceiling, he was making small notations in his mind of the mess needed cleaning, the cost for cleanup, and the time it was going to cost the opening of the movie and this house with delays.

Within moments of Peabody's entry, a man came out through the door near the fireplace mantle. The same door two men along with Sargent earlier walked from the control room to inside the house.

"Good evening, Mr. Peabody, please, this way." He pointed the direction to go. It was the creature controller who volunteered to escort Mr. Peabody to the restroom. It was decided he was to have the honor of escorting Peabody when he drew the small straw.

Returning into the hall, the escort led Mr. Peabody down the long corridor to another room. A lock was hanging from the knob. Taking a key from the ring of keys he held, he fumbled with several before finding the correct key. Peabody stood tapping that damn cane while his escort fingered through the ring of keys. Each tap made the effort that more difficult for his escort. With a short exhale, the escort found the correct key, inserting it into the lock. The lock opened.

Both him and the driver holding two luggage bags entered first. The driver spotted Peabody and his escort in the den. Quickly, he followed the two exiting the den room. Down several steps to a lower floor was the command room, and past the control room, they turned, following the hall passageway. On one side was a large dining area, and ahead was two doors. One door read Women, the other Men. Passing through the men's door, a row of stalls and urinals lined against the wall. On the other side was another opening. Rows of benches were positioned down the center of lockers.

Escort man spoke up. "Here, sir, this is our restroom and bath. Choose any locker on the left. The others on the right have been taken.

Up ahead are the showers. I'll be leaving you to your bath. If for any reason, all you need to do is speak up. These rooms have a listening device, ahem, intercom on every wall. Just press a button and talk."

Peabody waved him off and began to remove his soiled clothing. Looking to the driver, he sharply commanded him to get his other luggage from the car.

When the driver left, Peabody broke down and began a quiet cry. Never had he witnessed such a scene as what he had upstairs. "No one will know of me crying, no one," he said softly.

Stephen and Teddy Bear had, in the meantime, fashioned a litter from two planks torn from the walls. Ripping off the shirt of some of the men less bloodied lying on the floor, they created a pillow for Mike's head. Cho sat cradling Mike's head in his lap. Mike was quiet. He stared up at his master giving him loving care. Tears filled his eyes feeling Cho's love for him.

Tad led the way out the room. He made a path for them to walk unhindered. Most of Mike's friends watched both Cho and Stephen carry Mike's body with great care. Not one inch of shaking to disturb him as they walked was made to disturb him.

Everyone gathered by the side of the road to look at Mike being carried. Each one wanted to make sure he was alive. Each took a turn to touch Mike. Mike was tenderly carried to the cars. A long line formed behind the litter. All followed the litter to the cars. Many of the girls were crying and kept crying, seeing Mike all bloody on a litter. Some heard that he was okay, but that scene made them think otherwise.

Cho, Stephen, Bear, and Tad made their way through the tangled line of parked cars to Tad's car, carrying Mike on their litter. Tad had parked nearest to the road going back to the highway. Teddy Bear stood by the door waiting to open it as Cho came near. Cho went in first, and Bear held his end of the litter. Stephen and Bear held the litter and fed it to Cho. Tad walked to the driver's side and entered. Cho told Stephen and Bear to make sure the kids got off safely. "Have a talk with the man in charge. Find out what went down," was Cho's final words before the car door shut.

Stephen curtly responded, "You're damn right I will, Cho." Then he turned to face the small crowd of Rama Rowdies following after them to Tad's car. Waving his arms to get their attention, Stephen stared at each one, amazed at how well they fought through this situation.

Speaking loudly, Stephen started. "Well done to each and every one of you. You should be proud of yourselves. You handled the situation with courage and maturity. I ask one thing from all of you. Please, for the time being, tell no one. What you went through, you may have to repeat again. Mike has some enemies. They may use the information you leak to attack Mike. We need time to prevent any further attacks on him and hopefully not any of you."

Walking to one side, Stephen pointed to the house.

"Look at that house. Five men are dead tonight. Mike killed four of them. For all this gang knows is that Mike had friends, and they were at that house. This news will be spread across every newspaper and on the air. These reporters and media care little of you and the danger they will put you in. All they care about is a story and recognition to build their paper readers and viewers.

"We will be around to offer protection to each and every one of you. If you care for your friends standing next to you, remember, loose lips sink ships. In other words, no matter your way of thinking, and some of you will think this. You may believe what I say is a pile of hooey, okay, but think of this one thing before you run to a friend or talk to a reporter. If I am the tiniest bit correct in what I am telling you and you talked to someone, yourself and all of your friends will be in peril. Also, your families may not escape being harmed. Much will rely on you keeping your mouth tight-lipped. Just one person opening their mouth, and we won't be there to help."

Before Stephen finished, he made one more point to all of them.

"If you open your mouth and nothing happens, great. Just know this, if something does happen and this gang comes looking for any of you, I swear to all of you that person will hear from us. What happens to that loose-lipped person will not be pretty."

Everybody hearing what Stephen said and what he promised to do to the person talking turned to look at Bob.

Bob stood watching them turn and stare at him as if he would be the one to blab. Standing erect, he forcefully responded with a powerful denial. "I will never be the one to say a word to anyone about what had happened tonight."

The group seemed to be satisfied with Bob's answer, and they turned back to this tall man.

"Good." Stephen acknowledged that they understood and appeared to convey an agreement to his terms. Speaking to them, he said, "The only thing now is to make sure these people at this place understand the consequences they will place you in. Bear and I will give them our strongest language we can apply to make sure they keep this quiet for the time being."

Grabbing Bear by his arm, Stephen pulled him along toward the house. After getting past the group, he turned back to ask them all to go home. "We will contact you tomorrow at the Rama Theater and give you an update on what we did this night and the status on Mike."

Everyone started to return to the car they came in. Once they were in their cars, each car waited its turn to pull out of the driveway.

Stephen and Bear proceeded to walk down the drive to the house. Standing on the porch was Sargent; he appeared to be a man of importance to most people's first impression. To Stephen, he saw through his facade and noted his inferiority to Peabody.

Watching these two men walking to the house and the last car turning onto the road leading away from the house was like a fresh cold beer. He was glad it was over, and to Sargent's way of thinking, all the blame would lie on Peabody and maybe those men. He had to play this just right to absolve him from any blame. This could be his big opportunity to advance his career. Sargent was plotting his defense watching two men come near the house.

Two very big men walked to the edge of the porch. Sargent for the first time saw the size of these men. He began to double think his earlier plans about making them the fall guys. He became sure of that fact once he shook the tall man's hand, then the larger man's hand. Their handshakes implied they were powerful and wanted him to get the message, whatever that may be. Quickly, he was informed of that message when tall man spoke. A chill ran up Sargent's spine, not from what was said to him, but from the eyes staring at him. This man, Sargent reasoned, was a killer, no doubt about that. So was the other man. Then Sargent thought back to the smaller man that shoved him into the wall. He was the most dangerous one of the three. He remembered what the kid had done and what he said lying on the floor.

"My Sifu will not be please with me. I got cut, I got cut," echoed in Sargent's mind. *That Asian man tending to the kid taught him those skills. If a kid can do that to four men and with a knife cut and bleeding the way he was, hell, who are these men? What did we get mixed up with? What am I mixed up with?*

"You, your name is Sargent, is that right?"

Sargent snapped back to his two companions at the edge of the porch. Looking at them, he wanted to keep his responses as short as needed. "Yes, that is correct."

"Good, I see you are paying attention, for a second you appeared to be lost in thought. Good, now answer several more questions. Let me first tell you this, that kid lying on the floor with those four men you allowed in this house getting many kids nearly killed. This house you manage, you are responsible for all this. The well-being of twelve kids, whether they were here by invitation or trespassing, you are still responsible for their safety. Since there is little evidence that this place is indicated as private property, having no signs or fences to keep passersby from entering, it seems to me, you and your boss may have some serious legal problems to deal with.

"Five men were allowed to enter carrying dangerous weapons. Their intentions were made clear when they demanded the kid named Mike be surrendered to them. You monitored this happening and did nothing."

Sargent was about to respond to that last remark until the tall man asked him the next question.

"Where are the police, Mr. Sargent?"

Then Sargent remembered the lines were cut, and he couldn't call for the law. Somehow the tall man knew that he used another second backup line to call Mr. Howell. Again, Sargent was about to speak and tell him he couldn't due to the phone lines being cut.

Again, before Sargent had a chance to explain why he had not made a call for help, Stephen had interrupted. "Now, we inspected the outside of your house. Bear noticed the phone line cut. As he continued his checking, he also noticed a second phone line. From that I can safely guess you had backups for every problem. Now let me make this crystal clear to you, if I have to stand here and bandy words on who is to blame and what you think you can do and what we can't do, it will make me upset.

"Please look at my friend standing to my side. I want to have you ask him a question. Will you do that for me, Sargent?"

Sargent turned to look at Bear.

Teddy Bear stood next to Stephen with a friendly smile. He was bigger than the tall man to his side. He seemed like a nice kind of a fellow, one far nicer looking than this other man making or hinting to threats of them being responsible for all the carnage lying around the house. Once he determined the question was most likely nondiscriminating to him, he replied, "Okay, sure, what would you like me to ask him?"

"I want you to ask him, did he ever see me take a man who thought I was not serious and beat the hell out of him? Did he see me break his jaw in three places, and while that asshole lay on the ground staring up at me, I pulled my pecker out, pissed in his mouth, and stood watching that pig gag on my piss?"

Hearing what he just said, Sargent paused.

Not one for patience, that pause angered Stephen. "Well?" Stephen asked him. "Go on, ask him." It was more of a command than a request.

Seeing this man and listening to what he told him, Sargent felt sure if he delayed too long, the question would be mute. "Mr. Bear, did you see this man beside you?"

Interrupting Sargent to make a correction, Stephen said, "That is Stephen, Sargent. I have a name."

Sargent began with the correction to his first question. "Ahem, Bear, see Stephen break a man's jaw in three places and piss in his mouth."

"Sargent, you left out beating the hell out of him first," corrected Bear.

"Excuse me, Stephen. Bear, did Stephen also beat the hell out of the man?"

"Sure did. That man was a heap bigger than me and a whole lot tougher. He did just that and after he first worked his way through five of the baddest bikers this side of hell," Bear added for good measure.

"I got one thing to tell you, and this best not be repeated to you a second time. Believe this, Sargent, I will know everything about you this night. Where you live, eat, how many kids, your dog's name, barber's name, doctor, everything. I will know the whore you sleep with and when. How many tattoos she wears, etc. You will get a visit from me or a friend of mine. I don't care who you know or think you know. I could care less how many bodyguards you hire and any connections you think you have. I got more, and they owe me a lot. They will give me what I want, and if I want you, rest assured they will hand you over with a cherry on top.

"You, Sargent, think on this while I talk to Peabody. He has had a taste of what can be given to you ten times more. This will not leave this place. No one will hear about this little tussle and the five men dead. These bodies will be disposed of. I want this entire place so clean you eat rare meat off the floors by tomorrow. When I come back here, and I will tomorrow, I will not be happy if this place and all the recording and people are not here. You got that? Before we leave, I want everyone's name and phone number in Bear's hand. No one, no one, will leave here tonight.

"We best not have to drag this area to find anyone missing. So you make sure the six men in the command center know this. You tell Frank, Tom, Jessie, Jerry, Monroe, and Henry what I said."

Sargent stood there with a shocked look on his face. *How did he know their names? How did he know how many? What else does he know? My men must be watching this conversation and heard their names said. Damn, this will scare the heck out of some of them. They might run to the police. I got to get them make sure none will do anything rash. Mr. Howell will be here soon, what am I going to tell him? He is going to see all this and want some answers.*

Walking up the steps and giving Sargent a slight nudge out of his path, Stephen walked to the fireplace room. Over by the mantle, the door was still opened. Two men walked to and through the doorway quickly. They must have been listening, Stephen reasoned, seeing them enter the doorway. He followed them down into the large command center. All four men stood milling around the two men that just returned. They had rushed to their side upon hearing what Stephen said to Sargent.

"Ahem," came a loud sound of someone is here. Turning to the *ahem* sound, all six men saw the tall man upstairs in the command center with them. Looking at Stephen, his imposing stature, and his deadly glare with those two menacing eyes gave them good reason to worry. They believed what he said without a single question being requested by any of the six men.

Stephen stood staring at the six men before him. Peabody entered. He was clean and had no smell of his urine on his person. He recognized Stephen and his power and the wonderful, amazing power of his master, Mr. Cho. He did not want any part of them ever again. That long bumpy bike ride shook every bone in his body. His thighs were red raw from the chafing and pee covering his pants.

Seeing Stephen in the command center slightly annoyed Peabody, but he remained quiet.

"I was talking to your man upstairs. He was told to get this house clean and to not report this to the authorities until we have determined the nature of this attack. If for any reason someone does, and those kids are hurt due to that, I can assure you there will be serious consequences to those responsible, Peabody."

Peabody continued to remain quietly standing, watching Stephen lay the law down.

"As I explained to Sargent, we have many connections. You may think we are some no-account biker gang? Be advised, we are more than that. Much, much more.

"I have contacted some of my people to come here and remove the bodies. I want the walls and floors cleaned. No traces of this scene will be found. No one leaves until I get back here and inspect this site." Before leaving, Stephen told the command team, "Now get cleaning."

* * *

Turning down the main road in town, Tad was almost at the hospital.

"Stephen should be wrapping up with that house and be here within the hour," Cho told Mike. Mike was lying still without pain in the back of Tad's car as they sped through town.

At the hospital, they met the emergency staff. Mike was quickly taken into surgery. Not more than an hour had passed, and he was in a bed with an IV connected to him.

The doctor met with Cho and Tad. Looking at the two men before him, he noted no similarity to the boy. "Are you two related to this child?"

Tad replied, "No, he works for me. He was severely cut by a fall against a sharp edge by his car. When I was leaving the theater, he had to have been passed out by his car for thirty minutes or so. This man saw him, he is a friend of his family. It was by his car the accident occurred. He came and got me. We loaded him in my car and brought him immediately here. Is he going to be okay, Doctor?"

"Did you call the police about this?" the doctor asked Tad.

"No, Doctor, I did not. I hadn't time to call them, and besides, why would I do that? Far as I can tell, it was an accident that occurred in the parking lot at the theater."

Cho remained quiet as Tad continued to answer the questions posed to him by the doctor. He seemed to have all the answers and just watched Tad respond to each question with a calm and innocent manner. Thinking to himself, Cho thought, *He is an excellent liar.*

The doctor had one more question to ask. "We need to contact his parents and have them come down here to fill the paperwork out. May I ask you this one question, Tad?" the doctor inquired.

"Sure," Tad responded.

"Why did you not bring him in his car and instead take your car?"

That question startled Tad when he heard the words exit his mouth. He hadn't thought about that. Besides, he was answering questions as they were asked with a spontaneous, untethered planned excuse. *Really?* Tad thought he should have prepared some excuse on the way to the hospital. Both Cho and Tad were too busy with concerns for Mike to consider what kind of a story they should have been planning.

"Two reasons, Doctor. First, I was in my car and drove over to the accident where Mike lay. Second, Mr. Cho's car was giving him some trouble starting. It is an old 1956 Chevy and has had trouble getting it started from time to time. Many a time, Doc, I had to jump-start the car when Mr. Cho arrived to pick up Mike. He would stop and turn off the engine while waiting for him to get off. The hood was up when I got there."

The doctor seemed happy with his responses and told them they could see Mike. Cho finally spoke to the doctor. The doctor was walking away from them when Cho called him back. The doctor was young and newly out of med school from the looks of him, Cho perceived.

"Excuse me, any bill that needs to be paid, I will be responsible. His mom is a widower and has no job. Being a friend of the family, I will assume all debt from this injury. You seem to be new to this hospital. Are you a new intern here?" Cho inquired.

"Yes, I am, is that so apparent?"

Cho answered back, "Yes, but from the way you handle the accident, I feel you have performed most admirably. Thank you for making sure Mike was taken care of so professionally. If you like, I would consider making my contentment of pleasure known to your superiors."

Inside the room where Mike was resting, the doctor escorted the two men in. "Here he is." The doctor held out his hand as to offer a seat. Next to Mike was an IV plastic bag feeding him plasma while he was lying on the bed.

Cho spoke first to the doctor. "When can he go home?"

"Well, we usually want to keep patients overnight. He lost some blood, but nothing that should keep him here. Give him an hour to enjoy his meal I am feeding him. We had to put fifteen stitches in the arm and patch the small puncture on his side. Other than that, he is young and very fit. He will heal quickly. Just keep him off his feet for a day and not too much heavy lifting on that arm."

The doctor was beginning to turn to leave when he suddenly stopped. Not turning around to Cho or Tad, he made an off-the-cuff remark. "That leg he fell on was given an x-ray. He has a hairline fracture. Keep him off that leg for some days. That sure was some fall he had."

"Thank you, Doctor," Cho repeated. Cho knew exactly what the doctor was thinking. It didn't take no mind reader to know he told the doctor a fib, not with the types of wounds Mike sustained.

Tad offered his thanks as the doctor was walking out.

Mike looked up at both Tad and Sifu. "I am sorry for you having to bother over me so much."

Tad spoke. "Mike, Mr. Cho has taken on the bill and told the doctor to bill him."

Mike looked at Cho. "Sifu, that wasn't your responsibility to pay. I will pay you back, I promise. I got some money put aside. I hope it will cover the expenses."

"Mike, Mr. Cho knows your mom hasn't a job or insurance to pay the cost of this hospital bill. The theater can't because it wasn't on our property. It is very kind of him to do so for you and your family."

Looking a bit distressed from what Tad said, Mike replied to Mr. Cho, "I am truly sorry if I had insulted your kind gesture, Sifu. I didn't want you to think that this cut and injuries was any way your responsibility, and…and I guess that we needed some charity." Mike's eyes lowered not to have his eyes reveal his shame.

"Mike, this is not charity. I would never allow myself to show disrespect to you or your family by an offer of charity. You are part of our group. Didn't Chopper tell you that, you are a member of our group?"

Mike nodded to that fact.

"Then know that we take care of our own. Know this as well, Mike." Cho bent down and placed his hand on Mike's hand. Both eyes looked deep into Mike's eyes as he spoke. "Mike, if you in any way had shown fear or disrespect in dealing with these men, I would have not wanted to continue my training with you. You are worthy to learn my art. I am proud to have you as my student. Now rest, we will sit with you."

Turning to Tad, Cho mentioned, "If you have other duties to attend to Tad, I will understand, and please feel free to go. I will remain and take Mike home."

"Thanks, Mr. Cho, I do have to get home. I will remain until he is ready to be discharged from the hospital."

Within an hour, the doctor returned, and Mike was allowed to leave. Outside, Tad said he would see him later that same day. It was nearly three thirty before they allowed Mike to leave from the hospital.

"Now, you two get in the car, and I will take you back to the theater where your car is parked."

Neither Mike nor Mr. Cho spoke until they arrived at Mike's home. The door was locked as they tried to enter. Mike removed the key and opened the door. Inside, his mom was on the couch asleep.

"Mike, I will leave you, but I will see you tomorrow. Don't wake your mom. It would be best not to do so. She will be full of questions, and you need rest. Go to bed, and in the morning, you can deal with questions your family may ask."

"You are right, Sifu, it would be better if I don't wake my mom. I will see you tomorrow."

* * *

At 5:30 a.m., a small Lear jet was asking permission to land at the Macon airport. At the same time, a crew of six men just finished cleaning the blood off the walls and floors in a house deep in the woods.

Before they had completed their task, four bike riders drove into the driveway of the house. A small van was the last vehicle to turn in.

Two men and the four riders went to the leader man lying face up, still staring at the stars, and hoisted his still-cold body, placing it in a large plastic bag. Then two men toted the corpse to the rear door of the small van. Returning shorty with several bags, one in each arm, they partly dragged both bags across the dirt to the front porch. Entering the den, they placed each man into his own bag, then quietly removed each body bag. It took a matter of minutes before coming and leaving.

Once they removed the bodies, the spot they lay was swiftly mopped and cleaned with Clorox per instructions by Stephen. By 5:45 a.m., they began the painting. One half hour with plenty of sweat, the room was cleaned and repainted. When the clock read 6:00 a.m., they went down to the cafeteria and had several cups of coffee. Each control room personnel felt a relief knowing this was going to disappear and the job was done. Only worry that they had was what that tall man and that short man would say. Hopefully they would say nothing and leave.

Sargent and Peabody made a round inspecting the job their men had completed. Feeling satisfied the job was perfectly done and no trace of blood or damages remained, Sargent made an offhand comment that he should have kept to himself.

"Peabody," he said, "I hope this cleanup met with your satisfaction. I sure don't want to be in your shoes when Mr. Howell arrives."

Peabody was well aware of the animosity that the two of them shared. Hearing the slightest hint that he was to blame was enough to allow him to see through Sargent's plan, that he was to be the fall guy for what had transpired this night. He himself had already set in motion his own plan to make sure this incident fell squarely onto Sargent. Peabody silently snickered and said nothing to Sargent. He let him have his moment of self-acknowledgment that he believes he got one over on him.

THE DAY AFTER

TOUCHDOWN. A PLANE LANDED AND was coasting to the gate. Soon the jet's door opened, and a short pouty man in his early fifties disembarked the jet. He looked as if he came directly from a dinner engagement still wearing a tuxedo. As he left the plane, a secretary was behind him carrying a satchel. A large limo was waiting. The car engine was still warm and had not been turned off. It shortly arrived before the plane made its way to the gate. The driver was at the wheel with a thin, young, attractive blonde lady wearing what appeared to be a French maid's outfit. She was holding a tray. She was tall, having thin curvy legs adorned with fishnet stockings. The black very short frilly skirt with layers of underskirts and a white apron matched the intent she was to portray. Her hair was blonde, long in length, and placed in a bun, only to be unwoven when required. On the tray were two glasses of some alcoholic drink.

Mr. Howell with his secretary walked up to the limo with the young blonde attractive woman. She greeted them with a smile and softly spoke. "Here, sir, I have prepared your drink, a martini with two olives, dry, and only one ice cube. I hope you will enjoy it." Then she offered the second drink to the secretary, having no remarks for her. She of course was hired help; it wasn't necessary to make a remark.

Inside the car, the chauffeur asked for directions. It was almost six thirty in the morning. "Take us to our hotel. Call ahead, have them prepare our breakfast. I do hate to wait for my meal. Please let them be aware of this fact and to have it ready when we get there."

"Yes, sir," the chauffeur responded. "May I ask you what you would like them to prepare for your breakfast fare?"

"Yes, I should allow them some measure of lack of attention since this was a last-minute unexpected detour. Reply that I would like two poached eggs, three minutes no more. One slice of toast, lightly buttered with grape jelly on the side. I do hate it when they put my jelly on my toast. Hot and not warm or cold toast. Five strips of bacon, not overcooked. Each strip of bacon should be lying flat on the plate. Make double sure there is no grease dripping off the bacon. I abhor too much grease on my food. Have a hot urn of coffee with two teaspoons of sugar with milk poured in the cup until my coffee turns a light shade of brown. Lastly, a large glass of orange juice without pulp, and definitely no seeds. Chauffeur, please inspect my meal when you let us out. I want to be seated and ready for my meal when I arrive."

"Yes, sir. Anything for your secretary, sir?" Looking at the secretary in his rearview mirror, he was quick to notice her legs. They were long and thin. As he followed the legs up, he could see her stockings hem and girdle tabs attached. Just a little farther he could make out much more, until she saw him ogling her in the mirror. After that he kept his eyes forward on the road.

"Miss, have you decided what you would like for your meal when we arrive?"

"Yes, thank you. Please have them cook some scrambled eggs and add some hot sauce. Preferably Texas Pete. Coffee black, one slice of toast with butter, lightly coated, and sausage, two links, then some orange juice in a small glass. One more thing, I would like several extra napkins."

"I will call this in and make it clear they follow these directions as you have requested, sir."

In town, there was only one hotel and by no means the Hilton. When the limo pulled up to the door, the chauffeur opened the door for Mr. Howell and then rushed around the car to open the secretary's door. Before they had a chance to get erect from the crouching endured from both flight and drive, the chauffeur immediately went inside to check the meals of his clients.

Entering the restaurant, he saw with astonishment all meals were ready at the table as he requested. A quick once-over of each item revealed they did as they were told.

Returning immediately back to the limo, his assistant was unloading the luggage from the spare tire wheel well. Both the driver and assistant went to the counter to enter their guests into the register. A bellboy came taking the luggage from them. Both of them remained in the lobby while Mr. Howell and his secretary ate.

After remaining in their rooms for several hours to freshen up, both Mr. Howell and his secretary went to the lobby. Waiting by the counter was Peabody. Turning to greet his employer, Peabody walked over and offered his hand to shake.

Peabody quickly explained what had transpire before he arrived on the phone. Making sure all the commotion at the house was proceeding without any problems before Mr. Howell's arrival at the airport. He was careful to not mention the other incident. Stephen was quite persuasive. Then there was Mr. Cho. Peabody, as he had always done when reporting to his most demanding boss, provided details minute by minute on the house's readiness. Last item came the one incident he dreaded to bring up to Mr. Howell.

"Sir, I must assure you, this man I met at the theater is not to be treated in any way disrespectful. He will not consider that behavior as acceptable." Peabody was trying to be as tactful as he could, knowing Mr. Howell was about to meet a man he could not bully. Mr. Howell was about to be put in his place, and Peabody did not want the fallout that would follow if Mr. Cho found Mr. Howell as disrespectful as him.

At 11:00 a.m., the phone rang. A man still groggy from going to bed about four was still asleep when he answered the phone. "Hello."

On the other end came, "Hello, is this Tad?"

"Yes," Tad responded.

"Good, then will you please attend to the theater within the hour to greet Mr. Howell, the producer of NXC Movie Company? He is the owner of the house you had visited last night and would like a report from you this morning. Please be prompt, Mr. Howell will not tolerate tardiness." *Click.*

"What? What was that?" Tad found he was speaking to himself into his phone. Quickly he was up and out of bed. Looking at his clock, he spotted the time as twenty till the hour. "Gosh, I'm going to be late." Tad promptly put his tie on around his shirt while slipping his pants up. He fastened his belt and slid on both shoes. Neither foot had a sock. Still a bit sleepy, he got in his car and drove quickly to the theater.

Mr. Cox was already waiting once Tad drove up. Looking at his watch, Tad saw the time as two minutes till twelve. Just in time.

Mr. Cox looked at Tad. "Ahem, Tad, if I was you, before you meet with this Mr. Howell and his pretty secretary, you might consider zipping your pants up."

Tad was shocked at what might have been if not for Mr. Cox intervening with him, what would have been poking out of his pants.

Both Mr. Cox and Tad stood waiting for the arrival of Mr. Howell. At exactly 12:00 p.m., a limo entered the parking lot. The limo drove to where both of them stood. Stopping, the chauffeur exited the cars and opened the back door. A lady's voice asked them to come in and be seated.

Mr. Cox was about to begin a question, but Tad stopped him short of uttering a word. He knew Mr. Cox was totally unaware and uninvolved in any of the incidents that took place that evening at the house.

The limo's doors closed after seating Tad and Mr. Cox on one side and Mr. Howell and his secretary opposite them. Tapping on the window, the chauffeur turned, rolling down the window. Mr. Howell said three words to him. "To the house."

The driver rolled the window back up, and off they sped to the house. Mr. Cox sat there befuddled. Tad waited for the questions he knew were going to come from this man and his secretary. Each remained seated, and no questions and answers followed.

Turning on the dirt road Tad drove that night, he realized it would be about fifteen minutes before they reached the house. Mr. Cox sat contently looking out the window, enjoying the cocktail he was offered. Tad refused his drink and sat watching all three.

Eighteen minutes later, the limo turned into the drive. Around the house was parked many bikes. Tad recognized three of them. Well, he was glad they were there waiting. He wondered how Mr. Howell had contacted them. They left no phone, other than the one number he had from Mr. Cho. He never gave that number to anyone was his understanding.

The large limo stopped at the front door, and Sargent and Peabody stood waiting on the porch. Peabody walked down the steps to meet his boss. The chauffeur opened the door for Mr. Howell, and he pulled himself from the car.

Looking around, he gave a nod to Peabody. "This is better than I expected, Peabody." Looking up at Sargent, he remarked, "This looks fine. How soon will I be given a demonstration of all those gadgets I paid for?"

Sargent was quick to reply. "Sir, as soon as we have met our other guests and have concluded the reasons why they are here."

"Sargent, I am here for this demonstration and no other reasons. You take care of this minor inconvenience."

"Sir, I am sorry to tell you this, but this overrides any demonstration until this matter is taken care of."

"Really, Sargent, do you plan on continuing employment with this agency?"

Mr. Cho and Stephen made their appearance beside Sargent. Mr. Howell took one look and told Sargent, "If this is your important business I am intending to hear, then you will be terminated before the day is out. Now take them, those people, and leave. I have no time nor inclination of spending one second with either one of those…those… ahem, individuals."

Tad stood there by the car doors listening to the tone of Mr. Howell's voice. Knowing how Mr. Cho reacted to such bad manners in the past, he was waiting for what was surely coming soon to Mr. Howell.

Sargent hadn't yet experienced the Peabody treatment, but had a funny sense of foreboding if he was disrespectful to the short man. Peabody couldn't watch what happened next. He looked away wrenching. Tad grabbed Mr. Cox's arm and politely moved him closer to himself, farther from Mr. Howell.

Cho moved so fast, the last word that came out of Mr. Howell's mouth never completed the last syllable sound. Stephen took hold of Sargent by the cuff of his neck and held him in place. Sargent had no intention of moving, but just the same, Stephen held him tight.

Cho was standing beside Mr. Howell as he finished the last syllable and, with a much harder application, applied to the same spot Peabody was familiar with. Mr. Howell froze with a more intense pain Peabody first experienced.

The pain etched across Mr. Howell's face. One could see that he wanted to desperately cry out with pain. The secretary watched in horror. Tad had to reach out to her. The chauffeur was at her side first. Mr. Cox was simply dumbfounded at what happened.

Cho, after making his jump to the side of Mr. Howell, stood looking at this pompous fool who considered himself superior to them. He was filled with pride to know this fool was nothing as compared to Cho. Cho wasn't a man filled with pride; on the contrary, he prided himself with his lack of pride. These men he met, Peabody and Mr. Howell, had done what others never attempted nor had done before. That was to make him feel like a cur dog. They must be taught a lesson of humility to help them be better people was his aim upon meeting them. It was his duty to show them the error of their way.

"Now, Mr. Howell. If you please, I will inform you why this meeting is the utmost important decision you will make before leaving this place today. I will also convey to you why it would be most foolish to think when we leave, you can ignore this most wonderful advice I will leave with you. To do so even with a man such as you believe yourself to be would be a disaster, I guarantee you.

"I will after this meeting give you a reminder to carry with you. This little gift will stay with you for a time until I see fit to remove it. You may want to go to the best doctors around this country. It will be to no avail. Any measures you undertake to cure this ailment will only add to the pain. I know you will ignore this advice and seek to find a remedy. So be it. You will only prove my worst fears, and that is you are a bigger fool than I originally thought.

"If for any reason, I would have you seek counsel with this man Peabody. He has experienced this correction to his behavior. He understands what little he can comprehend, that I am no person, nor my comrades, you care to deal with. We can reach out and touch you with little effort. You have wealth and power, sir. We recognized that and hope with this small demonstration, you will also recognize that we too have certain powers and wealth."

Walking up to Mr. Howell's face, Cho almost touched noses with him. Slowly he spoke. "The next words I speak, I want no misunderstandings between us. We may look like a rowdy bike gang with little education and skills. That is the furthest from the truth. If you try to investigate us, we will become alerted to that. That will be okay by us. But—and I mean but—don't dig too deep. Too deep, and we will be upset, and I can assure you, sir, that a visit will be forthcoming."

Staring into Mr. Howell's eyes for a minute, Cho unfroze him from the pain coursing through his body.

Mr. Howell fell to the ground onto his knees. While staring down, panting, he said two words in response to Cho. "How dare you." Excuse me, my correction, three words I meant to say.

Before Mr. Howell had begun to raise his head, the pain returned, going through him once again. He knelt there on the ground; Cho reached down on the wet dirt. Mr. Howell had a similar event to Peabody's wetting his pants. For Peabody, it took three times before he wet his pants. Mr. Howell only twice. The ground received a full complement of a full bladder.

Cho scooped up a handful of the nasty dirt, and with his other hand, he pried open Mr. Howell's mouth. Then to everyone watching in shock, he shoved that dirt into Mr. Howell's mouth.

Mr. Howell's eyes bugged out. He wanted to spit the dirt out of his mouth but was unable to do so. Not one inch of his body could move. He tasted the dirt. It had a taste similar to rotten meat. It smelled the same. He was going to heave.

Cho took his hand and lifted Mr. Howell's chin for him to look at him. Tears were filling his eyes. "Sir, if you are going to talk with filth, then I will fill it with filth. So be it. I will not listen, nor will my comrades endure your filthy words. I will continue to fill your mouth with filth every time you utter any such words again. I do hope we have an understanding. I do so dread putting my hands in this nasty dirt."

Mr. Howell got the meaning, and Cho, for the second time, released him from his frozen pain. Mr. Howell spit the dirt out and waved to Sargent to get him water. Standing up, he leaned against the car. The chauffeur walked over to Mr. Howell. A nod from Mr. Howell gave the driver a signal to take out a gun and point it at Cho.

Cho, to his astonishment, was almost caught by surprise that Mr. Howell was not well mannered. Quickly and most devastatingly, the driver went flying through the air into and through the windshield of the rear of his car. He wasn't dead, but out. Then Cho turned to Mr. Howell. With the gun held in his hand, he requested Mr. Howell to take the gun. "Please take your gun. I have no need of it."

Stephen realized what was going to occur soon and slapped Sargent on his head with the same hand holding his neck. The slap was so fast, Sargent barely noticed him releasing his grip.

"Look, you got to see this. This is going to be a hoot. Watch this, Sargent," Stephen commanded of him.

Mr. Howell did not hesitate grabbing for the gun. Cho slapped him on the side of his head. This infuriated Mr. Howell getting slapped like a child. He reached for the gun again as Cho offered it to him. This went on for several times, and each time resulted in Mr. Howell getting his face slapped. By the fifth time his face was beet red and just as tender. He continued to reach for the gun.

Stephen watching from his vantage point on the porch quipped to Sargent, "Your boss isn't a quitter, I give him that." Releasing his grip on Sargent's neck, he set him down. "I see Cho do this to a man for an hour before the man figured out Cho wasn't going to stop and could do that all day. Sargent, I wonder if your boss can last that long. Hahaha!" Stephen laughed, and soon, most of the onlookers were giggling. Sargent knew better but couldn't resist a tiny giggle.

Mr. Howell kept at it for nearly thirty minutes. He was so ashamed that this little man could do this to him and make him look the fool in front of all these people. He wasn't going to forget this incident ever. He silently hoped the others would, and if they didn't, he would make sure they never work at his studio ever.

Finally back on his knees and totally exhausted from the slapping, he raised his hand to quit. Cho helped stand him on his feet, then froze him again. Mr. Howell was shocked to be placed back into this painful condition. He surrendered to that man. "Why is he doing this to me?" was the expression Cho read on his surprised look.

"Mr. Howell, not only did you have your man try to shoot me after you led me to believe we had an understanding, then I was forced to lay my hands on that most unfortunate fool you told to attack me. I do hope he will be well compensated for his injuries. We are of agreement on that?" Cho reiterated his meaning.

Mr. Howell, unable to speak, did so with his eyes, giving his response.

"Good, Mr. Howell. I do hope this third time will be enough, and we can begin our true purpose for this meeting. If you persist with this silly display of who is in charge and who has the biggest gun, I will put you back in that state leaving here and not return until this evening. Just one bad-mannered word, and we will meet later tonight."

Peabody realized Mr. Howell tied his record of three frozen moments from this man. In one way, he hoped Mr. Howell wouldn't break his record. He and Mr. Howell always had a private respect for each other's accomplishments and tended to outdo the other. This would give him the edge.

After the third freezing and thirty minutes of being slapped, Mr. Howell was wet with sweat and also his pee.

"Now, Mr. Howell, we may go in and sit at the table and have our discussion. That is if you don't have any other business more pressing." Cho gently touched Mr. Howell, releasing him from the thawed painful position he was in.

"No, no, no other business. This is my most important business of the day."

"Good," Cho responded.

All the people outside walked in and down to the cafeteria below. Mr. Howell was still exhausted, and any attempt to walk was made more difficult. Both his legs could barely support his weight. Peabody sympathized with his boss, knowing full well how that felt.

The pretty secretary had the opportunity to see and smell her boss in a new light. Unfortunately, it also meant to assist him walking inside. The smell was different than his customary aftershave.

Sargent had coffee and donuts on the table. Rolls still fresh and hot from the oven were near the front, containing everything one imagined having for breakfast. No one arriving had eaten. A brunch was prepared for them. The table was laid out for a king with platters of eggs, bacon, sandwich meats, and various fruits. Two sous-chefs offered to prepare steaks and eggs cooked the way one wanted at two stations. Each person made a round filling their plates, and within minutes, all were sitting at the tabled. Cho and Stephen were the only two with empty plates.

Mr. Howell entered the dining hall, but not before the odor preceded him. Peabody had a smirk on his face. He was thinking to himself, *Damn, I had to ride on that hot bumpy bike for nearly half an hour before I could move. Damn, he got lucky, he has a pretty helper to aid him. Oh well, I didn't get slapped for nearly thirty minutes. Aha, I do believe this still gives me the lead.* The smirk slowly was replaced with a slight smile. Not too big a smile, or Mr. Howell might take note.

The discussion began with Stephen recounting the evening's events. He conveyed all the circumstances that led to this confrontation with that gang. He went on to explain the disposal of the bodies. This he had to make very clear to Mr. Howell and Mr. Peabody. Some of the members present found recounting the incident was too much to take in. One of them was Mr. Cox. What happened was more than he was prepared to deal with. He remained quiet as Stephen continued to give a detail of the fight scene and how it unfolded with the death of each gang member.

Mr. Howell interrupted the story one time. "Excuse me, er, Stephen. You said this boy, Mike, the one we have been searching for, he did that to four grown men?"

"Yes. The fifth man was taken care of by Bear. I tell you this so you will have a better perspective of how serious this is. To you, Mr. Howell, this tragedy would mean a great deal of money in lawsuits, court fees, liabilities, and homicide charges to name a few. To add to this, the possible attacks on all the members at this house by this gang may occur later. You may feel you will be out of harm's way in Hollywood, and you may well be. But these kids live here, and they will be put in harm's way. If this story is released to the media, they will not care one bit for the kids' lives.

"I have explained this to Peabody and the crew working here. I will now make it clear to you. If one child is caused any harm from this incident, you will hear from us. You think you will be safe back home. Go ahead and think that. But but don't forget what I told you, we won't." Stephen leveled his eyes toward Mr. Howell. The movie mogul just sat expressionless. Cho saw in his lack of concern what was deeply held inside the man. Money, money, money, how can he capitalize on this horror.

"The bodies of that gang were delivered to Atlanta and laid in front of their hideout this morning. I have been informed that the bodies have been discovered. There will be consequences for this action. We are preparing at this very moment to deal with it. This will be a deadly fight. We might have some injuries taken on our side. But know this, we will prevail. We always have and will always again and again."

"How can you be so sure of that?" Peabody spoke to the last statement of Stephen's remark.

"Because, Peabody, we have the talent, skills, motivation, will, courage, know-how, and backing from several high-up places you can't even imagine. We will win. Now, if no more questions, we will be on our way," Stephen said as both he and Cho were readying to leave.

"Excuse me, one more question I would like to ask. I made this trip here for the purpose of contacting this boy, Mike. Will I be permitted to have a discussion with him, considering you seem to have a great interest in him?" asked Mr. Howell.

Cho spoke to Mr. Howell's inquiry. "Mr. Howell, I will be with the boy you are talking about, and you may conclude your business with him. I will offer my advice if he so wants it. Today, we are to meet all the kids at the Rama around two. This will be a good time for you to meet with him and the others."

"Fine, I will be there, Mr. Cho."

Not long after the meeting with the members at the house, Mr. Cox, Tad, Mr. Cho, and Stephen returned to the Rama. There was a concern raised by Mr. Cox. Mr. Cox was entirely absent of the knowledge and was a little on the edgy side of what he had been told. He was concerned for the theater and its liability from the incident. Needless to say, most of his concerns centered around his young people at the Rama Theater.

"I'm afraid, gentlemen, this incident last night might not be so contained as you seem to think it will. I think knowing about these kids, it will be difficult to secure this knowledge from leaking out. But that is not my main concern. What is my concern is how Mike is involved in this, and how is his involvement going to prevent any other occurrences with this gang? I have my people to worry about and the patrons who will enter this theater. If that gang decides to follow up with another attack on Mike, they will be in harm's way."

Both Cho and Stephen nodded to his concerns. Stephen spoke up. "Mr. Cox, I know your concerns, and they are valid. I can promise you this will go no further. Right now, there are plans being put into motion that should end this threat within days. I will tell you this, Mike has been trained. He has the capabilities to deal with this threat. Also, I want you to know, Cho and several of our team will be here every day and night to offer added protection."

Tad entered into the argument knowing where Mr. Cox was going and was afraid if he didn't make his knowledge known, Mike could be left alone to deal with the threat. All the attention will be to guard him and leave the Rama less protected. "Mr. Cox, the only reason you were left out of this was to keep as few people as possible aware of Mike. If this got around, his secret would be found out, resulting with a more dire consequence. Too many persons have become interwoven in this, and we kept all this unknown and secure for a good reason. This event last night occurred before the main assault will take place. Unforeseen happenings came about. Thanks to Mike, this happened without anyone getting hurt."

"Tad, don't forget those men that were killed," Mr. Cox reminded him.

"Yes, sir, people were killed last night as you heard there will be more. All we can hope for is for those evil people will get killed."

"If you do nothing, then they will win. More people and good people will pay the price. These men will stop at nothing to learn where Mike is. That simply means your involvement is always in a threat," answered Stephen.

Cho spoke. "He is right. There are bad people in the world, there have always been bad people in the world. Those who are afraid and don't do anything pay the price for their weakness. They expect others who are strong to come to their aid. They believe love and kindness win over this evil. They are wrong and have always been wrong.

"History is full of how wrong they were. The strong and powerful will make slaves out of the weak. They will make them depend upon them, thus become slaves to them. Fear grips them, and they bend a knee. Their lives are changed, and they become unhappy with their new lot in life. The weak will inherit the earth, and they will deserve what they wrought. A world full of fear, destroyed environment, corruption, slavery, sin, and perversions of morals.

"We are the strong, and we will do the fighting and die for you. We ask for support, hoping you will provide support as long as you believe you will not be involved. Your money and families will not be involved. You lie safe as we save you from others. It is okay for you to enjoy this safety and wealth you have accumulated. You pay for that security by supporting the governments for that protection. You are privileged and expect others to obey laws to protect your rights.

"Mr. Cox, you work for men who have wealth and power. We have done so in the past and continue to in the present. The one thing we have that separates us from those that want to take what they want and not earn it is that we believe in honor. We have faith in goodness. Understanding this truth, I regret my poor explanation is said with so few words. Our strength comes from that belief. We will die for those truths. Mike has become a force in these truths. He is pure, having a great love in his heart."

Mr. Cox stood listening to what Cho, Stephen, and Tad was explaining to him.

The kids started to drive up. Mike walked from behind the wall he practiced his finger jabs. Several dents marching across the length were forever permanent reminders he was here. Lindsey, leaving her car, walked toward the front. Soon all the people from last night met under the marquee.

Tad walked over to the main doors, telling everyone to enter. Once inside, Cokes were passed around by several candy bar girls. Everyone went into the auditorium taking seats.

Speaking up first was Tad. Mr. Cox remained quiet. "Okay, I know you all have a lot of questions to ask. First, I want each of you to tell me you did as you were asked to do. Each one of you will tell everyone here that you either told someone or did not tell someone. That means your parents, friends, dogs, the wall, whatever."

After everyone reaffirmed, they kept quiet.

Stephen stood, beginning to retell the events happening last night and then what happened this morning with the house people.

No one said much to Mike coming in the theater. He was bandaged on one arm, which was hanging in a sling. His waist could be seen through his white shirt to have a wrapping around it. He had a slight limp. Lindsey offered to carry his drink, handing it to him after he sat down. All eyes remained on him through the briefing made by Stephen.

Cho spoke after Stephen. He made a short comment on who he was, then gave all some understanding of Mike's training. He left out many things he deemed not necessary for them to learn about. Bob, who had doubts about what Mike was learning, was now convinced from the night events that transpired. Seeing Mike sitting with his wounds, he felt the need to ask Mike to forgive his bad manners. He remained quiet and decided it wasn't a need to do so at this time.

Stephen stood telling the group what they planned on doing and how important they remain quiet for some time. He went on to explain the dangers they will be in, and most of all their families. "If you care about your families," Stephen conveyed, "then keep quiet. These people will find you out and will seek revenge. They will kill everyone in your families. Remember that when you feel the urge to tell a friend or your parents. All it takes is one of those people to say something to someone else. They might promise they will keep it private. They will think it was okay to tell one person, and they will tell you that the person they told promised to keep quiet.

"If they promised not to tell anyone, then told another person making them promise, then what stops the next person to not tell a friend? We see this happening all the time. You speak of this out of pride and acknowledgment for being involved. It will be hard not to do. Let your love for your family guide you. You risk them and all your friends. This is not a game. This is real, these people mean business."

Stephens turned to Cho and walked out of the auditorium after some words quietly spoken between the two. Outside the auditorium, Stephen made a phone call.

Inside, everyone started to talk about what they did or what they saw and how they felt. Tad hearing them talk mentioned, "This is okay to talk within the group. Go ahead and talk with each other, but remember, this is the only place we discuss any of this."

Everyone gathered around Mike, assaulting him with all kinds of questions. What exactly went on in the house while they were running to the cars? What was all the screaming they heard?

"We thought you were killed," came from one of the girls. "Who cut you? Why didn't you get out when we did? Did you see us punch this one guy? Bob got knocked out. The girls helped drag one guy off me and Vic. When we got to the cars, the tires were flat."

So it went on and on, with one person telling what happened and another filling in on what they did.

Not until the movie was to open its doors did anyone stop talking about their part in the event last night.

After twenty minutes of discussion with Stephen, Cho entered the auditorium. He had Mike walk outside under the marquee. Stephen was waiting near one of the billboards of the coming show.

"Mike, Stephen has to leave soon. He will be leading the assault on the gang within a day."

Stephen reached over to Mike, giving him a hug. Looking at him with a sadness, Stephen told Mike to be safe, that he enjoyed training him. "Mike, when this is done, we will get back together. Cho and I will continue your training."

Mike felt inside his being a foreboding. What and how Stephen spoke to him suddenly made Mike afraid. Afraid that this was the last time he would see his friend and teacher.

Stephen shook hands with Cho, and before leaving, he walked back in the lobby. Stephen met with Tad and told him his plans.

Coming outside, he waved to Mike and Cho. Stephen and Teddy Bear kept watching their friends while they revved up their bikes to ride off.

Mike turned to Cho. "He is going to be all right, Cho?"

Cho looked back at Mike. Seeing concern in his eyes, he responded with assurance. "Yes, he will. That man is one of the best at what he does. He will be back after this business is finished, Mike." Cho thought about what Mike was holding back. Cho began to worry. While standing under the marquee, Cho explained the affair with the house people. He revealed some of the things said and what he felt they might do.

"If they do that, Cho," Mike asked, "are you really going to go to Hollywood?"

"Yes, and Stephen, maybe you will accompany me. Sometimes it becomes necessary to reinforce the meaning of one's intentions. I believe this may be one of those times it will be necessary to do."

A large black car turned into the parking lot. Cho pointed to the car driving through the entrance of the parking lot. "I do believe that guest I told you would arrive soon has now arrived, Mike."

The black limo stopped near the curve. The driver exited the car and opened the door to the passenger side. Both Cho and Mike entered the car. Inside sat three very large men and Mr. Howell. Both Cho and Mike were requested to sit between the two very large men. The third man sat directly across from Cho.

Cho turned to Mike and said a few words to Mr. Howell's dismay. "Mike, what I said earlier, this may be that reminder."

Mike was aware of the intention Cho made and prepared himself for what may come. Across from Mike sat Mr. Howell, a pretty blonde lady, and the third very large man closest to Cho.

"So, this is Mike. I have heard and read about all the adventures you had. I must say, you are younger and smaller than I thought you would be."

The secretary mumbled softly into Mr. Howell's ear. "He is a good-looking kid. That will be good for your movie. The teen girls will love him."

"Yes, and this should be easy to persuade him," Mr. Howell softly returned his reply to the pretty blonde sitting next to him. Neither of the two considered that both Cho and Mike could hear their conversation. Both were very wrong.

Cho grabbed hold of Mike's arm. Mike eased back in the soft cushioned seat and continued to listen.

"We are in the process of making a picture about your exploits, young man. It is going to make a great adventure story. You will be famous. All the girls will want to be with you. Then there's all this money you are going to make. I can tell you this, Mike, I have been searching high and low for you for nearly a year."

Mike watching this man telling him all these wonderful things he planned for him made him consider how this will help his family. "Thank you, sir," Mike replied.

"Yes, boy, you are welcome. All I need from you is your permission to allow me to tell your story."

"Ahem." Cho interrupted the talk. "I think the boy is too young to give that permission. His mother will need to consent first. Then and only then if Mike agrees to this."

"Mr. Cho, let me explain to you. This picture is being made. Many of the props such as the house and animatronics have already been created at great expense. I repeat, a lot of money has been spent so far. This will be made. You, sir, have little say-so in this matter. In case you haven't noticed, these men in the car are here to make you or assist you in understanding any confusion you may arrive at."

Really, you think I will be confused and in need of someone to clear up anything I don't understand? So, is this correct, Mr. Howell?" Mike eased farther back in his seat.

"I couldn't have said it clearer than that, Mr. Cho." Mr. Howell made a small hand gesture. Immediately, one large man on Cho's side reached for his hand. The other across from him sitting next to the pretty blonde reached into his vest. Mike saw the man reach inside his vest. Then a strong hand grabbed his hand.

Mr. Howell sat with a smile creeping across his face. Suddenly Cho's man received an elbow to a rib followed by a knife hand strike to his throat while still trying to take hold of his hand.

Mike at about the same time executed a less-effective elbow to his man's rib. His arm was still in a sling. The follow-up strike to his throat with his opposite hand offered had less effect as the elbow. The large man quickly recovered from Mike's blow.

Sitting across from Cho, the third man had his gun out. It was found after everything calmed down in his mouth. It was sticking out like a waterspout. Cho took hold of the large man's hand with the gun, twisting it back toward his mouth.

Later the secretary told Mr. Howell she thought she could hear Mr. Cho tell the man to say "ahh" prior to the gun being shoved into his mouth.

The gun in the mouth shut him up and momentarily stopped the gunman. The final decision to stop his attempt to draw a gun had come from the other large man next to Cho. The impact from the first big man Cho chopped in his throat was flung across the seat into the gunman, causing his head to enter the glass panel to the driver's front seat.

The pretty blonde screamed only after the third man next to Mike found him staring out the window with hair blowing in the wind. Mike was lifted and placed into the seat next to the pretty blonde. Cho's other hand assisted the third man into the window.

Cho moved Mike across Mr. Howell and his pretty secretary so fast, neither realized the damage done to his bodyguards. Both sat motionless, stunned by Cho's speed. Within the space of less than a minute, Cho moved Mike off his seat across to the empty seat vacated by the third man poking in the window to the driver's front with his gun stuck in his mouth. The first man went out the window sitting next to him.

Mike turned to the secretary. He could see her frozen with both eyes wide open and mouth in the midst of a yell. He gave her a slight nudge. Once the nudge woke her from the shock, she let out a most loud scream. Cho reached over to her, and soon she was asleep. Her head leaned against Mike. Then it slipped to Mike's lap.

Cho hit the second man Mike did not completely stop with a front kick under his chin. The roof of the limo was flimsily made. The company never expected it to stop a man's head penetrating it.

Mr. Howell suddenly awoke from his state of shock, only to quickly realize he underestimated this short man a second time. He soon felt the touch. After several minutes, Cho unfroze him. Cho's first thoughts were that of Mike and if he had reinjured himself. Mike was fine. He had a smile on his face. The pretty blonde with an overabundance of breasts kept Mike comfortable.

Mr. Howell sat staring at Mr. Cho. He screwed up and hoped this wasn't going to get him killed with his body dumped somewhere.

"Mr. Howell, I hope this is the last time I need to remind you. Believe me, I knew this was going to happen. I see now that a visit will be forthcoming to your home and office in the near future. Let me be honest with you, may I?"

Mr. Howell replied, "By all means, please."

"Good, when I come to see you, please do not have a greeting for me. I for the second time will tell you this. It will not end well with you."

Mr. Howell looked at this man and this time had a most unpleasant feeling Cho was not going to be nice to him as he was now.

Mike, sitting next to the pretty girl, asked Cho if he would let her rest her head for a while longer. Then he said, "Mr. Cho, they have spent a lot of money on this picture. My family surely could use the money. I will respect your wishes on this matter. You have more experience than I have. What you think is best is what I believe is the best thing for me."

Mr. Howell was looking at Mike when he said that, and his whole demeanor changed. His face went from hopeful to "Oh my god, this is going to be the biggest loss I will ever have."

Cho, seeing the wisdom his young student processed, was pleased. He turned to the sad-faced Mr. Howell and expressed to him, "Mike will take you up on his offer. Send me the paperwork. You will under no circumstances talk to his mother. I do hope this is clear to you. When you draw up the contract, make sure you do so correctly and fairly to Mike. There will be no, no second contract. I will read it, and if I deem it fair, you will have your movie. If not, that will be the end of it. Remember, no second chances. Now, if you will please return us to the Rama." Cho reached over to the secretary and awakened her.

She sat up and pulled her hair back. Looking around at the carnage, she started to scream again. The sight of the three large men dangling almost dead or dead was too much. She held her scream when

Cho reached over to put her back to sleep. He stopped when she waved him off, holding her mouth with her hand.

When the limo returned to the Rama, all three men were trying to reseat themselves. A few moans were heard and rubbing sore limbs felt. One man was given a handkerchief from the pretty secretary to halt blood dripping down his forehead witnessed by both Cho and Mike as they were exiting the limo.

Cho turned to Mike. "That went well, Mike."

Mike looked back and nearly broke into a laugh. "Yes, Sifu, that went well."

Cho and Mike walked to the Rama's front doors. Cho said one more thing to Mike before they went in. "Mike, we need to walk with people in the beginning to help us learn our way in this world. After a time, we need to walk alone to fine our own way in this world."

MAGIC'S AND MECHANIC'S DREAM HOUSE

A T THE CLUBHOUSE, A LONE biker, Stephen, walked in. Most of the members were arriving when he came in. It was to be the beginning of a struggle to finish this gang causing trouble. Mandy was nearly killed, and other innocents were put in danger of losing their lives at the house.

Razor was first to greet Stephen at the door entering the bar. Jack Knife and Chopper were seated at their table. Soon, everyone was surrounding the table. The conference began.

Jack Knife began with the morning dropping off five men in a lot near the Atlanta gang main warehouse. "Inside the main warehouse, gang members heard the roar of our bikes leaving. By the time they arrived where we left the bodies, we were out of sight. They definitely were upset."

Chopper spoke next. "Well, from our end, Stephen, we have the warehouse under watch. They made a silent move to another hangout. I had Magic Jack go to the old warehouse to prepare it for their return. That is, if we don't get them all."

Everybody started to talk after Chopper mentioned Magic Jack was preparing the warehouse. They all understood what he could do. Magic Jack, like the other members, had his unique skills in his Special Forces training. Magic's skill lay in his magic he trained in. That included some escape tricks as part of his skill sets.

"Along with Magic Jack," Chopper continued once the talk subsided, "I sent the mechanic."

Everyone began talking again about Mechanic and his skills. He could build anything. After the haunted house event to clean up, he acquired some fantastic ideas. Coming back, he and Magic Jack came up with a plan for the warehouse reception.

Once Chopper and Razor heard their plan, Chopper ordered them to set the plan into action. Right now, a crew was almost completed with warehouse preparations.

"No one in the gang had returned to the warehouse to check on the site. We figure they are trying to keep their old hideout a secret. The gang plans to use this new warehouse as a trap for us. If things go wrong, they figure they can leave this temporary place," reported Magic.

Razor spoke. "That is correct, if this place is destroyed by our attack, we believe they think they can safely return to their old hideout. All the damage will be at the new place. When they return, we will have it prepared with some special toys in their old warehouse."

Stephen asked Razor to explain what he means as prepared.

"Well, Stephen, since you were gone, you don't know. Magic and Mechanic have installed hidden cameras and listening devices. At the haunted house you were at, they talked to some of the techs and brought back some novel ideas to give to our friends."

Some chuckling was heard from the crowd.

Stephen hearing the chuckles said to Razor, "They must be pretty good ideas the way you are laughing."

"Yep, Stephen," Jack Knife responded. "We got some mirrors and hidden smoke generators. We messed with the air. Mechanic installed some ice machine, and when activated, it will lower the temperature, producing cold air with fog to descend from the roof. He placed it by the air conditioner on the rooftop."

"What the devil for?" Stephen asked.

"That house you were at, wasn't it a haunted house with ghosts and eerie things occurring?"

"Yes. Oh, I see."

Everybody began to laugh at the prospect of this attack and the aftermath if this gang's plans went awry.

Chopper added to the laugher. "Stephen, everybody wants in on this attack. After the second attempt on Mike, it got them all riled up. Then with what Magic and Mechanic got rigged, I can't keep them from not going. They all want in on this.

"Your job is to scout around the site as we are going too. You are to distract them so we can get in as unnoticed as possible. This is your skill set. Who you want with you?"

Stephen looked at Teddy Bear. "I'll take Bear, Flying Joe, and Tunnel Tim."

Mandy walked in. "Hey, don't you dare leave me out of this, Stephen."

Everyone turned. Mandy stood looking none the worse for wear.

""I figured you still recouping from that knife wound?"

"Yeah, I am. But that ain't keeping me out of this hit. Besides, all you plan on doing is ride around. All we be doing is keep them focused on us while the rest of our men do all the hard work, Stephen."

Teddy Bear spoke on that matter. "Hey, Mandy, love having you along, but this ain't no picnic we be riding into."

"Yeah, Bear, I know. They be focus on us. We are going to get the first hits. But I ain't not going."

Bear nodded his approval.

"Well, the next question I got is when is this all to go down, Chopper?"

"Soon, Stephen, soon," Chopper replied. "Now, Stephen, tell us all what went down."

"Well, our boy is going to have a movie made about his adventures. He's going to be famous. Cho is taking care of the finer touches." A slight smile edged across his face.

"With Cho finishing the final touches to the contract, I believe the businessman is needing some subtle persuasion."

"You might say that, Razor."

OPPORTUNITY HAPPENS

S EVERAL DAYS WENT BY, THEN a week. One day, as was Mr. Bach's routine, he walked under the marquee to his car. Ever since Mike began to work at the Rama, he would see him walk down the shopping center and walk past the Rama to his car. He would lock his jewelry store and go home. Every day at the same time when Mike was at the door, he would greet him, wishing him a good evening. On this day, Mike asked him if he was hiring. To Mike's surprise, he said yes. "I have been considering taking on an apprentice to learn clock repair."

Mike only asked Mr. Bach if he could get a better-paying job. He figured he may have to leave town and was going to need money to leave. Mike had money in his pack but planned on giving that to his sisters. With another job, he decided to work at the Rama on the weekends and hopefully work at the jewelry store on weekdays. After work, Mike planned to continue his training with Sifu.

After Mr. Bach had spoken to Tad, Mike was hired. Soon, he was being taught how to repair clocks. *Who would ever believe there were so many types of clocks?* thought Mike.

Mike began working on basic eight-day mantle clocks. Next came wall clocks, which were the same. Most clocks worked the same way. Some were different. Cuckoo clocks had a lot of wires, and some had music boxes. Finally, Mr. Bach gave him a book on anniversary four-hundred-day clocks.

Mr. Bach had him read a book to learn how to repair anniversary clocks. They were simple to repair, but had a suspension spring that had to be properly adjusted to work. That was the key to getting them to run. Finally, Mr. Bach started him on grandfather clocks. Mike quickly achieved mastery at repairing all clocks within weeks.

After hours working at the Rama or the jewelry store, Mike would run to class with Sifu. It had been three weeks since the house incident, and he was working at the Rama and Bach's Jewelry Store. Everyone at the Rama still was talking about that night. Orders were still to talk among themselves and not with anyone else.

On one night of not practicing with Sifu, Mike walked to the Rama for a night shift. Lindsey was at the booth, greeting him. Going inside, he walked in the storage room, grabbing his red jacket. On the way out, Sifu was waiting for him. He was not smiling.

"Come with me, Mike." Cho grabbed his arm, walking back outside. By the wall, he was still holding unto Mike's hand. Looking at him with sad eyes, he slowly began to speak. "Mike, it is with great pains to me as it will for you to tell you this news."

Mike looked at Cho's face. He was very upset, and it showed. "What is it?" asked Mike.

"Mike, Stephen and Bear, they have been killed."

"What? What do you mean they've been killed, Sifu? How, where, when did you know this? Why, why?" Mike started to tremble upon hearing this news. "Why?" he asked Cho.

Cho spoke slowly. "Mike, it was the night we planned our retaliation on that gang that attacked you and these kids. They were to decoy the gang for the others to sneak into their warehouse. They must have been prepared. Some of their men were on the roof waiting. When Stephen and Bear along with several others, including Mandy, rode by, they threw hand grenades and firebombs at them.

"Mike, the first bomb exploded nearest Stephen and Bear, killing them right off. Mandy and the others were hurt, and it looks like they will recover. I came here to tell you and Tad. We destroyed most of the main gang. Some got away. Chopper wants you back at the house. Will you come with me?"

Mike looked up and silently nodded. Cho had talked to his mom before coming to Mike. Speaking, Mike told Cho he needed to do some things and asked Cho to take him home.

Mike entered his home while Cho remained outside by the bike. Mike gathered his belongings he once toted. He left two envelopes for his sisters. Then he kissed his mom bye, walking out the door. Before leaving, he made a phone call to Mr. Bach.

At the Rama, Tad and Mr. Cox received the news Cho had brought to them. They told the crew later that same day. A report was made to the police and a call sent to Mr. Howell. Everything was taken care of. That day ended as Mike straddled the bike behind Cho. Both he and Cho rode away from the Rama before the sun set.

EPILOGUE

MIKE BEGAN HIS NEW LIFE at the clubhouse. Many hard cold hungry weeks would pass by. The bikers were Special Forces. Each was assigned to train Mike their skill set. Cho was the toughest of them all. Early before the sun had a chance to rise, Mike was running five miles with a fully loaded backpack. Both legs and arms were weighted down. Every biker's wife complained constantly on the harsh training being expected of him. Bell especially made it her priority to address Chopper.

New concerns were to plague Mike. The daughter of Stephen blamed Mike for her daddy's death. Threats at school on many of the biker's children caused much concern within the club. Then drug dealers began coming into their subdivision.

To add to all the strife in the club, Mike had to deal with a spirit. This spirit soon became a friend to Mike. He needed one when it discovered the whereabouts of the remaining gang surviving the warehouse battle that killed Stephen and Bear, good friends to Mike. Before the year ended Mike was engaged in an epic battle in the city, fighting every square inch, fighting to live. That fight was made difficult with his memory loss.

Other Books by the Author

Published

- Oz Book 1: One Fine Adventure

Pending Publication

- Oz Book 2: Rama Rowdies
- Oz Book 3: Battle in Atlanta
- Oz Book 4: Rumble in the Jungle
- Oz Book 5: Desert Storm
- Oz Book 6: Wicked City
- Oz Book 7: Tranquil Forest
- Oz Book 8: Ghost of Past
- Oz Book 9: The Gift
- Oz Book 10: Voodoo Queen
- Oz Book 11: Alien Agenda
- Oz Book 12: Sensei's Dilemma
- Oz Book 13: Wisp of the Willow
- Oz Book 14: Time Loop

ABOUT THE AUTHOR

MICHAEL OSBORNE IS THE SON of Robert F. Osborne (a navy chief torpedoman) and a Southern belle, Evelyn Spivey, both deceased. He is one of three siblings and a twin to one. He is the only one to graduate high school and college. He graduated with a BS in geology from Georgia Southwestern College and later received an MS in educational science from Fort Valley State College.

He created his own business doing clock repair, which he learned from a local jeweler. He entered the US Navy and was deployed on a WestPac, then completed twenty-one years total, active and reserves, attaining the same rank of his father, chief instrument man.

Michael went on to earn several black belts in several martial art disciplines as well as certification in sport diving. He set many goals for himself and strove to achieve each one. He refers himself to people as an overeducated fool. He trained on working on various office machines, postal machines, copiers, engraving, jewelry repair, and trained as a projectionist.

When he is not busy, he builds scaled handcrafted wooden ships, winning many firsts at the state fair. One of his greatest achievements was being a grade school teacher. The other was marrying his wife, Dorothy, his partner and friend for life, for thirty-eight years.

He has written fifteen books. This book is his first attempt in publishing. In this book, he hopes the many adventures and some of his life lessons can inspire others to take the bull by the horns and do it.

CPSIA information can be obtained
at www.ICGtesting.com
Printed in the USA
LVHW080258190322
713650LV00005B/6

9 781957 148878